ᚨ

**"...a worthwhile peek into the horrors of war."**
— Kirkus Rev̵

**An Exciting Boo**

A nicely writte            and was in
Vietnam himself serv           ˌst Airborne Division as a CH-47 pilot      ⌐ıays the feeling of time and place
extremely well. Well worth reading. — HELICOPTER LIFE,
Spring 2021

**Harrowing**

The subtitle "A Story About U.S. Assault Helicopter Pilots
at War in Vietnam" tells a potential reader exactly what this book
is about. There are more than enough harrowing flying scenes
and firefights on the ground that will keep readers of this genre
interested. For Army Aviators, "Chariots in the Sky" is a realistic
and fictionalized tale of what they endured during their time in
Vietnam. —The VHPA Aviator, May/June 2021

**Realistic Look At A Pilot's Life In The Vietnam War**

This book is an exciting and informative look into the life of a
helicopter pilot during the Vietnam War. It reveals that the
enemy was much more than the NVA. The enemy was lurking
around every corner, from "leadership" to weather to the pain of
losing multiple friends to the unimaginable stress of flying
extremely dangerous missions. — Paulette J. Brown

**One Word...**

"Outstanding!" — George Lean, AVCM (NAC/AW)

## Flying/Maneuvering Of The UH-1

As I read through the book and you described the actual flying/maneuvering of the UH-1 I found myself thinking, "Self, did you really do that?" It was so long ago. — AlexO-Medical Evacuation Helicopter Pilot, 57th Medical Detachment (DUSTOFF), Vietnam, 1965

## A Great Novel About Chopper Pilots At The End Of The Vietnam War

This is a great novel about chopper pilots at the end of the Vietnam war. I have read many books about this conflict both fiction and nonfiction and this one reads almost like nonfiction.

— Abibliofob

## A Must Read

A gripping novel of helicopter action in Vietnam. The characters were well developed and the plot was great. The action scenes were interesting and suspenseful. I really enjoyed this book and will look for more from this author. A must read.

— Ron Baumer

## Bravery Of All The U.S. Combat Helicopter Pilots In Vietnam

A compelling story of the life of a combat helicopter pilot in Vietnam. A tribute to the bravery of all soldiers who risk their lives daily for the freedoms we enjoy each day. — Greg Hodson

## Felt like I was there with the characters

Written in such a way that you could be forgiven for thinking this is non-fiction, the book handles the context of a terrible war with respect and also in a way which does not sugar coat the realities of a conflict situation. I enjoyed the writing style and really felt like I was there with the characters. — Louise Gray

## A Vietnam War Thriller of a dedicated U.S. Army assault helicopter pilot!

This book puts you into a combat helicopter pilot's seat for an emotional ride of your life time! It touches every emotion and every chapter draws you to the next! It is hard to put down! Very well written for everyone to read! — Dave-Amazon Reviewer

## Best book reflecting the human toll and courage of our troops

Well written book reflecting the trials and courage of American helicopter pilots and crews during the Vietnam war. This is the best book I have read on the Vietnam War as it reflects not only the military history but the human side of the War. — Whh-Amazon Reviewer

## An entertaining and eye-opening look at the life of Army helicopter pilots during the Vietnam War

This is a good read for those interested in aviation's contribution to the war effort in Southeast Asia. — Tom Lokey, Major, USAF, Retired

## Brings the reader to the war in Vietnam

The author brings to life the experiences of a combat helicopter pilot and crew in the Vietnam war. Chariots in the Sky places readers in the assault helicopter as the horrific insanity of war rages. It makes the reader appreciate the difficulties of a soldier who has been separated from his country and loved ones while he also must deal with the politics of his superiors in the chain of command. A good book to read and a war that should never be forgotten. — Powell Ennis

## Chopper Jockey

For any Viet Nam vet who depended on the choppers to take him to his objective or act as Medivac for wounded personnel in the battlefield, a great read. Also, this book has the protagonist, ie, an officer who sacrificed his men to climb the ladder of success. Although fiction, the author was a chopper pilot, who has been there, done that. Enjoy. — Sam Bell

## Right up there with some of the best

I loved the book! Anne and I do a lot of reading - Clancy, Patterson, Jeremy Waldron and a few others and I have to say Chariots In The Sky is right up there with some of the best. The book really held my attention and let me visualize all of the various scenes as they unfolded. I think the author is a very talented writer and I am looking forward to his next story.

— Tony Mancini

## Outstanding Book

My husband was in the USAF and says it is especially a great book for those who were pilots or anyone who served our country. —Louanne-Barnes & Noble Reviewer

## Great Vietnam Story

A gripping novel of helicopter action in Vietnam. The characters were well developed and the plot was great. The action scenes were interesting and suspenseful. I really enjoyed this book and will look for more from this author. A must read.

— rnb 777--Literary Reader-Barnes & Noble Reviewer

# CHARIOTS IN THE SKY

A STORY ABOUT U.S. ASSAULT HELICOPTER
PILOTS AT WAR IN VIETNAM

LARRY A. FREELAND

Publish Authority

*Chariots in the Sky*
*Larry A. Freeland*
*www.LarryFreeland.com*

First paperback edition April 2021

*Cover design lead: Raeghan Rebstock*
*Editor: Bob Laning*

ISBN 978-1-954000-05-6 (paperback)
ISBN 978-1-954000-04-9 (eBook)

Published by Publish Authority
Offices in Newport Beach, CA and Roswell, GA USA
www.PublishAuthority.com

Printed in the United States of America

# THE WALL

In Washington D.C., a short distance from the Lincoln Memorial and across from the Korean War Memorial, you will find The Vietnam Memorial. Passionately known as "The Wall." That V-shaped, black granite wall lists the names of 58,320 American servicemen and eight servicewomen who lost their lives during the Vietnam War. Their names are listed for visitors to see and be reminded of their sacrifices during a challenging time in our nation's history.

Like everything associated with the Vietnam War and its aftermath, the Wall was mired in controversy from the beginning. The Wall's unconventional design, black color, and lack of ornamentation were of particular concern. At the onset, some public officials voiced their displeasure. Two prominent early supporters of the project withdrew their support once they saw the design. Under President Ronald Reagan, the Secretary of the Interior initially refused to issue a building permit for the memorial due to the public outcry about the design.

Since its early years, however, criticism of the Memorial's design has subsided. It has now become something of a shrine.

Since The Wall was dedicated in November 1982, more than 400,000 items have been left there by visitors as remembrances and tributes to those whose names are etched into the black granite. It is now considered by most to be a beautiful memorial and is one of the most visited monuments in Washington, D.C.

*This novel is dedicated to the men who served as helicopter pilots and crew members during the Vietnam War. I believe these are some of the finest men America has ever produced.*

On 7 January 1967, John Steinbeck was at Pleiku, where he flew aboard a UH-1 Huey helicopter with D Troop, 1st Squadron, 10th Cavalry. He wrote the following about helicopter pilots:

I wish I could tell you about these pilots. They make me sick with envy. They ride their vehicles the way a man controls a fine, well-trained quarter horse. They weave along stream beds, rise like swallows to clear trees, they turn and twist and dip like swifts in the evening. I watch their hands and feet on the controls, the delicacy of the coordination reminds me of the sure and seeming slow hands of (Pablo) Casals on the cello. They are truly musicians' hands and they play their controls like music and they dance them like ballerinas and they make me jealous because I want so much to do it. Remember your child night dream of perfect flight, free and wonderful? It's like that, and sadly I know I never can. My hands are too old and forgetful to take orders from the command center, which speaks of updrafts and side winds, of drift and shift, or ground fire indicated by a tiny puff or flash, or a hit, and all these commands must be obeyed by the musicians hands instantly and automatically. I must take my longing out in admiration and the joy of seeing it. Sorry about that leak of ecstasy, Alicia, but I had to get it out or burst.

# PREFACE

## THE HELICOPTER WAR

During the Vietnam War, helicopters played a vital role in the overall strategy of fighting the war. During the thirteen years that Americans served and fought in Vietnam, approximately 12,000 helicopters from all services saw action, with the United States Army being the main force. There were 5,086 helicopters classified as destroyed, representing 42% of the helicopters that saw action in Vietnam. Many of the remaining helicopters flown but not destroyed in Vietnam sustained some form of battle damage. Over 40,000 helicopter pilots and 60,000 crew members served in Vietnam. During the war, 2,165 helicopter pilots and 2,712 crew members were killed. Many more were wounded. When totaled, the number of pilots and crew members killed represents over 8% of the men and women whose names are inscribed on the Vietnam Memorial in Washington, D.C.

# PROLOGUE

## REFLECTION

I t is a clear and brisk fall morning in 1990. The sun is rising over the Vietnam Memorial in Washington, D.C. It is early, and as the morning mist slowly begins to burn off, the usual daily crowds have not yet begun to gather.

Halfway up the right side of the wall, a lone figure dressed in civilian clothes is leaning against the wall. His head is lowered as if praying, and his right arm is outstretched, his hand touching the wall. His face is not visible. He seems lost in time, drifting back into his past. As he leans against the wall, a reflection begins to emerge. The reflection is not of him, but of an Army Aviator clothed in a flight suit, wearing his helmet, upper body armor, survival vest, and a shoulder holster carrying his army-issued .45 pistol.

The reflection's face is not visible. His head is bowed down with an arm outstretched, touching the hand of the lone figure at the wall. The lone figure and the reflection are motionless, as if frozen in time, seemingly intertwined and connected.

The lone figure is totally absorbed in the moment. His mind

slowly drifts back to early 1971, and he begins to hear the faint sounds of helicopters, radio traffic, and gunfire. The sounds become louder, more distinct, and grow ever closer.

# CHAPTER 1

## HOT LANDING ZONE

I t is late morning over Laos in early February, 1971. I'm leading the last section of four Hueys in a trail formation of twelve Hueys on a combat mission into Landing Zone (LZ) 30. My name is Captain Taylor St. James, called TJ by my friends. I'm somewhat of a cocky fellow with a low tolerance for bullshit. I grew up surfing in Southern California, enjoying the California lifestyle, and driving any muscle car I could get behind the wheel of, with a particular fondness for Pontiacs and Corvettes. My military call sign is Eagle 25.

We are being escorted by four Cobra gunships, two flying on each side of our formation. Proud to be one of the famed Screaming Eagles, our helicopters have the distinct markings of the 101st Airborne Division. We are on our second trip back to Firebase 30, ten miles inside Laos. Earlier this morning, we inserted the first of two groups of Army of the Republic of Vietnam (ARVN) soldiers seemingly without incident. These men are our allies in the fight against the North Vietnamese Army (NVA) communist regime. *I hope this is a good sign and we're in for another good day. But, I doubt it.*

We are flying under a low hanging cloud bank. Although the cloud cover is beginning to burn off, the sun is barely visible. Directly below us is Route 9, a big name for a narrow dirt road with a river running parallel. Our formation is flying "nap of the earth," about fifty feet above the ground, creating dust storms on the road below as we pass over. We use "nap of the earth" staying as low to the ground as possible to avoid enemy detection and reduce the threat from incoming fire being directed at us. We work our way winding and twisting up the valley toward Firebase 30 for the second time today. As expected, the air is humid and chilly since it is the monsoon season in Laos and the northern part of Vietnam.

Initially, we thought our mission was without incident, but we now learn Firebase 30 came under attack shortly after the insertion of the first load of ARVN troops into the LZ earlier this morning. Their job was to establish a defensive perimeter around the LZ to help protect the next flight of troops being inserted right behind them. Now we realize the enemy has been alerted and is expecting us. An estimated force of over 200 North Vietnamese Army troops is now engaged in attacking the LZ from all sides. *So much for a good day!* Our Hueys will be going into a Hot Landing Zone, the LZ is under attack.

The ARVN soldiers from the first insertion have already sustained some casualties and will need to be flown out. As we close in on the LZ, we adjust our upper body armor, affectionately called chicken plates, and pull our protective armor plates, attached to the side of our seats, as far out as they will go. Those of us wearing side holsters pull them between our legs. Many of our "packs" (troops being airlifted) notice what we are doing, and some take their helmets off to sit on them.

Major Hutchins is our Company Commander. We are B Company, the Eagles, one of several Huey Assault Helicopter Companies of the 101st Airborne Division. The Major's military call sign is Eagle 1, and we call him Pappy. He knows it's a sign of affection, but at the age of 43, he may feel a little ancient compared to most of his men who are in their early twenties. He is a somewhat crusty, middle-aged career officer with two previous military tours in Vietnam. His first tour was as a Company Commander, and on his second tour of duty, he was an Adviser to the ARVN. Having experienced the unpleasant life of a "grunt" (infantryman) in his first two tours, he went to flight school and came back on his third tour as an esteemed helicopter pilot. He only has a few months left on his tour before he rotates back to the States.

He often says, "From what I saw my last two times over here, pilots seemed to live the good life. They generally got some hot meals, occasional showers, and a bunk to sleep in. That seemed good to me!"

As we approach the LZ, Pappy, flying the lead Huey in our formation, leads us out of the valley, up through the dissipating cloud bank to a higher altitude. Firebase 30 occupies the top of a high ridgeline, partially covered in low vegetation, and surrounded by trees. The designated landing area is relatively open, but will only allow four Hueys to land simultaneously in trail formation. Two Cobras escort Pappy's lead flight group of four Hueys as they approach the LZ.

Pappy yells over his radio, 'Eagles, Eagle 1. We're going into a hot LZ. Stay alert! When you start receiving ground fire, call out the locations to our Cobra support. And for God's sake, we need to get these packs in there. Over!' To acknowledge his radio transmission, his radio crackles with the double-clicks of multiple pilots depressing their radio transmit button twice, and some of us reply with 'Roger that!'

Pappy transmits again, 'Eagles, Eagle 1, One more thing. They have some wounded men in there. They'll be placing them on any chopper that can take them. Be ready. If it gets too hot, bug out! We'll get them later. Over!' Once again, we respond with a flurry of double-clicks and 'Roger that!'

The second group of four Hueys is led by Warrant Officer Ron Thomas, whose call sign is Eagle 7. He is also a short-timer with only two months left on his tour. Leading the second group of four Hueys, he will take his flight into LZ 30 when Pappy's group clears the LZ.

In a calm, matter-of-fact voice I transmit over the radio, 'Eagle 1, Eagle 25, can I take a rain check on this one? Over!'

'Eagle 25, this is Eagle 1. Not today, TJ. Uncle Sam pays us big bucks to get the job done, and we certainly don't wanna cheat him, now do we? Over!'

I jokingly respond, 'Eagle 1, this is 25. No. No, I guess not, but I can think of a few other places I would rather be, earning my paycheck today. Over! '

Some of the other Eagle pilots join in on the banter and transmit their thoughts in the clear. 'At the beach! Back home! With my girl!' Pappy has to cut them off as we are closing in on our LZ. 'Eagles, Eagle 1, okay fellows, I get it! Let's focus and get this done. Beers are on me tonight! Over!'

I reflect on how cool and level-headed our guys are, knowing they are going into a hot LZ, and some of us might not be coming back. The other two Cobras escort my group. Flying the Cobra on my left side is Captain Greg Owens, a tall, lean, weathered-looking Texan with a somewhat boisterous personality. He reminds me of the Marlboro Man, the famous cigarette icon for the Marlboro Cigarette Company. Greg's a gunship pilot assigned to A Company, the Butchers, a Cobra Gunship Company of the 101st, his call sign is Butcher 12.

Greg and I met in Army basic training. We continued to train together through Advanced Infantry Training and Infantry Officer Candidate School (OCS) at Fort Benning. After OCS, Greg went on to flight school, and I followed him several months later. Our paths crossed once again when I ran into him at the Pilots Club, which is the watering hole on the main airfield at Phu Bai Base. The A & B Companies, Butchers, and Eagles are located there. Greg had been in the country a few months when we ran into each other by chance a few days after I arrived at B Company. As we flew many missions together, we rekindled our friendship and would meet at the Pilots Club for beers and relaxation after long hard days of flying.

Greg joins in on the banter and transmits, 'Eagle 1, Butcher 12, does that include me and my guys? Over!'

Pappy responds, 'Affirmative, Butcher 12. Over!'

I can see Greg from my window, and I give him a hand wave motion while calling him. 'Butcher 12, Eagle 25, see you tonight!'

'Looking forward to it!' he responds, as he waves back and then transmits to his flight group, 'Butcher flight, you heard the man...beers later tonight. Make damn sure we keep them covered! Over!'

As Pappy approaches the LZ on a short final (short descending flight path into the LZ) with his three Hueys following, they begin receiving small arms fire from all sides of the weakly defended perimeter. He can see several NVA troops to his front and side, firing into his flight formation.

Pappy calls out to his Cobra support. 'Butchers, this is Eagle 1. We are catching hell in here, lay down some heavy shit now! Over!'

'Eagle 1, we're on it. Over!'

The two Cobra gunships escorting Pappy and his Hueys close in on the LZ and begin firing their rockets and mini-guns at the enemy positioned around the LZ. All the Huey door gunners are blazing away with their M-60s, and the ground troops are ferociously firing at the enemy. This concentration of firepower has an immediate effect on the enemy positions, as their firing begins to taper off. Pappy's flight of Hueys can land in the LZ, drop their packs off, and pick up some of their wounded soldiers. Once loaded, Pappy leads his men out of the area, sustaining only multiple bullet holes in their Hueys.

As Pappy and his flight are clearing the LZ, Ron sets up his approach and leads the second group of four Hueys toward the LZ. Ron transmits, 'Eagle 1, Eagle 7. We are on a short final now. We'll pick up any of their remaining wounded. Over!'

'Eagle 7, Eagle 1. Roger that. Be careful in there, Ron. I thought I saw some gooks back in the tree line with Rocket Propelled Grenades (RPG's). Over!'

'Eagle 1, Eagle 7. Roger that. Just my frigging luck! Over!'

The Cobras that escorted Pappy's flight into the LZ have continued to provide covering fire for Ron's flight. As they close in on the LZ and settle their skids on the ground, a tremendous mortar barrage rains down on them. Chunks of earth are kicked up into the air, and pieces of shrapnel from the exploded shells fly through the landing area, heavily impacting many of their Hueys. ARVN troops are scurrying from the Eagles' choppers and heading for cover. The Eagles don't have that option as they have to wait for the troops to clear their choppers before they can lift off. They pay a heavy price, as several men are hit and slump over their guns or fall forward in their pilot seats.

Ron transmits in the open, 'We are getting creamed in here. Eagles pull out now! Butchers, get after them! They're back in the tree lines. I can see their mortar tubes from here; they're about 100 meters out from my front. Over!'

With that transmission, the other two Cobras join in the fight and begin unloading their tools of death on the enemies positioned below. Ron's group of Hueys is unable to wait to load the remaining casualties and he starts to lead his flight out of the LZ. His world suddenly goes to hell in a handbasket when one of the mortar rounds hits next to his Huey as he lifts off. His Huey explodes in a massive fireball. There is no hope for the men. They and their Huey are blown to pieces and consumed in fire.

The other three Hueys, in Ron's formation, are able to get out of the area with several wounded men. Pappy's Huey has remained over the firebase, helping to guide the Cobras to their targets. He has witnessed all that has transpired below him and transmits to his Eagles. Having just lost a Huey with four men killed, Pappy calls for his men to give him a headcount of his remaining crews. Eagles, 'Eagles, this is Eagle 1. Give me your crew status. Eagle 25, assume a holding pattern south of the LZ until further notice! Over!'

I respond in the affirmative as the other Eagles give Pappy their crew status. 'One pilot dead, two pilots and three gunners wounded.' The Hueys reporting wounded and dead on board are directed by Pappy to head back to Khe Sanh base. The remaining Hueys are instructed to stay with him, gain altitude, and go into a holding pattern south of the LZ.

'Butcher 12, Eagle 1. See if your guys can soften them up some more before I send in Eagle 25. Over!'

Greg responds, 'Roger Eagle 1. We'll see what we can do! Over!' Greg leads his group of Cobras on repeated gun runs as they rain death down on the enemy's position around LZ 30. This concentration of firepower seems to have worked, and I am directed to take my flight into the LZ. *I hope that is the case, and we get in and out of that LZ alive.*

As I lead my group in, I call out to my friend. 'Butcher 12, Eagle 25. This doesn't look good! Stay close and keep us covered! Over!' Greg responds, 'Will do! Good luck, Amigo!'

As the LZ comes into view, I push my cyclic (controls movement sideways, forward and backward) forward and push down on my collective (controls movement up and down) to maneuver my Huey forward and down. These coordinated movements result in my Huey beginning an immediate fast descent approach into the LZ.

Over the intercom, I tell my crew, 'We're going in, keep it sharp! Gunners, watch the tree lines! Open fire and blow away any of those little bastards you see as we go in!' I hear double-clicks on my intercom, signaling they heard my transmission.

As we clear the treetops in front of us, the LZ where I need to drop my packs becomes visible. Approaching the spot, with my three Hueys following, I pull back sharply on the cyclic and pull up on the collective, bringing the Huey to a fast flaring stop. It's so extreme that my tail rotor almost hits the ground. As the nose of the Huey points up, dust and dirt is blown everywhere, and the Huey seeks its equilibrium as it settles into a controlled hover. It's a beautiful thing to behold from a bystander's point of view.

Hovering about three feet off the ground, we rock back and forth as our packs jump out on both sides and head for cover. As they are jumping out, we once again begin receiving heavy ground fire from machine guns and AK-47s. Red tracer rounds are coming at us from several directions, but it is difficult to gauge from where because of the dust generated by our rotor blades. Red tracer bullets, when fired, burn red which allows the shooter to follow the bullet's trajectory and adjust his aim as necessary to hit a target.

It is not until several rounds start smashing into my Huey that I realize we are under heavy fire. The rounds hitting my ship sound like popcorn popping, and I think to myself, *My god, am I really in Vietnam?* Just as I start moving the Huey forward, some ARVN soldiers run over, carrying three of their wounded comrades and throw them like sacks of flour onto the floor of the Huey. As the packs run back to cover, I have to stop my forward momentum temporarily. *Damn, this is too long in a hot LZ! We need to get the hell out of here now!* With their wounded on board and my engine running at full throttle, I pull up and resume my takeoff.

I call out to Greg. 'Butcher 12, Eagle 25. We are under heavy fire down here. These little bastards are shooting the shit out of us! Get them off my ass!'

Just as we start to lift off, an RPG goes flying right past my window. I yell out over the radio, 'Damn, did you see that? Let's get the fuck out of here, guys!'

From his vantage point, Greg, in his Cobra, can see over the battlefield from where the firing is coming and dives down from the sky to begin his gun runs. Greg calls out to me, 'We have them in sight, hang on, this will only take a minute.'

With the packs unloaded, and the wounded on board, I begin a desperate climb into the sky with my bullet-riddled Huey. My flight of three Hueys follows me. As we gain altitude, our choppers receive more heavy machine gun fire from many directions. As I clear the tree line on the backside of the LZ, Ethan, my right door gunner--the kid from Arkansas--screams into the intercom. 'I'm hit...oh God! Help me! Help...'. Then he goes silent.

I glance back into the compartment and see Ethan slumped over his gun. Over the intercom, I tell my left door gunner, Will, to check him. Will moves over to the right door, checks on Ethan, and yells into the intercom, 'He's dead, Captain!'

Before I have a chance to process what just happened, my Huey shudders as it's being ripped to shreds by 51-caliber machine gunfire. In this hail of machine-gun fire, Will falls, mortally wounded, having taken a round to the head. Half his face and helmet have been blown away. He too slumps lifeless to the floor of the Huey.

No time to think about it. Reacting instinctively, my pilot and I scan our instrument panel. No warning lights, oil and hydraulic pressures are okay, and rotor RPM is holding steady. Believing no severe damage has been done to our Huey, we continue our climb out. As I concentrate on keeping our Huey in the air, while gaining more altitude, we continue receiving heavy ground fire.

I call out to Pappy. 'Eagle 1, 25, we're pretty damn shot up, but I think we can make it back to Khe Sanh. Our gunners are dead! We have three wounded packs on board. Over!'

Just as I finish my transmission, the Huey following directly behind me receives devastating fire from the same machine gun that was focused on me three-seconds ago. However, they are not as lucky as we are. Their Huey explodes, sending burning debris plummeting to the earth. We can all hear the pilots screaming into their microphones over our radios as they spiral toward the ground. Their radios go silent as the burning Huey crashes into the earth and disintegrates, killing all on board.

I instinctively and unconsciously transmit in the open over my radio, 'Oh, christ...did you see that?'

Pappy has been flying a holding pattern above the LZ as the Command and Control (C&C) ship. He is our leader, whom we respect and will follow anywhere. He does more than his share of combat flying, never asking a man to do anything he did not do, or would not do, himself. His style is to fly over the assigned LZs we work until all his Eagles clear them.

'Eagle 25, this is Eagle 1. We saw it! I'm coming down to join you!'

Pappy does a free fall from his high-altitude position, causing his Huey to vibrate excessively as the rotor blades begin to exceed their maximum RPM. As he closes in on my Huey, he pulls back on the controls before his Huey shakes itself apart.

The other two Hueys in my flight manage to follow me out without any casualties and join up with me. Their bullet-riddled ships attest to the ferocity of the shitstorm we have just been through.

Before Pappy realizes it, the rest of his Eagles who were south of the LZ, flying in a holding pattern, have joined us. Having lost two Hueys and sending three back to Khe Sanh with our wounded and dead, we are now a group of seven Eagles flying in a V-shaped formation. Our door gunners are firing their M-60 machine guns on any target they can locate. By joining me, we all begin receiving ground fire. This has the intended effect of redirecting some of the incoming fire away from my Huey. This courageous action by the other Eagles increases the chances of my crew and I making it back to base alive. *This is how we roll in Vietnam.*

As we head back toward the border and away from LZ 30, Greg and his Butcher flight continue working over the area surrounding the LZ. He and his men continue to rain death down on the enemy, trying to relieve the pressure on the ARVN troops in the LZ. With the action on the ground tapering off, and also running low on fuel and ammunition, they break it off and head out to join us.

As we fly back toward the border and out of harm's way, I notice my oil pressure is dropping fast, and my engine is starting to lose RPMs. This is not good. I call over to Pappy. 'Eagle 1, Eagle 25. We are losing oil pressure fast and RPM is dropping. I'm not going to make it back across the border. Over!'

In a calm, matter of fact voice, Pappy transmits. 'Roger, 25. Look for a place to auto-rotate into, and we'll pick you up. Over!'

Looking down at the terrain below, I locate a large clearing devoid of any visible activity next to a stretch of Route 9, which should work—with a hope and a prayer. I respond, 'Roger, Eagle 1. I have a clearing to my right front about 500 yards out. That's where we're going. Over!'

At this point, my Huey is getting harder to control. We are about 600 feet up and closing in on the chosen spot. I push my collective to the floor, stabilize my foot pedals, and push the cyclic a little forward for some additional airspeed. We drop rapidly toward the ground, and at about thirty feet in the air, I pull back on my cyclic and pull up hard on the collective. This causes the Huey to flare up with its nose rising and the tail section dropping down. The wind from our rotor blades causes a dust storm in front of us as our airspeed drops to almost zero. My control movements have the intended effect of slowing our rate of descent and help cushion our drop to the ground. We hit the ground hard, bounce several times, and eventually settle to the ground. *For a controlled crash, that wasn't a bad landing!*

Pappy and my fellow Eagles have been flying over me and have observed our autorotation to the ground. Greg and his Cobras have joined them. Pappy calls out to his flight group. 'Eagles, Eagle 1. There's enough room down there for two of us. Eagle 20, follow me in, and we'll extract TJ and those with him. The rest of you remain up here on station. Over!' As the men respond to him, we hear double-clicks and 'Roger that!'

'Eagle 25, Eagle 1. Good job. We're coming in right behind you. Clear your ship and get ready. Over!'

'Roger, will do!' I respond.

Landing behind me and to one side of my Huey, is Pappy and Eagle 20. Their door gunners run over to help us carry the two dead bodies of my crew, as well as the wounded ARVNs we have on board, over to the waiting Hueys. This only takes a few minutes, and our Hueys, loaded with our men, dead and alive, take off.

We get out of there just in time, as several enemy soldiers emerge from the brush shooting at us with their AK-47s. I'm in Pappy's Huey. I plug into his radio system, and we communicate over the intercom. 'Thanks, Major. That was too damn close! This has been one hell of a day.' Pappy responds, 'Yeah, it has, TJ...and this is just our first week into this operation! Terrific!' I respond sarcastically.

Looking down on my bullet and shrapnel-riddled Huey with smoke billowing out from the engine compartment, I can see the enemy crawling around it. They are celebrating the loss of another American chopper. This pisses me off, and I ask Pappy to call Greg and have him and his Cobras do a gun run on them and destroy my ship. I can't call out to Greg on the Huey's radio, since I can only use the intercom. So, Pappy makes the call for me.

We then watch as Greg and his Cobras do a full-throttled, two abreast gun run on them. It is over in a flash as their rockets and miniguns rip up the ground, cutting down several NVA, and hitting the Huey. It explodes in a huge fireball, sending pieces of the helicopter and body parts flying everywhere. Watching the scene below us unfold, I feel no sympathy or remorse—only a numb indifference toward the enemy we just killed. *So much for their celebration party!*

Pappy leads Greg's Cobras and us back across the border to Khe Sanh. Once there, we drop off the wounded ARVN soldiers at their Battalion staging area, take on fuel, and fly back to our airstrip at Phu Bai Base. Upon landing, we are directed to hover over to the Mobile Army Surgical Hospital (MASH) unit, where the dead bodies of my crew members are removed from the Huey and taken into the morgue. I will be required to come back later to identify the bodies and prepare an official report.

The bodies of the eight crew members of the two Hueys we lost earlier in the day, were recovered by ARVN troops at the LZ. They had already been placed on two other American Hueys that came in sometime after we completed our mission. They will be returned to us by tomorrow. As I did with my fallen gunners, Pappy will go over to the MASH unit to identify their bodies, ensure the necessary paperwork is completed, and schedule a Memorial Service for our fallen comrades.

It has been another long and terrifying day, in which several men lost their lives. I came too damn close to being one of them! I've had enough for one day and head back to my room to crash. My room is one of several included in a hastily constructed, one-story, long wooden structure, serving as our pilots' quarters. As rooms and pilots' quarters go, it's not too bad. We have our own outdoor showers, covered latrines, a fire pit, and a small shack that serves as a bar. Near our quarters are sandbag bunkers to dive into when rockets slam into the base. This is our home, our safe haven, a place to try and relax, unwind, and get ready to go out and do it all over again tomorrow.

# CHAPTER 2

## LAM SON 719

L ater that evening, after a hot meal and a cold shower, I lie
back on my cot reflecting on the day's events and wonder if
I will make it through Lam Son 719. It has only been a week
since the operation started, and it becomes more intense and
deadly as the days drag on. It all started about two weeks ago
when the Company was presented with a major operational
briefing for all pilots and crew members. It was at that meeting
the 101st Airborne Division's Operations staff laid out what was
to come.

The operational campaign is named Lam Son 719 and is
designed to stop the flow of men and supplies from moving down
the Ho Chi Minh trail in Southern Laos. The job of the 101st
Airborne Division's helicopter force, numbering over 650 helicopters, is to support the ARVN forces in Laos. The 101st
Airborne Division's air assets will be augmented, as needed, by
other U.S. Aviation units in South Vietnam. South Vietnamese
Armor and Infantry components, numbering over 20,000 men,
are to make a deep thrust into Southern Laos along Route 9.
Along the way, they will set up several Firebases and LZs on the

highest ridgelines and peaks. Their purpose is to guard their flanks as they move deeper into Laos and engage enemy units in their areas. In essence, South Vietnamese forces will do all the groundwork and fighting inside Laos, and we Americans will provide air support. Lam Son 719 is supposed to last 90 to 120 days. This will be the first real test of Vietnamization, which is President Nixon's plan for turning the war over to South Vietnam.

As part of our briefing, we were all provided forms and told to sign them. The forms stated in part that we were not to land in Laos, unless it was an emergency, and then under no circumstances were we to get out of our helicopters. I've seen and heard some crazy things over here, but this is beyond anything I could've imagined. Apparently, Nixon has no authority to send American forces outside of Vietnam. He caught hell last year when he sent Americans into Cambodia. This is probably some kind of an effort to circumvent that restriction.

Much to the disappointment of Division Operations personnel, nobody would sign the forms. As the joke goes over here, what the hell are you going to do, send me to Nam?

Lam Son 719 seemed to go well the first few days, but as South Vietnamese military operations bogged down inside Laos, the situation started to deteriorate. The North Vietnamese Army began rushing massive reinforcements to the entire region, and the ARVN forces found themselves under heavy attack. It has now fallen to us, American helicopter aircrews, to keep them in the fight.

# CHAPTER 3

## SANDY

Realizing I haven't finished dictating my tape to Sandy, I move over from my comfortable cot to what serves as a desk. A piece of plywood supported by two wooden crates underneath. Lam Son will have to wait. It's time to think about Sandy and give her my complete attention. Since I do not currently have a roommate, I am able to enjoy some privacy when I need it, such as now. Sitting at my work table, I grab the tape machine, insert the tape I'm currently using, and start dictating. "It's late evening over here Sandy, at the conclusion of another boring day. I flew several hours and managed not to crash, so it was another rather successful day! The days seem to be going faster now, but they tend to blur."

Leaning back and looking up at the ceiling, I try to control my emotions—it's been another rough day. How do you talk about the things you saw and did today with your wife? I try to keep my emotions in check and continue dictating. "Sandy, I miss you so much...But each day that goes by is a day closer to you. I received your tape three days ago and have already listened to it several times. It's so good to hear your voice, and it's almost as if I were there lying next to you. God, I wish I were."

It's no use. I can't. I stop dictating and get up and walk over to my cot. I lay down and stretch out on it. As I do, I look over and stare at Sandy's picture on the wall next to my pillow.

Sandy is an especially attractive young lady with long wavy blond hair, a light tan and bluish green eyes. She is an accomplished tennis player, who enjoys swimming, running, and playing golf. Being outgoing, understanding, and confident contributes to her being an excellent high school teacher.

Sandy's first husband and college sweetheart, Mike, was killed in Vietnam the year before we met. We met on a blind date shortly after I finished OCS at Fort Benning, Georgia. We dated for several months and decided to get married halfway through my flight training program. To this day, I'm not sure what drew Sandy to me, especially after losing Mike. For me, it was love at first sight. Here was a woman I could spend the rest of my life with and love every minute of our time together.

After completing phase one of my flight training, I had a three day leave to travel from Fort Wolters, Texas to Fort Rucker, Alabama for the second phase of flight training. Between Texas and Alabama, I made a short detour to Fort Benning. It was there at the Fort Benning Infantry chapel, we got married, had a small reception at the Officer's Club, and headed to the Florida panhandle beaches for a one-night honeymoon.

Arriving at Panama City Beach, we were lucky to have found a hotel room on the beach for our honeymoon. It was summer, and there were not many places to choose from. While checking in, I just happened to notice the surf was up. A storm had recently blown through and churned up the Gulf. This caused larger waves to roll in and crash onto the beach in front of our hotel. So, what did the surfer do? I rented a surfboard and spent the afternoon riding waves. This did not go over very well with Sandy. It could have been a short marriage. But it all worked out, and we moved on. Sandy was understanding, but there was a limit. There was to be no more surfing for me when we managed to go to the beaches before I shipped out.

We spent the next five months living in a trailer park just outside of Fort Rucker. Because of the heavy demand for helicopter pilots, the U.S. Army Aviation School was running at full capacity throughout the Vietnam War. Fort Rucker could hold only a limited number of military personnel, thereby creating a massive overspill of service personnel into the surrounding communities. This need for temporary quarters resulted in an explosion of trailer parks surrounding Fort Rucker.

We shared our first home with Sandy's Scottish Terrier puppy, Angus. Sandy acquired Angus the day before we met on our blind date. Angus was a one-person dog, and that person wasn't me. There were many early mornings, well before the sun would come up, that I had to leave for training. Angus slept at the foot of our bed and between us. On many occasions, he made small deposits on the floor next to my side of the bed. One could say we had a love/hate relationship. When I would drink my Michelob beer, Angus would crawl up on my lap and join me for a sip. Eventually, we became good buds, much to Sandy's delight.

Our tour at Ft. Rucker consisted of socializing with other pilots and their wives or girlfriends, which included parties at the club, getting together at each other's trailers, going to the movies, and eating out occasionally. When it was girl time, they would play some golf, tennis, swim, or shop.

Our pilot's training was intense, demanding and at times it could be deadly. We were preparing to go to war in a very hostile environment for helicopters. From the beginning of flight school, through graduation, we were continually reminded of and trained for the many challenging and deadly situations we would face in Vietnam.

However, some of the fellows adopted an attitude that we were all "living on borrowed time" and would probably not make it home alive. Thus, although they trained hard, they tended to live their lives for today, and not think of or plan for a future.

When flight training was over, and new Army Aviator wings had been pinned to our chests, we received our orders for Vietnam. We were instructed to ensure all legal affairs were in order and then sent home on leave.

At the end of my training, Sandy and I packed up and headed for San Diego, California. While I serve in Vietnam, Sandy lives in an apartment near my parents, who live on the beach. She is working as a teacher at a nearby high school, stays physically active, and enjoys the companionship of her many new friends.

Sandy continually worries about me serving in Vietnam. She fears for me and is always asking herself, *Will he be alright? Will he get wounded? Will he get captured? Will he be killed, and I'll lose another husband?* These haunting questions shouldn't be on the mind of any wife for a day, let alone an entire year of their life.

# CHAPTER 4

## LAST NIGHT--LEAVING ON A JET PLANE

Wh ile looking at Sandy's picture, my thoughts begin to drift back to the last night we were together before I shipped out to Vietnam. Sandy's presence begins to overpower me as my mind slips back in time.

~

It's mid-evening in early November 1970 at the Miramar Naval Air Station Officers Club, crowded with Navy Officers, wives and dates. With few exceptions, the military men are wearing their dress uniforms. Sandy and I closely embrace as we dance to a slow song "Leaving on a Jet Plane," played by the club's band. Sandy whispers into my ear, "Oh Taylor, I wish this night would never end." She clings to me tightly. "Why you? Why do you have to go?"

I loosen my embrace on her just enough to look down into her eyes. "Sandy, let's just forget about tomorrow, and enjoy tonight. I want to remember this night with you forever." Sandy responds.

"And I want to remember this night with you. I'm sure I'll relive it many times while you're gone. God, I love you so much."

We finish our dance and stroll over to the large, round table we share with several other couples. All the men at the table are military. I have on my Army dress greens, and the other men at the table are wearing their Navy dress uniforms. They are all Navy fighter pilots.

As we approach the table, one of the pilots stands up, pulls out Sandy's chair, and helps her into it. While she is being seated, I sit next to her and simultaneously cast a frown at the pilot. Pilots are a notorious breed, and you can never be too careful around them with your lady.

Realizing I disapproved, he returns an apologetic look and asks me how the two of us met. I look around the table to see if anyone else is interested. They are, so I proceed to tell them our story. "We met on a blind date about a year and a half ago. After I graduated from OCS at Fort Benning, I roomed off base with two OCS buddies. One was of Irish descent and the other from Britain. The Irish guy loved to drink, and he and I would go out after work, hit the bars, and try to bring some ladies back to our place to party. The British guy had a girlfriend, and didn't much appreciate some of our activities as they interfered with his love life."

I look around the table to see if I'm still holding their attention. No one has tuned me out yet, so with some embellishment, I continue with our story. "Well, the British guy considered his girlfriend to be a proper lady. He figured that maybe I would slow down if he could find me a proper lady. He didn't hold out much hope for the Irishman, so he had his girlfriend bring us together. Soon we were dating, and one thing led to another, and here we are."

One of the pilots looks over at me and asks, "Well, did your

British roommate's love life improve? What happened to your Irishmen?"

I reply, "It did, and the Irishmen spent many a lonely night drinking his Irish whiskey and watching television in his room."

The table erupts in light laughter, and as the evening progresses toward midnight, there are many questions directed at me from the other pilots. How long have you been in the Army? How did you end up flying helicopters? How many hours do you have? What kind are you qualified in? I do my best to oblige them with answers that keep the conversation light and somewhat humorous. Then one of them asked me if I've been to Vietnam yet. The table goes silent.

Sandy chimed in. "He leaves tomorrow morning!"

"That's a hell of a way to go into the end of the year!" says another pilot. He continues. "I just returned from there. My hats off to you guys in the choppers. You're a rare breed. You have to have balls of steel to do that kind of flying!" After that, I didn't have to buy another drink. They just keep landing in front of me —compliments of the Navy.

The evening moves on as Sandy and I enjoy ourselves, socializing with everyone at the table, and dancing the night away. It's after midnight when it dawns on me how late it is. It's been a great evening, and I hate to see it end. But we have to leave, so I inform our new friends that we are headed out since I have a long few days coming up. After saying our goodbyes, hugging, and shaking hands, we depart the club for our apartment near the University of California, San Diego, and the beach.

Realizing that I've had a few drinks and may not be in the best condition to drive, Sandy insists I give her the keys to my Corvette. With some trepidation, I hand them over. I'm a car guy, whose pride and joy is my red 1960s, second generation, Zo6. No one drives my Corvette but me, that is until Sandy came along. She drives us back to our apartment, taking advantage of her opportunity to push the Vette. Arriving back at the apartment, Sandy helps me navigate the stairs to our place. Once inside we both drop everything on the floor that we've been carrying. I take my coat off and throw it over a chair and we slowly move out to the balcony.

We are standing on our balcony, looking out at the beach a short distance away. It's a beautiful early morning with a full moon shining off the water, and the waves slowly drifting onto the beach. We are embraced and softly caressing each other. Sandy whispers, "I can't believe we only have a few hours left. I don't think I can bear this again." She starts to cry. I try to comfort her as I tighten my embrace. "I know, I know, but we'll make it!" Looking into her eyes and trying my best to comfort her, I say, "You have your teaching job to keep you busy, and you'll make plenty of new friends. My parents are close by. As you know, they've been in our situation many times over the years. They know how we feel...and they'll certainly be there for you."

As Sandy regains her composure, I gently wipe the tears from her eyes. She struggles to speak, "I know, but it still isn't going to make this any easier. After losing Mike, I swore not to look at another man in uniform. Then you come along. God help me. I can't bear the thought of losing you!"

"I'll be alright! Mike was an infantryman. Those poor bastards have it rough all the time over there, always stuck out in the bush, never knowing when they will be hit. It's different for pilots. I'm coming back!"

Sandy, "You promise?" In a soft voice, I respond, "Yes, now let's go back inside." Sandy, after a long pause and in a seductive kind of way, says, "What's on your mind?

I slowly back off the balcony and into the living room, gently pulling Sandy with me. Once in, I close the sliding door. The room is dimly lit by the moonlight, which is shining through the sliding glass doors.

Softly stroking Sandy's long blond hair as we come together hard and tight, our bodies start to quiver. We kiss, and kiss again. Our hands travel over each other's bodies, and as the tempo increases, so does our desire for each other.

As I work feverishly, unbuttoning her blouse, then her skirt, my hands fumble at every attempt. You would think that after being married this long, I could undress my wife. Finally, success as her blouse slides off her back and to the floor. This is followed by her skirt as it falls to the floor around her ankles. Sandy kicks off her shoes and the skirt. She momentarily draws back from kissing me, and as she does, I loosen my coat tie and pull it off over my head and let it fall to the floor. We kiss again. Sandy unbuttons my shirt, and with some help from me, slips it off. Her hands work with the precision of a surgeon as she unfastens my belt and pulls down the zipper.

I kick my shoes off as my pants slowly slide down my legs to the floor. It is almost comical as I struggle to kick my pants off without falling flat on my face. No doubt that would be a mood killer! My breathing is heavier, and my hands are shaking slightly as I move to release Sandy's bra strap and pull at her panties. Releasing her strap, the bra falls to the floor and with Sandys help I slide her panties down her legs. She kicks them off.

With heartbeats rising, I draw back from Sandy and gaze at her beautiful naked body bathed in the moonlight. I think to myself—*my god it's going to be a long year!*

As Sandy draws closer to me, her body begins quivering with desire, and her breathing quickens. With increasing expectations rising within both of us, we tighten our embrace. I pick Sandy up and carry her into our bedroom. I close the door behind me as we clear the doorway.

# CHAPTER 5

## FLIGHT OPERATIONS OFFICER

S uddenly I'm brought back to reality. "Captain, Captain, wake up, Pappy wants to see you!" The Company First Sergeant (Top) has entered my room and nudged me several times, trying to wake me up. "Captain! Wake up, dammit!"

It's mid-morning the next day, and I slowly shake myself awake. "Yes, what is it, Top?"

"Pappy wants to see you in his office. He's with Captain Norton."

"Okay, alright, tell them I'll be right there!"

As the First Sergeant leaves the room, I slowly rise from my cot, looking around the all too familiar room, reality sets in again. I'm still in Vietnam. My night dream, as so many before it, seemed so real. One day maybe, I'll wake up and be lying next to Sandy. But not today as I put on my shirt and cap, head out the door of my room, and head towards Pappy's office while still buttoning my shirt. The morning air is already hot, heavy, and muggy.

The Major's office is one of the smaller rooms in a large air-conditioned trailer which serves as the Eagles' Company headquarters. Arriving there, I am met by Pappy and Captain Norton. Captain Stan Norton is the Company's Flight Operations Officer. He is a large, husky career officer, who graduated from Virginia Military Institute many years earlier. He is considered by many of the men to be a frustrated career man who thinks he should already be a Major, and commander of his own Company. He can be difficult to reason with, and sometimes loathful of anyone who questions him. As the Flight Operations Officer, he is responsible for assigning pilots their flight schedules and specific daily mission assignments. In this capacity, he controls his own assignments, which do not include many combat missions.

"Take a seat, TJ. That was one hell of a day yesterday! Are you doing okay?" Pappy says. Looking around the room as I walk over to the sofa next to the Major's desk and slowly settle myself into it, I notice Stan in one corner. "I think so, Major, thanks for asking."

Pappy, with a nod of approval, says, "It doesn't get any easier over here, does it, son?" I respond with a slight grin, "No, sir, it sure doesn't."

Removing my cap, I wipe the sweat from my forehead with the same arm. Then I flap my shirt lightly, taking in as much of the stale, not very cool air, as possible. Although the trailer may be air-conditioned, like most everything else in our operations area, it is not very reliable, nor does it function well.

Stan, who has been leaning against a wall in one corner of the office, straightens up and walks toward me. He works his way over so that he is looking down on me with that smug look of his, one of his many annoying characteristics. Stan says, "Taylor, tomorrow we're going back into Laos and LZ 30 to try and resupply them and get some more ARVN soldiers in there. I was going to assign you as the lead ship for the mission, but the Major wants to keep you back for a few days of light duty."

I look over at Pappy, who has been sitting on the corner of his desk and nod my appreciation. "Thanks, Major, I think I could use some slack time." Pappy reciprocates as he stands up and walks toward the door. "Taylor, we had another new pilot arrive today, and on the recommendation of Stan, I'm assigning him to you. When the First Sergeant finishes processing him in, he'll bring him by."

I shoot a fiery-eyed glance over at Stan, and as I stand up, give Pappy a weak salute as he leaves the office. "Right, Major, I'll do my best to take care of him." As Pappy closes the door, I turn to Stan and unload on him. "What the hell are you doing to me? This is the fifth new guy you've given me in the last three months. Are you telling me there is no one else who can do this right now?"

As a slight smirk appears on Stan's face, I can see him thinking to himself—*I've got him riled up now.* He then says, "We're a little short on seasoned pilots right now, and besides, this is light duty."

I have to restrain myself when I realize I've involuntarily started to clench my fists. As I turn to leave the office, my eyes become fixed on Stan, and I angrily respond, "Short on pilots! Light duty! That's bullshit, and you know it. You've been here much longer than I have, and if breaking in new guys is your idea of light duty, why the hell don't you ever do it?"

Stan doesn't respond, but my comments have hit a raw nerve. It does no good, but it sure makes me feel better. Just a little agitated, I turn and walk out of the office, ignoring anyone I pass, as I head back to my room.

# CHAPTER 6

## THE NEW GUY

Entering my dimly lit room while slamming the door behind me, I let out a frustrated shout, "Damn, I don't understand that guy!" I don't notice 1st Lieutenant Scott McGregor lying on a cot in one corner of the room. Scott is a good-looking young man who has an all-American quality about him. He is one of those fellows who just doesn't look like he belongs here. But then who does? Scott is well-spoken with a calm, soft, and somewhat whispering voice, yet reassuring.

With my abrupt entrance, Scott leaps up from his cot. "You don't understand who, Captain?" Startled, I look over in the direction of Scott.

"You'll meet him soon enough. You must be the new guy, Lieutenant McGregor!"

Scott crosses the room and extends his hand, and we shake. He explains to me that the First Sergeant processed him into the company and said that he was assigned to bunk here with me. "I guess we're to be roommates, Sir!"

I step back some and respond, "You can cut the sir shit, just call me Taylor or TJ, and I'll call you Scott. Okay by you?"

Scott replies, "Sure, no problem."

Scanning the room as I sit down on my cot, I look over at Scott. "It's damn sure not The Ritz, but you'll get used to it eventually. Put your stuff wherever you can find a place. After lunch, I'll get us a jeep, and we'll drive around the Phu Bai base, our Company area, and I'll introduce you around. Tomorrow I'll give you a check ride, and we'll start getting you acquainted with our operational area. Then it will hit you!"

Scott, with a quizzical look, asks, "What will?"

"You'll realize you are in Vietnam, or as you will soon learn, you are in the shit now!" With that happy note, I get up from my cot and lead Scott out of the room and over to the mess hall.

On our way there, Scott asks if it is always this hot and muggy. I respond, "Yeah, the weather is lousy like this most of the time, but don't worry, you'll get used to it pretty quick."

With a concerned look, Scott asks, "Are you used to it yet?"

I reply emphatically, "No!"

Scott asks, "How long have you been here?"

My response, "Just a little over three months now!"

Scott stops momentarily and looks around at his surroundings and the sky above him and says, "And you're not used to it yet—damn, I'm a mountain man from the northwest—I don't handle heat and humidity well!"

With a grin and a chuckle, I respond, "Well, good luck with that, Scott! Ah, hell, enough about the weather, you married?"

I had continued walking toward the mess hall, and as Scott catches up with me, he responds in a low melancholy voice, "Yeah, I'm married to a terrific, good looking school teacher."

"What a coincidence, me too! God, how I miss her! I was just dreaming about her again last night!"

In a subdued voice, Scott says, "I've only been in this country a few days, and I'm going nuts!"

With another grin and chuckle, I tell him, "Don't worry, you'll get used to it."

Scott cracks a small smile. "Yeah, right, kinda like the weather!" We both laugh.

Changing the subject as we approach the mess hall, I ask Scott, "How'd you end up in the Army? Are you going to make it a career?"

Scott responds, "No, it's not a career for me. I got drafted after graduating from college—I had no desire to come over here, so I kept volunteering for every Army school that I could attend. Then I ran out of schools!"

I stop dead in my tracks and look at Scott, "No shit!"

Scott responds, "Yeah, no shit, why?"

I resume walking and, with a smile, look over at Scott, "I did the same damn thing!"

Scott, who had kept walking, stops and looks over at me and says, "No shit! I thought I was the only guy crazy enough to do that, hoping this damn war would end before I finished all their schools!"

We continue walking, and I respond, "No, my friend, not hardly! I've met others over here who did the same damn thing!" Both of us laugh at the absurdity of continually volunteering for more training in hopes of not being sent over here. Arriving at the mess hall, both Scott and I sense we will become good friends.

After lunch, I check out a jeep from our motor pool and take Scott on a tour of our Company area and the Phu Bai base. Although the jeep is no muscle car, I tend to drive it like I'm behind the wheel of my Corvette. This is much to Scott's discomfort, as he occasionally grabs for handles to keep from falling out of the jeep.

Our Eagles Company area consists of the pilots' quarters, separate NCO and enlisted men's quarters, sandbag bunkers to use as protective cover in the case of rocket and mortar attacks, headquarters trailer, mess hall, motor pool, arms room bunker, ammunition bunker, and the large helicopter staging area. We are located on the west side of the Phu Bai base and are responsible for a large portion of the berm line on that side.

The berm line is a defensive structure, manned 24 hours a day, much like the ramparts of a military fort. It consists of long connected trenches, guard towers with machine guns, searchlights, and small bunkers. Outside of the berm line are large open/cleared areas allowing for an established field of fire and placement of mines and claymores. The difference between these two weapons of death is that a mine is placed in the ground and explodes up, whereas a claymore is set on the surface and explodes outward. They are both deadly and effective. Several layers of barbed wire stretch from one end of the berm line to the other. Some refer to this area as "no man's land." This is all designed to provide security for the base and make it more difficult for sappers, enemy commando units, to penetrate the base and wreak havoc on our helicopter groups.

The central part of the Phu Bai base is a fully operational airfield with a runway, taxiways, large helicopter staging areas, control tower, and fire equipment. The airfield is capable of handling U. S. Air Force transport aircraft. The base has several of the 101st Airborne Divisions Huey, Cobra, Chinook, and medical evacuation helicopter companies. In the hopes of reducing their vulnerability to sapper attack, they are set up at strategic locations all around the base. Our base also has a PX (Post Exchange—a place to purchase personal hygiene items, reading material, and light snacks), medical facilities, and various small clubs where men can enjoy their free time and buy beer and some liquor.

This is the limited world of the men stationed at Phu Bai Combat Base, and home for Scott, our fellow pilots and crews, and me. After a long afternoon showing Scott around his new home, we head over to the Pilots Club for some relaxation and a few beers.

The Pilots Club is a large, wooden shack that serves as the watering hole for us helicopter pilots assigned to the different Companies located at the 101st Aviation Group's Phu Bai base. The Eagles and Butchers Cobra Company are part of that Group.

Entering the Club, we find it crowded with pilots, smoke so thick it's hard to breathe, and a radio blasting away with the latest stateside hits. I see Greg standing at one corner of the bar and head toward him with Scott following me.

"Greg, you have some room for two more thirsty pilots?" Recognizing my voice, he turns to greet his friend. "Damn TJ, that was close the other day! You almost bought it out there. You know, you should consider another line of work!"

With mild laughter, I respond, "Good idea, what would you suggest?"

Greg says, "What about a General's aide or a staff officer in Saigon?"

I crack a grin. "Yeah, right, I'll keep that in mind." After a pause, I continue. "Greg, this is Scott McGregor, my new roommate. We'll be flying together for a while. Scott, meet Captain Greg Owens. He's a Cobra pilot with Butcher Company. He's not a bad guy, just keep an eye on your wallet, liquor, and women when he is around."

Greg and Scott shake hands as Greg grins at me. "Thanks, TJ, what did I ever do to you to deserve that? Scott, good to meet you."

Scott replies, "Good to meet you, Captain."

Greg, not being a stickler for rank either, says, "You can call me Greg, forget the rank bullshit."

Scott, thinking to himself, *why in the hell do we even have a rank at all?* Responds, "Sure, no problem, Greg."

I yell down at the bartender to set us up with three beers. He pulls them out of the cooler, pops off their tops, and slides them down the bar to me. I hand one to Greg and then Scott. Taking a sip from his beer, Greg says, "So TJ, you drew some more light duty, who the hell did you piss off again."

Scott is confused by Greg's comment and asks, "Greg, what does that mean, light duty?"

Greg responds, "It's kinda a play on words, Scott...it's not light duty."

Seeing that Scott is confused by his answer, Greg continues in a matter-of-fact tone. "Scott, nothing against you, I'm sure you have your shit together and are a good pilot. But breaking in new guys can be a dangerous business over here. Now with this Laos operation, the pucker factors are way up there, and it is pretty damn hairy right now! It's not a good way to become a short-timer over here."

Scott asks, "What is considered a short-timer over here, Greg?"

I answer that question. "Anybody that's been here longer than you!"

Scott retorts, "Oh, this might be a dumb ass question, but how does a new guy live long enough to become a short-timer if nobody wants to break the new guy in?"

Greg and I both shrug our shoulders while saying nothing, and I think to myself, *That's not a dumb ass question. There is no answer—that's just the way it is over here.*

Not really satisfied, but realizing there is nothing he can do about it, Scott gazes around the Pilots Club. While doing so, he notices there are several comments scribbled on the wall behind the bar under the caption Helicopter Wisdom. They catch his attention, and he reads them to himself.

. . .

## HELICOPTER WISDOM

Cover your Buddy, so he can be around to cover for you.

The terms Protective Armor and Helicopter are mutually exclusive.

Chicken Plates are not something you order in a restaurant.

Loud, sudden noises in a helicopter will get your undivided attention.

Having all your body parts intact and functioning at the end of the day beats the alternative.

It's not a good idea to run out of airspeed, altitude, and ideas all at the same time.

A free-fire zone has nothing to do with economics.

The further you fly into the mountains, the louder the strange engine noises become.

Medals are OK, but having your body and all your friends in one piece at the end of the day is better.

Being shot hurts, and it can ruin your whole day.

Flying is better than walking. Walking is better than running. Running is better than crawling. However, all of these are better than extraction by Medevac, even though it is technically a form of flying.

After reading them, Scott asks me where all those sayings came from. Looking over at them, I respond. "After some drinking and long days of flying, some pilots just feel the need to express themselves poetically with words of wisdom to live by you might say."

Scott's reaction is pensive as he reads them over again. By his facial expression, it appears as if he is committing them to memory. Scott continues to look around and notices several carved wooden eagles behind the bar on a shelf. Most of them have last names taped to them.

Scott again asks, "Taylor, what are all those wooden eagles on the shelf over there for?"

"Those are our eagles. When a new guy goes through our initiation into the Company, they get to choose one for themselves. That'll be your official welcome, and as part of the initiation, you'll select one of those unassigned wooden eagles, tape your name to it, and if you make it through your tour here, you'll take it home as a memento."

Scott asks Taylor, "What happens if you don't make it?"

I respond, "After the tape with your name on it is removed from the eagle, it'll go back on the shelf for another new guy to possibly choose."

Scott looks over at Greg and asks if his Company does the same thing? With an anguished look and emotional response, he tells Scott, "We still do initiations, but stopped giving out mementos because we were losing too many pilots. It was not helping our morale any as we kept having to remove taped names off of dead men's mementos and place them back on the shelf."

As our conversations taper off, a melancholy mood settled in over us. We each drifted off momentarily into our own thoughts as we slowly finished our last beer. Tomorrow comes early, and we call it an evening. Since I had a jeep, we all climb aboard and I drive Greg over to his Company area. Scott and I then head back to our quarters for some rest. From the look on Scott's face, I sense he is wondering just what the hell has he gotten himself into over here. I remember when I first had that same feeling. The problem is, I still have it!

# CHAPTER 7

## AREA OF OPERATIONS (AO)

The next morning is like any other, hot, and muggy, with that distinct and unpleasant smell in the air that permeates everything. I long for the scent of a fresh ocean breeze. For Scott, it's the smell of a Northwestern forest. After breakfast and checking in at Operations for the day's weather and situation reports, we stroll through the Company area on our way to the arms room.

"Well, Scott, it looks like we lucked out for your first day, good weather, and not much activity in the areas we'll be flying around in."

Scott belches as he says, "That's a relief, I'd hate to buy it my first day in the air over here!" After a long pause and with a look of embarrassment, he continues, "Sorry about that...I like milk, but that stuff they serve in the mess hall leaves a lot to be desired. Do you have any idea where it comes from?"

Looking over at Scott and laughing, I respond, "As to your first point, don't believe everything you hear over here. Our situation reports are not exactly accurate and usually understated. Our little friends from the north can come out of nowhere and shoot your ass off before you know what hits you. As for the weather, it can change in a heartbeat."

I pause to see if he has any questions or comments, hearing none, I continue, "As for the milk we are provided...well...there's a rumor that it comes from a Company in the states which is owned by Lady Bird Johnson. It's not very popular with the men in our Company!"

Scott replies with a smirk, "Interesting!"

Arriving at the arms room, I open the door and enter the sandbagged bunker complex, with Scott following. The arms room Sergeant looks up from behind the counter, sitting and reading a Playboy magazine.

Strolling over to the counter and looking over at his magazine, I blurt out, "Good morning, Sergeant. This is Lieutenant McGregor. He's my new roommate. I'll expect you to take care of him like you do me. If not, I'll hear about it and cut off your supply of Playboys. Got it?"

Scott and the Sergeant exchange hand salutes casually.

The Sergeant reaches over to shake his hand and says, "Welcome to the Eagles, Lieutenant."

Scott extends his hand and responds, "Thanks, Sergeant!"

The Sergeant looks over at me, and his facial expression conveys a sense of concern for his magazines. "Cap'n, you're just kidding about the magazines, right?"

Leaning over to see the playgirl of the month centerfold at which the Sergeant was looking, I respond, "Yeah, don't worry. I wouldn't want to deprive a man of his only source of enlightenment."

"Thanks, Cap'n!"

"Sergeant, I'll take my usual and give the Lieutenant the same!"

The Sergeant starts moving around, gathering up our equipment as he speaks. "Yes sir, let's see now. That'll be two shoulder holsters with .45 pistol's, two waist holsters with .38 pistol's, two survival vests, and four chicken plates, two for each of you. That should do it, Cap'n!"

Scott watches with a puzzled look on his face as the Sergeant lays the equipment on the counter. I pick up my weapons from the counter and strap on a shoulder and then a waist holster. Once I've adjusted them for comfort, I grab two chicken plates, a survival vest, and head for the door. Scott follows my lead.

"Cap'n, you and the Lieutenant be careful out there today." I give him a thumbs up and, turning toward the door, say, "Thanks, we'll try, see you later." Scott follows me outside.

As we walk toward the helicopter staging area carrying all our equipment, Scott inquires why I drew two pistols and two chicken plates. "I'll show you when we get to the chopper. Trust me, when you go into a hot LZ, this stuff just might make a difference!" I respond.

We arrive at our assigned helicopter, located in one of several revetments housing the Eagles' helicopters. Revetments are designed to protect the Hueys from enemy rocket and mortar attacks. They consist of sandbags, wood, and some metal sheeting built as high as possible on both sides of the helicopters. They allow for enough space so that the helicopter blades can rotate within the revetment without hitting the sides of the revetments. Needless to say, this can be challenging when it comes to hovering in and out of them.

Our helicopter's assigned crew chief/door gunner today is Charlie, a clean-cut, serious young man from New York. Our other door gunner is Rick, a young surfer from Southern California, who has his own colorful language. Both men have been busy performing their pre-flight assignments of the Huey when we walk up to them.

I explain to Scott that each helicopter in the Company has an assigned crew chief responsible for the aircraft. Pilots and door gunners are assigned daily to whatever helicopters are available for the day's missions. I then introduce Scott to our crew for the day. "Charlie, Rick, this is Lieutenant McGregor. Scott, this is Charlie and Rick, our crew today."

Both Charlie and Rick walk up to Scott as they salute him. Charlie extends his hand and says, "Scott, you're flying with a good pilot, he has his shit together. Oh, and let me add, you also have a good crew today!"

Before Scott can respond, Rick steps forward and tries to give Scott the brother's handshake. Scott just grabs his hand and shakes it. Rick blurts out, "Lieutenant, I look forward to our day together. Just don't get me killed!"

Scott responds to them. "Gentlemen, good to meet both of you, and I'll do my damnedest not to kill any of us. How's that?"

To which Rick replies. "Bitching man! Tubular...no wipeouts today!"

Scott shakes his head slightly, while casting a quizzical look at me and responds to Rick. "Yeah, right, bitching!"

I open the door on our Huey's left side and drop the chicken plates and survival vest on my seat. Scott does likewise on the other side. Looking at Scott and without speaking, I point to the top of the Huey and motion to him that I will take the bottom. We begin our detailed pre-flight check of the Huey.

I walk down one side of the Huey, scrutinizing it closely for any holes or fluid leaks. Moving down the side, I open every compartment and look inside, checking to ensure there are no tools, such as wrenches, pliers, screwdrivers, or other working tools left in the compartments by the maintenance team. I'm also checking to ensure there are no loose wires or any fluid lines leaking inside the compartments. Reaching the tail of the Huey, I check the tail rotor for freedom of movement by shaking it, and visually inspect it for any discernible damage. I then move down the other side of the Huey, performing the same diligent check.

Scott has climbed on top of the Huey and is checking the rotor blades for freedom of movement. He peers into the engine compartment and looks for any discernible damage or leftover debris. Finishing on top, he climbs down the side. Once on the ground, he squats down, and reaching under the Huey, presses the fuel sump valve releasing some fuel from the bottom of the fuel tank. This procedure is performed to remove any moisture caused by condensation or bad fuel and to remove any sediment that might have collected.

Having completed our outside checks, I pick up one of my chicken plates and slip into it. When that is securely fastened, I place my survival vest over it and tighten the vest. I'm not sure how much good this vest would be if I really had to depend on it. I never made it past Tenderfoot in the Boy Scouts. In other words, I'm not a survivalist by nature. So, I hope we're extracted very quickly by our fellow pilots if we ever do go down..

The other chicken plate I gently place in the chin bubble of the Huey directly in front of my seat and below the foot pedals. Scott observes me doing all of this and proceeds to do the same thing. Charlie has moved to the front of our Huey and removed the rotor tie-down rope. Wrapping it up, he steps back, waiting for the engine to start and movement of the blades.

Scott and I climb into the Huey, adjust our seats, and strap ourselves in. Rick has climbed in and adjusted his M-60 machine gun as he settles himself in.

Scott says, "Taylor, the fuel tank is clear. Everything is secure and okay on top!"

I respond, "Good! Everything checked out okay on my walk around."

Scott looks over at me, "I see why you bring along an extra chicken plate but does it really help any?"

Looking over at Scott, "You never know over here, Scott, but it might just stop a bullet or some shrapnel from coming up at you through the chin bubble. Hell, I'll take any little advantage I can get."

As I pull the waist holster, with the .38 revolver inside it, around so that it is resting over my crotch, I gently tuck it between my legs. "Scott, see what I've done? Do the same thing. It might seem uncomfortable at first, but you'll get used to it."

With a smirk on his face, Scott follows my lead and says, "You've got to be kidding!"

With a serious tone, I respond, "No, not really, I slip it there before flying into hot LZs. Doing this and bringing the extra chicken plate were two extra precautions shown to me by more experienced pilots shortly after I got here. Some guys take one or both precautions, and others don't. It's your call!"

We both adjust our waist holsters so that they are once again by our side. We slip our helmets on, tighten the straps, and plug the radio connections to the Huey's radio system. Scott and I go through our start-up checklist. While I move the controls through their range of motion, Scott adjusts the radio frequencies and does a scan of the instrument panel, hoping he hasn't forgotten anything. It has been almost a month since he last flew before arriving at this moment in time.

Over the Huey's intercom, my crew and I communicate as I transmit, 'Controls feel good. Everything okay, Scott? Rick?'

Scott responds, 'Looks good!'

Rick responds, 'Everything is fine back here, Sir.'

'All right, gentlemen, we're ready to fire this puppy up.'

I lean out my window and yell to Charlie, "All clear?" Charlie responds, "All clear!"

As I press the engine start switch, our Huey begins shaking as the turbojet engine fires up, and the rotor blades slowly begin to turn. Scott is monitoring the instrument panel and keeps me informed of his observations over the intercom, 'Oil pressure online and okay. Hydraulic pressure on-line and okay. Rotor RPM increasing and approaching the red line.'

Our Huey's rotor blades reach their normal RPM, and the vibrations subside. It feels light on the controls as I pull up on the collective enough to bring the Huey to a hover. Once stabilized in a controlled hover, I slowly move forward out of the revetment, as Charlie guides me. Over the intercom, I hear Scott and Rick tell me we have cleared the revetment. 'Roger, I'm setting her down, and we'll pick up Charlie.'

As I set the Huey down, Charlie jumps in and settles into his seat. He fastens himself in, plugs in his radio connection, and adjusts his M-60. With Charlie secured, I bring the Huey back up to a hover and move to the end of the helicopter staging area. Once there, I call the main base control tower for clearance to launch. 'Phu Bai Tower, this is Eagle 25, we are ready to depart. Over!'

'Roger, Eagle 25, this is Phu Bai Tower. You are cleared for take-off. Maintain a heading of 150 and climb to 2,000 feet. Maintain that altitude until clear of Camp Evans airspace. Over!'

'Phu Bai Tower, Eagle 25, Roger that, tower. Out!'

I pull in more power and move all the controls, simultaneously, in a well-coordinated manner. Our Huey slowly and gracefully takes off into the mid-morning sky. At altitude and well clear of Camp Evans air space, I speak to the crew over our intercom. 'Okay, fellows, test your guns'. With that, Charlie and Rick load their machine guns and fire small bursts directly out into the open sky around us. I look over to Scott, 'Scott, you have the ship!'

Scott slowly takes the controls as he responds, 'I got it.'

Relinquishing the controls to Scott, I settle back into my seat. I continue to scan the instrument panel and look outside the cockpit over the areas below. Helicopter pilots are trained from the beginning to be ever vigilant of what is going on inside the helicopter, and outside in the environment around them.

After settling in for the first phase of our flight today, I begin a dialogue with Scott over the intercom.

'Scott, you may have heard this already, but I'm going to share it with you anyway. There are four general categories of helicopter incidents over here, which can ruin your whole day. Enemy fire, bad weather, mechanical trouble, and human error. I've already experienced all of them. As you know, I've just started my fourth month over here. I dare say you will experience all of them, too, at some point.'

I pause for a moment to give Scott a chance to digest what I just said and then continue. 'So, learn well, learn fast, stay alert, and keep your shit together, and you may just make it home. Having said that, you can rest assured some asshole is going to come along and try to ruin your whole fucking day!'

Scott responds, 'Wow! Thanks, I feel better already. I guess you're not the morale officer.'

'No, I'm not. We lost him a few weeks back!'

Scott says, 'No shit?' I respond, 'No shit!'

'Okay, Scott, today we'll be doing your check ride while flying around our AO. This will help you to get the lay of the land. Remember the locations I'm going to show you today, particularly the landmarks. They can be a big help around here when the weather gets shitty.'

With an apprehensive look spreading across his face, Scott says, 'Just how bad can it get?'

'It can get pretty damn bad. I've flown into some firebases where the ceilings were only a few hundred feet or less, and the visibility was piss poor!'

'Damn, we didn't do that kinda flying in flight school!'

'You're in Vietnam now, Scott—you're going to do a lot of flying you never trained for. We fly in all kinds of weather, day and night, and all kinds of conditions. There is no such thing as flight minimums or conditions if the grunts need us! Okay, turn to a heading of 240, climb to 6,000 feet. We'll go over to Firebase Sarge first. Anyone for some music?'

Rick comes to life. 'Yeah, bitching, dude, I mean... yes sir!'

Charlie responds. 'Damn surfers, don't you guys have a bigger vocabulary than that? Can we trade him in for another door gunner?'

I respond, 'I can't do that to a fellow surfer Charlie. Besides, without him, we wouldn't be up on all the stateside hits and surfer tunes!'

Rick looks over at Charlie and says, 'Yeah, well, what about rad, tubular, awesome, bitching. Is that a big enough vocabulary for you, Charlie? Being a surfer, the Captain knows what I'm talking about. Right, Cap?'

Wanting to get into the moment and provide a little levity, I respond to Rick, 'Fucking A!'

Adjusting our ADF radio frequency to the local Armed Forces Radio Station, we hear some of the latest stateside music over our helmet radios. Rick asks, 'Sir, can you see if we can get the Beachboys or Dick Dale and The Del Tones.' I respond, 'Well, Rick, I would like that, but unfortunately, we only have the one station to choose from, and they control the music.'

Knowing that is the case, Rick injects some more levity into our conversation by going into a profanity-based tirade about the lack of good music. Charlie reacts, 'Damn, he does have a bigger vocabulary.' We all laugh at that.

With that exchange, we settle back down and concentrate on today's flying objectives. I take some time to explain to Scott what the Operational Area is for the 101st Airborne Division. 'Scott, we are responsible for much of 1 Corps in the northern part of South Vietnam. Our area of operations stretches from the coastline on the east to the mountains on the west, which border Laos.

North to the DMZ (Demilitarized Zone) and south to DaNang. Included in this area are Phu Bai, Hue City, Quang Tri City, Khe Sanh, A Shau Valley, Camp Eagle, which is the 101st Division HQ Combat base camp, Camp Evans, and several other smaller firebases established in the mountains and around the A Shau Valley.'

Scott looks over at me and says, 'Damn that's a lot of territory, it's going to take time for me to get familiar with all the various areas and their landmarks.'

I look over at Scott and with a grin respond, 'Don't worry Scott, with all the flying we do, you'll pick it up quickly.'

For the remainder of the day, we fly around many of the areas included in our AO. As we fly low over some American firebases, several men on the ground look up and wave at us. When we fly low over some Vietnamese villages, many people look up, but no one waves. I spend much of my time commenting on the different locations and points of reference. I do this to acquaint Scott with landmarks and give him some history of previous activity in our area. We eventually wrap up our day and head back to base.

The next day we are at it again, but this time, we're flying some "milk run missions" (non-combat, routine, low risk related missions) to give Scott a chance to get some stick time on low-risk missions. Once again, Scott does most of the actual flying. This is done to give him an opportunity to gain confidence and become more comfortable with our area. As usual, the weather is bad, with low ceilings in some areas, wind, and some light rain.

The countryside we fly over is beautiful, picture-postcard kind of stuff, with hills, mountains, streams, rivers, waterfalls, and land mostly covered with trees and lush vegetation. I express my thoughts to Scott that someday this area, with its terrain and beaches, would make a great tourist haven for people from many countries. Scott agrees with me, but not anytime soon. This we both agree on.

Our flying day ends with me doing a slow, spiraling descent into Phu Bai Base. After landing, I hover our chopper over to the Eagles staging area and into a revetment. Shutting down the engine and sitting back in my seat, listening to our rotor blades wind down and come to a stop, I think—*it was not a bad day of flying, and it passed quickly. Scott's a good pilot, with good instincts and a fast learner.* I look forward to flying with him on regular missions and can only hope we have many uneventful days of flying in the future. However, I know we won't, not with this Laos operation in full swing.

# CHAPTER 8

## EAGLES INITIATION

After a long day of flying, Scott and I head up to the Pilots Club, where Greg meets us outside. We walk into the Club, which is full of pilots from different Companies. In one corner, near the shelf holding the wooden eagles, a large contingent of Eagles pilots are gathered. Pappy, standing in the middle of them, waves us over. I guide Scott in their direction, with Greg following.

As we close in on Pappy, he reaches out and shakes our hands, saying, "Good to see you, fellows." He then pulls Scott next to him, looking out at the pilots standing around, and motions for their attention. "Gentlemen, I want to present to you, for initiation into our fine brotherhood, Lieutenant Scott McGregor."

The group roars their approval. Pappy says, "Scott, I give you your fellow pilots, the Eagles. After tonight, you will be part of the finest group of chopper pilots in Vietnam. They will take care of you, and you will take care of them!"

Scott looks around at the group surrounding him, surveying their faces while trying not to show any trepidation concerning what is to follow. "Thank you, Major, I am looking forward to becoming a member of the Eagles and flying with the best!"

"Well said, young man!" Pappy guides Scott over to the bar and points to the wooden eagles on the shelf. "Pick one out for yourself, and we'll tape your name to it."

Scott surveys the selection on the shelf behind the bar and points to one. An Eagle pilot standing behind the bar grabs the eagle and sets it on the bar. He then places a piece of tape on the base of the eagle carving and writes Scott's name on it. His eagle is then placed back on the shelf with the others.

"Okay, Scott, we're ready, are you? Oh, do you like to drink?" Pappy asks.

"On occasions!" Scott responds a little nervously, even though he tries to conceal it.

The Major, laughing, says, "That'll work just fine son. On with the games!"

With that exchange, Stan emerges from the group and walks over to Scott. Being the most senior officer next to the Pappy, he leads the initiation. As he moves next to Scott, the group becomes more subdued in anticipation of what is to follow. Pappy steps back and out of the way.

Stan, looking directly at Scott, says, "Are you ready to join us and become an Eagle?"

Scott tries to reply in a confident, self-assured voice, but it comes out a little weak, "Yes sir."

Stan looking out at the group with a smirk starting to spread across his face again says to Scott. "Are you sure?"

Scott responds, "Yes!" Stan says, "Well then, let's start with a toast to the Eagles."

Stan hands a beer to Scott and picks up one for himself. He then raises his beer and offers the first toast, "To the Eagles, the best chopper company in Nam!"

The group of Eagles raise their beers in a toast. Drinking

them down, they show their approval with hoots and hollers. Scott finishes his beer, and Stan slaps another into his hands while making another toast. "To Pappy!"

Looking over at their Major, they give him nods of approval and shout out comments of, "You're the best!", "Great guy!", "Fucking A" and on it goes, as another round of beers bites the dust.

Now the group starts to get into the act as some of the Eagles pilots make toasts.

"Going back home on the big Freedom Bird!" This brings on a hearty cheer and roars of approval.

"To the Cobra pilots who cover our asses!" More cheering, as many in the group look over at Greg, who nods his acknowledgment.

I get into the act and shout out a toast over the noise. "To Greg, one of the best, just don't let him near your women!" My toast sparks more laughter as some of the pilots throw their empty beer cans his way. For some reason, in our little world over here, that is taken as a show of respect.

"To R&R, which can't come soon enough!" yells out another one of the Eagles. "Amen to that!" is heard from several in the group.

By this time, we are all well on our way to feeling a little inebriated. Scott is already wobbly when Stan moves to the next phase. Stan has one of the pilots behind the bar hand him a bottle of whiskey, a shot glass, and a wet towel. As they are handed to him, he sets each one on top of the bar in a slow and deliberate manner. As he does, the Eagles pilots quiet down and watch with eager anticipation as to how Scott handles this part of his initiation.

Stan puts his arm over Scott's shoulder and pulls him closer. "Scott, we've come to that part of your initiation, which separates the men from the boys."

To which Scott replies. "No shit?"

Stan responds, "Yeah, no shit! Get through this, and you'll be one of us. An Eagle!"

Scott replies, "No shit?"

Stan pulls back Scott's head, so it's resting on the top of the bar, and replies, "No shit!"

Scott finds himself looking up at the ceiling, anxiously anticipating what comes next. Pouring whiskey into the shot glass until it pours over, Stan pulls out a lighter and lights it. He then ignites the whiskey in the shot glass and holds it up for all to see. Placing the wet towel over Scott's chin, he hands him the flaming drink. Stan, with a look of anticipation, says, "Okay, all you need to do is drink up, make it quick, it's much easier that way. I'll put out the flame if any of it gets on you—bottoms up!"

Scott takes the drink, and with his hand trembling, slowly lifts it to his mouth. In one swift movement, Scott gulps the flaming whiskey down. Some of it spills on his chin and is still on fire. Stan is a little slow to put it out as Scott jerks up from the bar. Scott's not very happy about it, but he's too drunk to do anything.

Stan guides his head back down on the bar and repeats the process several more times. With each succeeding drink, more of the men lose their zest for the initiation. Seeing that Scott can hardly stand up and he's had enough, I step forward and put an end to it. As I do, I look over at the Major, who nods his approval. "That's enough, Stan, he's one of us now!"

Our group of Eagles cheers and congratulates Scott. Many of the pilots try to shake Scott's hand. By now, Scott is semiconscious and not aware of much of anything as Greg and I carry him between us and head for the exit. As we open the door to leave, Stan and I exchange staring glances that momentarily silence many of the men witnessing it.

Once outside the Club, we head for Greg's jeep and do the

best we can to settle Scott into the back. This proves to be somewhat challenging since we are both a little drunk, and Scott is dead weight, having lost all consciousness.

While driving Scott and me back to our Company area, Greg asks. "What is with that guy Stan? Was he born an asshole, or does he just take an asshole pill every day?"

"Probably both. You know, you asked me the other day who I pissed off? You saw him in action tonight."

"Taylor, there is some loose talk in our Company that he's more talk than action, and not a very good pilot. We rarely hear his call sign, in or around the hot LZs we work."

With a slow, somewhat slurry voice, I respond. "He doesn't assign himself the more dangerous missions...and no one wants to fly with him. I haven't been in the Company that long, but I've heard this from those who have. Another thing he hasn't done is assign himself any new guys to break-in since joining the Company. He apparently prefers to fly a desk!"

Greg replies, "What an asshole!" Arriving at our Company area, Greg pulls up next to the Pilot's quarters. He helps me lift Scott out of the jeep and carry him into our room. We lower Scott into his bunk and throw a blanket over him. Greg turns to leave the room and says as he's walking out the door, "Catch you later, TJ."

"Yeah, see you later." As Greg leaves, I collapse on my cot, and I'm out for the night.

# CHAPTER 9

## THE MAJOR-PAPPY

I t's late morning the day following Scott's initiation. We both struggle to get out of bed, but somehow, slowly manage to rise from our cots. It was a long night, and Scott is nursing a severe hang-over. It always takes at least 24 hours for the new guys to recover from their initiation, so the next day is a stand-down day for them. I luck out and get to hang back also. I think to myself, *that is a good thing, for I got pretty damn wasted myself last night.* After showering and putting on fresh fatigues, we head out into the midday sun and over to the mess hall.

Although neither one of us is hungry, we go through the chow line, drop a few food items on our trays, and head for a corner table. Very few men are in the mess hall. We are both thankful for this since our heads are still throbbing and feel like they might explode any minute. We sit there quietly, picking at our food, each of us is lost in our thoughts. Our peaceful bliss is shattered when the mess hall door swings open, banging hard against the wall. The arms room Sergeant rushes in and, in a highly distressed and emotionally quivering voice, yells out to those of us in the mess hall, "Pappy has been killed."

We are suddenly awakened from our stupor, and throwing our chairs to one side, run out of the mess hall. We are followed by everyone else and head directly over to the headquarters trailer. A large group of men has already started to gather. Reaching the trailer, we push our way into the operations area. It is a small area that is overflowing with men, to include the First Sergeant and Stan. No one is talking. Many are in a state of shock.

Hearing me enter the room, Stan turns from looking out the window to face me. He's desperately trying to hold back his emotions, but it is clear he has been shaken. I ask him, "What the hell happened?"

"Major Hutchins chopper got hit on short final going into LZ 30. They crashed nose-first into the ground and exploded on impact—no one survived!"

There are low murmurs and whispers as the news sinks in among the men gathered. Stan continues. "From what we know so far, Pappy got hit pretty bad as they were coming into the LZ, and his co-pilot took over the controls."

I ask. "Who was it?"

Stan looks back out the window. "It was our newest Warrant, Officer—Steve. He apparently panicked and lost control." A long pause, "Goddamn new guys!"

Steve had arrived at the Company a few weeks before Scott. Until Scott arrived, he had been the "new guy." I respond, "That can happen to any of us—you should know that!"

Turning back to look at me, eyes glazing and intense, Stan says, "It's damn sure not going to happen to me!"

There is no response I can make to that comment, so I turn and start to leave the room. Scott and the other men follow. Stan motions for us to stop as he wants to say something. "Gentlemen, there will be a memorial service tonight at 1900 hours for Pappy and his crew. It will be held in the Company formation area. Pass the word."

The room starts emptying, as Stan turns to look back out the window. Scott stops, turns around, and walks over to Stan. As he does, I stop and look on. "Stan, you don't blame this on Steve because he was a new guy, do you?" Stan continues staring out the window and doesn't acknowledge Scott, who slowly turns away and walks out of the room behind me.

Later that evening in the Company formation area, the men of Company B are standing around in small groups as a very somber mood prevails. Scott, Greg, and I are with a small group standing nearest the stage, which was set up in the formation area for the service. On the stage is the Eagles Battalion Commander, Battalion Chaplain, and Stan.

Arranged in a neat row across the front of the stage are four sets of aviator boots. Behind each set of boots is an aviator helmet. On the left side of the stage is the American flag, and on the right is the 101st Airborne Division flag. The Battalion Commander is speaking to the men.

"Gentlemen, we lost four good men earlier today. Unfortunately, they will not be the last. I know how all of you felt about Major Hutchins. He was a good man and a fine leader. Always leading from the front and never leaving a man behind. A leader's job is to set the example and mold his men into good pilots and leaders. I firmly believe, as your beloved Pappy would, that the greatest honor you could bestow on his memory would be to follow in his footsteps."

The Battalion Commander pauses to let his words settle in and then continues. "In a few days, your new Company Commander will be here. I know all of you will give him your support and ensure that the Eagles carry on. Pappy would expect nothing less of you, and neither will I!"

The Battalion Commander turns toward the Chaplain and motions for him to come forward. Reaching the front of the stage, he looks up into the night sky with its sparkling stars and shining half-moon and brings his hands together for prayer. "Dear God in heaven, we commend to you this day, the souls of four good men. We know that you will welcome them into your house for eternity. We also ask that you watch over their families back in the States, as this will surely be trying times for them."

The Chaplain looks down at the boots and helmets arranged on the stage in front of him. I can tell from the expression on his face that he has grown weary of performing these services. He invites us to join him in a moment of silent prayer for our fallen comrades. Almost in unison, we bow our heads. After a moment of silent prayer, the Chaplain raises his head and looks out over us. Many of the fellows still have their heads bowed as he continues the service.

"To ease our pain and give us strength in this time of sorrow, I will now read from the Holy Scriptures, Psalm 23. The Lord is my Shepherd: I shall not want. He maketh me to lie down in green pastures: he leadeth me beside still waters. He restoreth my soul: he leadeth me in the paths of righteousness for his name's sake. Yea, though I walk through the valley of the shadow of death, I will fear no evil: for thou art with me: thy rod and thy staff they comfort me..."

His service is very emotional, and many of those present are overcome by grief. Tears stream down our faces and sobs can be heard from around the formation area. I am one of them who is overcome by grief and struggle to hold myself together. Although I didn't know the other three crewmen very well who died with Pappy, I had grown to respect and admire Major Hutchins, very much. I will miss him. I feel immense sorrow and grief for the families back home of all four men.

Having listened intently to the Chaplain reading from Psalm 23, I find myself repeating part of it over and over again in my mind. *Though I walk through the valley of the shadow of death, I will fear no evil, valley of the shadow of death, fear no evil, shadow of death, fear no evil.*

# CHAPTER 10

## NEW COMPANY COMMANDER

A few days later, the Battalion Commander arrives at B Company with our new Commanding Officer, Major Parker Stewart. Parker is an arrogant, self-centered, pompous, long time career officer on his second tour of duty in Vietnam. His first tour was as a staff officer in Saigon. This is his first combat command, which is critical for him to complete. Without this command, it is doubtful he would be considered for promotion to Lieutenant Colonel.

When the Battalion Commander and Major Stewart enter his new CO office, they find Stan and the Company First Sergeant waiting on them. Upon entering, the customary hand salutes are exchanged. The Battalion Commander speaks first. "Captain Norton, First Sergeant, this is your new CO, Major Parker Stewart. He has been down in Saigon, working with a South Vietnamese aviation unit as an adviser."

Stan and the First Sergeant shake his hand as they each welcome him to the Company. Parker acknowledges them and directs the First Sergeant to see that his gear and personal items are moved into the trailer as he plans to bunk there.

The First Sergeant and Stan exchange puzzled looks as there is no bunk area in the trailer. Parker notices their looks and says to them, "I noticed that Major Hutchins' room was not air-conditioned. I don't think I can put up with this heat. So see to it that a space is set up somewhere in here for my room."

As the First Sergeant salutes the officers and turns to leave, he acknowledges his new CO's order. "Yes, sir! I'll see to it right away. Anything else, sir?"

"No, that should do it for now."

The Battalion Commander, with a bemused look on his face, gazes at Parker. When the First Sergeant leaves the room, he speaks to Parker. "Do you really think moving into the only air-conditioned structure in your new command is a prudent thing to do?"

Parker responds, "It won't bother the men, sir!"

"You're sure of that, are you Major? I would be careful about making too many changes around here right away. This is a good Company, with a good record. The men were close to Major Hutchins and respected him. Hell, they loved the guy and called him Pappy for Chrissake. He is going to be a tough act to follow, Major!"

Parker's arrogance comes through as he responds to the Battalion Commander, "Yes, sir, I will take that under advisement, sir!"

The Battalion Commander lets this one slide by but is not impressed by Parker's attitude. With his command voice, he says, "Major, you'll need to get yourself acquainted with our operational area as fast as possible. We are in the early phases of a massive operation in Laos, as you know. Division is demanding a maximum effort every day from all our Aviation units. It is very taxing on the men and proving to be very costly!"

Sensing the Battalion Commander's irritation with his previous comment, Parker responds more respectfully. "I understand, sir. If it's alright with you, when I get settled in here, I want to meet with you and get a better idea of what we're up against."

"Good idea, Major. Call my office and set up a time when you're ready. Again, Parker, it's good to have you with us!"

Parker responds, "I will, and thank you, sir!"

The Battalion Commander looks over at Stan, "Captain, I'll be looking to you to ensure the Major settles in down here!"

"Yes sir, I'll see to it!"

Hand salutes are exchanged as the Battalion Commander leaves the office. Parker walks over to the window, looks out at the Company area, and addresses Stan. "Captain Norton, as my Operations Officer, you're the man that can make or break my career here. I'm going to expect you to work closely with me to make this the most operationally efficient Huey unit in the Division. We're going to launch every available Huey on every mission the Division gives us. I expect our maintenance unit to keep a maximum number of choppers operationally ready at all times. I want our downtime to be minimal and will accept no excuses. Do you understand, Captain?"

"Yes, sir, I understand! But, as the Commander said, this is a good Company, I don't think they can give much more!"

Parker turns from the window and stares into Stan's eyes. Stan becomes uneasy. "Look, Captain, I don't give a damn what you think. They can and will give much more. There's always room for improvement!"

With that said, Parker walks over to Stan and places his hand on Stan's shoulder. "Stan, work with me on this. I assure you our careers will both benefit from it. Work with me."

Parker releases his grip on Stan and steps back. Stan replies as he does so. "Like you, Major, I'm a career man. I'll do my job to the best of my abilities, and as your Operations Officer, I'll support you—yes, Major, I'll work with you!"

"Good! One more thing Stan. I did a brief walkthrough of the

Company area when I got here and before our meeting. It's a mess. Just because we're in Vietnam doesn't mean we can't run this Company like a stateside unit. It'll be good for discipline and improve our efficiency if we shake this place up some!"

Stan, with hesitation in his voice, says, "What exactly do you have in mind, sir?"

Again, Parker stares into Stan's eyes, with almost a crazed look. "Basic military discipline! We'll start with routine inspections of the men's living quarters, full parade Company formations for reveille and retreat, and the wearing of proper military attire at all times."

Stan, disbelieving what he is hearing, and without hesitating, snaps back at him. "Sir, this is a combat unit. They've been in some heavy action, that kinda stuff just isn't done."

Parker cuts him off. "Let's get something straight right now! This is my Company. It will be the best! I'll prepare a list of directives. You and the First Sergeant will see they are carried out. Understood?"

Parker turns back to look out the window and gives Stan a faint hand salute as he does so.

"Yes, sir!" Stan returns the salute, heads for the door, and as he leaves the office, whispers to himself, "Oh my god, what have we got here? Another frustrated Major who wants to make Colonel. This can't be good!"

# CHAPTER 11

## DIARY

Over the next several days, our Company flies multiple combat missions into hot LZs. Scott and I fly together on many of the missions and are accompanied by Greg and some of his Cobra pilots. Parker and Stan fly together on shorter missions as a C&C ship and always at high altitudes. Stan is acquainting Parker with our Area of Operations.

Lam Son 719 has been in full swing for the last few weeks, and we have helped establish several firebases inside Laos. These bases are located on higher ground to the north and south of Route 9 inside Laos. This dirt road is the main invasion route used by ARVN mechanized units as they penetrate deeper into Laos. We have been flying into Firebase 30 and 31, which are north of Route 9, and Firebase's Delta, Delta 1, and Brown, which are south of Route 9. All of them have been experiencing heavy contact with the enemy. We are routinely subjected to small arms and heavy weapons fire as we fly in and out of these firebases. Mortar rounds and artillery shells explode on impact all over the landing zones as we approach them, and RPGs are fired at us as we land or hover. In a nutshell, it is one hell of a mess when we cross the border into Laos. By some accounts, we have a 50/50 chance of making it back across the border into Vietnam without losing someone. This is no way to make a living.

During this period, our new CO spends most of his time overseeing the implementation of his Company directives. There are constant inspections of the men's living quarters, our arms room and maintenance area, motor pool, and mess hall. Company formations are held in the morning with reveille and uniform checks, and retreat in the evening after dinner. Wherever Parker goes in the Company area, he is pointing out things he doesn't like. Comments like, "That's wrong, soldier," "Fix that, soldier" "You're not doing it the right way, soldier," "Clean that area up," "That's a mess, soldier" can be heard all over the Company area as the days drag on. As these scenes progress, the men grow increasingly bewildered and frustrated. It shows in the looks they give each other, and the glares they give our new CO behind his back.

One of the main distractions from daily life that I established for myself was keeping a diary. I did so shortly after arriving in Vietnam. I briefly record my daily experiences, many of which are not shared with Sandy in the letters and tapes I send her or my parents. There is no need to give them more cause to worry about me than they already have. At the end of each entry, I close with—I love you, Sandy! Should I be killed or captured the next day, I want her to know that my last thoughts were of her.

Sitting at my desk late into the evenings, I record some of my experiences over the last few days.

## FEBRUARY 1971

Today Scott and I flew for 9 hours out of Khe Sanh and into Laos all day. It was quite an experience. We had gunship coverage every time we rolled into LZ 30 and 31 that we were working. We took mostly light machine gun ground fire. Not a lot of fun. Once, while refueling at Khe Sanh, a medevac helicopter made an emergency landing on the field. It was all shot-up, and one of the pilots had been killed. The two medics on the ship had been hit, and the other pilot was hurt. We could hear their conversations over our radio. That pilot kept his cool the whole time.

An H-53 Marine helicopter was shot down near the river by the border with Laos, all the crew members were killed. We flew by the scene shortly after it happened. Those guys didn't have a chance. This Laos operation is getting very costly. We are losing several crewmen and pilots. We are only in the early weeks of this operation and have many more to go.

I love you Sandy!

## FEBRUARY 1971

Scott and I flew together again for 10 hours today inside Laos and around Khe Sanh. We flew into LZ 30 once and received heavy fire. After that, we made several trips into a new LZ just south of LZ 30. I don't think they named it yet. They are using it as a temporary LZ to fly supplies and troops in. The new troops will then move up to LZ 30, carrying their supplies with them. Right now, it is just too damn hot to send helicopters into LZ 30.

Unfortunately, it did not take long for the NVA to figure that out. When they did, we started receiving fire every time we went into the new LZ. On our last flight there, we got hit several times by ground shrapnel. The aircraft was banged up pretty bad, and we were very slow to regain some altitude. Because of this, we continued to draw a lot of ground fire. We were finally able to gain enough altitude to get out of the line of fire and then limped back to Khe Sanh. Scott was flying us back and did an autorotation on a dirt road near one of the helicopter staging areas. Although we hit the ground hard, no one was hurt, just shaken up. It is getting progressively worse inside Laos, and harder to relax or unwind.

Our helicopter was banged up so bad we couldn't take a chance on flying it back to base. So, we left it at Khe Sanh and caught a ride back to our Company in another Eagles' chopper. A Chinook slung loaded the Huey and brought it back to the Company staging area this evening. It's a mess and will take considerable time to repair and have it ready to fly again.

I love you Sandy!

## FEBRUARY 1971

I flew today for about 2 ½ hours, and it was another bad day over Laos. I was assigned to fly with another one of our pilots named Jim. We flew into LZ 31 on our second mission into Laos, which was under attack again. Approaching the LZ on short final, we were hit on the right side of the ship by heavy machine gun fire. Several rounds hit the cockpit on Jim's side. He was hit in the legs and neck and was severely wounded. The right door gunner was hit in the head. He didn't have a chance and was killed instantly. I had our crew chief pull Jim out of his seat and do what he could for him. The ship was shuddering badly, and we lost several instruments, and our engine power was shaky. The crew chief did a good job helping Jim and probably saved his life. I was lucky and managed to fly us back to Khe Sanh, where I made a crash landing on the airstrip.

Everything happened so fast. When we first got hit, it seemed like I was in a slow-motion movie, and it became surreal to me. I was scared as hell but was too busy trying to get us back to the airstrip at Khe Sanh. I'm lucky to be alive tonight and hope that doesn't happen again. I still have many months to go over here.

It's really a bad feeling in your stomach to be scared. I think it's worse knowing there is nothing you can do about it because you cannot control the events going on around you. You just keep going and have to believe you will make it. I do not think I can live like this the rest of my life should I be lucky enough to make it through this tour.

Great news, Jim made it and will be medevaced home.

I love you Sandy!

## FEBRUARY 1971

Today was quite exciting. My crew and I almost got killed again. Scott and I were flying together, and we were doing an approach into Camp Evans. At 800 feet, we ran into a heavy downpour, which caught us by surprise. I was at the controls when I lost sight of the ground and couldn't see anything outside the cockpit. We went into an inadvertent IFR (instrument flight rules) situation. This is scary stuff. Your inner senses are telling you one thing and your flight instruments another. Which do you believe and then follow? I went with our flight instruments. It was shaky for a while, but I was able to regain control of the aircraft and get us out of the storm. We flew up through the cloud cover and punched out of the soup at about 3,000 feet. At that altitude, we were above the storm and flew a large holding pattern until we regained our bearings. Eventually, we were able to get back under the storm and fly into Camp Evans. I thought for sure we were going to crash.

Scott thought I did a good job of saving our asses. I'm sure of one thing, he gained a new appreciation for the weather conditions we have to fly in over here. I told him we were lucky on this one, and let's hope we don't face that again. This was just another in a long line of experiences where I've come close to dying over here, and I've only been here a few months.

I love you Sandy!

# CHAPTER 12

## THE BIG JUMP

I t's late evening, and I'm lying on my cot relaxing and listening to my new tape from Sandy.

"Your Mom, Dad, and I went to a movie earlier this evening called "The Last Picture Show" and Jeff Bridges was in it. I enjoyed it more than I thought I would. I surely did miss your not being with me. I kept thinking I could reach over and hold your hand. But it wasn't there. I can't begin to tell you how much you mean to me! I'm counting every day until your R&R, and we can be together again, and I'm in your arms. The look on your face the last time we were in each other's arms is still so vivid in my mind. The look in your eyes, the way you held me then, showed me how much you cared for me, and I love you so much for it. I wish I could be there now and show you just how much I love you."

I'm momentarily startled when Scott walks into the room. Sitting up and turning off the tape recorder, I wipe the moisture from around my eyes.

"Oh hell, I didn't realize you were listening to Sandy. I'm

sorry to barge in on you like this, TJ. I'll go get another beer and come back later."

"No need, Scott. It's late, and I'm ready to call it a night."

"You're sure, TJ?"

"Yeah!"

As we go about our personal business, getting ready to turn in, our conversation continues.

"TJ, this new CO is really a piece of work. He's managed to piss off most of the fellows in the Company. This can't be good for their morale!"

I respond, "Yeah, he's running this place like we're back in the states. That sure isn't winning him any friends or earning him the respect of his men, but I don't think he gives a damn about it. I understand he's got eighteen years in the Army, and this is his first combat command. You know what that means!"

Scott says, "If he wants to make Colonel, he needs this command."

I nod in agreement and respond, "You got that right. But, if he wants to keep his command, he better lighten up and start treating these men with more respect. That includes cutting them some damn slack."

Scott says, "What do you mean?"

As we crawl into our bunks, I respond, "I've been told our Battalion Commander and members of his staff have heard some stories about what he's been doing around here."

"I heard that too. You know TJ, there's a rumor going around the Company that Parker thinks you're the source."

"Yeah, I know, I heard that one also. I'm not! If I were, you can bet your ass he'd know it!"

Pulling the sheet up to his head, Scott turns to me and says, "I've also heard some of the men referring to the Major jokingly as Major Altitude." I ask, "Why's that?"

Scott replies, "He always stays way up in the sky, at altitude, and never comes down from his perch up there to where the action is on the ground."

Reaching over and turning the light out, I jokingly and somewhat sarcastically say, "Hell, that's not a very catchy name, but it does seem to kinda fit. Let's get some sleep—good-night."

Early the next morning, we are called into a special briefing at our mess hall. When Scott and I arrive, all the other Eagles pilots and crews are seated around tables, making small talk. Standing in front of them is Parker, with Stan seated near him. Behind them, hung on the wall, is a large map depicting our area of operations around Khe Sanh and inside Laos. Scott and I work our way over to Captain Barnett, whose call-sign is Eagle 16, and take a seat next to him near the front.

Captain Barnett is the third most senior officer in the Company, behind Parker and Stan. He insists we call him by his rank and last name. Usually, that would infer he's rigid, a stickler for details, and hard to please. Actually, he's quite the opposite and gets along well with the men. I like him and enjoy flying with him. He has the most logged flight hours of any pilot in the Company and is on the downside of his tour. As the saying goes over here, only 151 more days and a wake-up, and he goes home.

Charlie, Rick, and two other crew members are seated near us. Having checked the flight operations board before coming to the meeting, I'm aware that Scott, Charlie, and Rick will be flying with me on today's missions.

Parker motions for the men to quiet down and begins speaking. "Quiet down and give me your attention! As most of you are aware, the rumor mill has been working overtime the last few days with speculation that another major thrust deeper into Laos is in the works. It is not a rumor. Today, we will be helping to insert several ARVN Companies into new firebases deep inside Laos."

The men start talking among themselves, and Parker again

motions for them to quiet down. "Gentlemen, these insertions will take us deep into enemy territory and further away from friendly forces. It's going to be very intense, and we know the enemy will throw everything they got at us when we fly into these LZ's. We expect some losses!"

Again, many of the men break out in small talk, and Parker quiets them down. As he continues to talk, he points to several locations on the map. "As you're aware, we have helped to resupply these firebases on both sides of Route 9 since they were set-up at the beginning of this operation. They continue to run into heavy resistance and haven't made much progress beyond those firebases. These new insertions are intended to leapfrog further west and are a considerable distance beyond their current bases. It is hoped this new drive will take some pressure off them. The bigger goal here is to get as deep inside Laos as possible and continue with their objective of cutting off NVA forces and their supplies moving to the south."

Parker takes a moment and surveys the room. It has become noticeably quiet as we are entirely focused on the Major's presentation. He points to three locations on the map as he continues.

"The firebases are located here, here, and here. They are Brown, Sophia, and Lolo, which is the furthest west. That is our destination today. They have been bringing in fresh troops and more supplies for the past several days to Khe Sanh in preparation for this assault. At 1200 hours today, several Assault Helicopter Companies in the Division will be airlifting troops into their assigned LZs. Before dusk, all troops are to be on the ground and have their LZs secured. Any questions before I turn it over to Captain Norton?"

There are none. Parker motions to Stan, who rises from his chair and takes the floor. "As Major Stewart said, and you can see on the map, our LZ is the furthest out. We will be the first American unit to go this far into Laos. According to our available intelligence, the NVA does not expect South Vietnamese forces to go out that far. Having said that, these little bastards have proven to be very adept at getting to wherever we go and quickly. Sometimes it's like they already have our playbook. So, expect it to be a rough go out there this afternoon."

The men start talking among themselves again, and Stan has to quiet them down. He continues. "We have to be at our staging area in Khe Sanh by 1100 hours. We will refuel once we get there and shut down while we wait for the go signal. American advisers and ARVN officers will coordinate the loading of all assigned ARVN troops to our choppers. Liftoff is set for 1200 hours!"

Stan looks over at Captain Barnett and me. Stan continues. "Fifteen of our choppers are available. For this assault, we'll have three flights. Captain Barnett, you will lead the first flight of five ships into the LZ, Captain St. James, the second flight of five ships, and I'll take the last flight of four ships. Major Stewart will fly the C&C ship above Lolo."

Scott leans over to me and whispers, "Fifteen ships, who the hell is he kidding? I wonder how many are held together with duct tape and baling wire?"

I whisper back. "Well, if there are any, you can bet that Parker and Stan won't be flying them today!"

Many of the other men grumble about Stan's comment concerning the number of Huey's available for this mission. Stan has to quiet them down, as he realizes they are questioning the number of Huey's scheduled for today. "Gentlemen, I realize that fifteen ships are questionable, but we are operating at a maximum commitment today. No exceptions, no excuses. Just accept that, and deal with it. Any questions now?"

There are none, but our faces reflect our doubts. Stan continues. "The Butchers are flying cover for us, and the Air Force will be on station in case things get out of hand. There will be an Air

Force spotter plane in the area, and we'll contact him when we get out there. Captain Greg Owens, call-sign Butcher 12, will be the lead for his flight of six Cobras. If there are no more questions, I am going to give it back to the Major."

There are none. Parker steps forward as Stan returns to his seat. "Today will require a maximum effort by each of us to do our part and get those soldiers in and keep them supplied. To meet this challenge, I'll expect 100 percent from each of you at all times out there, no exceptions! Thank you, that is all!"

With the briefing completed, we slowly rise from our chairs and head for the doors. As Scott and I stand up, we momentarily stare at each other. The haunted dread in our eyes speaks volumes. We are certainly not alone, as the only noise heard is the shuffling of feet as we head out of the mess hall. Each man is lost in his own thoughts and dreading what awaits us later in the day.

# CHAPTER 13

## KHE SANH

After the meeting, we go about the business of securing our helmets, chicken plates, survival vests, weapons, and any other gear we might need. My fellow Eagles and I head out toward the flight line to our assigned chariots of the sky. It is a clear day, but as always, very hot, muggy, and that distinct fishy smell hanging in the air. Just another day in Nam. Uncomfortable as hell.

Arriving at our choppers, we go through pre-flight inspections. Many of us could do this in our sleep. I speak figuratively, of course. There's no flight station in the sky we can pull into for help, so we better get our checks right while we're still on the ground. Once completed, the aircrews settle into their choppers. As if we're all connected to the same switch, we fire up the engines, bring our choppers to a hover, and move into position for take-off.

Parker is the lead ship. He calls the tower for clearance to launch his Company. Upon receiving clearance, he barks over his radio, 'Eagles, this is Eagle 1. We are cleared to launch on me.

We'll climb to 2,000 feet on a heading of due north. Over!'
Double-clicks and the response 'Roger that!' are heard as the
other fourteen ships acknowledge his transmission. Parker brings
his Huey to a hover and slowly moves forward, gaining speed and
altitude as he climbs skyward.

Captain Barnett starts moving forward as he leads his group
out, following Parker. Lifting up and gaining airspeed and altitude, I lead my group out, following behind Captain Barnett.
Stan and his flight follow us. Once at altitude, we go into a triple
V formation, one flight behind the other. Parker is flying solo in
the lead ship. We head north toward Quang Tri City, which is
our first marker. Once there, we'll bank left and head west toward
Khe Sanh.

Scott and I have been busy trying to dial it down a notch and
relax as we fly closer into harm's way. Conversations occur
between my crew and me over the Huey's intercom system.

'Scott, all the instrument readings look good to me. Do you
see anything?'

'No problems here TJ, we're looking good to this point.'

I say, 'Charlie, Rick, test your guns.'

They both respond. 'Roger!'

Short bursts are heard as they fire their M-60s.

'You good, Charlie?'

'Affirmative!'

'What about you, Rick?'

'My gun jammed at first, but it's okay now.'

'You're sure about that?' I respond. 'I don't want our guns
jamming when we go into Lolo.'

Rick, 'Yes, sir, I would bet my next month's paycheck on it.'

Scott responds, 'Hell, you're betting more than that!'

Rick comes back with, 'No problem, I have a good feeling
about today. When we reached our assigned altitude, I could see

that the waves were up and peaking nicely. If it's a good day to surf, it's a good day to fly.'

Charlie chimes in with, 'Surfer logic escapes me, but if it works for you, I'm in!'

After a momentary pause in our back-and-forth banter, Scott directs a comment to me. 'TJ, it looks like Parker is going to sit this one out again and stay well above the action. What the hell do you think is wrong with him?'

'Who the hell knows? One of these days, he's going to have to lead this Company from the front. He's going to have to come down on the deck with the rest of us. Today would be a good day to start!'

Scott, who has become no fan of Parker, blurts out, 'It'll be a cold day in hell before that happens!'

'Roger that,' is the response I hear back from my crew.

As our formation nears Quang Tri City, we make a slow banking turn to the left and head due west for Khe Sanh. The DMZ, to our right, is not too far off. In the distance, we observe several U.S. Air Force planes flying in a low, slow formation on this side of the DMZ. They are spraying defoliant along their flight paths.

Conversions continue over our intercom. To my crew, I blurt out. 'Ranch Hand's hard at work again!'

'Ranch Hand, what's that, TJ?'

'Scott, those are the guys who spray defoliant all over Vietnam. It's supposed to deny the enemy a place to hide.'

'Is that Agent Orange we're talking about?'

'Yeah, that's it.' I respond and continue. 'You know why they call it that?

'No!' Scott replies.

'They call it that because the barrels that shit comes in are painted with orange stripes to help identify them!'

Charlie jumps in. 'That shit kills everything it comes in contact with.'

Scott, 'Including people?'

Charlie, 'No one knows, but I wouldn't be surprised if it does!'

Scott, 'I thought chemical warfare was against the Geneva Convention.'

In my best authoritative voice, I respond to Scott. 'Yeah, well, we all did. One thing's for sure, though, in a few days, that whole area will be dead, and hopefully, it will help keep the bad guys away. But I wouldn't bet on it!'

Our formation is coming up on Khe Sanh, a massive combat base built on top of a large, flat plateau. Back in January of 1968, during the Tet Offensive, the base was operated by the U.S. Marines and some South Vietnamese units. For two months they fought off an intense siege by the NVA. The Marines finally prevailed, and shortly after winning the battle, they abandoned the base and moved back east toward the coast. The famed combat base of Tet, 1968, has now been reopened and expanded for Lam Son 719.

The plateau at Khe Sanh is at a very high elevation. It is surrounded by hills and ridgelines, which fan out in several directions from the base. Small firebases, manned by the 101st Airborne Division units, have been placed on surrounding hills with the highest elevations. The job of the troopers on those hills is to provide more security for Khe Sanh. The base has one long runway down the middle, which can accommodate Air Force C-130s. There are taxiways at each end of the runway, leading to parking areas for aircraft and helicopters. For Lam Son 719, Army Engineers have built several large staging areas all around Khe Sanh for our helicopter units. At the height of this operation, there will be over 700 helicopters using them.

As we close in on Khe Sanh, we hear Parker contacting the American Adviser on the ground. His call sign is Baker Leader. He is assigned to work with the ARVN Commander that we are supporting today.

Parker transmits over his radio, 'Baker Leader, this is Eagle 1, over.'

'This is Baker Leader. Go ahead, Eagle 1, over.'

'Roger, Baker Leader, we are inbound to your location with three flights. We'll be landing one flight at a time. The first and second flights have five ships each, and the third has four. Are you ready for us? Acknowledge. Over!'

'Roger Eagle 1, we are ready and standing by. Over!'

Parker transmits over his radio to us. 'Eagles, this is Eagle 1. They're ready and waiting for us. Flight leaders, it's your show. Take them on in, refuel your ships, then hover over to our staging area. Go ahead and shut down. I'll see you there. Over!'

Parker receives our acknowledgments. 'Eagle 16, Roger! Eagle 25, Roger! Eagle 8, Roger!'

Remaining in the air flying circles above his Company, Parker watches as we lead our flight groups into the staging area. Following Captain Barnett's flight, I take my group in for a landing and hover over to the refueling area. Crew chiefs climb out of our Hueys and perform hot refuels. A hot refuel is the practice of refueling while the Hueys engine is still running. Refueled, we follow the ground guides as they direct us to our assigned location. Once there, we shut down, exit our Hueys, secure the rotor blades, and look around the area while waiting for Parker to join us.

Parker has followed the last ship in, refuels, then hovers over to where we are parked. Once there, he shuts down the engine and has his crew secure the ship. Walking toward us, he motions at us to join him in a large camouflaged military tent. The sides of the tent are tied up to allow for a free flow of air. This will serve as our forward HQ and operations location for the next few days. During this time, we will help establish new firebases inside Laos and resupply them with ammunition, food, water, and medical supplies, and take out their wounded and dead.

Inside the tent, Baker Leader, a Colonel in the Infantry, and some of his staff are waiting for us. As our aircrews walk into the tent, Parker walks over to the Colonel. They exchange salutes and shake hands. "Welcome to Khe Sahn, Major Parker. This is Captain Nan Tran, the CO of the ARVN Company you will be airlifting in today, and this is Captain Le Duan, his Executive Officer." They exchange military salutes, and Parker shakes their hands. The two ARVN officers look around at the aircrews gathered in the tent and acknowledge them by nodding. Most of us reciprocate their gesture by nodding.

The Colonel turns to address us. "Welcome, gentlemen. You're in for a long day. Please make yourself comfortable, and I'll briefly explain the situation as we currently understand it." Looking out over the room and making eye contact with us, he begins. "Supposedly, there are no indications the NVA suspect we are going this deep into Laos. You will be the first Americans to go out that far. Our G-2 staff thinks you'll only have minimal contact in the area you're going into. I personally doubt that. You should expect heavy resistance once you start going into Lolo. The conditions at most of the established firebases you'll be flying over on your way out are constantly under some form of enemy fire and harassment. If you get hit and must go down in Laos, try to make it to Route 9. Your chances of getting lifted out should be better. Any questions?"

There being none, he continues. "We'll be loading twelve packs on each chopper. It should allow us to get most of the Company in there on the first insertion. When you return, we'll load the rest of your packs, their heavy machine guns and mortars, and as many supplies as we can onboard your Hueys.

Once loaded, you'll head back out again. Three sorties should do it, but if needed, we may have to send a fourth. Once the LZ is set up, Chinooks will follow with artillery and building supplies. Again, any questions?"

There being none, the Colonel turns to Parker. "I'll leave you with your men. Good luck out there!" The Colonel turns back to face us and renders us a hand salute. "Good luck out there, men!" He then walks out of the tent with his staff and the ARVN Captains following him.

Parker turns to look out over us as he speaks. "Remember, I want 100% out there today, no exceptions. We will get our packs in there! Our flight paths over and back will parallel Route 9 and a little south of the road. We will be flying there and on the return trip back at altitude and in our V formations. Once we close in on Firebase Lolo, we will drop down and use "nap of the earth." I want minimal distance between flights, so be alert with your spacing."

He pauses, as if we needed to let that sink in, and then continues. "The LZ itself should allow us to land five ships in a tight V formation at the same time. If not, you'll land in trail formation with the lead ship going as close to the end of the LZ as possible. This should allow room for the other ships behind you. Once we're out there and I can see the LZ up close, I'll make a judgment call on this. Any questions?"

None are heard. "Okay, let's go."

Scott and I converse with each other as we head out to our Huey. I say to Scott. "Twelve ARVNs to a ship! They're little guys, and we can handle the weight okay, but if we get in the shit out there, it will take longer for them to get out of our chopper. This just gives those little bastards out there more time to shoot at us while we're in the LZ. Just thought I would throw that out there!"

"Thanks, TJ, I really needed to hear that!"

"No shit, Scott?"

"No shit, TJ!"

"Do you think they'll be waiting for us when we get out there?"

With concern in my voice, I respond, "You can bet on it!"

# CHAPTER 14

## LOLO-AIR ACTION

We return to our Hueys, settle ourselves in, bring the engines on-line, and increase rotor RPM to maximum. The noise is almost deafening, and the downward force of our rotor blades creates a small dust storm in the staging area. We are ready. I feel for the ARVN packs being loaded into our Hueys. They are headed straight into a living nightmare, from which many will not awaken. We watch anxiously, knowing we are flying into the same nightmare, and there is no turning back.

With our packs on board, Parker transmits to us. 'Eagles, this is Eagle 1. We'll climb to 2,000, form on me. Then we'll head over to our holding station and wait for the command to head west. Over!'

Double-clicks and the response of 'Roger that!' are heard over our radios as his men respond to the command. Parker receives clearance from the control tower to launch, pulls pitch, and slowly begins to climb into the sky above Khe Sanh. Flights one, two, and three follow his lead and slowly gain altitude. Once at our assigned altitude and flying in formation, we follow Parker to the holding station.

It is just south of Khe Sanh, where we go into a slow turning, oval-shaped, holding pattern at 2,000 feet. We try to relax by rechecking our equipment, adjusting our chicken plates, and those wearing waist holsters slide them between their legs. Our door gunners recheck their machine guns. Lord knows we will surely need them before this day ends.

Flying in a holding pattern while waiting for the go signal has many of us on edge. Finally, we hear Parker call the 101st Aviation Group Commander, his military call-sign is Tango 6, over our radios. 'Tango 6, Tango 6, this is Eagle 1, over!'

'Eagle 1, this is Tango 6, go ahead, over.'

'Tango 6, Eagle 1, we are on station and ready, over.'

'Roger, Eagle 1. Your escort should be there now. All units are ready. H-hour is still a go. Acknowledge, over.'

'Tango 6, Eagle 1, Roger that, understand it's still a go! Over!'

Scott and I have been monitoring Parker's radio communications and scanning the horizon for the Butcher group. Out of my left seat window, I see the six Butchers Cobras closing in on us. Over the intercom, I tell Scott, 'Here they come!'

Scott replies, 'Yeah, I got them. Hope they are well-armed and ready!'

I respond, 'We're working with Greg. You can bet your ass they are!'

Scott laughs lightly and watches as Greg's group closes in on the left side of our Eagle's flights. Greg is in the lead ship, and as he and I make eye contact, he transmits over his radio, 'You guys call for some backup?'

Giving him a thumbs up, I respond, 'Good to see you. I do believe we can use some help today.'

Parker cuts in on our radio traffic and is livid. 'Eagle 25, Butcher 12, this is Eagle 1. You characters, knock off the bullshit. This is a military operation! Keep the radio talk to a minimum and keep it military! Do we understand each other, gentlemen? Over!'

Looking over at Scott and with a grin on my face, I respond to Parker. 'This is Eagle 25, Roger that! Over!'

Greg comes back with 'Eagle 1, Butcher 12, copy that! Over!'

'Butcher 12, this is Eagle 1. We have three flights. The first two have five ships each, and the third has four. I want all six of your Cobras to go in with each flight for max cover! Do you copy? Over!'

Greg responds with double-clicks over his radio transmitter. With a grin on his face, he speaks to his copilot over their intercom. 'This guy is a real asshole! I think we know how to fly cover for them. One thing you don't do is send in all your ships at the same time. We'll leave two flying a cap over the LZ. We can react faster should they get into some deep shit down there!'

Greg's copilot responds to his comment, 'Works for me, damn that guy's an idiot!'

Over the radio, Greg instructs his Cobra pilots to join him on their alternate frequency, one which Parker does not have available. I know Greg will provide cover for them his way, and is now sharing that with his group on their alternate frequency. Since I just happen to know their frequency, I switch over and listen in.

'Butcher flight, this is Butcher 12. We'll be providing cover for the Eagles today, but we'll do it our way. You heard the Major's line up for his flights. Butcher 10 and I will provide a cap over the LZ. Butcher 6 and 8, you'll provide cover on their left flank, and Butcher 2 and 4, you guys will do the same on their right flank when the first flight goes in. After that, do your hammerhead turns so you can stay on station, and provide continuous cover for flights two and three. Any questions?'

There are none, as all the Butcher pilots 'Roger!' Greg's transmission. Greg then transmits to them, 'Okay, guys, let's go back to our primary frequency. Be safe and good hunting! Over!'

It's H-hour, the operation begins with Tango 6 transmitting over the radio. 'All units, all units, this is Tango 6. H-hour is a go. Commence operations. Godspeed, and good luck! Over!'

Parker transmits to his Company and the Butcher group, 'All Eagles and Butchers; this is Eagle 1. We're a go. Follow me and keep it close, tight, and stay alert! Over!'

With that transmission, we head west, flying across the border between South Vietnam and Laos, staying at 2,000 feet. Our three Eagles groups are flying in V formations, one behind the other. The Butchers have split into two groups of three. One group is now flying on each side of the second flight of Eagles. They say there is safety in numbers. Seeing this massive formation from the ground, one might say it looks impressive and almost immune from any serious enemy threat. We know from experience that is not likely, and yet we still fly into the valley of death.

Flying deeper into Laos, we can see from our vantage point, above the action, that many of the firebases are under some form of attack. There are pillars of smoke rising high into the sky from all of the fighting in and around many bases. Gunships are rolling in, firing their rockets and miniguns. American fighter jets roll in, dropping their devastating bomb loads on various targets at the direction of their Forward Air Controllers (FAC). FAC's fly in small, single-seat, single propeller-driven airplanes that stay on station and fly above the action. The job of a FAC pilot is to work with ground forces and any aircraft in the area to locate and then guide ground attack aircraft to their targets. They risk their lives to help men on the ground they don't know and will never meet.

In the distance, and to the north, we observe massive explosions on the ground. Entire grid squares, measuring 1,000 meters on the ground for each side, erupt shooting massive chunks of earth high into the air, and large columns of smoke billowing up into the sky. This is followed by shock waves emitting from the ground explosions and radiating out from their centers. Even at our distance and altitude, we feel the shock waves as they roll over the ground below. We have just witnessed an "Arc Light" by the U.S. Air Force. This is a concentrated bombing of a large target area by several B-52 bombers flying high over the target and dropping their massive bomb loads. Some of us consider them a thing of beauty to behold but wouldn't want to be in the neighborhood receiving one.

*All in all,* I think to myself, *this is just another day at the office for the men I'm flying with today.*

Approaching Lolo, Parker, from his altitude, can see the area and believes there is enough space to land each flight of five ships staying in their V formation. He yells into his radio transmitter, 'Eagles and Butchers, this is Eagle 1. There's plenty of room on the LZ for each flight to go in together. Stay in your V formation and keep your spacing. Do you copy? Over!'

Receiving acknowledgements from his pilots, Parker instructs Captain Barnett to lead his flight in. 'Eagle 16, this is Eagle 1. Lolo is at your 10 o'clock, drop down to "nap of the earth," and begin your approach. Over!'

Captain Barnett responds, 'Eagle 1, Roger. Eagle 16 is going in now.'

Captain Barnett leads us in with the Butchers providing cover as we begin our descent from altitude into the LZ. Parker stays at 2,000 feet, where he will observe the action as it unfolds.

Greg responds to Parker, 'Eagle 1. This is Butcher 12. We have you covered! He continues transmitting, Butcher group, Butcher 12. It's showtime. Assume cover formation.'

Approaching the LZ on short final, Captain Barnett finds himself looking out at a large clearing located in the middle of a plateau. Many low trees and thick vegetation surround the edges of the LZ. He leads his flight in and comes to a low hover on the far side of the clearing. This leaves room for the other choppers in his flight to come in behind him.

As soon as his flight of Hueys is in the LZ, a murderous volume of small arms and machine-gun fire opens up on them. Their packs scramble from the choppers and run for cover. All the door gunners are pouring lead into the surrounding terrain, trying to slow down the rate of incoming fire. The men in the choppers are under heavy attack as the machine gun fire starts taking a toll on crew members. Many are hit and slump over in their seats.

Scott and I are watching the action as we begin our approach into the LZ. Over the intercom, I say to Scott, 'Jesus, look at that mess in front of us. They're shooting the shit out of them. There's tracer rounds coming from all directions.'

Scott responds, 'Damn, it looks like they were expecting us!'

I respond with, 'Yeah, so much for Army Intelligence! There has to be some high-level spying going on somewhere in our command structure. This shit is just happening too often.'

On Lolo, Captain Barnett increases his engine throttle giving him all the power his engine can produce. He pulls up pitch and takes off with his flight following him out. As they slowly move forward, gaining altitude, they continue receiving heavy fire.

Captain Barnett calls Greg over his radio, 'Butcher 12, can you get a fix on those little bastards? You need to waste them now! Over!'

Greg responds back, 'Eagle 16, Butcher 12. Hell, they're everywhere down there. Just get the fuck out of Dodge. We'll take care of them! Over!'

Parker transmits over the radio to Captain Barnett. 'Eagle 16, this is Eagle 1. What the hell is going on down there? Over!'

'Eagle 1, it's hotter than hell down here. Those little bastards were waiting for us. We got our packs in. Some were hit as we landed. We were able to bring some of them out with us. We also have our own casualties. Over!'

Parker doesn't hesitate to send me in next. 'Roger that! Eagle 25, this is Eagle 1. Take your flight on in. Over!'

I respond to Parker, 'Roger! We're headed in now!'

Greg's Cobras have been working over the LZ's perimeter area by continuously rolling in on different targets. The ARVN soldiers on the ground called in for artillery support as soon as they found some cover. Incoming rounds are now tearing up large chunks of turf and laying waste to trees around Lolo's perimeter.

Over the intercom, I ask, 'You guys ready? We're going in!' They all respond, 'Yes', as Rick says, 'And I thought this was going to be a good day to fly!' In my mind, I know everyone's pucker factors are about to go off the chart.

I call Greg over the radio, 'Butcher 12, Eagle 25, we're going in. Don't let me down, good buddy! Over!'

Greg responds, 'Roger, Eagle 25, we have you covered. Watch out for the far side of the LZ when you begin to pull out. There's a heavy concentration of fire coming from that area. Also, be advised, I think they may have some RPGs. Over!'

I respond, 'Roger, Butcher 12.' I then transmit to my group, 'Eagles, stay on me, we're going in, keep it tight and watch the far side as we lift off. We could see some RPGs. Over!'

Leading my flight in, I stay just above the treetops and go as fast as possible. Clearing the trees on the edge of the LZ's perimeter, I head for the far side of the landing area. Enemy fire from all sides of the LZ is still very intense as red tracer rounds are seen coming at us from everywhere. Again, I hear the familiar sound of bullets ripping into my Huey. There's that popcorn popping again! Artillery rounds are landing all over the place, and the Cobras are making their gun runs. All this activity adds to the noise and confusion around me and my flight of Hueys. We have descended into helicopter hell. I blurt out over the intercom, 'What a fucking mess!'

Closing in on the far side of the LZ, I bring my Huey to a sudden stop. I was going too fast, and the sudden stop caused my Huey's nose to pitch up and our tail to hit the ground hard. I struggle with our chopper's flight controls, trying to keep from losing my ship. It's like riding a mechanical bull at a Texas Roadhouse. The only difference between being there and here is I could kill everyone if I'm thrown off the bull, so to speak. I stay on the bull, and we settle into a low hover. Over the intercom, I yell, 'Holy shit. That was close. Everyone still with me?'

My crew responds in the affirmative as they clear their throats and wonder what their shorts look like. Hovering my Huey three feet off the ground, we rock back and forth as the packs jump out and head for cover. Looking around, getting ready for a quick departure, I see Scott has drawn his pistol and is shooting out his window into the tree line.

Over the intercom, I bark at him, 'Scott, what the hell are you doing?'

Without stopping, he yells back at me while continuing to fire his pistol. 'I don't have to take this shit from anybody!'

Before realizing it, I'm laughing, even though all hell has been unleashed on us. Over our intercom, I try to reason with him, 'Scott, put that damn thing away, we gotta get out of here. You'll get a chance soon enough to shoot back, I'm sure of it.'

As Scott settles back down and holsters his pistol, I call out to my flight group. 'Eagles, let's get the hell out of here!'

My Huey lurches forward and up as it starts to climb out of Lolo. The Hueys in my flight follow me up and out. Miraculously no ship is lost. However, a few men have been hit. As we clear the treetops at the far side of the LZ, a terrifying scream is heard over the radio.

Butcher 6 is heard screaming into his radio, 'Oh God, we've

been hit. We're going down. Help, help, please, dear God, help!' Their radio goes silent.

Greg calls out over his radio to the Cobra pilot. 'Butcher 6, Butcher 6, pull up, pull up!'

No one can help them. It's all over in the blink of an eye. Butcher 6 has been hit by an RPG and spirals to the ground, with smoke and fire billowing from the engine and tail sections. The Cobra crashes nose-first into the ground and explodes on impact. The aircrew doesn't survive.

Just as I look over at Scott, there's a loud explosion as our own world goes up in smoke and fire. We've been hit by an RPG. I fight to maintain control of my Huey as it vibrates violently. Our engine begins to lose power, and the cockpit has filled up with smoke from the burning engine compartment. Talking between the crew occurs over the intercom.

'Holy shit, we've been hit. What the hell was it?' says Scott.

'An RPG. Watch the instruments. Do we have an engine fire? What's the RPM doing?'

Scott responds, 'No firelight, but our hydraulic and oil pressures are dropping fast. RPM is okay but slipping.'

'Are you sure about that firelight, Scott? Something is sure on fire back there. Pull the fire switch!'

Charlie says to me in a choked-up voice, 'Sir, it's Rick. He's...dead!'

As the smoke begins to clear some, Scott looks back at Rick. The RPG hit on his side and killed him instantly. His body is hanging over his M-60, and he is only held in by his safety strap.

Scott says, 'TJ...Rick is gone!'

I do not have time to respond as I'm struggling to keep us in the air. Realizing it's useless and that we're going to crash, I pull back on the cyclic and simultaneously push hard on my left pedal. My control movements are spontaneous, without thinking, as they cause my Huey to flare up and do a hard turn to the left.

We are now facing back toward the LZ and only a few hundred feet from the ground and rapidly losing power. As we close in on the ground and are dropping fast, I pull up on my collective just before hitting the ground and yell out to the crew, 'Hold on, we're gonna hit hard!' Our burning Huey hits the ground hard. We bounce a few times and settle into mother earth.

I don't know how I did that, but we're down. Thank God for some good flight instructors who drilled into us, "Don't think about your situation. React to it!"

Our chopper is on fire, and we have to move quickly. I switch off the engine, and the rotor blades begin to slow down. Scott, Charlie, and I unstrap ourselves and slowly climb out of the Huey. We have to be careful of the rotor blades as they're tilted slightly to one side and are slowly coming to a stop. The last thing I want to do is get decapitated exiting from my own Huey. Looking around at the scene on the ground, we find ourselves in the middle of a hurricane, as ferocious fighting rages all around.

Witnessing what has happened to us, two ARVN soldiers run over to help. They help Scott remove Rick's body from the chopper and carry him back to where they are digging in. Charlie and I follow them to cover. Within moments after finding some protection among a fallen clump of trees, our Huey explodes, sending pieces flying everywhere.

Watching this unfold in real-time, an incredibly empty feeling overcomes me, and I feel it in the pit of my stomach. We're stranded in this hellish environment and have no way out at the moment. We are now infantry grunts, along with these ARVN soldiers, and will be fighting for our lives with the very men we flew in here today.

# CHAPTER 15

## LOLO-GROUND ACTION

Having secured some relative safety in a large ditch, partially covered with fallen trees, I check on Scott and Charlie. "You guys alright?" Scott gives me a thumbs up, but Charlie is sobbing over the body of Rick as he holds on to him. I move over to Charlie, who by now is covered in Rick's blood from the massive wounds that shredded him. I check Charlie over to see if he has any wounds while I try to comfort him. Kneeling next to him and placing my arms on his shoulders, I speak to him as a father would to his son. "Charlie, he's gone...We're gonna need your help to get out of here alive, so you need to pull yourself together now!"

Charlie looks at me and shakes his head slightly, acknowledging that he will try. He lowers Rick's body gently to the ground and slowly rises with a look of intense, blazing hatred in his eyes.

Scott looks over at me and says, "That was too fucking close. What do you want me to do?"

I respond, "See if you can find us some rifles. There should be plenty around here somewhere. And Scott, see if you can find out who is in charge here. I need to see him."

Charlie says, "I'll help him!" I respond, "Good!"

Scott asks, "What are you going to do?" Responding, I say, "Contact Greg and give him some targets to shoot at down here!"

"Good idea!" With that, Scott crawls out from the area we are in, with Charlie following behind him.

I pull out my survival radio and make radio contact with Greg. 'Butcher 12, Butcher 12, Eagle 25! Over!'

Greg and his wingman, who had dropped down from flying cover and joined in on the battle as I took my flight group in, hears my call and responds. 'Eagle 25, this is Butcher 12. You guys alright down there? Over!'

'Butcher 12, Eagle 25, Rick bought it, but the rest of us are okay for now. It's hot as hell down here. Let me get my bearings, and I'll spot you some targets and guide you in. Did the rest of my flight make it out? Over!'

Greg responds, 'Roger that. Your other four choppers got out. As for targets, you give us their locations, and we'll do our best to screw those little fuckers up!'

As I attempt to respond back to Greg, Parker cuts in on me and once again is livid as hell. 'Eagle 25, this is Eagle 1. What the hell is going on down there, goddammit? Over!'

Responding back to him, 'Eagle 1, this is Eagle 25. It's deadly down here. We have a hot LZ right now. Recommend you delay the third flight until it cools down some in here. Over!'

Parker responds, 'Eagle 25, I'll be the judge of that! You direct Butcher 12 to all the targets you can. Over!'

He continues, 'Butcher 12, the third flight will be going in next, keep them covered! Over!'

Greg responds, 'Eagle 1, Butcher 12. Roger that. We'll do the best we can, but you should reconsider what Eagle 25 suggested! Over!'

Parker ignores Greg's last transmission. Greg realizes it, and his facial expression shows the disdain he has for this man. Over the intercom, he says to his copilot, 'What a fucking asshole!' To which his copilot responds, 'No shit. If he's so damn brave, why doesn't he come down here and lead the third flight in himself?'

Fighting is raging all over the LZ as I attempt to identify targets for Greg and his Cobras. I'm trying to call Greg over my survival radio when Parker interrupts me again. 'Eagle 25, this is Eagle 1. Give me a goddamn situation report. ASAP. Over!'

I'm fed up with the man and respond in a fit of anger. 'We're a little goddamn busy right now! Why don't you just fly your ass down here and see for yourself? Eagle 25. Out!'

This has the intended effect of keeping Parker off the radio so Greg and I can work together, trying to take out enemy positions without his interference. Parker is furious, I'm sure, but restrains himself from responding and apparently has decided to deal with me later. *Good idea!*

Turning my attention to locating targets and calling them into Greg's Cobra flight now becomes priority one. Our radio transmissions are very brief and to the point. Locating several enemy gun emplacements, I'm able to direct Greg and his Cobras in on them. 'Mortars one hundred meters out and near the tree line to my right. Gooks in a shell crater 75 meters to my front. Beau-coup Gooks in the open, 50 meters out from the tail section of my burning Huey!'

We are working together just fine as Greg's Cobras roll in firing their miniguns and launching rockets at targets on the ground I identify for them. I'm awestruck as I witness the devastating effect their gun runs have on the targets they hit. I'm a pilot, and until now, I haven't been this close-up and personal when this kind of firepower is unleashed on the enemy.

Watching the action below from his vantage point far above,

Parker grows more impatient and sends in the third flight. 'Eagle 8, this is Eagle 1. Take your flight in now! Over!'

Stan responds, 'This is Eagle 8, Roger that!' He then tells his crew over their intercom to stay alert as they approach the LZ. Each man knows what awaits them. Being the last flight in, they have seen the devastation going on in Lolo and heard the harrowing screams of their comrades over the radios.

Surely these men fit the description of courage attributed to the actor John Wayne. "Courage is being scared to death, but saddling up anyway."

Scott and Rick have rejoined me, bringing with them some M-16s. Scott tells me, "I found their First Sergeant, and he is going to have their CO, Captain Tran, work his way over here to see you as soon as he can." I take one of the M-16s from Scott, check to ensure it's loaded, and point to the far end of the LZ, where the third flight is starting to come in.

As Stan leads his flight in, they come under intense ground fire. Approaching the LZ's far side where we have taken cover, Stan brings his Huey to a high hover. Suddenly he pushes the nose of his Huey forward and starts a slow, gradual climb. As he does, the packs in his chopper jump out, and some are hurt as they hit the ground hard. The other Hueys in the flight come in behind Stan and bring their choppers to a low hover, allowing their packs to jump out without falling from ten feet up.

Stan has already cleared the LZ when his other three Hueys pull pitch and start their lift-off. As they do, two of them are hit by RPGs. The Huey following Stan takes a direct hit to the engine compartment and blows up. What's left of it falls 20 feet to the ground. The crew is gone, killed in an instant! The other Huey is hit in the tail section. The pilot has no way to control his torque since the tail rotor is destroyed. His Huey begins spinning around like a top as it crashes to the ground hard. The rotor blade beats itself against the ground and eventually comes to a stop. Their Huey is now resting on one side and burning.

Crew members are crawling out of the chopper and trying to get away from it as fast as possible. We have been watching this tragedy unfold and make a mad dash over to the chopper. Several ARVN soldiers follow us as we all come under enemy small arms fire.

As we run to the downed Huey, Scott yells over at me, "Christ, can you believe what Stan did?"

"Yeah, screw him, we're in deep shit right now! Let's get these guys out of here and undercover!"

Reaching the burning Huey, we help three of the crew members who have managed to crawl out. They're all in a state of shock, and each man has sustained multiple injuries. They can move with help. The copilot is unconscious and still strapped to his seat, with flames closing in on him. Without thinking, Charlie goes over to the copilot, reaches in, and unbuckles him from his seat. He falls partially out of the chopper and into Charlie's arms. Scott goes over and helps him pull the copilot completely out of the chopper and onto the ground. He is still alive and bleeding from a severe head wound.

Scott and Charlie, who are holding the unconscious copilot up between them, start back toward cover. I'm helping the pilot to safety, and two ARVN soldiers are helping the other two crew members. The remaining soldiers are doing their best to provide covering fire as we work our way back to safety. Almost reaching safety, one of the soldiers providing covering fire is shot and killed instantly. Charlie is grazed in the leg by a bullet and nearly falls over. He manages to stay up and limp his way back toward our position while still supporting the copilot. We make it back. But I'm tired, scared, and just want to get the hell out of here. I'm sure we all feel that way. The day is not over yet, and our fates are still to be played out. However, there is no time to dwell on it. We attend to the wounded crew members.

Stan and his remaining Huey make it out of the LZ. They gain some altitude and rejoin the other Eagles. Parker transmits over the radio. 'Eagles, this is Eagle 1. Form on me, and we'll head back to our staging area at Khe Sanh. When we get there, refuel your choppers, pick up the remaining packs and supplies, and we'll head back out here to finish this mission. Do you copy, over?'

Double-clicks are heard as the pilots acknowledge the order. Stan responds, 'Eagle 1, what about Taylor and his men? Over!'

'Eagle 8, Eagle 1. They'll be okay for now. We'll extract them when we come back! Over and Out!'

I don't hear these transmissions over my survival radio because it operates on a different frequency. However, Greg does and calls me on the survival radio frequency. 'Eagle 25, Butcher 12, over.'

'Butcher 12, this is 25. What the hell is going on? I see our guys bugging out and heading back toward the border?'

'Taylor, buddy, you're on your own for now. Parker is taking them back to Khe Sanh to pick up the rest of the troops and supplies and then return. He plans on extracting you when they get back!'

'Nooo shit!'

Greg responds. 'Yeah, no shit! Look, I'm staying on station as long as I can with my wingman, and we'll supply what cover we can. My other three ships are escorting your guys back to Khe Sanh. Hang in there!'

'Roger that, thanks, Greg!'

Lolo is still under heavy fire from many sides. ARVN soldiers are working to set up some form of a defensive perimeter so that more troops and supplies can be flown in. With all this chaos around, Captain Tran has managed to work his way over to me.

Tran looks distressed and confused as I speak to him. "Captain Tran, have you established any contact with the Air Force FAC on station?" Captain Tran, in broken English, says to me, "No Daiuy.... been in shit...too busy!"

Seeing his condition, I suspect he hasn't tried or couldn't communicate with the FAC in discernible English. Unfortunately, that has been a real problem for the Americans supporting this operation. There are severe communication issues with ARVN soldiers on the ground. Most do not speak English. For those who try, it is very broken English and hard to understand. With few exceptions, the Americans speak no Vietnamese. Americans supposedly are prohibited from being on the ground in Laos. Unfortunately, the ARVN soldiers are on their own when trying to communicate with us. Since we are providing all of their support, this is not a good situation for anybody in this hell hole.

Sensing that I have no other choice, I take control of the situation and tell Captain Tran I'll contact the FAC and get some heavy ordnance (bombs) dropped around the perimeter of Lolo. I hope this will cause the enemy to break off contact for now. Captain Tran agrees.

Using my survival radio, I call the FAC flying on station somewhere above us. 'Foxfire Leader, Foxfire Leader, this is Eagle 25, over!'

Foxfire Leader comes back with, 'This is Foxfire Leader, go ahead, over.'

'Foxfire Leader, Eagle 25. I'm on the ground at Lolo with surviving crew members and the ARVN CO. It's a cluster fuck down here, and we need some immediate assistance. Over!'

'Eagle 25, Foxfire Leader. What do you have in mind, over?'

'Foxfire Leader, Eagle 25. Request you drop as much ordnance as you got around the perimeter of this LZ. Cluster and napalm, if you have some, would do just fine! Over!'

'Eagle 25, Foxfire Leader here, Roger that, we can arrange it. Give me a minute. Over!'

There is a brief pause, and then Foxfire leader comes back with, 'Eagle 25, this is Foxfire Leader. We're a go! Mark your positions with smoke. Make it clear to your troops down there that anyone outside that smoke will be toast. Over!'

'Roger that!'

With this communication, I tell Captain Tran to have his men around the perimeter to throw out some smoke and then take cover. Captain Tran tells his radio operator to put the word out for his men to throw red smoke grenades to mark their positions. He also tells them that fighter-bomber support is rolling in and to take cover. Within minutes, red smoke grenades are going off everywhere around the perimeter of the LZ

I transmit again, 'Foxfire Leader, smoke is out. Identify. Over!'

Foxfire Leader responds, 'Eagle 25, Foxfire, we have red smoke all over the damn place down there. Over!'

'Foxfire, Eagle 25, Roger. They might have gotten a little carried away with the smoke. Over!'

'Eagle 25, Foxfire Leader. Not a problem. We have your position and will be making our runs now. Suggest you hug the ground until we're done. Over!'

'Roger Foxfire, Eagle 25, out!'

Turning to the men around me and Captain Tran, I yell out. "Get down, get down! Hug the ground like it's your mother. The Air Force is coming in."

The men do their best to burrow into the ground around them. As we lay there clutching mother earth, four jets streak by us. They are low to the ground with two jets on each side of the LZ and flying in trail formation. They drop their bombs. As they hit, the ground shakes, and the earth around Lolo erupts, sending dirt and vegetation raining down on us inside the perimeter.

They are followed by four more jets streaking in. Like the first flight, two are on each side of the LZ, flying low and in trail formation. The air is instantly filled with fire, and intense heat from the napalm bombs dropped around us. I feel like I'm in an oven as the smell of napalm permeates the air making it harder to breathe. As the roar of jets fades into the distance, the LZ area quiets down as a deathly silence settles in for the moment.

Several of the men begin to emerge from their hiding places. Pulling myself up, I'm amazed at the sheer devastation that surrounds us. Trees are down everywhere, debris litters the ground, the air is thick with smoke, and fires are raging around the perimeter where the napalm was dropped. I can hear men screaming in the distance and wonder how anyone could have survived what I just called in on them. I feel no remorse and take solace in the fact that the firing has stopped, and the LZ is quiet. We are relatively secure for now. I wonder to myself. *Why didn't we just bomb the hell out of this place first and then fly these men in here?*

Checking on my men, I'm glad to see that no one sustained additional wounds. Charlie, who has dressed his own wound, along with Scott and I, help our injured comrades. We tend to their wounds and give them as much aid as possible under the circumstances. Captain Tran walks over to me and renders a crisp military salute. He then extends his hand out to me in a gesture of appreciation for my help. We exchange looks that can only reflect what we have just experienced together. Turning away, he walks off and goes about the business of checking on his men and organizing their defenses.

The relative silence is broken when over my survival radio, I hear 'Eagle 25, Foxfire Leader. You guys okay down there?'

'Foxfire, Eagle 25, I think so. That seemed to break their back. For now, it's pretty quiet down here. Thanks for your help! Over!'

'Eagle 25, you're welcome. You have our number. Just give us a call when you need some more assistance, and we'll be there! Over!'

I respond, 'Roger that! Again, thanks, Air Force! Out!' I hear a double-click.

As my adrenaline rush starts to wear off, I have a moment of reflection. *How in the hell am I ever gonna survive this war and make it back home?*

Greg radios me, 'Eagle 25, Butcher 12, that was one hell of a show. You guys, okay? Over!'

'Yeah, we're doing okay. It got a little warm down here, though. Over!'

Greg responds, 'Glad you made it, TJ! We're low on fuel and headed back to Khe Sanh. We'll return as soon as possible. Also, be advised that Eagle 1 is headed back your way with the rest of the troops and supplies. He should be about five minutes from your location. Over!'

'Thanks, Butcher 12. The first round is on me when we get back to the club. Over!'

Greg responds, 'You got it, buddy. Be safe! Over!' I respond with double-clicks over my survival radio and watch Greg and his wingman fly east towards Khe Sanh.

Within minutes, two flights of Eagles appear on the horizon as they approach the LZ with some Cobra gunships. My attempts to reach Parker on the survival radio are unsuccessful. I guess he's pissed at me, and this is his way of showing it. Man, how I miss Pappy.

The first flight lands and drops off their troops. As they leave, I gather up the men, and we work our way to where the second flight is preparing to land. When they touch down and unload their cargo, several crew members step out of their helicopters. They run over to assist us with our wounded and dead comrades.

Scott and Charlie carry Rick's body to one of the choppers

and carefully place him on the floor of the Huey. Captain Tran had some of his men recover the bodies of our comrades killed when their choppers went down in the LZ. His men help to place them into our waiting Hueys. Ensuring that all our men are loaded up, wounded and dead, I climb aboard one of the Hueys. Once loaded, the flight lifts off, and together we fly back toward Khe Sanh as the sun slowly slips below the horizon in the west.

For the next two days, our Company stays busy flying in and out of Lolo with supplies and more troops. After the first day, the LZ has been quiet, and we can fly our missions with no losses. During this time, Parker has totally ignored me and my room-mate, Scott. Both of us have been too tired and busy to notice or give a damn.

# CHAPTER 16

## CONFRONTATION

Scott and I are exhausted after flying support missions into Lolo for three long days in a row. After our first harrowing day of inserting troops into the LZ, Parker kept us in the air until our Company was given a down day to recover. Lying there on our cots, waiting for the mess hall to open for dinner, and staring up at the ceiling, we engage in some conversation.

"TJ, I don't believe I've ever been this scared! These last few days have been real ball busters! I thought we bought it on our first day into Lolo."

"Yeah, me too. That was a bitch!"

Scott says, "It's a goddamn shame about Rick. He was a good kid, and so were those other fellows we lost. I really hadn't gotten to know any of them very well. Is Rick the first crew member you've lost?"

"Rick was a good guy, as were the other fellows, and no, he wasn't the first man I've lost over here."

Scott asks, "How many have you lost?"

Rolling over to look at Scott and feeling melancholy, I respond. "Five, counting Rick."

After a long pause, Scott says, "After going through something like this, do you always feel this way?"

"What do you mean, Scott? Like what?"

Scott replies. "I don't know if I can describe it. It's kinda like being in a bad dream that you can't wake up from, and there's nothing you can do about it. When I go to bed, I hope that when I wake up in the morning, I'm home, and this was all just a bad dream. But, when I wake up, I'm not at home, it wasn't a dream. I'm still here!"

"Scott, this whole damn thing is like a bad dream, a nightmare. I've gone to bed many nights wondering if I'll live through the next day. I've wondered to myself many times, why me? What am I doing here? Will this madness ever end? What happens to Sandy if I don't make it?"

After a long pause, Scott says, "Do you ever wonder about the guys who came before us and what pulled them through? What made them do it? How did they keep going, mission after mission?"

"I have Scott. If you're looking to me for answers, I have none. Every man has to look within himself for answers to those questions."

The door to our room swings open, momentarily startling us. In walks the First Sergeant. "Sorry to bother you, Captain, Lieutenant. I know you've both had a rough few days, but Major Stewart wants to see you in his office ASAP, Captain."

Standing up, I adjust my jungle fatigues and look over at the First Sergeant. "What does he want?"

He responds, "I'm not sure, but he is pissed. I think it has something to do with what happened between you two on the first day at Firebase Lolo."

As Scott sits up, he looks over at the First Sergeant, "How do you know what happened?"

The First Sergeant looks at Scott and then over at me, "With all due respect, sir, it's all over the fucking Company what happened out there."

I walk toward the door and touch the First Sergeant on the shoulder as I pass him. "Let's go, First Sergeant."

Scott says to me, "Let's meet at the Pilots Club when you're done!"

"Yeah, sure, see you up there!"

The First Sergeant and I walk out of the room and head for the Headquarters trailer. On the way there, the First Sergeant says, "Captain, that was pretty damn gutsy what you said to the Major the other day."

I respond with some noticeable irritation in my voice. "Oh! There wasn't anything gutsy about it. It was just total frustration!"

"Whatever it was, the men loved it! Captain, I don't know quite how to say it, but many of the men..."

I stop him in mid-sentence. "I know what's on your mind. Forget it for now. Eventually, someone at Battalion or Division will figure this guy out. Then the problem should go away!"

"Well, sir, I certainly hope so! The men in this Company are getting pretty damn fed up with him!"

Reaching the Headquarters trailer, the First Sergeant opens the door for me and says, "Good luck, Captain!".

I respond, "Thanks, Top!" as I step inside. The First Sergeant closes the door behind me and turns to walk away.

Walking through the operations area on my way to Parker's office, I pass by Stan. He's slouched over in his chair and, with a grin and look of anticipation, says, "He's waiting on you, Taylor!"

Not looking back at him, I just keep walking and respond, "Go to hell!" Stan's grinning slowly turns to a cold stare as he watches me walk over to Parker's office door and knock.

From inside his office, Parker yells, "Who is it?"

"Captain St. James, sir!"

Parker yells back, "Get your ass in here!"

I enter his office and close the door behind me. Parker is seated at his desk, smoking a cigar, and glares up at me when I enter. I move over to the front of Parker's desk, come to attention, and render him a hand salute.

"Captain St. James reporting as ordered, sir!"

Parker doesn't return the hand salute, so I assume an at-ease position.

In an agitated voice, Parker says, "Who the hell told you to stand at-ease, mister?"

I snap back to attention and remain calm. Parker starts working himself into a rage.

"No one," I respond back to him.

"No one, no one, who the fuck do you think you are? I'm a Major, and you're a Captain. You'll address me at all times as Sir or Major. Do we understand each other, Captain?"

"Yes, Major!"

Stan can hear the verbal exchanges through the thin wall he is leaning against and is enjoying every moment. On the other side of the wall, Parker, who is livid, stands up, puts his cigar down, and moves from behind his desk to a position next to me.

"Don't fuck with me, Taylor. I'll bury your ass!"

I can't resist and respond, "Literally or figuratively, Major?"

"Oh! So, you're a smart ass too?"

I've had enough of his abuse and step back from him. "Look, Major, if you have a problem with me, or have something on your mind, spit it out."

Parker cuts me off. "Yeah, I've got something on my mind. It's called insubordination. People can be sent up to Division for a court-martial around here for that kind of thing!"

I snap back at him, "Insubordination? What the hell are you talking about, Major?"

"Yeah, Captain. Insubordination. When I ask for a situation

report, I expect to get one. I don't care how heavy the enemy contact is; you respond to me ASAP. Don't think I don't know some men in this Company consider you their hero for your insubordination the other day. If that ever happens again, I'll put your ass up for a court-martial. Do you understand me, Captain?"

I've relaxed my stance and stare directly into the eyes of Parker. "I don't think you'll do anything of the kind, Major!"

"You don't, Captain?"

"No, Major, I don't, and I'll tell you why. After we got shot down that day, we were up to our ass in trouble. That LZ was in complete chaos and could have been overrun. Directing our Cobras in there and having them place accurate fire on the gooks helped stabilize the situation. Calling in the Air Force to drop their ordnance around the perimeter broke their back and gave the ARVN time to get their shit together."

Pausing for more effect, I deliver the coup de grace. "While all this was going on, where were you? Somewhere up in the clouds. We could have used your help! A leader would have been down close to the action. We both know that's a fact! Do you think maybe the Group Aviation Commander and Battalion Commander might feel the same way?"

I hit a raw nerve with Parker. Parker is about to go ballistic and struggles to regain his composure. As he starts pacing around the office, all the time staring coldly at me, he says. "Let's you and I get one thing straight right now, mister! I'm the CO around here, and I'll run this Company my way. Do you understand?"

I respond, "Yes, sir, but Major, in my opinion, if you don't start exercising some real leadership around here, you're probably going to lose your Company."

Parker turns to look out his window into the Company area and says, "I'll be the judge of that. Dismissed, Captain!"

"Yes, sir!"

Coming to attention, I salute Parker, who does not turn to see me exit.

Leaving his office and entering the operations area, I notice Stan has been standing near the wall to Parker's office. Stan says, "Was the Major a little upset with you?"

With a grin slowly emerging across my face and looking at Stan as I cross the room, I say in my best sarcastic voice, "You heard it through the wall, did you?"

Stan responds, "Fuck you, Taylor!"

I don't respond to or look back at Stan, and I walk out of the Headquarters trailer, quietly laughing to myself. The Major yells for Stan to come into his office. Stan, who is furious, turns and walks into Parker's office without knocking.

Entering the office, Stan slams the door and walks over toward Parker. Both men are furious with me. Parker is looking out the window watching me walk across the Company area as I head back toward the Pilot's quarters.

"That guy's an asshole, and I am fed up with him. He doesn't say it, but I know he has a low opinion of me!" Stan says.

Parker is straining to control his emotions and responds. "Yeah! I know. I think we have a mutual problem, and his name is Taylor."

Parker turns from looking out the window, walks over to his desk, and sits on top of one side of it. He picks up his cigar, takes a few puffs, and looking over at Stan, says, "What do you think, Captain?" Stan nods his agreement as he settles himself onto the couch and slowly calms down.

Parker says, "Taylor, damn him! The men look up to him and seem to despise me. This is my goddamn Company, and I'm tired of him upstaging me!" Gathering his thoughts and carefully trying to choose his words, Parker continues. "Look, Stan, we're both career officers and want to be promoted up the chain of command. You're still young and have more time than I do. I'm closing in on 18 years, and this is my first shot at real command. I need this to work! I view Taylor as a fucking troublemaker for me, and quite frankly, he seems to get under your skin too!"

Stan, listening intently now, nods his agreement.

Parker stands up and moves back to the window. Looking out, he continues. "I haven't quite figured out Lieutenant McGregor yet. He seems to be cut from the same cloth as Taylor. I believe it's in our mutual best interest to deal with both of them. Ideally, it would be better if they would just request transfers out of this Company. Less red tape, and certainly less of a hassle for us!" Turning to look back at Stan, he says, "Do you agree?"

Stan nods yes and asks, "Just what do you have in mind?"

"According to regulations, they each have a few days of light duty coming because of what they've been through these last three days. When their time is up, I want you to ride their asses!"

Stan nods his agreement again as Parker looks back out the window and continues. "Scott is due for another check-ride. I want you to do it and give him a rough one! Then make him an Aircraft Commander (AC)!"

"Are you sure about that, Major? I don't think he's ready to be an AC yet. He hasn't been here long enough to gain the experience he'll need to be one."

Parker turns around and walks back toward Stan. "Yes, he's ready! Just do it! Then, I want you to assign Taylor and Scott every shit mission we get! Maybe they'll both request transfers!"

Stan rises from the couch and, with some trepidation, says, "Major, this is full of risk! If something goes wrong and can be blamed on Scott's lack of experience or that we pushed him and Taylor too hard, it will lay at my feet as the Operations Officer…"

The Major cuts him off. "Just do as you're told and make their lives as miserable as possible. The sooner they're out of here, the better for both of us!"

# CHAPTER 17
## PILOTS CLUB

Returning to my room, I find a note from Scott saying that he has secured a jeep and gone to the Pilots club. There is a light, comfortable breeze blowing this evening with a dimly lit sky. The Pilots Club is near the main flight line and about two miles from our Company. I decide to stop by the mess hall, grab a sandwich, and then walk to the club. After what I've just been subjected to, exercise will help release some of the tension and anger that grips my body. Trying to make sense of what took place in Parker's office consumes my thoughts as I nibble on my sandwich while walking to the club, thinking to myself. *What the hell is wrong with Parker? I thought we're on the same team. Don't we have enough to deal with over here? The enemy is supposed to be outside the wire, not inside!*

Entering the club, I notice Scott and Greg seated at a small table in the far corner. This was no small feat since the club is always full of pilots. As usual, they are drinking, being rowdy. Some are trying to outdo each other with tales of flying skills and daring aerial feats they performed during the day.

I walk over to the bar, buy a beer, and head for their table. As

I approach their table, Scott notices me. "That didn't take too long!"

"Long enough!" I respond as I pull a chair out and settle in for some drinking.

Greg reaches over and taps his beer to mine. "Is Parker giving you a rough time, TJ?"

"Yeah, I guess he can't take a fucking joke!"

Greg chuckles, "A joke? Hell, man! I would venture to say he's just a little pissed at you for telling him to fuck off the other day!"

"You think!"

Greg responds, "Fucking A! You know, TJ, that's some pair of characters you're working for over there!"

Scott jumps in, "You referring to Parker and Stan?"

Greg responds, "Yeah, Scott. One stays as high as possible above the action all the time, and the other guy goes out of his way to avoid flying combat missions, which isn't too difficult since he is the Operations Officer. And what's this crap about making his packs play airborne and have to bail out of his chopper?"

With a serious look on his face and remorse in his voice, Scott says, "Hell, one thing is for sure! Major Stewart is no Major Hutchins, and Stan, well, I don't know what the hell he is!"

With that said, we all raise our beers, tap them together, and finish them off. "Anyone for another beer?" as Scott gets up and heads for the bar. Greg and I give him a thumbs up.

Scott returns with three beers, passes them out, and conversation resumes. Looking at Scott, I say, "Thanks." Greg nods to Scott, his appreciation. Looking at both, I say, "Three ARVN soldiers were hurt on that first day in Lolo when Stan started to pull up before his packs had a chance to get out. They all jumped from higher in the air than they should have. Did either of you hear anything about why he pulled out like that?"

Scott replies. "I ran into his crew chief yesterday after we got back from flying and asked him what happened. He said Stan told him they were losing RPM and had to make a go-around. He didn't realize his packs were going to jump off as he was going up."

Greg grins and, in a sarcastic voice, says. "Loss of RPM. That sounds like bullshit to me!" Pausing for effect, he continues. "Why not just land and let your packs jump out? That should have solved his problem. Wouldn't you think?"

I reply, "Who the hell knows. I can tell you one thing, though, I really don't want to fly with him. He's too unsure of himself and seems to lack confidence in his abilities. Not a good combination!"

After a long pause, I mentioned to them in a serious, reflective way, "You know, Stan could probably be a pretty good pilot and not a bad guy if he would just lighten up. It seems to me he spends too much time worrying about his Army career." Neither Greg nor Scott react to my comment. Apparently, they want to think it over for a while before commenting.

Continuing, I look over at Scott and say, "The Major really has it in for me. And Stan is probably siding with him! I wouldn't be surprised if you're in their sights. Just be careful!" Finishing my comments, I stand up, stroll over to the bar and order another round of beers.

While standing there waiting on my beers, several pilots gather around me and insist I join in with them singing our favorite song. It doesn't take much to coax me into joining them. We start to bellow out, "We gotta get out of this place if it's the last thing we ever do." The rest of the pilots in the club join in. Although we claim this song by the Animals, the truth is that troops universally adopt it across Vietnam.

Our frolicking abruptly ends with the sounds of rockets whistling in as they rain down and explode on the far side of the base. Men scramble from their chairs and places at the bar, and head for the exits. I hook up with Scott and Greg and run like hell for the nearest sandbagged bunker. Unfortunately, they're not that well-constructed and will not stand a direct hit from a rocket. We seldom get rockets raining down on our location for some reason. Because of that, we have become somewhat complacent in this regard.

As we run for shelter, the night sky lights up as rockets explode on impact around the base. Making it to one of the bunkers, we scramble inside, joining other men who are trying to make themselves as small as humanly possible. How contorted can a human body become? In a situation like this, every man tries his damnedest to wrap himself into a ball, including me. All of us are gasping for air, both out of fear and exertion from running. Almost as soon as it started, it's over. As the all-clear signal is heard, we begin crawling out of the shelter.

Standing a short distance back from the club and dusting ourselves off, Greg looks over at Scott and me and says, "Why is it we never hear a damn siren before rockets rain down on us?"

There is no time to respond to Greg as we hear another whistling noise closing in on our position. It grows closer and closer. We dive to the ground just as the rocket hits the ground. A terrific explosion occurs right in front of us as the Pilots Club takes a direct hit. Chunks of dirt, splinters of wood, and pieces of metal rain down on us. Slowly picking ourselves up from the ground, we check for any wounds. Everyone at this location appears to be okay. However, we are all going to have one hell of a severe headache and ringing in our ears for the next few days.

Scott blurts out, "Damn, will I ever make it back home?"

Greg, always one to try and lighten the mood, says, "Well, Scott, if you stay out of bars like your mother told you, you just might make it home!"

All three of us manage a laugh while turning to look at our Pilots Club, which appears to have sustained considerable damage. Looking around for the jeep, the one in which Scott drove over, we have more bad news. His jeep, along with several others, is on its side, burning.

"Well, I guess we're walking home, gentlemen!" As we start to head out, I continue, "This just hasn't been my fucking day!"

Within 24 hours, our beloved Pilots Club is rebuilt and ready for use. Since there isn't much else for pilots to do in our limited downtime at Phu Bai, the Pilots Club received top priority. Aviation units, especially Chinook Companies, are notorious for their abilities to acquire materials and other items deemed necessary for a pilot's well-being.

# CHAPTER 18

## CHECK RIDE

The next morning, Scott and I are awakened by a runner sent to our room with instructions for Scott to grab his flight gear and report to the Operations room. Rubbing his eyes and stretching out as he sits up, Scott asks the runner what's going on. He doesn't know and just tells him to hurry up.

We exchange puzzled looks as Scott puts his flight suit on and grabs his helmet heading out the door. "See you later, TJ." I respond, "Yeah, see you later," and I roll back over in my cot and try to go back to sleep.

Arriving at the Operations room, Scott finds Stan waiting for him. "Lieutenant McGregor, I'm giving you an AC check ride today!"

Scott replies, "A what?"

"A check ride to make you an Aircraft Commander. Do you have a problem with that, Lieutenant?"

Scott replies sarcastically. "Captain, I know what an AC check ride is, but I haven't been in the country long enough to become an AC. Hell, I'm still learning..."

Stan cuts him off. "You're ready. We need all the ACs we can to get qualified, so just suck it up, and you'll be alright. Now let's go!"

Leaving the Headquarters trailer, they go by the Arms room to pick up their remaining gear and weapons. From there, they head out to their assigned Huey. Walking up to the revetment housing their chopper, they are met by the crew chief and door gunner. Salutes are exchanged as the gunner jumps in the chopper, and the crew chief moves to the front of the ship and takes off the rotor blade tie-downs.

Scott looks at Stan and says, "What about our pre-flight check?"

Stan replies, "It was done earlier by the crew and me. It's ready. Jump in!"

Both men put on their chicken plates and survival vest and climb into the Huey. Once in, they adjust and secure their seat straps, and put on their helmets. They plug their helmets into the radio system, and intercom conversations occur as they go through their start-up procedures.

'Scott, you look a little concerned, maybe even apprehensive!'

'Christ, Captain, in my position, only a fool wouldn't be!'

Stan ignores his comment and says, 'Instruments check, radios are set, everything checked out okay on our pre-flight walk around. So, we are good to go. Fire it up, and let's get the hell out of here, Lieutenant!'

'Right! Fire it up and get the hell out of here!'

Scott starts the engine, monitors his instruments as they approach their normal readings, and brings the rotor RPM up to the red line. Their Huey is getting light on the skids. With everything looking good, he brings the chopper to a low hover and gingerly hovers out of the revetment as the crew chief guides him forward. Once clear of the revetment, Scott settles his Huey back on the ground. The crew chief jumps in and straps himself down.

Scott feels uncomfortable already as he senses Stan is just looking for an excuse to jump his ass.

Hovering to the end of the Company's staging area, Scott calls Phu Bai Tower. 'Phu Bai Tower, this is Eagle 13, ready for takeoff. Over.'

'Eagle 13, Phu Bai Tower. You're cleared for takeoff. Climb, and maintain 1,000 feet until clear of Phu Bai air space. Be advised; there are low hanging clouds and some light weather when you get north of Hue and closer to Quang Tri. Over!'

'Eagle 13, Roger.'

Stan jumps all over Scott, admonishing him for making an incorrect radio transmission to the tower. Over the intercom, Stan tells Scott that he should have said, 'Phu Bai tower, this is Eagle 13, Roger, understand. Climb and maintain 1,000 feet until clear of Phu Bai airspace. Over.' This is not a big deal. Many pilots respond as Scott initially did. If he had any doubts earlier that this would be a rough day, they just vanished.

Scott strains to keep his cool and not go off on Stan. Instead, he focuses his attention on taking off. Scott pulls up on the collective and edges the cyclic forward while keeping pressure on his foot pedals. This orchestrated and choreographed movement of hands and feet on the Huey's controls moves the chopper forward and up as it lifts off into the clear mid-morning sky.

At their initial assigned altitude, Stan informs Scott over their intercom of what to expect for the day. 'I'll be giving you a series of emergencies during your check ride today. Some you will respond to verbally, and others you will have to react to as they are thrown at you. Clear so far?'

Scott responds, 'I got it!'

'When we clear Hue, you will climb to 5,000 feet, contact the Quang Tri tower and request to shoot an instrument approach into the airfield. We will not be landing there. This will be an IFR approach into the field, and then we'll do a fly around.

You'll then fly on to Khe Sahn, where we will land, take a break for lunch and refuel. When ready, we'll launch and do some work in that area. When done, we'll head back to Quang Tri, shoot another approach, land, and refuel. Then head home. You can expect an emergency any time during your check ride today. Stay alert and try to relax. Any questions?'

Scott is pissed. This is not a usual check ride. Having been through several check rides to get this far in his Army Aviation career, he knows bullshit when it comes his way. 'Damn Captain, this is bullshit! I know we're in Vietnam, but this goes well beyond a regular check ride.'

Before he can finish, Stan rebukes him. 'Lieutenant, just concentrate on your flying, stay focused, and don't fucking talk back to your superior. Got it?'

Scott replies, 'Yes, Sir!' while thinking to himself, *superior my ass!*

Later that evening, I'm seated at a table in the mess hall, having dinner with Captain Barnett and some of the other Eagles pilots. The subject revolves around the low morale and piss poor attitudes of many of the Company's men. Parker has managed to destroy much of the "esprit de corps" and teamwork attitude that the Company enjoyed under Major Hutchin's leadership.

"Company formations, spot inspections of living quarters, article 15s (allegations of minor misconduct by a soldier) being given out like candy, and now he's closed the enlisted men and NCO's club facilities until further notice. Thank god, we have a separate Pilots Club up on the main field." Captain Barnett says in a sarcastic voice.

"What's this about the clubs for the men? I hadn't heard that yet!" I bellow out.

"Oh yeah, that happened earlier today when Parker conducted a surprise inspection of the enlisted men's quarters belonging to the maintenance group! He thought it was a mess and out of compliance with his Company directives. As a result, he chose to punish all the enlisted men and NCOs in the Company for their lack of military discipline!"

"My god!" I respond. "Does he have any idea how hard those men have been working to keep this Company's choppers in the air so we can meet our operational requirements for this damn Lam Son operation? He's a damn fool to screw around with those men!"

Noticing more men are looking my way, I realize my voice has increased in volume to the point where it carries beyond my immediate audience. Dialing it back, I continue. "Hell, they spend all their time now in the hangar and revetments working on our Hueys. Good maintenance men are hard to find, and when you have them, the last thing you want to do is fuck with them. Who gives a shit if the Major can't bounce a quarter off their cots or that their boots aren't spit-shined to his liking? That has nothing to do with their ability to do their jobs and keep us in the air! What a damn fool!"

The men around him agree. Captain Barnett says to me, "Do you think some of us should approach the Battalion Commander about what has been going on here?"

Before I can respond, the door to the mess hall swings open and slams against the wall. In walks Scott, drenched in sweat, exhausted, and mad as hell. All eyes in the mess hall are fixated on Scott as he makes his way over to the chow line. Once there, he grabs a tray, slowly works his way down the chow line while not saying a word to anyone, and throws food on his tray. Reaching the end of the line, he turns and walks over to where we are seated.

As Scott takes a seat across from me, I look over at him and jokingly say, "Have a rough day, Scott?"

Settling into his seat, Scott replies, "Yeah, one could say that!"

"What happened, Scott?" Captain Barnett says.

"I had my AC check ride today with Stan!"

"Aren't you a little green around the gills to be an Aircraft Commander?" Captain Barnett replies.

"That's what I said to Stan when he dropped it on me first thing this morning!"

Suspecting what is going on here, I ask Scott, "You mean you've been at this all day?"

Scott, just a little pissed off, responds, "Fucking A. All damn day, all over our operational area, in and out of firebases, flying in weather and shooting instrument approaches. It was one damn emergency procedure after another. This shit borders on harassment!"

Speaking directly to him, I respond, "Scott, this has something to do with Parker and me. Unfortunately, I think he's pulled you into it with me. He views me as a threat, and by association, you. I think he wants to run us out of the Company!"

Scott, still upset, says, "Damn! Isn't it enough that we have to worry about getting our asses shot off by the gooks? And now Parker's after us too! What a hell of a way to fight a war!"

Scott picks at this food and begins to settle down as the conversation continues.

"So, you're going to be an AC, right?" Captain Barnett asks.

"Yeah, I passed," Scott replies.

I say to Scott, "That's good! You'll do fine, Scott. None of us thinks we're ready when we first make AC. Being an AC is no guarantee you'll make the right decisions or not make any mistakes. The most experienced ACs can make mistakes and screw up!"

One of the pilots sitting near Scott asked him what the worst part of his day was. Scott replies, "That's easy. We were flying at 10,000 feet, and Stan cut our power. If we were not fighting on the same side in this war, I would have thrown his ass out of the chopper!"

I try to inject a little humor. "At least he gave you plenty of time to find a place to land!"

Except for Scott, the group laughs. Scott replies to our reaction. "The rest of the story follows. We were several miles inside Laos when he killed the engine!"

The laughter stops abruptly. Another pilot says, "That wasn't too fucking smart!"

Scott, looking tired, angry, and wasted, says, "I didn't think so either!"

A long silence follows as the First Sergeant enters the mess hall and walks over to me. "Hey, Captain. Captain Norton wanted me to let you know you're flying standby with him tomorrow morning. You're to meet him on the flight line for pre-flight at 0600. Okay?"

Grinning, I look up at the First Sergeant, "You got any other good news for me, Top?"

"Well, sir, it seems like another day of light duty for you. You certainly deserve it!"

"Light duty...where have I heard that before? Thanks. Top, let him know you gave me the message, and I'll see him at 0600."

"You got it," says the First Sergeant as he leaves. Scott and the rest of us pilots get up and head out the door grinning. "Light duty, don't you just love it!" I say as I'm thinking, *there's no such thing as light duty over here when you launch in a Huey!*

On our way back to the room, Scott informs me he's exhausted and calling it a night after showering. I respond, "I got a tape from Sandy today, and I'm going to listen to it if that's alright with you?" Scott replies, "Not a problem, go ahead. I'm so damn tired; nothing will bother me tonight."

# CHAPTER 19
## STAND-BY

S cott wasted no time. When his head hit the pillow, he fell fast asleep. We've all been there; a long, intense day of flying can drain you of every ounce of your energy. You are physically and mentally wasted from the strain, fear, and constant need to be at the top of your game. If not, it could be game over!

Laying on my cot with my head supported by pillows, I'm in a state of temporary bliss listening to Sandy's tape. Sandy's voice comes through clearly on the tape, and I can hear in the background waves rolling onto the beach and Angus barking occasionally. It was early evening as the sun slowly set in the west when Sandy dictated her tape while jogging along the beach with Angus by her side.

"From your tapes, it sounds like you're not involved in any real fighting. That's good but hard to believe. The nightly news broadcasts and the newspapers are full of stories about Laos and the invasion. They talk about our American helicopter aircrews' heavy losses and the South Vietnamese not pulling their weight. Knowing you're with the 101st, there's no way you're not involved in some of the fighting over there. God, I hope you're safe! When we're in Hawaii and together again, you and I will talk about what you're doing. I want to know, yet I don't, for fear it would make it harder to live with. I know this. I just want this war to end and for Nixon to bring all of you home. Taylor, you mean the world to me, and I want you home safe and beside me. That can't happen soon enough. I can't wait to see you again and feel you against me. Hawaii can't get here soon enough for me. God, I love you!"

Switching the tape off, I wipe the tears from my cheeks, which have slowly flowed from my eyes. The emotions welling up within me are almost too much to bear. Turning off the night lamp, I roll over in my cot and try to go to sleep. It could be a long day tomorrow. *Light duty, we'll see!*

Stan, feeling quite good about his performance today with Scott, has been drinking the night away at the Pilots Club. After landing earlier that evening, he reported to Parker and gave him the details concerning Scott's check ride and his reactions to it. They both seemed pleased that Scott did not take well to his treatment and may well request a transfer. Parker praised Stan, which made him feel good and drove him to celebrate at the club with heavy drinking.

Tomorrow he is on stand-by, which seldom results in much aerial activity, so in essence, it's a down day for Stan. Most helicopter pilots know how to drink and certainly do some drinking while in Vietnam. However, one should take precautions if they are scheduled to fly the next day, regardless of their missions.

Early the next morning, as I walk up to our assigned Huey and greet Stan, I notice he is nursing a severe hang-over. "Stan, you look like shit!"

"Oh?" Stan replies.

"Yeah. Did you get drunk last night?"

Stan replies in a defensive voice, "I had a few beers, so what?"

"So, what, just a few beers, you say? Like I said, you look like shit! Why don't you go sleep it off, and I'll get another pilot?"

Stan retorts, "Look, Taylor, why don't you mind your own fucking business!"

The crew chief and door gunner have walked up to the Huey and can hear our verbal exchange. Not intending for this conversation to happen in front of our crew, I try to get Stan to join me and move away from them. Stan ignores my gestures and throws his gear onto his seat in the chopper.

"All right then. Stan, it is my fucking business when you're risking my life and the crews!"

"Hey, look, Taylor, I'm all right. Besides, this is just stand-by duty, right? We just crank her up, go around the pattern, land in the Battalion area, and shut her down. And unless someone needs our help, we just lounge around and relax the rest of the day. What could possibly go wrong?"

"A lot could go wrong. You're the senior officer here, so I'm telling you right now in front of the crew. This is a mistake, and you should stand down!"

Stan replies, "We're going! Put your damn stuff in the chopper, and let's get our pre-flight done."

I know this is a mistake, but Stan is not going to listen to me. I help perform the pre-flight procedures, then climb into my seat and settle in. Stan and the door gunner have climbed into their seats and are settling in. The crew chief has removed the rotor tie-downs and is standing out in front of the Huey. He has placed himself a considerable distance back from our revetment, just in case.

We put on our helmets and plug the radio chords into the ship's radio system. Stan takes the controls and starts the engine. I'm checking our instruments, calling their readings out as they come online, and stabilize in the green zones. As our rotor RPM reaches the red line, conversations continue over the intercom.

Stan to me, 'Everything looks good to me, what about you?'

'Looks good to me, Stan, but I'm not sure.'

Stan cuts in on me, 'Okay then, let's get this day over with!'

'For Chrissake, Stan, just be careful!'

As Stan starts to pull up on the collective and bring it to a hover, he yells into the intercom. 'It's starting to get away from me! I'm going to set it back down.'

'Easy, Stan, you want me to take it?'

'No. I got the goddamn thing!' Stan replied angrily.

Instead of easing down on the collective, Stan pulls up on the collective, which takes our Huey to a higher hover. Simultaneously, he overreacts with his cyclic, moving it sideways and back to front. These control movements cause the Huey to begin to sway just above the revetment. Suddenly the nose dips forward, and the rotor blades hit the front of the revetment. The crew chief sees what is happening and instinctively dives for cover behind another revetment.

He does so just in time, as chunks of the blades go flying everywhere. Some of the fragments hit and impale themselves into other Huey's parked in their revetments. Stan panics, and I take over the controls. I push the collective down to the floor and throttle completely back on power. As I do, the chopper hits the ground hard and bounces several times before settling to rest.

In a panicked voice, Stan says, 'Holy shit, what just happened?'

'You said, "What could go wrong?" Well, look outside your damn window. You just made one hell of a mess, Captain!'

What's left of our rotor blades slowly wind down. I shut down the engine and look back to see if our gunner is alright. The gunner's expression is one of comical disbelief and total relief that we are fine other than our chopper. Stan is in a state of shock and confusion. He's mumbling into our intercom, 'What'd I do?

What happened? What have I done? Oh my God, there goes my fucking career!'

As the Huey's rotor blades come to a complete stop, I remove my helmet and climb out of the chopper. I run over to the area where the crew chief dove behind another revetment to check on him. He's sitting up and leaning against the backside of it. He is dazed and shaken, but otherwise alright. He says, "That was too damn close. What the hell happened?"

I respond, "You okay?" The crew chief says, "Yeah, I think so!"

"Good! There's going to be an investigation, and each of us will be required to give our statements. I can't say anything right now, nor should you, until we are questioned. Got it!"

"Yes, sir."

I help the crew chief to his feet, and we walk back over to the beat-up chopper. The door gunner has climbed out and is looking it over. Stan, who has also climbed out, is still in a state of shock. He just stands there staring at the mess he's made. By this time, several men from around the Company area have come running over to the site to see what happened and view the damage. Some of the other Hueys parked in their revetments are damaged. As the rotor blades were destroying themselves against the revetment, pieces were flung out everywhere. Many of them slammed into and impeded themselves in choppers closest to us.

When tallied up, three Hueys sustained mild damage from flying debris. They should be repaired and back in service within 24 hours. However, our Huey sustained considerable damage. It will be out of service for weeks. This does not bode well for Stan since he was the AC.

There went my light duty day!

# CHAPTER 20

## INQUIRY

P arker, sitting behind his desk, is fighting to control his growing rage. Stan and I are standing in front of his desk at attention. Parker stares at us as Stan is still visibly shaken, and I'm calm but concerned. We are both avoiding eye contact with Parker.

Parker, "What the hell happened out there?"

Stan can't bring himself to answer, and after a long pause, I respond. "We had an accident, Sir!"

Parker yells back at me, "Always the smart ass! Aren't you, Taylor?"

Looking directly at Parker, I respond back to him. "No, sir. The fact is, we had an unfortunate accident."

Parker cuts me off. "Unfortunate accident? Unfortunate? You have got to be shitting me! I'm trying to make this the best damn Aviation Company in the Division, and you two fuckers go and have a dumb ass major incident. You notice I said dumb ass, not unfortunate?"

I look away, "Yes, sir."

Parker gets up from his desk and walks around to stand in

front of us. Stan has started to relax his stance, and Parker goes nuts. "I didn't say you could relax! Son of a bitch! This isn't going to ruin my career. One of you bastards is going to take the fall for this. Now, who was flying that ship? And what the fuck happened? Taylor!"

Parker's verbal abuse of us finally awakens Stan from his stupor, and he looks straight into Parker's eyes. "I was flying the goddamn thing, and I don't know what happened. It just seemed to get away from me. She just got light on the skids, so I brought her to a hover, and then... It's all a blur right now. I need some time to think this through."

A long silence ensues as Parker moves back behind his desk and settles into his chair. He's slowly calming down and alternates his stares between Stan and me. Stan appears remorseful; I'm just impatient and want this to end. I can only imagine what is running through Parker's mind. Parker's eyes betray him, as you can see him trying to figure out how to spin this so he can come out the other side untouched. He is the CO and ultimately responsible for what happens in his Company.

Parker looks calmly now at both of us. "Gentlemen. There will be an inquiry as to what happened. You're both grounded until it's complete. Since we're in the middle of this damn Lam Son business, the inquiry will be over and done quickly. We need every pilot and every ship. Stan, I suggest you figure out what the hell happened out there and what you're going to say before meeting with them. They might just fry your ass! Dismissed!"

We salute Parker, who doesn't reciprocate, then turn away and leave the office. I retreat to my room, where I try to relax and wait for the inquiry, which should start later in the day.

Sandy and I regularly record and send tapes to each other. I try to dictate some each day until a tape is full. After which, I mail it to Sandy and begin a new one. Having some time before the inquiry, I believe this would be an excellent opportunity to dictate a little on my current tape. Stretching out on my cot, I turn on the tape recorder and begin dictating.

"Sandy, I've got a little time, so I'll continue with this tape. Not much has been happening around here lately. Most of our time is spent flying routine, resupply missions around Khe Sanh. Laos is still a mess, but we are fortunate and seldom have to cross the border into Laos. Parker is his usual self-a real asshole! I think he's trying to make things more uncomfortable for Scott and me, hoping we'll request transfers. We don't plan on going anywhere. This was a good Company, with good men, until he showed up. Good leadership can make all the difference-Ah hell, enough of that. I sure do miss you and can't wait to wrap my arms around you. I dream constantly about making love to you. In a few months, we'll be together in Hawaii for some R&R. I'm on the list now. I was able to secure a date range for this summer, which should not interfere with your teaching schedule. When I get a firm date, I'll take care of the hotel and plane reservations--not much longer."

I'm interrupted by a knock on my door. Turning off the recorder and standing up as I look over at the door, "Come in."

In walks the First Sergeant. "Captain, I was sent here to tell you to be up at Battalion HQ at 1200 hours. Apparently, it's going to be a quick inquiry taking place this afternoon and ending by dinner. There will be a truck at our Headquarters trailer at 1120 to take the four of you up to Battalion. And, sir, the Mess Hall Sergeant told me to tell you that his mess hall will not be open early enough for you to get some food before you have to go up there. He wants you to know that he can take care of you anytime, so just stop by well before you have to leave, and he'll see that you get something to eat."

I respond, "Thanks, Top. Tell the Sergeant I appreciate that and will swing by there sometime before 1100. Oh, has he included the other fellows in this? I believe we're all in for a long afternoon!"

"He has."

After the First Sergeant leaves, I sit back on my cot and turn the recorder back on. It's no use. I've lost my concentration and turn it off. My mind has shifted to the inquiry I'm about to face. I lay back and stretch out on the cot. I need to relax and ponder the possible questions I might be asked later in the day.

It's hopeless. My adrenaline rush has been high and has not worn off since the accident only a few hours earlier. The uncertainty about what's to follow haunts me. I know this incident has all kinds of potential ramifications and could result in a court-martial.

Not being able to relax, I stand up, adjust my flight suit to ensure it's presentable, and head over to the mess hall for some chow. After picking at some food provided by the Mess Sergeant and thanking him, I head out. Slowly and deliberately, I walk to the Headquarters trailer, all the while dreading what is to follow. There I'm met by Stan, our crew chief and door gunner, who are waiting in the Operations room for Parker to exit his office. We all have a look of dread, uncertainty, and stress in our eyes. The body language we exhibit betrays our apprehension.

Parker exits his office and walks right by us without speaking as he motions for us to follow him. We follow him out of the trailer and over to the truck, which is waiting for us. Parker jumps in the front seat opposite the driver, and we climb in the back. Arriving at our Battalion HQ without a word spoken between us, we leap from the back of the truck. Stan tries to engage Parker in some conversation as we're following him into the building. Parker ignores him. I could almost feel sorry for him, but at this moment, I'm more concerned about my immediate future. The building we enter is a large, one-story wooden structure, with sandbags stacked halfway up all four sides of the structure. This indistinguishable place serves as the Battalion Commander's office and those of his staff officers.

Upon entering the building, we go straight to the Battalion Commander's office. Parker knocks on the office door and is told to enter. He disappears into the office. As the door closes behind him, the other men and I are told to wait in the staff area until called upon. There is a Major from the Division's JAG (Judge Advocate General) office sitting behind a desk in one corner of the staff area. He has a serious nature about him and advises us not to talk to each other. We're further told to take a seat and be quiet while we wait to be called.

Looking around the room, I notice two other pilots from another Company sitting in one corner and looking serious. As instructed, no conversations take place. We sit in silence. The atmosphere in the room is solemn and foreboding. Just because we almost destroyed a quarter-million-dollar Huey is no reason to treat us like criminals. After all, the North Vietnamese damage and destroy several of our helicopters every day in Laos.

Parker finally emerges from the office with a distressed look on his face. It seems like he was in there for an eternity. Looking over at us, he says in a low melancholy voice, "I'm returning to the Company. You guys can find your own ride back!" I think to myself, *Thanks, asshole, we're the ones who Stan almost killed out there. Can't you wait to give us a ride or promise to send someone back for us?*

Stan is called into the room next.

When he eventually emerges, Stan's demeanor is one of distress and total exhaustion. Not looking up, he just walks by the other men in the waiting area, and out the exit. I'm called in next.

When I walk into the office, I'm greeted by the Battalion Commander, who introduces me to another Major from JAG, and two helicopter pilots from another Battalion. They will serve as impartial investigators. The Battalion Commander informs me that they want to hear from me what happened this morning on stand-by. Following any questions they may have of me, I will then be required to make a written statement. Once advised of my legal military rights, the Battalion Commander tells me to please take a seat and give them my story.

I proceed to inform them of everything that occurred in great detail, except for the drinking suspicions I had of Stan. I do not mention that during the interview. I do tell them that Stan didn't look good to me when I first saw him. I also mention to them that I recommended we get another pilot to replace him for the day. Stan refused, saying he was fine and would fly the mission. He duly noted my concerns.

After answering the few questions I was given, I wrote a statement in their presence and was dismissed. Returning to the waiting area, I inform the crew chief and door gunner that I'll secure a jeep, return here, and wait for them to finish.

Later that evening, after dinner, Stan and I are called into Parker's office. As we are standing before him, Parker proceeds to tell us the outcome of their inquiry. He is not happy.

"Thanks to you, gentlemen, I have a black mark against my record here. Being the Company Commander makes me ultimately responsible for all that goes on around here."

I think to myself, *that's part of your damn job description and comes with the territory.*

Parker continues. "I got my ass reamed today by the Battalion Commander. It seems that you, Stan, spent last night drinking, and apparently, you had several. Did it ever occur to you that maybe, just maybe, you should have replaced yourself with another pilot? You're the damn Operations officer here, Stan!"

Stan tries to say something, but before he can clear his throat, Parker stops him and continues. "And you, Taylor, it seems you were the hero out there and saved the day. Everyone thinks if you hadn't acted, it would have been much worse. On the other hand, I could make a case for dereliction of duty against you for not stopping Stan from flying. If you had, maybe this whole sorry episode would not have happened!"

Looking at Parker, I struggle to restrain myself. I desperately want to get in his face and tell him to go to hell. Parker is just waiting for me to mouth off and give him another opportunity to unload on me. Discretion being the better part of valor, I remain silent.

"What, no response, Taylor?"

To myself, I think., *None, no comment, no response, no hay problema!*

After a long pause, Parker continues. "Here is the deal, gentlemen. Stan, you will receive a reprimand, and it will be placed in your file. You will remain as my Operations Officer for now. Taylor, you were not judged to be at fault in this incident, and no action will be taken. If we were not in the middle of this damn Lam Son operation and needing every pilot and ship we have, you might have been up shit's creek, Stan." With that, he dismisses us.

After returning to my room, I lay on my bunk and doze off. I'm just getting into my first dream of Sandy when Scott walks in and closes the door hard behind him. That has the intended effect of waking me up. It was his first day as a new AC, and he wants to share his experience of flying up north around Khe Sanh. "Taylor, old man. Wake up. Let's go get a beer."

Scott walks over to his cot and throws his flight helmet and other gear on top of it. I slowly awaken and, sitting up, say, "It's been a long frigging day for me, Scott. I'm guessing you heard what happened?"

"I did. Let's go have a few beers and share stories. How's that?"

Even though it's been a long day, I could use some buddy

time with the guys. We both grab our fatigue caps and head for the Pilots Club.

This is our first time back to the club since it was hit by a rocket two nights ago. We're both impressed by the speed at which it was repaired and opened for business. Arriving at the rebuilt club, we notice a wooden sign hanging over the entrance. Looking up at it, we both manage a grin. It reads:

"Enter at your own risk! Subject to rocket attacks!"

Scott says, "As Rick would say, bitching sign!"

We swing open the door and enter the Pilots Club, full of pilots enjoying their evening. Looking around, I am struck by how casual and relaxed many of the pilots appear to be. *They're all relaxing as if we're back in the States enjoying the company of business associates after a long hard day at the office. There's one enormous difference; no one working in the States has had a bunch of people trying to kill them all day.*

Scott leads me over to the bar where he buys the first round. A sign hanging on the wall behind the bar says that new wooden eagles have been ordered and should arrive soon. The old ones were destroyed in the rocket attack. Again, I think, *The good news is we don't have to go through another initiation to pick out a new one when they come in.*

Looking around the club for some familiar faces, I notice Greg. He signals for Scott and me to join in at the table he shares with two of his pilots. We work our way over to the table and pull up two more chairs to join them. Greg, looking at me with a grin, says, "Heard you had another bad day. Not a shot fired, and four choppers were damaged. That would have been a good day's work if they didn't belong to the good guys!"

There is laughter, but it takes me a little longer to join in on the fun since I'm the subject of their humor. Lightening up and with a grin on my face, I look over at Greg and say, "Real frigging funny. I seem to remember a while back you nicked a revetment yourself!"

Greg responds, "Touche', my friend!" We tap our beers together and finish them off. Greg introduces the other two pilots at the table as new men in his Company—telling me that they were called in on the inquiry as witnesses. Looking at them closer, I recognize their faces from earlier in the day.

"Well, I'll be damned. What were you guys doing there today?"

One responds, "We were up here drinking last night before the incident and had a few beers with Stan. He could sure down them but didn't seem to know when to stop!"

I inquire, "Just curious, how did they identify you as drinking with him?"

The other pilot responds. "We wondered that too! The only thing we could come up with was that the Club had just reopened, and the word hadn't gotten out yet. There were only a few of us here last night, so we guessed it was easy to locate us."

Out of nowhere, five more beers are laid on the table in front of us, having been delivered by one of the enlisted men tending bar. Greg asked where these came from. He points to a group of Eagles pilots drinking at the bar and says they sent them. Looking over at the bar, I recognize the men and give them a casual salute of thanks. They reciprocate.

Turning back to our table and knowing that Greg and Scott are both interested in my take on what happened, I indulge them in some conversation. My comments are general and somewhat compassionate for Stan's situation. I stress to them that we were lucky no one was hurt in the incident. Parker got his ass reamed by the Battalion CO and was not happy about it. Stan was given a reprimand, a second chance, and placed back on flight status. I was cleared and placed back on flight status.

Finishing my comments, I look over at Scott and say, "So Scott, how did it go for you as a new AC up at Khe Sanh today?"

Scott replies, "Wasn't bad! We stayed on this side of the border all day, just flying supplies and troops around where needed. The weather was lousy as usual! I don't think I'll ever get comfortable flying into firebases shrouded in fog and mist."

Greg, smiling, says to Scott, "Maybe you should switch to Cobras. We don't have much of a problem with that kind of weather. We have to see what we're shooting at!"

Scott grins, "Somehow, I find that hard to believe!" That lightens the mood. Smirks spread across our faces as we all raise our beers and touch them together at the table center. We do this in recognition of the risk we share every day in the air.

Scott proceeds to entertain us with some of his daring exploits and experiences during the day as the Eagles' newest AC. He ends by telling us about how much the North Vietnamese have been raising hell all over, up north. Laos is a mess, and the NVA is becoming much more active around the Khe Sanh area.

This does not bode well for any of us.

# CHAPTER 21

## ANOTHER WEEK IN PARADISE

Over the next several days, our Company flies a series of dangerous combat missions into hot LZs inside Laos. The only difference from a few weeks earlier is that these LZs are much deeper inside Laos. Our Eagles aircrews are helping to make possible the continued movements of South Vietnamese troops. They are desperately trying to cut off NVA supply routes headed south through Laos. Using Khe Sanh as our staging area, we fly an average of ten missions a day into Laos. We routinely come under enemy fire after crossing the border, and not until we cross back into Vietnam does it let up. Both men and ships are taking a heavy beating. We are now openly questioning how much longer this operational tempo can continue. Hanging over us like a bad storm is Parker. He continues his relentless drive to make Colonel at the expense of his men.

During this time, I continue to fly my share of combat missions. Later in the evenings, I record the daily events and experiences in my diary. I have found this ritual of mine helps me to unwind and relax. At least I like to think it does.

## MARCH 1971

I flew for 9 hours today out of Khe Sanh into Laos again. Every time we flew back across that damn border into Laos, I got pretty shaky. It's a mess over there. However, we were lucky today, as the only incoming fire received on the LZs we worked on was small arms. Thank God, it was not highly effective. Another Company's Huey was hit on short final going into Firebase Sophia. Both pilots were hurt but could fly out of the area and head back toward the border following Route 9.

We happened to be returning to Khe Sanh for another load when we heard their radio transmission for help. They were too battle-damaged to make it back across the border. So, they landed on a section of Route 9 and requested extraction ASAP. We were coming upon them and had some Cobras with us. With the Cobras flying cover over us, we flew in and managed to pick them up. We took them back to our MASH unit at Khe Sanh. I don't think they were severely wounded. "Cover your buddy, so he can be around to cover for you."

In the evening, when I got back to the Company, the First Sergeant informed me that I was going to be awarded a couple of medals. Apparently, some of the combat action I participated in during the last few weeks warranted them. I'm not here for medals. I mean no disrespect toward any man who has been awarded medals for bravery. I've known many men who have received medals and respect every one of them. One of my personal heroes is Audie Murphy, who was awarded every medal the U.S. Army had for bravery during WWII. I'll accept what-ever they award me with honor, but I would rather they just send me home!

I love you Sandy!

MARCH 1971

I had another standby mission last night at Quang Tri, which is right up there close to the DMZ. The entire area, from Quang Tri to Khe Sanh, is continuously being harassed in some fashion. Some choppers are always placed on overnight standby to help if any units get in trouble and need assistance.

We were an hour late for our takeoff to head up to Quang Tri. We had all kinds of problems with our first assigned Huey, which couldn't be resolved. We were assigned another Huey that also had problems but, finally, we were able to get it off the ground. We made it up there well after dark and had to shoot an instrument landing into their small airstrip. There is no room for error because we are right on the border with North Vietnam. If you miss the airfield and cross over the DMZ into the North and get lost, you might be having breakfast with the NVA. That's an optimistic scenario since they would probably just shoot us. We are not very popular up that way.

The night was uneventful, and we didn't have to launch. On the way back to the Company this morning, our engine blew up internally, and we lost most of our power. We pulled the fire switch on the engine and auto rotated to the ground. Thank God we were close to Camp Evans. I was able to set it down inside the wire at Camp Evans. We were lucky to be close to the base and had some altitude before losing the engine. Our outcome could have been much different. I've almost been killed over here so many times now, I've lost count. I don't need this kind of excitement. I still have a lifetime to go over here before my tour is over.

I love you Sandy!

## MARCH 1971

I flew today for 10 hours up north. We didn't have to fly into Laos but worked all the areas around Khe Sanh. Our missions involved resupplying firebases on this side of the border, which are supporting Lam Son 719. They are manned by 101st troopers. What a good feeling to fly into and out of these bases and have no one shooting at us. I could get used to this very quickly.

On one of our sorties, we were severely overloaded with supplies, and had a tough time bringing the ship to a hover. The weather up there is still in the monsoon season. But it can get sweltering and humid, making the air less dense. The less dense the air, the more the engine must work to hover and climb out. We should have set back down and unloaded a few crates. You know how helicopter pilots are, we live on the edge. We were able to come up to a low hover, and I started inching forward with my cyclic. I didn't gain any speed or height and started to bleed off our RPM. I almost put us in a small swamp just in front of our staging area. However, I was able to come back to a hover and set it down just before we reached the swamp. After that, I had the crew unload some crates. My next attempt was successful, and we were able to lift off with no problems.

We heard a story while taking a lunch break, that a Cobra flying at high altitude over Laos was shot down by a "ground to air missile." Damn, I hope that's not true. That is the last thing we need to be dealing with over there. We're already subjected to more intense anti-aircraft fire, artillery, rocket, mortar, and ground fire than at any time since this war started.

I love you Sandy!

MARCH 1971

I flew today for 8 hours in and out of Laos. We worked two new firebases that were recently established and have already been under heavy pressure. They are about 35 miles inside Laos. If you get hit and go down out there, it's a long way home.

Most of our sorties consisted of supplies, and a few involved ARVN troops. One of the problems we are experiencing when we fly into many of their firebases involves ARVN troops jumping into our Hueys. They are getting creamed over there and just want to get the hell out. After we unload, some of them jump onto our choppers and won't get out. We can't stay on the LZ, so we take off with them. I feel for these guys, but that's not going to win this war for them.

This whole Lam Son 719 operation is one giant clusterfuck. The South Vietnamese are losing their firebases to heavy enemy attacks and retreating toward Khe Sahn. We've already had to rescue their troops on LZ 30, 31, and Ranger as they were being overrun.

Today, we took several rounds of small arms fire on many of our LZ approaches and liftoffs. Although no one was hit, our "pucker factor" was high as rounds penetrated the Huey, making their usual popping noises. Occasionally, some mortar rounds would land near the area where we were dropping off our loads. This can be quite unnerving as they kick up a lot of dirt, debris, and shrapnel. It does get a little annoying.

On another note, the morale in this Company has hit a new low. At dinner this evening, I learned that one of our crew chiefs pulled out his .38 revolver and shot himself in the foot on his way to the mess hall for breakfast this morning. He's been on the verge of cracking up and didn't want to have to go up north and fly into Laos again. He was scheduled to launch after he had breakfast. Because he pulled this stunt, another crew chief, who had the day off, was assigned to take his place. I understand he tried to claim it was an accident, but unfortunately for him, several men saw what he did. He's on his way to Da Nang for a court-martial.

Parker is out of his damn mind. In keeping with his way of handling individual cases of military infractions, he is punishing the entire Company again for what this crew chief did. What few privileges we had left are temporarily restricted. He's had the movie projector locked up until further notice, so no movies at night for a while. He had our next USO show postponed and has restricted our use of Company jeeps. I'll be walking to the Pilots Club on many nights. Getting over there won't be difficult. It's coming back after drinking that could prove challenging. I don't know how much longer this can go on. The latest rumor circling here is that some of our enlisted men have put out a "fragging contract" (kill him with a grenade) on him. Welcome to Nam.

Hawaii can't get here soon enough.

I love you Sandy!

# CHAPTER 22

## LONG RANGE RECONNAISSANCE PATROLS

The morale and general mood within the Company has grown increasingly disturbing for the pilots and NCOs. Laos is taking a real toll on us, and Parker has made it worse. Maintenance downtime has increased and sick calls have gone way up. Article 13s are continuing to be handed out like candy, and there is suspicion that a fragging contract has been placed on Parker. As a precaution, he has instructed the First Sergeant to place a guard near his room every night.

Such is the environment we find ourselves having to endure. Scott and I have discussed the situation between ourselves over the last few days. Surely the Battalion knows what is going on within the Company. If they don't, what is to be done about our situation? The Division's operational tempo has been so demanding and mission-focused that it's possible no one has really bothered to investigate what has been going on around here. Under the circumstances, we have been considering going over to see the Battalion Commander and appraise him of our concerns.

On our first down day from flying missions every day for a

week, we are resting comfortably in our room. Our peace and quiet are interrupted by a knock on the door. The First Sergeant enters the room and informs me that Parker wants me in his office now.

Slowly standing up and stretching, I adjust my flight suit, grab a hat, and head for the door. "Scott, I'll see you later."

"Have fun!" He says. "Thanks!" I respond as I walk out of our room with the First Sergeant following.

Stan is waiting for me when I enter the Operations area. It's the first time we have crossed paths since the incident.

"Taylor, how have you been? Haven't seen you in a while."

Surprised by his friendly demeanor, I respond. "Stan, I've been pretty busy up north this past week, but other than that, okay. What about you?"

Stan, struggling to find the words, continues the conversation. "I've been okay, but that damn hovering incident really shook me up. I can't believe they only gave me a reprimand. Hell, it could have been really bad."

"Yeah, you were lucky!"

"Look. I don't know how to say this, but I want to thank you for not making things worse for me. I know I've been a real asshole to you."

"Yeah, you could certainly say that!"

Stan responds, "Like I said, you could've made it worse for me. But, from what I heard, you kept it low key and gave me the benefit of the doubt. I want you to know I appreciate that."

"Stan, I just answered their questions. Besides, I'm not sure which is worse, doing time in a stockade somewhere or getting your ass shot off just about every day over here!"

Stan manages a grin and extends his hand out. "For what it's worth, thanks, Taylor!" I reciprocate with a handshake and a nod of approval.

Our conversation is abruptly halted when Parker walks out of his office and sees us shaking hands. "Well, isn't that nice! You two want to get your asses in here?" Parker turns and heads back into his office as we follow him in. Stan closes the door behind us as we walk over to the front of Parker's desk. Parker sits down, picks up the cigar he's smoking, and casually takes a few puffs.

"Good of you Captains to join me!" Parker's attitude toward Stan has soured since the incident. It's clear that he has become much harsher with him. As for his treatment of me, nothing has changed.

"Sorry." We both respond.

He brushes it off. "Yeah...right! I'll keep this short and to the point. Division Intelligence believes very strongly there's a large concentration of NVA troops gathering on the northern side of the DMZ around Khe Sanh and just inside Laos. They're expecting a major offensive any day now, intending to inflict heavy casualties on our troops at Khe Sanh. They also anticipate the NVA will do everything they can to destroy what's left of the ARVN forces as they retreat back across the border into South Vietnam."

Stan and I exchange forbearing glances while wondering what is to be asked of us. Parker can sense our anticipation as our eyes give it away. He slowly rises from his chair and begins pacing around the office, trying to avoid eye contact. The whole time he is puffing on that damn cigar of his. As he's moving around, a cloud of smoke hovers over his mostly bald head and follows him. I find a little humor in it, as I'm envisioning a hilltop LZ covered in smoke, fog, and mist. My facial expression must have betrayed my thoughts. Parker stops pacing and shoots a blazing, intense, hate-filled stare at me and yells. "What's so damn funny, Taylor?"

"Nothing, Major!"

"Then wipe that shit-eating grin off your face, Captain!" "Yes, Major!"

Parker goes back to pacing the room and continues talking while not looking our way. "Division wants to insert four Long Range Reconnaissance Patrols (LRRP) teams into the area up there. Each team will consist of four special forces men. Two teams are to go just over the northwestern border with Laos. The other two teams will be inserted north of Khe Sahn over the DMZ. They'll be in North Vietnam. The job of these teams is to find enemy concentrations and direct the Air Force in on their locations. They will proceed to bomb the hell out of those little bastards. This should set their plans back for a while. Any questions?"

Parker stops and turns to look at us. Before we can respond, he continues talking. "Good! Now, this is where you guys come in. You'll each have a wingman, and your Cobra support will be the Butcher group. Taylor, you and your wingman will take the two teams going across the DMZ. Stan, you and your wingman will take the other two teams going inside Laos. You'll pick up your LRRP teams at Khe Sanh. They must be inserted tonight. Stan, you work out the details and coordination. It's imperative we get those teams in there. Any questions?"

Moving over to his desk, Parker squats down to sit on one corner and continues smoking his cigar. He's obviously enjoying this, and it doesn't go unnoticed by myself or Stan. After a long pause, I speak up. "I've been flying missions every day now for a week, and this was my one down day to get some rest. With all due respect, isn't there another pilot who could fly this?"

I'm cut off in mid-sentence when Parker stands up and yells. "You have your orders, Captain. Carry them out! You're dismissed. Stan, stay here. I want to see you for a minute."

Once again, struggling to control my temper with this guy, I salute him, turn, and head for the door. Parker, with a slight grin, returns the salute and says, "Taylor, if you don't like it around here, you can always request a transfer. Hell, I might even approve it!"

That comment stops me dead in my tracks. Turning back toward Parker, I shoot him a wicked stare. "Major! From what I hear, you might not be around long enough to approve one."

"Get the fuck out of here!" Parker fires back with malice in his voice.

I leave his office, satisfied I've managed to piss him off again. Parker starts pacing the office again as he talks to Stan. "I want you to assign Scott as the AC on the second ship flying with Taylor. For their copilots, assign them the newest pilots we've got."

After a long pause, Stan replies. "Are you sure about this? Flying long-range reconnaissance missions into enemy territory at night is a very dangerous business. Hell, assigning new guys as pilots makes it even worse. I don't feel good about doing this."

Parker stops pacing and slowly turns toward Stan. "Stan! I don't give a shit what you think. Just do what you're fucking told!"

Stan salutes Parker, who ignores him. Stan, thinking to himself, *you really are an asshole,* turns, and walks out of the office. Parker moves over to the window and watches as Taylor walks across the Company area on his way back to his room.

# CHAPTER 23

## NIGHT MISSION BRIEFING

Stan has been struggling with Parker's orders to give Scott and me the newest Company pilots for the night mission. He cannot bring himself to follow through with it. Ordering him to place men's lives at risk unduly like that is wrong and may border on being unlawful. The truth of the matter is, the Company has been operating well under the number of pilots we should have available for some time now. We have lost six pilots, and five have been wounded since Lam Son 719 started. Three of the five pilots are still recovering from their wounds at Da Nang, while the other two were sent home. The experience level of many of the available pilots averages less than three months in the country. This mission requires the most seasoned pilots available. Just because they may be more experienced is no guarantee they will fare any better than the newest pilot. It's called war. There are no guarantees.

In preparing for our mission plans, Stan assigns the most experienced pilots and crews available. Later in the afternoon, Stan calls Captain Barnett, Scott, and me to the operations room for a mission briefing.

With all present, Stan proceeds to brief us on our night mission. "Captain Barnett and I will be flying our choppers into Laos with our LRRP teams. Taylor, you and Scott will be flying your choppers across the DMZ into North Vietnam with your LRRP teams. Each flight will be assigned two Cobras from the Butchers Company to fly cover for us. We'll depart here at 1700 and head for Khe Sanh and should arrive there around 1800."

Pausing for questions while surveying our facial expressions for any hints, Stan realizes we have none at the moment and continues. "Once there, we'll be directed to our staging area, refuel, shut down, and wait for our LRRP team members. Our Cobra support will join up with us there. When the LRRP teams arrive, we will be briefed by their commander. This will include going over the locations where they are to be inserted and the decoy locations we are to use."

Stan gives another pause, looking for any questions. I believe we're all taken aback by the potential for disaster with this night insertion. We have no questions, the mission is on, and we have to follow orders. Stan continues, "The plan calls for us to take off from Khe Sanh and head for our respective insertion points at dusk. After we have inserted our teams, we are to return to Khe Sanh. We'll be spending the night there in case any LRRP teams are compromised and need extraction. If not, we'll return back to base tomorrow morning."

Stan concludes his briefing with, "If there are still no questions, check the flight board for your assigned aircraft and crews. And gentlemen, I would suggest you get a good meal before we leave, as we're in for a long night."

Scott and I are pleased with the pilots who have been assigned to fly with us. They each have several months in the country and some valuable experience under their belt. With some peace of mind, we go about getting ready for our mission.

Stan, who has returned to his room and is getting ready for

the mission, is summoned to Parker's office. When he enters the office, Parker is visibly upset and doesn't wait for Stan to salute. He yells at him, "I thought I told you to assign our two newest pilots to Taylor and Scott. I noticed earlier on the flight board that you assigned them two of our most experienced pilots for tonight. What the hell happened? Wasn't I clear enough for you?"

Stan doesn't have a chance to answer him as Parker says, "Don't answer that—I've changed their assigned pilots—they now have our two newest pilots for tonight. The First Sergeant has made appropriate notifications!"

Stan, who was expecting to catch hell for what he did, wasn't expecting this. He wants to say something, but nothing comes out. He turns and heads for the door while muttering to himself. "The hell with saluting him."

In a controlled manner and with every word he speaks deliberately chosen, Parker says to Stan, "If you can't follow orders, you have no future in the Army, and certainly not in my Company!"

Stan stops momentarily and, looking back, responds, "If there are many more like you, I don't want one!" Turning back and moving toward the door, he continues. "I can't work with you anymore. I'll complete my transfer request when I get back tomorrow and have it on your desk!" He exits the office.

Parker ignores him, goes over to his desk, takes out a cigar, and sits down while lighting it. Putting his feet up on the desk and leaning back to look out his window, he settles in to enjoy his cigar.

While doing his best to relax, he thinks to himself. *I'm not going to let any subordinates of mine hurt my chances for promotion ever again. This is my third opportunity to prove to my superiors that I'm ready to move up. If it doesn't work for me, my military career is done. The problems I've had in the past were not of my doing. I can't help it if people who worked for me couldn't do their jobs. It's not going to happen to me again. I will make Colonel.*

# CHAPTER 24

## NIGHT MISSION KHE SANH

Scott and I have some chow, gather up our flight equipment, and head out to our Hueys on the flight line. Approaching them, we see that the two pilots waiting on us are not the ones originally assigned. They are the Company's newest two pilots with very little flight time in the country. Stan meets us before we reach our choppers. He painstakingly explains to us what happened. Stan goes on to say he disagrees with it and will be submitting his transfer request when we return to the Company tomorrow.

My first reaction is to challenge Parker and refuse to fly the mission with our newest pilots. Upon thinking it through for a moment, I realize this is not a good option right now. We have a shortage of experienced pilots, our mission is considered critical, and our operational tempo demands maximum effort from everyone. Because of our current circumstances, I choose to go forward with the mission. With Stan and Scott in agreement, we decide to meet the Battalion Commander and apprise him of Parker's situation when we return tomorrow.

Approaching our Hueys, I look over at Scott, "I'll take John as my pilot, and Paul will fly with you, Scott. Okay by you?" Scott nods his agreement. We walk up to our assigned pilots, exchange greetings and handshakes.

Both John and Paul are young Warrant Officers, and the Company's newest pilots. Paul has ten days more experience with the Company than John, who just joined the Company three days earlier. Both men are apprehensive about the mission and openly express concerns about their lack of experience. I try my best to give them more confidence in their abilities and reassure them about our mission. However, from their body language and facial expressions, I sense it's not going well. My situation and attempts at calming their fears remind me of an old baseball adage. *I'm swinging for the outfield fence, but I'm not connecting with the ball.*

We separate as John and I head to our Huey, and Scott and Paul to theirs. Both Hueys have been checked by their assigned crew chiefs and door gunners thoroughly. Given the dangerous nature of this mission, it doesn't hurt to have more eyes looking over our helicopters before departure.

When we get to our Huey, I place my gear in the left seat and begin pre-flight procedures. John places his gear in the right seat and joins me. He checks out the top while I work my way around the body of the Huey. Scott and Paul are performing their checks. We go about these inspections at a heightened level of attention and detail. Pilots flying a dangerous mission such as this would be foolish not to. Once completed and satisfied, we climb into our seats, strap ourselves in and place our helmets on.

Stan and Captain Barnett, working with their assigned pilots, have performed the same diligent flight checks. Stan confirms with Captain Barnett, Scott, and me that we are ready to go. We transmit over our radios, 'Affirmative.' On Stan's command, we start our engines, monitor our instrument readings, and slowly increase RPM up to full power. Following our crew chief's guidance, we bring our Hueys to a hover. We slowly hover out of the revetments, stop to pick up our crew chiefs, and then hover over to the staging area.

Lined up in trail formation behind Stan and ready for take-off, Stan contacts Phu Bai Tower. We are cleared for take-off. Following Stan, we launch into the early evening sky, slowly climbing to our assigned altitude like a flock of birds.

I continue to sense the apprehension and fear that John has bottled up inside. I resolve to try and get him to relax as much as possible, for it's going to be a long night. Once we reach our assigned altitude and settle in, I begin a conversation over the intercom with John. 'John, you take the controls and maintain our position in the formation.'

John replies, 'Yes, sir!'

'Forget the "sir" shit, and just call me TJ. Sorry, I should've told you that earlier.'

'Okay, sure, TJ.'

I continue in a relaxed, calm voice. 'How many flight hours have you logged since joining the Company, and was any of it at night?'

John replies, 'I've only flown two days so far, and none of it at night.'

'What about in the States? Did you log much nighttime while you were in flight training?'

John replies, 'Not really, just enough to meet our training requirements.'

I'm not surprised by his response since none of the Company's pilots had accumulated very much night flying experience during training. With few exceptions, we were not trained in flight school to a level where we would be proficient enough to obtain an IFR (Instrument Flight Rules) certification. With this certification, we would be better qualified to fly on instruments at night and in bad weather. All Army pilots receive IFR training, just not at a level where we would qualify for an IFR certification. Instead, we are trained to a level the Army designates as Tactical Instrument qualified.

Many men are naturals at flying on instruments and pick it up quickly. Not everyone is that fortunate. Some of us just learn enough to be dangerous. It's not until we accumulate more experience at night flying and in dangerous weather that we gain sufficient confidence in our instrument abilities. The Army's need for helicopter pilots during most of the Vietnam War was so great that the minimum training necessary to qualify men was the norm.

Responding to John, I proceed to give him some pointers. 'Look, John, night flying over here is a lot different than what little you experienced back in the states. It's dark over here. There are no city lights to help guide us, and the damn radio signals we home in on are not always reliable. This is going to be particularly true tonight.'

I let that sink in and continue. 'As you know, we're not trained on night vision goggles, so we have to rely on visual sightings, landmarks when we have them, and hope that we have enough of a moon-lit night to fly in.'

John, who is busy flying the chopper, has been listening intently to me and seems to be settling in some. *This is good!*

'John, the weather guys tell us there will be clear skies and a three-quarter moon tonight. This should provide us with sufficient visibility. Let's hope so.'

John looks over and says, 'Yeah, let's hope so.'

'Just do what I tell you and when, and we'll be okay. Have any problems with that?'

John responds, 'None, TJ, you're the boss.'

For the rest of the flight to Khe Sanh, I have John fly our Huey hoping to build his confidence and settle his nerves. With some music playing in the background over our ADF radio, I continue to share with him what I've experienced over here while flying at night. It just might help him and, by extension, the whole crew. The cold, harsh truth is, the only way to learn and gain confidence is the hard way. *Just do it!*

Arriving at Khe Sanh, Stan contacts the control tower. We are given clearance to land and hover over to our staging area. It is the same staging area we used when participating in the initial Lolo insertion. Being familiar with it, we easily maneuver around to the refuel tankers and then over to our designated parking area. We notice that the Butchers are already parked there. We shut down our Hueys, secure them, and follow Stan into the operations tent.

Entering the tent, we see Greg and his pilots lounging around and engaged in small talk. Scott and I walk toward Greg, as the rest of the Eagles find a place to settle into for the moment. Greg sees us and yells, "Hey TJ, some more light duty for you tonight?" While grinning at him, I casually display my middle finger. This momentarily lightens the mood as mild laughter breaks out among those who see my gesture.

Greg welcomes us over. "Haven't you been flying long days for a week now? I thought you had the day off?"

I respond to him with, "I have been, and I did have the day off! But Parker changed all that."

Scott joins in, "That's not the half of it. Stan initially assigned us the most experienced pilots he could. When Parker found out, he changed the line-up and gave us the two newest pilots. Then he reamed out Stan's ass!"

Greg looks over at me, "Is that for real?"

"Yeah, it is, and it only gets better. Stan told Parker he'd had enough of his bullshit and was going to submit a transfer request to get the hell out of his Company."

Greg, "NO shit!"

"NO shit!"

After that brief verbal exchange using the "Queen's English," Greg looks over at Stan. Stan noticed us talking and happens to be looking our way when Greg gives him a thumbs up and grins. His way of showing approval. Stan surmises Greg was just informed about the situation and appreciates Greg's gesture. As he reciprocates the gesture, the LRRP teams enter the tent. They are heavily armed, well camouflaged, and are ready for action. Their senior officer, a Captain, asks who the officer in charge of their aviation support is. Stan steps forward, extends his hand, and introduces himself. With that, the Captain gets straight to the mission at hand.

He briefly describes their mission to us, the high importance that Division HQ places on it, and emphasizes that time is critical. His teams have to be inserted tonight. Having made his point, he walks over to the operational map hanging on one side of the tent and proceeds to point out the LZs where we will be inserting his teams. He also points out the locations of the decoy LZs we'll be flying in and out of tonight.

All the LZs are well dispersed, and his teams will only disembark at their designated LZ. All the others are just a ruse. Hopefully, this will confuse any North Vietnamese soldiers who might be in the area and hear our Hueys. Call signs and radio frequencies are noted and recorded by each pilot. Coordinating with Stan, the Captain designates which Huey crews his four teams will fly with to their LZs. As they are assigned to our Hueys, we briefly exchange greetings with each other.

With our briefing completed, the LRRP team members exit the tent. Before launching, their time will be spent drawing the rest of their ammo allotment and performing last-minute checks of their equipment. These men are special. They're a rare breed. They are tough, independent-- highly motivated, trained, and skilled—the kind of men you want on your side when the shit hits the fan.

Stan has us join him at the map when the LRRP teams leave. He wants to recap the mission to ensure we all know our assignments and LZ locations. He instructs everyone, pilots, crew chiefs, and door gunners, to study the map closely. We are looking for any distinguishable land features which might help us out there later tonight. These include rivers, streams, hilltops, plateaus, clear areas, anything to help guide us.

Since this is our first time flying into these areas, identifying land features and remembering all of them is difficult. We do our best. He also reminds us to tune our ADF radios to the Khe Sahn beacon. We can use it as a navigational aid. With coordination and planning completed, we settle down to relax while studying the map and wait on orders to saddle up and head out. During this period, an eerie silence settles in over us as our mood is subdued. *Will any of us live to see the sunrise tomorrow morning?*

# CHAPTER 25

## NIGHT MISSION INSERTION

The sun is setting over Khe Sanh when the order to saddle up and launch is given. The Eagles and Butchers hustle out to our choppers. We settle ourselves in, go through our start-up checklist, and then fire them up. With our choppers ready, the LRRP teams climb on board their assigned Hueys. To ensure a quick departure from our choppers when we land in their LZs, they position themselves on each side of the Huey with their feet resting on the skids.

Stan makes radio contact with his flight group. 'Eagles and Butchers, this is Eagle 8. Are we ready to go? Over!'

After receiving an affirmative response from everyone, he calls the Khe Sanh Tower, 'Khe Sanh Tower. This is Eagle 8. We are ready for takeoff, request clearance. Over.'

The tower responds, 'Eagle 8, Khe Sanh Tower. You are cleared to launch; night conditions are favorable. Good luck out there! Over.'

Stan replies to the tower, 'Roger. Thanks, out.' He then transmits to his group, 'Eagles and Butchers. This is Eagle 8. We are cleared to launch. Follow me out, and good luck, gentlemen, over!'

Stan lifts off into the night sky as Captain Barnett follows him out, then me, followed by Scott. Greg's Butchers lift off behind us, one at a time. As we reach altitude shortly after take-off, we go into our respective formations. Stan, with Captain Barnett trailing him and one cobra on each side of them, form a diamond-shaped formation. Scott and I, with our Cobra escorts, are in a similar formation. Greg is flying one of the Cobras next to me and is visible out my left door window. We make eye contact, exchange a short wave, and a thumbs up signal between ourselves.

As we fly in a northwestern direction toward the border with Laos, Stan radios me. 'Eagle 25, this is Eagle 8. We are closing in on our separation point. I'm breaking off and heading west. Good luck. See you later tonight. Over.'

I respond, 'Roger, and good luck to you. Out!'

Transmitting to Scott and Greg, 'Eagle 21, Butcher 12, this is Eagle 25. We are turning north and are headed toward our first LZ. I'm taking us down on the deck to get us as close as I can and still see where we're going. Over!'

Scott has been busy flying and watching his instruments. He tried to do what I did on the way up from Phu Bai. He worked with Paul, attempting to ease his apprehensions about night flying and concerns about our mission. As a new AC with little experience himself, Scott is dealing with his own night-flying issues. Because of that, he believes his efforts were not very effective in easing Paul's anxiety.

His own self-doubt and uncertainty come through in his transmission back to me. 'Eagle 25, this is Eagle 21. Roger. Over!'

Sensing it, I reply, 'Eagle 21, this is 25, stay on my six, do what I do, and keep your visuals outside the cockpit. We'll be back at base in no time. Over!'

Scott realizes that I picked up on his anxiety and responds with more confidence, 'Eagle 25, Eagle 21, Roger. Will do. Over!'

Greg responds to my transmission, 'Eagle 25, Butcher 12, Roger. We're going to gain some altitude and provide cover for you from above. Over!'

In a joking manner, Scott replies to Greg, 'What? You're not going to stay down here on the deck with us?'

Greg, laughing, says, 'Eagle 21, Butcher 12, what happened to your radio discipline? It's bad enough you guys dragged me out here tonight. I think we'll just have to stay up here where it is safer. Over!'

I've been at the controls flying and intermittently scanning my instruments and navigation equipment while looking outside the Huey at the night sky and darkening landscape below. There is enough moonlight for us to have reasonable visual awareness of the geography below us. Looking out our window at the vast horizon in front of us is like peering into a dark closet.

According to my navigational equipment and the landscape I can see immediately in front of me, we have just crossed over the DMZ and are now inside North Vietnam. *The pucker factor does not get any higher than this!*

Over the intercom, I say to John, 'Okay, John, we're in North Vietnam and should be in the right area. We'll be making an approach into the first LZ. This is our first decoy. We're just in and out. Stay focused.'

John nervously adjusts his seat harness and then slides his holster between his legs. 'I'm ready, TJ.' I look over his way and try to give him a reassuring grin.

It's showtime, as I call Greg and Scott. 'Eagle 21, Butcher 12, we're in North Vietnam and coming up on the first LZ. Beginning our approach now. Remember 21, we're in and out. This is just the first decoy. Over!'

Scott transmits, 'Eagle 25, this is Eagle 21. Roger, we'll be right behind you. Over!'

'Roger, 21. Just keep your distance.' Scott replies with a double-click.

Greg transmits, 'Eagle 25, this is Butcher 12. We'll be up here on station. Give us a call if you need us. Over!'

I double-click my acknowledgement of Greg's transmission. Over the intercom, I tell the crew to keep their eyes open and stay sharp.

With Scott following, I fly my chopper in and come to a quick hover. Just as quickly, I pull pitch and take off from the LZ without incident. I transmit to Scott, 'Eagle 21, this is 25, you okay back there? Over!'

Scott, who is on his way out of the LZ, responds with some trepidation in his voice. 'Eagle 25, this is 21. We're okay. Damn, there's not much light down here. It's hard to see and stay focused. Over!'

I respond, 'You're doing good. Just concentrate on looking outside your ship, stay focused on the terrain right in front of you. Don't look at your flight instruments, especially your attitude indicator (artificial horizon). They won't help us this close to the ground. Over!'

Scott comes back with, 'Roger, understand, over!'

After a short flight and staying just above the ground, we land at our next LZ. My LRRP team jumps out and heads for cover. As they do, I pull pitch again and take off, with Scott following. The next two LZs are decoys, and we fly in and out without incident. We are now headed to the LZ, where Scott's team will jump out.

Scott has been doing all the flying and instructs Paul to take the controls for a few minutes. Scott has become a bundle of nerves, his back and neck are tight from the stress, and he's sweating profusely. Paul is reluctant to take over the controls. He has been dealing with his own anxiety and doesn't feel confident enough to do so. Scott must order him to take the controls, which he does.

Scott pushes back in his seat, stretches out his arms, and wipes what sweat he can from his face. He then adjusts his seat harness and chicken plate to get a little more comfortable. As we approach the next LZ, Scott takes back the controls. Scott senses that Paul is relieved as he takes them back. Scott doesn't feel good about it. He may as well be flying solo.

The night has become darker, making it harder to distinguish the terrain features we are flying over and into. On short final and following me in, Scott almost loses sight of the horizon in front of him, and a mild panic momentarily grips him. Straining to see the immediate terrain in front of him and focusing on my tail rotor light, he's able to control the "panic beast" and lands his chopper. The LRRP team jumps out and heads for cover. I've already lifted off. Scott hesitates, then follows me out, transmitting over his radio. 'Dammit, that was too close; I'm getting tired of this shit.'

'You're doing good. Just hang in there, Scott!' I respond.

We gain some altitude and head for our last LZ. It's another decoy, and after that, we can head back to Khe Sanh. We have flown a good distance from our last drop off and are now closing in on the last LZ. This one is near the DMZ.

Greg, who has been flying cover with his wingman and listening to the radio traffic between myself and Scott, contacts us. 'Eagle 25 and 21, Butcher 12. You guys doing alright down there? Are we about done here? I'm ready for a beer! Over!'

I respond, 'Yep, one to go, then back.'

I take us into the last LZ, which proves to be the most challenging. Clouds have moved in, which results in the moonlight becoming more intermittent. This makes it harder to discern features on the ground and maintain a visual horizon.

Approaching the ground with Scott following me, I make a quick "stop and go" without coming to a hover.

Scott, flying and drenched in sweat, is trying to control his nerves as he follows me in and out of the LZ. He intermittently scans his instruments and looks outside the Huey, trying to maintain his visual horizon. As he starts to gain some altitude, his visual horizon goes dark, and suddenly panic overtakes him.

Scott over his intercom to Paul, 'Holy shit. I'm losing it! I'm losing it! Take the controls. Take the controls!'

Paul, who is dealing with his own state of panic, says, 'I can't. I can't see the horizon!'

Scott, in a panicked voice, screams into his radio, 'We're going down! We're going down! We have vertigo. We're going..'. His transmission ends as they crash nose-first into the ground, exploding on impact.

Gaining altitude as I fly out of the LZ and bank to the left, I see Scott's Huey exploding on impact through my window. Emotionally shaken and with tears welling up in my eyes, I instruct John to take the controls. John says to me, 'I've got it, my god, do you think anyone survived that?'

After a long pause, I respond, 'No— I don't think anyone could've lived through that!'

Greg, seeing the explosion, transmits over his radio, 'Holy shit, we're coming down and joining you!'

Slowly regaining my composure, I respond. 'Butcher 12, Eagle 25. We're going back down there and see if anyone is alive — maybe someone made it. Over!'

Greg responds, 'We're with you!'

Taking the controls back from John, I fly back to the scene and circle above the burning wreckage of Scott's helicopter. My crew chief and door gunner are standing on the Huey's skids, leaning out and looking in vain for any survivors. John and I look out our windows for any movement below. With the flames from the burning wreckage lighting up the area below us, we now can see the terrain. Greg has joined us in the search. His wingman stays at altitude to provide some cover if needed.

Scott's Huey is engulfed in flames, and no one has crawled out of the burning chopper. Even though we are low on fuel, we continue to circle the area, not wanting to give up on them. Reality sets in. We're flying on fumes now and have to make a beeline back to Khe Sanh. There is nothing we can do for Scott and his crew tonight.

The short flight back to our staging area in Khe Sanh is devoid of any conversation. Not until we reach the airspace around Khe Sanh do we communicate. It is limited to obtaining clearance to land and hovering over to our staging area. After shutting down and securing our choppers in the staging area, Greg and I walk over to the operations tent. We are followed by the other crew members keeping a respectful distance behind us. They give us some space as we deal with our grief over the loss of a good friend.

Entering the tent, we are met by Stan and his group of pilots. The mood within the group is a somber and grief-stricken one. Scott was well-liked by everyone who knew him, and they all know how close he and I had become. The loss of Scott and his crew weighs heavily on all of us.

Stan walks up to me and pulls me to one side. In a low voice, he says, "Taylor, I'm really sorry about Scott. He was a good man. This is one hell of a tragic loss, and it shouldn't have happened." I nod my agreement as Stan continues. "We're going to bunk here tonight. Before dawn, we're going back across the DMZ and pick up Scott and his crew, and bring them back!"

With resolve in my eyes and grief in my heart, I look directly at Stan and say. "I'm in."

Stan asks the pilots and crew members who just returned from our mission to gather around him. Speaking to us in a somber and defiant voice, he says, "We are spending the night here, and let's hope the LRRP teams don't need us to go back out there and get them. If we are not called upon during the night, we are going back across the DMZ to get Scott and his crew at first light. I'm asking for volunteers to join Taylor and me."

Before he can finish, every pilot and crew member says, "We'll go!"

# CHAPTER 26

## NO MAN LEFT BEHIND

What remains of the night passes by very slowly for me. I've lost a good friend and will not be able to rest until we go back out there and retrieve Scott and his crew. I do not sleep, only toss and turn, waiting for the night to end. Luckily, we had no calls for help from any of the LRRP teams during the night.

After our brief meeting last night, Stan requested and received approval for us to mount a recovery effort. We will take a group back across the DMZ into North Vietnam and retrieve the bodies of Scott and his crew. Greg's Butchers group consisting of four Cobras, will fly cover. Stan, Captain Barnett, and I will take our Hueys. Each Huey will carry a small squad of infantrymen from the 101st Airborne. They will set up a perimeter and provide ground defense after we land at the crash site. Crew members from the Hueys will recover the bodies from the downed chopper.

While we snack on c-rations for breakfast, Stan briefs us on our mission. After the briefing, Stan looks over at me while directing his comment to the men present. "Taylor will be leading this recovery mission."

My mood and that of the men is still somber and grieving from our losses. Acknowledging Stan with a nod, I choose to say nothing. I know we all have a grim determination to recover the bodies of our fallen comrades. We have an obligation, a responsibility. We can not do otherwise and owe it to ourselves and their families, hoping it will give them some closure.

It is still dark when we emerge from the tent and head for our choppers. The night sky is just beginning to lighten to the east. Walking to our Hueys, we see large flashes of light across the horizon to our north and west. Almost immediately, the ground shakes beneath us, followed by explosive shock waves. This would be the U.S. Air Force's B-52 "arc lights" being dropped over North Vietnam and inside Laos. Apparently, the LRRP teams are enjoying some good hunting.

Our recovery mission will take us across the DMZ and just inside North Vietnam. The area where Scott went down is fairly rugged but relatively flat, with considerable room to land three Hueys simultaneously. This will help in our recovery effort and should require less time on the ground. We'll be flying "nap of the earth" over and back while keeping our radio chatter to a minimum. In some respects, this is more dangerous than the night mission. Several factors come into play on this mission. It will be light soon, and the North Vietnamese know we have inserted some teams. They will be watching for us and can hear and see our choppers coming easier in daylight.

Undaunted, we saddle up and head for the DMZ. I lead us out and head north. On route, our door gunners check and test fire their M-6os. The Butchers check their systems to ensure they are armed and ready. Crossing the DMZ, we are now flying just above the ground. Our Hueys are in a V formation, with the Cobras in a diamond formation following just behind us.

Approaching the wreck site, I spot it first and notice the Huey has not completely burned up. There is still some structure left. I also see several North Vietnamese soldiers mulling around the wreckage. I call out, 'This is Eagle 25. The wreckage is just to our right at three o'clock. Gooks are all over it. Eagles, turn right on me. Butcher 12. They're all yours! Fry their asses! Over!'

'Roger that!' and double-clicks are heard over my radio as I bank to the right with the other Eagles following me. This clears the way for Greg and his Cobras to have a clear field of fire as they unload on them with their tools of death. It only takes a few minutes to clear the area as miniguns tear into the men on the ground, and rockets explode around them as they try running for cover.

This clears the field. I bring my flight back around to the crash site and land next to the wreckage. The 101st troopers jump out as soon as the skids touch down and fan out to form a defensive perimeter. They're followed by some of our crewmen, who run over to the downed Huey. They recover the charred bodies of Scott and his crew and place them in body bags. With their bodies loaded onto our choppers, our crewman, followed by the troopers, jump back into their Hueys. We lift off. Our time on the ground was minimal, and we did not receive any ground fire. *The angels must have been watching over us this morning.*

I lead my flight back across the DMZ without incident and return to the staging area. We drop off the 101st troopers, and hot refuel the choppers. Stan confirms we have completed our LRRP support and are released to head back to our Company. I take the lead and set us on a course back to Phu Bai. I have two bodies on my Huey, and Stan has two with him. It is a very quiet trip flying back with our fallen comrades lying prone on the floor of our Hueys with their bodies sealed in heavy plastic bags.

As we approach Phu Bai airspace, I transmit over the radio, 'Eagles and Butcher 12. Eagle 25. We're approaching Phu Bai.

Eagle 8 and I will land on the main airfield and take Scott and his crew to our MASH unit. Butcher 12 and Eagle 16. You're released. Good work, gentlemen. Eagle 25. Out.'

I hear their acknowledgments and then contact Phu Bai Tower. 'Phu Bai Tower, Eagle 25. We're approaching from the north carrying four body bags. Request permission to land and proceed to the MASH unit. Over!'

Phu Bai Tower responds, 'Eagle 25, tower. Understand you're a flight of two and are bringing home four bodies. Over!'

I respond, 'Roger, four souls, over!'

The tower responds, 'Eagle 25, Phu Bai Tower, Roger. You are cleared for immediate landing and proceed directly to the MASH unit. We will advise them of your arrival. They will be waiting. Over!'

'Tower, Eagle 25. Roger. Thank you. Over!'

Phu Bai Tower transmits in the open to all aircraft in their airspace, 'This is Phu Bai Tower. All aircraft in Phu Bai airspace be advised we have two Hueys inbound with four souls on board. Hold your positions until notified by tower. Over!'

With Stan following, I land at Phu Bai and hover over to our MASH unit, just off the north end of the flight line. Once there, we shut down, unbuckle our seat harnesses and climb out of the choppers. The medics, who have been waiting for us, remove the bodies of Scott and his crew and place them on gurneys. They roll their bodies into the morgue. Here is where they begin the process that eventually returns their bodies to the United States and their awaiting families.

Stan and I follow them into the morgue while the rest of our crew members wait with the choppers. The morgue is a cold, silent, depressing, and very uncomfortable place. It is set up to hold many bodies and has been a remarkably busy place lately with Lam Son 719. Stan stays back as I walk over to the area where the gurneys with the bodies of Scott and his crew have been moved.

I want to stand over Scott's body before they place him in a refrigeration unit, but I have no idea which is his. They were too severely burned, and identification will take some time. Physically and emotionally drained, I bring myself to attention and salute all four men as they are gently laid on metal slabs and slid into their refrigeration units.

Turning towards Stan, I start wiping the tears from my eyes before Stan can see them. Approaching him, I realize he's just as emotional as I am. I leave the tears alone as they stream down my cheeks. We exit the morgue and return to our Hueys.

Strapping in, we start our Hueys, and after receiving clearance from the tower, come to a hover and return to the Eagles' staging area. When we arrive, several of the men in the Company have gathered to meet us as we climb out of our Hueys. Their mood is one of great loss, mourning for Scott and his crew. Attempts are made between us to console one another as words of sorrow are shared, with some hugs. Many of us struggle with controlling our emotions.

I'm just too drained to engage and yearn to be alone. I work my way through the men as quickly as possible. Just as I clear the group, Stan comes up behind me. "Taylor, would you throw this stuff in my room for me? I have a few things to take care of. Oh, and don't worry about an action report right now. I'll take care of it. Get some rest!"

I take his stuff, and say, "I got it, and thanks!" and head directly over to the pilot's quarters.

After dropping Stan's stuff off, I head for my room. Upon entering, I throw my stuff on the floor and just stand there, staring at Scott's empty cot. That's when the full realization of what happened over the last twenty-four hours comes crashing down on me. Completely exhausted and just wanting this whole nightmare to end, I stumble over to my cot and collapse on top of it. I'm totally out for the night. No dreams, no nightmares. Just total emptiness and darkness.

# CHAPTER 27
## AFTERMATH

The following day dawns late for me, and the weather is dreary and depressing. It's not helping my mood any. I'm slow to awaken and struggle with my emotions. Looking around the room and seeing Scott's personal effects really hits me hard. My mind is now racing with "what ifs." What if Parker hadn't reassigned us the less experienced pilots? What if Scott would have had more nighttime experience before being assigned the LRRP mission? What if Parker was a leader and not an utterly self-absorbed jackass with no leadership qualities? What if? What if? What if?

The 101st Airborne Division's Aviation Group Commander (AGC), a Brigadier General, and the Eagles' Battalion Commander have been meeting with Parker in his office most of the morning. The Eagles Senior Commanders have been monitoring Parker's performance for some time. They're aware of the Company's deteriorating morale and the rumors circulating about a possible fragging contract. Stories of Parker trying to make my life and Scott's more difficult have been circulating for the last several weeks. Neither Scott nor I had spoken out about the abuse, choosing instead to go about our flying duties.

The entire 101st Airborne Division's senior command structure has been totally focused on supporting Lam Son 719 and meeting their daily operational requirements. The military depends on our leaders at all levels to be professional, to fulfill their operational requirements, and provide leadership. This dependency is paramount to mission success. However, there are instances where some officers fall well short of these expectations. Parker is one of them, and B Company's Senior Commanders have no choice but to step in and deal with him. They believe the way he handled the LRRP mission was way over the line and directly contributed to the loss of Scott and his crew.

The AGC has grown increasingly agitated by Parker's always defending his actions. He finally reaches a point where he's had enough of Parker's ramblings and cuts him off. Closing in on Parker so that he is looking directly into his eyes, the AGC proceeds to admonish him severely.

"Major, in all my years in the service, I've only relieved two other officers. They were bad, but your behavior in this Company has been atrocious! Your total lack of leadership and your disregard for the lives of your men is the worst I've ever encountered, Parker. How'd you get this far?"

Parker, visibly upset and highly emotional, starts to respond, "I don't understand, General. What did I do that was so wrong? We were meeting our Company's mission requirements—"

The General cuts him off again. "Parker, you didn't do much right here! You could've met your Company's requirements by providing some leadership! Not by abusing your men. You've heard of the concept that "leaders lead from the front." How many missions in Laos did you actually fly into the LZs when you were over there? Don't answer that. You didn't! Flying a C&C

Huey well above the action on the few missions you did fly into Laos, is not leading your men!"

The General pauses for effect and closes with, "If we had acted sooner, maybe we wouldn't have lost Lieutenant McGregor and his crew. Why would you send your newest pilots on a dangerous night mission when you have more experienced pilots available? What the hell were you trying to do? You've given us no choice but to relieve you of your command, effective immediately!"

Parker is devastated. Saying nothing, he steps back from the General, and while lowering his head in shame, moves toward the office window to look outside.

I've been pacing in my room, slowly working into a rage as I try to control the anger and frustration that swells up within me. It's too much, and I let loose with some profanity, "Goddamn that son of a bitch! Goddamn him!"

Grabbing my helmet and throwing it against the wall, I storm out of the room. "I've had enough of that son of a bitch!" Walking out of the pilots' quarters, I move briskly through the Company area, speaking to no one on my way to the HQ trailer. I'm focused like a heat-seeking missile homing in on my target, Parker. As I pass other men, they stop and watch me heading for the trailer.

Storming into the trailer and walking through the operations room, I do not notice Stan, Captain Barnett, or the First Sergeant in the room. Heading directly for Parker's office, I hear Stan. "Taylor, don't go in. Parker's in there with our AGC and Battalion Commander!" The First Sergeant says, "Captain! You can't go in there now!"

Frustration, anger, and yes, pure hate overwhelm me at this moment in time. I ignore them and burst into the office. Slamming the door behind me, I cause the wall to shake, and the men in the office turn to face me. *I couldn't have made a more dramatic entrance, even if I had planned one!* Looking around the office, I see Parker starring out his window, as usual, the General near him, and the Battalion Commander seated in a chair in one corner of the office.

Parker turns from the window and finds himself staring into the eyes of an enraged Captain. Without hesitating, I tear into him. "Parker, you son of a bitch! You're responsible for killing four good men. Scott and his crew. Why did you replace our more experienced pilots with the newest pilots in the Company? What the hell is wrong with you?"

I'm hoping for a response, but Parker ignores me. Verging on losing control, I close the distance between us until I'm right up in his face. "You've been riding my ass and Scott's almost from day one. I've had enough of your bullshit. Tell me, Parker, how'd you ever get this far?"

The General looks at me and, in a calm voice, says, "Son, calm down. Get control of yourself. The Major has been relieved of his command."

Turning to look at the General, I'm aware that my facial expression must be conveying my reaction to his news. *Well, it's about goddamn time someone did something about this situation. Particularly given what it has cost us!* I step back from Parker as he lowers his gaze at me and turns back to look out the window. I struggle to control my inner rage. I desperately want to beat the living shit out of him.

My better angel takes over, and I slowly begin to calm down. *What are you doing? Are you crazy? It is not a good idea with a General and Colonel in the room to witness it!* I begin regaining some self-control. Thinking about Scott, I respond to the General in a low, calm, and somewhat emotional voice. "With all due respect, Sir, it's too late to do Scott and his crew any good."

Continuing in a calm and fatherly manner, the General says,

"I know, son, and for that, I will forever regret not acting sooner. Captain, would you step outside for a few minutes, please?"

"Yes, sir!"

The General turns his attention back to Parker as I leave the office. "Major, I want you out of this Company before the day is over. You can bunk in Battalion HQ for the night. In the morning, you'll be shipping out to Saigon, where there will be an inquiry into what has been going on here. You may or may not receive new orders after your review is completed."

Parker responds, "An inquiry? Oh my god! If I get new orders, where will I go? What will I be doing?"

"Major, if you survive the inquiry, I have no idea where you might end up. And I don't give a shit! So long as it is not another command of any kind. Now, get the hell out of here!"

Parker comes to attention, salutes both the General and Battalion Commander, turns, and exits the office. Neither man returns his salute. Stan, Captain Barnett, and I are sitting in the operations room when Parker emerges from his former office. He's dejected and walks by without looking or speaking to any of us. The Battalion Commander steps out from the open doorway and directs us to come in.

I close the door behind me as we enter the office. We find the General standing by Parker's desk, and our Battalion Commander moves over to the other side of the desk. We come to attention and salute our senior officers, who reciprocate. The General says, "Please, gentlemen, take a seat."

As I relax my stance and move to sit down in a chair, I'm aware that both Commanders are looking squarely at me. *Now what!* I angrily thought. *Here it comes. I'm going to get it now!*

The General says, "Captain St. James, Captain Norton came to see your Battalion Commander and me yesterday after your flight group returned. He had quite a story to tell us about Major Stewart's behavior. I can't begin to understand what drove him to act that way and direct his wrath at you and Lieutenant McGregor. It's unbelievable how he got this far."

The General takes a long pause and looks over at Stan and back to me, and continues. "Captain Norton also told us about the part he played in it. We can't condone his behavior in this whole sorry affair. What we are about to say has already been covered with Captain Norton. I am going to turn this part over to your Battalion Commander."

We've been listening intently to what has been said so far and turn our attention to the Battalion Commander. "Captain Barnett, you will assume temporary command of this unit until we get your new CO in here. He is due within a few days. Captain St. James, you and Captain Norton will be the Eagles' two senior flight leaders, effective immediately. Captain Norton, you will also remain as temporary Operations officer until your new CO arrives. Upon his arrival, Captain Barnett will assume the duties of Operations Officer. At that time, Captain Norton, you'll function solely as the second senior flight leader. Any questions so far?"

Captain Barnett asks, "Do you know who our new CO is?"

The Battalion Commander replies, "Yes, we do, Captain. He's Major Charles Breckenridge. He's been operating in the Saigon area as a Chinook Company CO. Your new Major has considerable command experience and stick time in Hueys. He'll have his hands full when he gets here and will need all the support you gentlemen can give him. We don't have the luxury of standing down the unit right now for any length of time. We still have our hands full with this Lam Son operation."

He pauses to give us an opportunity to ask any more questions. There are none, so he closes with, "The General has something he wants to say to you men."

We turn our attention back to him. "I want you to know your LRRP mission is considered a complete success. Those teams have been wreaking havoc with the North Vietnamese troops all over the areas you men inserted them. Division believes this has taken some of the pressure off the ARVN troops in Laos and our men in the Khe Sanh area. Well done. Gentlemen. We have put each of you in for the Distinguished Flying Cross, and one for Lieutenant Scott McGregor posthumously!"

# CHAPTER 28

## ANOTHER NEW CO

Returning to my room after the meeting, I'm drained and just want to rest. I can't yet, as it's my job to gather up Scott's personal items for shipment home to his wife. This is extremely difficult for me, as we had become good friends. Although we only served together a short time, we had shared many of our personal and family experiences. I feel like I know Scott's wife and immediate family. I can't begin to know how they will react to Scott's loss or imagine the grief they will experience when they learn of his death.

Thinking of Sandy and my family and how they might handle their grief if it were me, makes me feel guilty. Men, who see other men die in combat, sometimes, down deep within, experience a sense of relief that it wasn't them. I have a momentary sense of shame for having a thought like that and push it back into my subconscious.

Finishing my task, I place Scott's personal effects in the supplied boxes and set them on his cot. The First Sergeant will come by later to pick them up and ensure they are sent home to his wife. Two days ago, Scott was lying here on his cot. Now all that was his is in a few boxes laying there on his cot instead of him. How quickly a man's fortune can change over here. I can't help but think, *What if this was my stuff someone had gone through and laid it here on my cot?*

It's now late afternoon. And growing hungry, I realize I haven't eaten anything since late yesterday. Not wanting to be around anyone just yet, I send a request to the Mess Sergeant to have someone bring over some food. This is not usually done, but he sends some over without hesitation.

Sitting at my desk and nibbling on some food sent over by the Mess Sergeant, I continue dictating some of my thoughts onto the current tape I'm preparing for Sandy.

"Sandy, it's been a long two days, and a lot has happened. I normally wouldn't share this with you, but I believe I need to say something to you. We lost Scott the other night. He was killed flying another Huey on a night mission I was leading. He got disoriented shortly after we took off from our last LZ. His pilot either panicked or got disoriented himself, and they crashed. No one survived. As you know, Scott and I became good friends. I feel like I've lost a brother. This is tough. He would have had a better chance if only, but I better not go into that right now. Parker played a role in this tragic situation. You've heard some of my previous comments about him. Well, finally, our senior command took action. They relieved Parker earlier today, and we'll have a new CO in here in a few days. He's supposed to be very experienced and well qualified for the job. He will have his hands full, but any new CO will be better than the fool we just lost."

Parker suddenly bursts into my room, slamming the door against the wall. He's been drinking and borders on uncontrolled rage. He directs that at me and screams, "You did me in. You fucked me over, you son of a bitch!"

Jumping up from my chair and throwing it aside, I square off on him. It takes all the self-control I can muster at that moment. I so desperately want to deck the SOB. "Bullshit! You wanna know who did you in? Just look in the fucking mirror!"

Parker, still in a fit of rage, says, "My career is over. It's over, thanks to you, motherfucker! Why wouldn't you work with me? You cost me my goddamn career!"

Looking at Parker with an intense, blazing hatred for the man, I respond. "To hell with your fucking career. You're partially responsible for the loss of Scott and his crew. And the really sad thing is, you just don't give a damn about that!"

I pause, looking for a reaction, and when there is none, I continue. "You just saw this command as a ticket to punch so you could make Lieutenant Colonel! But you forgot something."

Parker replies with some hesitation, "Oh, what's that?"

Responding with authority in my voice, like an adult to a child. "The men under your command! They don't give a shit about you getting your ticket punched! They're just trying to do their job, survive around here, and live to go home to their families!"

Parker struggles for a comeback reply, but as a child to an adult, all he can come up with is, "I made this Company meet our daily launch requirements from Division, didn't I?"

Trying to keep from laughing in his face, I respond to him. "Do you really think you made that happen? Before you took over this Company, it was well-led, trained, and motivated. You stepped into a good situation and then proceeded to fuck it all up. In case you didn't notice, the morale in this Company deteriorated steadily since you took over. We've been long overdue for a change of command around here!"

After a long pause, I conclude our encounter with, "Now get the fuck out of my room!"

A subdued and drained Parker turns away and slowly

lumbers out of the room, whimpering to himself, "My career! My career! You guys ruined my career."

Watching Parker stumble out the door, I find myself wanting to give him a parting shot, but I don't. I do not pity him and only regret that we crossed paths here in Vietnam. I can only hope our paths never cross again.

The Battalion Commander has given our Company a two day stand down to train while we wait for our new CO's arrival. Over the next two days, Stan and I spend our time flying local missions with the newest pilots. The remaining pilots pair off, the most experienced ones flying with the less experienced pilots. The maintenance and ground crews spend their time repairing whatever needs the most attention. However, at the direction of Captain Barnett, they work at a more disciplined and controlled pace. These men have been working at a feverish, non-stop pace for weeks now. They need to slow down, catch up on their rest, and regain some sanity.

To help with Company morale, Captain Barnett has dispensed with Company formations and barracks inspections, and reopened the NCO and Enlisted men's club bars. Captain Barnett, Stan, and I have set a goal to reduce, if not eliminate, Major Parker Stewart's memory from the men's minds in the Company. We're hoping the men will give the new CO their full support when he arrives. This will give us a better chance to restore the Company's morale and "*esprit de corps.*" Many of the men who served with Major Hutchins before he was killed, hope the new CO is cut from the same cloth.

The next few days I spend flying with two of the Company's newest pilots. Our missions are low risk and flown within the borders of South Vietnam. As always, I record some of this activity in my nightly diary entries.

~

## MARCH 1971

Today I flew with our newest pilot, a Warrant Officer named Jake. Not a bad guy. He seems to be a natural, with good pilot instincts and reaction time. I enjoyed the day. We flew for 7 hours and worked three firebases: Sarge, Holcomb, and Fuller. They're up near Quang Tri Combat Base and the DMZ, and they are all manned by 101st troops. Our missions consisted of supplying them with ammunition, food, mail, and other necessities of life for troops on a remote firebase. We also ferried some troops back and forth between the three firebases and Quang Tri base.

The situation in Laos has totally deteriorated. The South Vietnamese forces are in full retreat and streaming back across the border into South Vietnam and the Khe Sanh area. It looks like the 101st Aviation Group will assist in bringing the ARVN forces back into Quang Tri. Rumor has it they will regroup and eventually assume total operational responsibility for the area north of Hue. This will include the area between Quang Tri Combat Base and the DMZ and west toward the Laotian border. Basically, Quang Tri Province. This will be a vast area of responsibility for them.

I hope they can handle it. If Laos indicates their abilities as a significant military force, I would say it does not appear very promising for them. From what I've seen over the last two months, the problem is a lack of leadership at many levels within their combat units. I'm in no way impugning their ability to fight, as many of their soldiers I saw did so bravely. However, without effective leadership, it has proven to be very costly and disastrous for them.

I love you Sandy.

MARCH 1971

Today was not a bad day, just a long one, as we flew for 9 hours up north. Most of our flying time was between Quang Tri and Khe Sanh. I took another of our newer pilots with me today; a Warrant Officer named Bert. He's an amiable fellow and seems quite sure of himself. This is good, so long as he gives himself some time to gain more experience with the way things are done over here. Time will tell.

We flew several missions to extract small equipment and wounded ARVN soldiers from around the Khe Sanh area. They sure are a dejected group of men who look like they have been living in hell for the last two months. You can't help but feel sorry for them. I have no idea what the future holds for them, but I have to hope it is better than what they have just lived through. On our third flight back to Quang Tri with several wounded men on board, two died before we could get them to the MASH unit. To make it that far and then die within minutes of potential life-saving, medical help is heart-wrenching. I feel for them and their families and hope we in America never have to go through what these people are having to endure to secure and then enjoy their freedom.

Once again, the rumor mill has it that Lam Son 719 has been officially brought to an end. Not sure if that's true or precisely what that means, but it sounds good to me. The big unknown is, will the North Vietnamese keep coming into South Vietnam through Khe Sanh and the DMZ. If they do, will they continue their drive into Quang Tri and down south toward Hue and into our AO? I'm sure the NVA feels pretty damned emboldened by what they did to the ARVN in Laos.

If Lam Son 719 is ending, I wonder how it is being reported back in the States. We really have no idea right now what they're saying about it back home. However, from what I've seen over here, I would say without a doubt it has been one big friggin mess. Unfortunately, it has resulted in the loss of several good men. What did we accomplish? What effect did it really have on the North Vietnamese? More importantly, will it shorten this damn war?

I love you, Sandy.

∼

As the Battalion Commander indicated, our new CO, Major Charles Breckenridge, reported to B Company on the third day following Parker's departure. Captain Barnett, Stan, the First Sergeant, and I have been called to the Major's office to meet him. When I walk into the Operations area, I'm met by the other men, all of whom are waiting to be called into the office. When the door opens, our Battalion Commander steps out and directs us to join him inside. The First Sergeant is the last to enter and closes the door after entering.

Standing in front of his new desk is Major Charles Breckenridge. He is a big man and looks like he could have played professional football as a lineman. My first thought is, *how the hell does he fit into the cockpit of a Huey?* After entering the office, we all come to attention and salute our new CO. He returns our salutes. The Battalion Commander then introduces him around. With each introduction, we shake hands and exchange greetings.

The Major looks us over as if we are a new car he's considering for purchase. His facial expression warms up to us and conveys one of satisfaction with what he sees. We notice it, and our apprehension levels begin to ease. The Battalion Commander shares that he's gone over our situation and current status with Major Breckenridge.

He excuses himself, turns it over to our new Commanding

Officer, and walks toward the door. He abruptly stops, turns to face us, and says, "Gentleman, you have a good man here. He will work with you, support you, and listen to you. I'm sure you will give him your full support. We all want this Company to return to the high state of performance and morale that existed under Major Hutchins. Good luck!" He turns back toward the door, and as he exits the office, our new CO thanks him for his support and comments.

After the Battalion Commander leaves, Major Breckenridge speaks to us. "Gentlemen, please take a seat." We settle ourselves in, and the new CO continues. "As the Commander said, he brought me up to speed on what has been happening around here under your previous CO. It's unfortunate. But I want to assure you that you will not be subjected to anything like that from me."

He pauses and, in a calm, deliberate manner, continues. "I want your thoughts on the current status of this Company and how we can bring it back up to par on all levels. I didn't know Major Hutchins, but I've heard nothing but good things about him. I hope, in time, I will earn your support and respect. I will work hard to do so, and I expect each of you to work hard to earn mine."

He looks us over and proceeds, "First Sergeant, you and I will meet later today and go over some items I want to cover with you. For now, you're dismissed, and thanks for your help in getting my things here." The First Sergeant stands, salutes, and leaves the room.

He resumes, "Beginning tomorrow, and for the next few days, I'll be flying some missions with each of you. This will help me to get more acquainted with you and the area up here." Looking over at Captain Barnett, he says, "Captain Barnett, as our new Operations Officer, will you post our flight schedules." Captain Barnett nods his acknowledgment, and Major Breckenridge continues. "I'll be looking to each of you to familiarize me with our AO, and the caliber and abilities of the men we fly with. Your views on what needs the most attention around here and what can be done to improve the men's morale will be most appreciated. According to the Battalion Commander, you three have already made progress in that respect. Good job! Any questions for me?"

Captain Barnett asks, "Major, when do you want to meet the other officers and men in the Company?"

The Major looks at him and responds, "I would like to meet the officers as a group when the last pilots return from their missions today. If possible, I would like to do it over dinner. Later tonight, say around 2100 hours, we can have a Company meeting in the mess hall, and I can talk with all the men at that time. How does that work for all of you?"

Looking at each other, it's evident from our facial expressions; we believe we have another good CO. We respond to him in the affirmative. With that, the Major dismisses us but asks me to stay back for a minute.

I stand up with the other officers, who then step out of the room. The Major approaches me and speaks to me as a father would to his son. "Taylor, I am aware of what you and Scott endured with Major Stewart. Frankly, I'm a little surprised you didn't deck the SOB a few times. Not that I would condone that kind of behavior, you understand!" A little grin crosses his face as he continues, "I'm also aware of what you've done for this Company and many of the men in it. They look up to you. You're a natural leader and a damn good pilot from what I've been told."

That is a welcomed comment from him, and it makes me feel appreciated for the first time since we lost Major Hutchins. A slight smile crosses my face as I respond. "Thank you, Major, but I'm just one of the many men in this Company that fit that description."

"Taylor, you're too modest. But I'll take your word on that. I'll be looking to you for help in identifying them. Lord knows, we are going to need all we have. This Lam Son Operation is winding down, as I'm guessing you've heard. But you may not know that Division and MACV Headquarters in Saigon believe the North Vietnamese are planning another major incursion. They believe their plan involves crossing the DMZ and attacking South Vietnamese installations across a wide area in the northern part of the country. If this is true, we are going to be in for more heavy fighting and combat insertions."

I do my best to respond in a positive tone and with confidence. "Major, I've heard similar rumors to that effect but was hoping they were just rumors. What the NVA did to the ARVN in Laos surely has emboldened them. I'm guessing they feel pretty damn confident right about now."

The Major steps away from me and walks over to his desk. Turning back to look at me, "Taylor, we'll talk more about that later. I've kept you too long. I look forward to us working together and flying with you. I'll see you at dinner."

With that, I come to attention and salute our new CO, who reciprocates. Leaving his office and walking across the Company area, a feeling of contentment and calm settle over me. Any apprehension about the caliber of our new Commanding Officer I had before meeting him has vanished. Major Charles Breckenridge is a leader. *I believe I'm going to like this man!*

# CHAPTER 29

## MARINE RESCUE

After our Company meeting in the mess hall that evening, Captain Barnett and I borrow a jeep and head over to the Pilots Club. It's been a few days since I've seen Greg, and I yearn to be around a close friend and spend some time with him.

Entering the Club, we have no problem finding Greg, who has secured a table with a few of his Cobra pilots. On the way to the table, I stop at the bar and direct the bartender to send over a round of beers to Greg's table. As we approach, Greg stands up and greets me with a handshake and a guy hug. He then gives Captain Barnett a hardy handshake and motions for both of us to have a seat. Greg says, "Taylor, old buddy, it's been a rough few days. Are you doing alright over there?"

Both of us take a seat while greeting the other pilots at the table with head nods. "Yeah, I feel better about our situation than I did twenty-four hours ago. The Battalion Commander brought in our new CO today, and I think we have a winner!"

Greg responds, "We heard about the changes over there earlier today. Sounds like you might be catching a break with the new CO!"

Captain Barnett responds, "We think so, by all accounts, he has a distinguished record. Time will tell! Oh, before I forget, you need to ask Taylor about his close encounter with Parker before he left the Company!"

"What's this about Parker, old boy? We didn't hear anything about your latest run in!" Greg says with a sense of anticipation.

Grinning, I look over at Greg, "Nothing to it, really. The night before he left for Saigon, he busted into my room, drunk, blamed all his problems on me—we had a few words, and then I threw his sorry ass out. End of story!"

The table erupts in laughter as we all raise our beers in toast and tap them together. The rest of the evening revolves around small talk. We share our general opinions about Lam Son 719, and the rumors we're hearing about another major North Vietnamese incursion headed our way. Also bantered around are the usual complaints about the weather, lack of good food, lousy USO shows when we do get one, and any number of other minor annoyances soldiers tend to complain about. The evening slowly winds down, and eventually, we head back to our rooms for the night.

The following day, Major Breckenridge flies with Captain Barnett and the day after, with Stan. These two days provide the Major an opportunity to familiarize himself with our AO and his direct reports. It also gives him a better appreciation of the overall situation with Lam Son 719 and its continuing aftermath. During those two days, I fly with our two newest pilots, Jake, and Bert, on missions around Khe Sanh. The 101st Division's Aviation units continue to relocate ARVN soldiers and equipment from Khe Sanh to the Quang Tri base area.

On the evening of the second day, the Major calls a meeting with Captain Barnett, Stan, and me. During this meeting, he informs us that our Company has been directed to send two flights of Eagles to an area about five miles inside Laos early the next morning. The remnants of a South Vietnamese Marine Battalion have been cut off in their attempts to reach the border. They are holding on but need to be evacuated ASAP. An ARVN Armored Company had been trying to break through to them all day but without success. They ran up against heavy resistance and took a hell of a beating. What was left of their Armored Personnel Carriers and tanks had to pull back. So, it's up to us to go in and get them out.

Major Breckenridge informs us that two CH-47s from one of our Chinook Company's is already on station at Khe Sanh. They will be dropping night flares over the Marines' position during the long night. The Butchers have six Cobras on station up there and will provide whatever firepower they can during the night. The objective is simple—keep the Marines alive and give them a chance to be extracted early the next morning.

The Major concludes his briefing with, "Gentlemen, I will be leading one of the groups and Captain St. James the other. We'll have six ships in each group. Captain Barnett, you will fly one of the ships in my group, and Captain Norton, you'll fly one of the ships in Captain St. James' group. You men will assume command of our groups if either Taylor or I go down."

Looking at us with an intensity we never saw in Parker, he continues. "This is going to be another rough one, gentlemen. Captain Barnett, please take care of positing the crew assignments for tomorrow. Do your best to spread out the experience levels of the crews. I want everyone to know as soon as possible. We will leave here by 0500. We're to be on station at Khe Sanh by 0600. Our jump-off time is 0630. We're going in at first light. Any questions?"

We have none. We know the score and what's expected of us. Turning to leave, we each render him a military salute. He returns our salute and says, "Get some rest, gentlemen. We're going to need it. Goodnight!"

Walking back to my room, a sense of foreboding once again begins to overtake me. This Lam Son operation is going to kill all of us before it ends.

I don't sleep well, and the next morning arrives very early. My morning starts with a flurry of activity that unfolds before me. I'm in a fog. I go through all the motions I've performed numerous times before when going out on missions, but this seems different to me. My mind hasn't engaged yet, just my body as it takes me through the motions. One minute I'm getting out of bed, and the next, we are arriving ahead of schedule at Khe Sanh.

Slowly I shake off whatever was going on in my subconscious and focus my attention on the here and now. *It's going to be a long day, TJ, so get your mind in the game!* Landing at Khe Sanh, we refuel our Hueys and shut down in the staging area. Within minutes of shutting down, the pilots are directed to a large wooden structure near the staging area for a briefing. There we are met by two Full Colonels, one from the 101st and the other from the South Vietnamese Marine Division. They will conduct the briefing.

The 101st Colonel introduces himself and his South Vietnamese counterpart and then continues with the briefing. "Major Breckenridge, you and your men have a very critical mission this morning. You men are the only hope those Marines have of getting back across the border. They're a tough bunch. They've been fighting like hell just to get this far. They are critically low on ammo, have several wounded men, and have had no rest in over four days."

He pauses and looks over at his counterpart to see if he has anything to add. He doesn't and motions for the Colonel to continue. "You will be flying into an extremely dangerous situation, as the area is not secure. It's under constant attack, and as of a few hours ago, we received a report that some North Vietnamese tanks moved into the area."

At this point, there is some talk among the men, and it's clear our anxiety levels and pucker factors have gone up considerably. Major Breckenridge quiets us down and motions for the Colonel to continue. "Gentlemen, you need to be in the air and on your way by 0630. It's only about a fifteen-minute flight time to your LZ. When you launch from here, we'll initiate a massive bombardment of the area surrounding the LZ. Our artillery will hit them with HE (high explosives), white phosphorus, and smoke. This will last until you call it off, Major." Again, he pauses and asks, "Are there any questions?"

I speak up, "Sir, how big is the LZ area we're flying into, and where will we pick up our Cobra support?"

The Colonel responds, "Good questions, Captain! The LZ is large enough to land six Hueys at a time. There appears to be plenty of room. The Marines are dug in near what is left of the tree lines along most of their outer perimeter. You may want to use a diamond formation with three ships in the front and three in the back when going into the LZ. This should place you closer to the Marines when you get in there, as they'll have less ground to cover getting to your choppers. You'll have less time on the ground that way. Major, it's your call on how to proceed with your formations. As for your Cobras, they've been here all night flying around the LZ, providing what support they could. They should be refueling and rearming now and will join you at 0630 hours. Butcher 12 is their commander. That's about it, gentlemen, any other questions?"

There being none, both Colonels render a hand salute and wish us good luck as they exit the structure. Returning their salute, we break out in small talk among ourselves. If my morning started as a big blur, that just ended. I'm wide awake now.

The Major quiets us down and takes a moment to talk with us. "Gentlemen, this is going to be a ball-buster, so keep it sharp, call out your targets to the Cobras and stay focused. Once we cross the border, we'll fly "nap of the earth" and stay that way for the return trip. If anyone goes down in the LZ, get out of your chopper and over to another one quick. We're not going to leave any man behind."

The Major pauses for a minute to let what he just said sink in and then continues. "As for there being any tanks in there, that's gotta be a new wrinkle! We'll go in fast, touch down, load our packs, and get the hell out of there. That should make it harder for a tank to get a lock on you. The Butchers should be able to deal with them. So, if you see one, call it out and be precise! Anyone have a question? If not, take this time to double-check your choppers and equipment. Let's head to our ships! Good luck out there, men!"

There are no questions, and we slowly disperse. Heading back to our choppers, some of the men indulge themselves with small talk.

I'm flying with Bert, and as we head to our Huey, Bert strikes up a conversation. "Sir, have you ever come across any tanks in LZs you've flown into before today?"

"Bert, call me TJ or Taylor, not sir, remember? And no, this will be my first time, if there are any!"

"Sorry, Taylor, I forgot. I guess I'm just anxious to get this one over with and hope I don't screw it up!"

"You're not alone, Bert. We're all anxious! Just do what you've been trained to do. When the shit hits the fan, just react to the situation at hand and do what's necessary to stay alive. Don't worry about it, and you'll do fine! Besides, you didn't have anything else planned for this morning, did you, Bert?"

Bert tries to crack a smile, but his apprehension and fear of what's to come will not allow one.

The order is given to saddle up as soon as we reach our

Hueys. Men scramble into their seats, buckle up, put their helmets on, adjust their chicken plates, and extend out the armor plating on the sides of their seats. After confirming with my crew that they're ready, I fire up the chopper as Bert monitors our instruments. The Eagles are prepared to launch and once again fly straight into hell.

# CHAPTER 30

## PURPLE HEARTS

Confirming with his Eagles that we are ready to launch, Major Breckenridge contacts Khe Sanh Tower. Receiving clearance to go, he transmits calmly and authoritatively. 'Eagle flight, this is Eagle 1. We have been cleared to launch. Climb to 800 feet and form on me with two V formations. My group followed by Eagle 25s. We'll drop down to treetop level when we approach the border. Over!'

His ACs respond to his transmission with double-clicks, and some of us with 'Roger that!'

I communicate with my crew over our intercom. 'Are you doing okay over there, Bert?'

Bert responds, 'Yeah, I think so. It's the best I can hope for right now!'

'I'll take that. Don't think about it. Just react to whatever happens out there, as it happens, and you'll be alright.' I respond, trying to keep the crew from dwelling too much on what awaits us five miles inside Laos.

'How's it going back there, Bob?' He's one of our newest

Crew Chiefs, and this will be his baptism by fire. 'Your M-60 ready to rock and roll?'

Bob responds, 'I'm doing fine, sir. My M-60 is locked and loaded. I'm ready to unload on any of those little bastards that show up today!'

'Good, stay sharp!' I then ask our door gunner, Tom, the same question. 'Tom, are you doing alright back there? How's your M-60?'

Tom responds, 'Yes, sir, my gun's ready, and I'll let you know when we get back how I'm doing, Sir!'

'Tom, sounds good. We'll be back in plenty of time for chow tonight and maybe even a few beers. How's that sound?'

'Good, sir!' Our conversations over the intercom are interrupted when the Major transmits to his Eagles.

'Eagles, Eagle 1, we are crossing the border. Drop down with me and stay sharp. We're only a few minutes out. Over!' The Major receives acknowledgements from his group via double-clicks and a few radio transmissions of 'Roger that!'

After his transmission, Greg transmits over his radio. 'Eagle 1, Butcher 12. We are joining up with you. We are a flight of six, heavily armed angels of death, flying at your six and above you. Over!'

'Butcher 12, Eagle 1. Good to see you and your angels of death. We have two flights of six each. I'm going in first, and Eagle 25 will lead in the second flight. Over!'

'Eagle 1, Butcher 12. Roger. Understand. Over!'

'Butcher 12, Eagle 1. Good. I understand you fellows have been over there all night. What's it like? Have you seen any tanks in there? Over!'

'Eagle 1, Butcher 12. In two words—fucked up! There are some tanks. We hit one of them on our last trip out. They appear to be on the south side of the LZ and way back in the tree line. Get in and out as fast as you can! Over!'

'Butcher 12, Eagle 1, thanks. Over!' After transmitting to Greg, the Major calls in a request to have the artillery barrage lifted as we're closing in fast on the LZ.

Looking out of my window, I can see large columns of smoke in the distance and assume we are coming up on the LZ. The artillery barrage has been going on for some time, and I hope it's been effective.

Greg calls me, 'Eagle 25, Butcher 12. How are you doing, TJ? Keep your head down when you go in there. It's another fucking mess! Over!'

I can see Greg's Cobras high above us as I transmit. 'Butcher 12, Eagle 25, thanks, buddy. Got you in sight. Stay with us. What about a beer or two later tonight? Over!'

'You're on!' Greg responds. Thinking to myself, *Here it comes, radio discipline. Stay off the radios.* But nothing is said. Major Breckenridge is not Parker.

As my fellow Eagles and I close in fast on the LZ, we see that the artillery fire has lifted. Major Breckenridge has contacted the Marine Commander on the ground, who has informed him they are ready for extraction. The artillery barrage has had its intended effect. Enemy ground fire has tapered off for the moment. The Major radios his group, 'Eagles, this is Eagle 1, the artillery has lifted. They're ready for us on the ground. Flight one, on me. We're going in! Butcher 12. Keep us covered! Over!'

Greg responds, 'Roger, Eagle 1, over.'

Leading his flight into the LZ, they land in a diamond formation as suggested. Once down, Marines scramble from their hidden positions around the LZ to the nearest choppers. Several are wounded and are being assisted by their comrades. The Major's flight is on the ground for a brief time and lifts off once their packs have jumped on board. They were in and out without receiving enemy fire. He radios me. 'Eagle 25, Eagle 1. We are out with no contact. You're clear to go in. Good luck. Over!'

'Eagle 1, Eagle 25, roger that, going in now! Over!'

The smoke, which had covered most of the area, has almost cleared when my group approaches the LZ. Those North Vietnamese that survived the artillery barrage have now come out from their covered positions to greet us. They are once again laying down a heavy field of fire over the LZ. As I clear the tree line and land my flight in a diamond formation, we are caught right in the middle of their field of fire. Red tracer rounds whiz by my window from all directions. The remaining Marines are scrambling for the nearest choppers they can get to as the firing intensifies. Their wounded were loaded on the first flight, making it easier for the remaining Marines to cover the ground to our waiting choppers.

As Marines jump into my chopper, I notice two tanks off to my left and set back in the tree line. I call out to Stan and Greg, 'Eagle 8, Butcher 12, this is Eagle 25. We have two tanks to our left front inside the tree line. Stan, let's get the hell out of here. Butcher 12, can you kill those bastards?'

Stan calls out to me, 'Eagle 25, Eagle 8, I'm right behind you. Let's go!'

Greg, hearing the desperation in my voice and radios, 'Eagle 25, have your gunners shoot at them. Over!' My gunners direct their fire toward the two tanks. Their tracer rounds ping off the tanks. Greg, flying high above them, can see where their tracer rounds are going and spots the tanks.

Greg radios, 'Eagle 25, we have them in sight—rolling in.'

As he does, the tanks open fire on the LZ with their machine guns and turret cannons. The shells from their cannons miss hitting any choppers but kick up considerable dirt and debris as they hit the ground around us. However, the machine guns are raising havoc with our choppers. With all the Marines loaded, I take off and lead my group out of the LZ. As we start to lift off, Stan's chopper gets hit with several rounds. Thankfully, he's able to keep flying and follows me out. The last chopper in the diamond formation also gets hit as they lift off. Their pilot and door gunner are both wounded. Smoke is billowing out one side of their chopper. By some miracle, they manage to stay in the air. As we clear the end of the LZ, Greg and his group are firing rockets into the tanks' location. They score direct hits on both tanks as large explosions erupt in the tree line where they were hiding.

I call the Major, 'Eagle 1, Eagle 25. We are on our way out of the LZ. Two ships hit, some wounded. We ran into two tanks.'

My transmission is stopped cold as several rounds hit us in the cockpit and down the right side of our Huey. A third tank is hidden further back in the tree line, and one of its gunners was firing their turret-mounted machine gun at us. This is what wreaked havoc on us. Bert has been hit in the leg by one of the rounds and is screaming in pain. Bob has taken a round to the chest and is slumped over his machine gun.

I've not been hit by a bullet, but one of the rounds that came into the cockpit was a red tracer. It shattered some of the plexiglass when it hit, and the cockpit is full of smoke. I've been hit by some of the small fragments of plexiglass, but that's not the problem. My real problem is all the smoke in the cockpit. Embedded in the smoke are tiny particles of plexiglass that get into my eyes. It's like getting sand thrown in your eyes. I can still see, but it's very uncomfortable as I struggle to maintain my vision.

Major Breckenridge realizes that something is wrong and calls me. 'Eagle 25, Eagle 1, you guys alright?'

'Eagle 1, Eagle 25, we just took several rounds of machine-gun fire from another tank, which was set way back from the tree line. Bert is hit in the leg, our crew chief may be dead, and I'm struggling. We took a tracer round in the cockpit, and the smoke particles are irritating the hell out of my eyes. Over!'

'Eagle 25, Eagle 1. Roger, understand. I'm coming around

and will join you on your left side. Eagle 16, take over my flight and get them back to Khe Sanh. Eagle 8, take over Eagle 25's flight and bring them back. Over!'

Both pilots respond in the affirmative.

While I'm trying to calm Bert down, who is screaming in pain, Tom moves over and checks on Bob. He tells me we've lost Bob. He was killed by one of the machine gun rounds. It penetrated his chicken plate and hit him in the chest—no time to mourn now. I'm struggling with my eyes as they are becoming more irritated and scratchier by the minute. It is becoming more difficult to see very far as my vision deteriorates and is very blurry.

The Major has flown in close to the left side of my chopper. We are both flying back toward Khe Sanh at a low altitude. I'm struggling to keep the Huey in the air as it shudders, and my controls are going stiff. Looking over at my hydraulic gauge, I notice the pressure is steadily dropping. Bert is in a lot of pain and is of no help right now. Over the intercom, I yell out, 'Tom, see if you can pull Bert out of his seat and back there with you. Do what you can to help him.'

Tom works his way from the back of the chopper to Bert's seat and unstraps him. With the help of two Marines, Tom pulls him out of his seat and settles him on the Huey floor. Bert's leg is a mess, and he is bleeding heavily. One of the Marines is a medic and jumps in to help Tom. They place a tourniquet on his upper thigh and do what they can for him as he continues screaming in pain. As this was unfolding, two of the Marines had taken over the M-60 machine guns mounted on each side of the Huey. They begin shooting at any target they can find on the ground below our Huey.

These South Vietnamese Marines are a tough bunch!

Tom, who has been working on Bert, tells me, 'Bert is losing a lot of blood, his leg's a mess, we need to get him to a MASH unit fast!'

'Do what you can, Tom. I've got my hands full up here. We're losing our fucking hydraulics!'

Tom says, 'Oh shit! This just keeps getting better!'

Seeing what's going on inside our Huey, the Major calls me. 'Eagle 25, Eagle 1. How are you fellows doing over there?'

'Not good. I'm having a tough time with my vision. The smoke and plexiglass particles are really getting to me, and I'm also losing my hydraulics! But I think we can make it back to Khe Sanh! Over!'

Major Breckenridge realizes the only chance I have to come out of this alive is to make a running landing on the airstrip back at Khe Sanh. A Huey can still fly without hydraulics, but it's a real challenge. The hydraulic system on a Huey is the lifeblood of its controls. This system allows the controls to move freely and with little effort on the part of pilots. With no hydraulics, the controls are stiff and require herculean efforts to move them. Under these conditions, a Huey cannot perform a slow approach and come to a hover. The only choice is to land like a fixed-wing aircraft. Army pilots train for this emergency, but the real thing is tough and tricky.

I'm also aware that this is my only option.

'Eagle 25, Eagle 1. Good. I'm right next to you. I'll help guide you in. I've called the tower and requested an emergency approach for you. Medics will be standing by when you land. We're about five minutes out. Copy. Over!'

'Eagle 1, Eagle 25. Roger, I understand, over!'

Greg and his Cobra group destroyed the third tank that ruined my day. They've now joined up on the Major and me and are flying cover above us. Greg calls me. 'Eagle 25, Butcher 12, hang in there, TJ. I'm looking forward to a few beers with you later—I'm buying. Over!'

Although focused and totally immersed in flying our Huey and doing my best to keep it in the air, I manage a brief response. 'Thanks, Greg, see you soon!'

Approaching Khe Sanh from the west allows me to make a straight-in approach to the runway. The Major has been working his radios and keeping me on course as we close in on the runway. My eyes are extremely irritated. It has become very difficult for me see objects at a distance outside my cockpit window. Without the help of Major Breckenridge acting as my eyes, the outcome would be in serious jeopardy. If we make it down safely, we'll owe our lives to him.

My hydraulics are gone, and the controls are stiff and hard to move. I have to maintain enough airspeed and forward momentum to keep our Huey from falling out of the sky. This requires a coordinated effort between the cyclic and collective while maintaining enough pressure on my foot pedals to keep the tail rotor from getting away from me and spinning out of control.

Sweating profusely and struggling with my eyes to see outside the ship, I coax our Huey down on the runway. As we hit the runway, our landing skids bounce and slide along on the surface for a considerable distance before the helicopter comes to a complete stop. Once we stop, I shut down the engine, sit back in my seat, and take a deep breath. We're down. We made it. My shoulders and back ache from the stress. I'm exhausted and try to relax while straining to watch the rotor blades slowly come to a stop.

The Major lands behind me, hovers to one side of the runway, and sets it down. He tells his pilot to take the controls and shut the chopper down. Exiting his chopper, he heads straight for us. As he's doing so, ambulances converge on our Huey. We are a beehive of activity as medics jump out of their vehicles and begin tending to our wounded and dead.

The Marines disembark the Huey as medics tend to Bert and

remove Bob from the floor of the Huey. Once they remove Bob from the chopper, they slip him into a body bag, and gently place his body in an ambulance. Some of the medics are helping me out of my seat when the Major reaches our Huey. "Taylor, that was a fine piece of flying. Well done. You saved a lot of lives over there today."

He looks at me, trying to determine how much damage may have been done to my face and eyes. All he notices is little red spots around my lower face where small pieces of plexiglass have hit me. My eyes are red, watery, and almost swollen shut. I was flying with my helmet visor down, which is standard practice. Our helmet visor can be lowered to our cheek line, which helps protect the eyes. This prevented any plexiglass fragments from directly hitting my eyes.

The Major is relieved to see that it doesn't appear to be too severe, and asks, "How are your eyes? Can you see anything? Do they hurt much?"

"Thanks, Major. I think I'm okay. But my eyes are bothering me. How is Bert doing?"

"The medics are working on him now. His leg is in bad shape, but he should make it. We need to get you two to our MASH unit back at Phu Bai right away. We'll take care of everything here. We'll see you back at base." With that, the Major pats me on the back while looking at me with a sense of pride that a father might have with a son who just did something worthy.

"Thank you, sir. See you tonight."

The medics place Bert and me onto a Medevac chopper, headed back to Phu Bai. Bert is doing better. The bleeding has been controlled, and he was given some morphine. He's in a mild state of bliss right now. En route to the MASH unit, one of the medics places gauzes, soaked in a water solution, on both of my eyes. He then wraps a bandage around my head, thereby holding the gauzes in place. I find this to be somewhat soothing, and then

I have a frightful thought. *Oh my god, am I going to be blinded by this?*

Later that evening at the MASH unit, I'm resting on a hospital cot, and my eyes are covered with new gauze. Everyone has been trying to assure me I'll be okay. I appreciate their caring and good intentions, but I can't help worrying about it. Until these gauzes and bandages are removed, and I can see for myself, I'll continue to worry.

It's been some time since I've been in the company of a woman. I find all the attention I'm getting from the nursing staff a pleasant byproduct of my situation. While eating, Major Breckenridge and Greg drop in for a brief visit. They interrupt my dinner as I'm nibbling on some food with the help of a nurse, guiding it to my mouth. Walking up to my bed, the Major says, "Taylor, they tell me you'll be alright and that you just need a few days bed rest along with some eye treatments. This is great news! It was pretty tough over there this morning. You did a good job." The nurse stops feeding me and stands up to leave so they can visit but tells them they only have a few minutes.

Greg thanks the nurse as he looks her over and checks to see if she has a ring. Recognizing his voice, *I know he is checking her out.* Looking in the direction of Greg's voice, I say to him, "She married, Greg?"

Greg, surprised, says, "How'd you know I was checking her out?"

"Well, she sounds really nice, and knowing you—it just somehow seemed appropriate to ask."

Greg looking down at me, says in a low, calm, and light-hearted manner, "As a matter-of-fact, old buddy—she's single. I think I'll get her number!"

We all share a little levity for a moment. The Major then says, "Taylor, I understand the Flight Surgeon is sending you down to the 95th Evacuation Hospital in Da Nang tomorrow morning so an eye doctor can check you out."

"Yes, sir. They want to continue my treatments for a few days down there and make sure I don't have any permanent eye damage."

"That's good. I'll just mention a few things, and we'll be on our way. While you're there, you will be visited by two officers from Saigon who are involved in the Parker inquiry. I've been told they will wait until the doctors clear you before they see you. They'll do their interview down there before you return to the Company. Any questions?"

"No, sir. Sounds fine. I was expecting to be questioned at some point."

The Major continues. "Our actions earlier today saved many South Vietnamese Marines, and there will be some medals awarded. You will be recommended for two, another DFC, and a Purple Heart!"

After a long pause, I look up in the direction of the Major and say, "Sir, I would appreciate it if you would pull any recommendation for the Purple Heart for me. I do not consider what happened to me today to be worthy of it. Bob lost his life, and Bert is headed back home with a severe leg injury. They deserve to be awarded that medal, not me. I just got some smoke in my eyes."

Both the Major and Greg looking down at me can see I'm very serious about this request. The Major tells me he will consider it. Before we have any chance to continue our conversation, my nurse returns. "Gentlemen, you need to call it a night. The Captain needs his rest." With that, they both shake my hand, turn away and leave so I can follow the nurse's orders to get some rest.

Walking out of the MASH unit, the Major looks at Greg and says, "I've been in the Army a long time. I've never had a man to turn down a Purple Heart because he didn't consider his wound to be worthy of one. I've known some who requested on their own to be awarded a Purple Heart to beef up their medal chest, but never one to turn it down. That young man is something!"

Greg says, "That he is! That he is!"

# CHAPTER 31

## REST AND RECUPERATION (R&R)

I t's my last night at the Hospital in Da Nang. I will be returning tomorrow morning to my Company. I'm not particularly looking forward to going back since what I've experienced being here would definitely qualify as "light duty." It will be good to be back among my friends and comrades and get on with completing my tour of duty over here. Since I have the use of my eyes, I'm going to record an entry in my diary of this experience and then retire for the evening.

APRIL 1971

I'm returning to my Company tomorrow morning after being here five days. I'm rested, a little less stressed, and enjoying normal sight again. While recovering here at the 95th Evacuation Hospital, I enjoyed air-conditioned rooms, good food, and some casual conversations with other men recovering from their wounds. Most of all, I enjoyed my evenings and going to bed at night, knowing I would not be flying combat missions the next day. My only regret was not seeing and enjoying any of my surroundings visually since my eyes were bandaged until my last day.

It was an interesting experience, not being able to rely on my eyes. I could not fully appreciate my surroundings or move around without some assistance. I found myself relying more on my other senses of sound, touch, taste, and smell.

Being in Da Nang and close to the beach, I found the smell of the sea air most refreshing and invigorating. The one smell I didn't notice, or miss, was the smell of jet fuel, JP-4 in the air. I'll probably never forget that smell, along with the distinct whooping sounds of a Huey's rotors. Something I seldom heard during my five days here. They placed me in a wing of the hospital that was the furthest away from the helicopter pad. Apparently, I requested that, but I have no memory of doing so.

Yesterday morning, the medical staff removed my eye bandages and determined I was fit to return to flight status. They scheduled my release for early tomorrow morning. During most of yesterday, I was restricted to the inside of the hospital because my eyes were very sensitive to the light. As the day progressed, they became more adjusted to the light, and I was able to go outside last night and enjoy the sunset. What a relief that was!

Today I was interviewed by two officers from Saigon concerning Major Parker Stewart. Their questions were very thorough and probing in nature. I did my best to answer them. They spent several hours with me, and when it was over, I was totally drained of energy. At times I wondered if I was the subject of their inquiry. As it continued, I found myself being less responsive to some of their questions. I have no respect for Major Parker Stewart. However, he is a career officer with eighteen years of service. His Army career could all end because of what occurred while he was CO of B Company. I understood that and wanted to be as fair and impartial as possible. When it was over, and they dismissed me, I couldn't get out of that room fast enough. Hoping that's the end of it, I headed straight to the nearest bar for some beers. I never want to hear the name Parker Stewart again.

I love you Sandy.

The next morning came early. After breakfast, I met Stan, who flew down to pick me up at the hospital's landing pad. It's a clear day, and the air is refreshing as we fly back to our Company. When we return, most of the men are still out flying missions, including the Major. Only a few are there to welcome me back. Those that are, greet me with kind words and some hand slaps. It's good to be back, and I thank each man for their kind words and gestures. I then help Stan and his crew perform their post-flight of the Huey. When completed, Stan walks with me over to my room as we engage in conversation.

"Taylor, it's good to have you back, and I'm glad your eyes weren't damaged. That's gotta be a relief!"

"Thanks, Stan. Yeah, it is. All I could think about was what if my eyesight doesn't return to normal. Being bandaged for five days and not being able to see was pretty intense. I can't begin to imagine what it would be like to be blind."

"Me neither," Stan replies.

"So, what's new, Stan?"

"In a nutshell, Lam Son 719 was officially declared over. All the South Vietnamese troops lucky enough to get out of Laos are back in this country now. We have been pulling them out of Khe Sanh and redeploying them around the Quang Tri Province as directed. Our troops are pulling out of the Khe Sanh area and moving back into the 101st AO. It's been pretty quiet around here for the last few days."

I respond, "Sounds good to me. Let's hope it stays that way for a while!"

Reaching my room, Stan opens the door for me and says, "Get some rest. The Major will be by to see you later today when he returns. Good to have you back!"

"Thanks, Stan. See you around."

Entering my room, I notice several letters and some small packages stacked on my nightstand. I hadn't received any mail while I was in the hospital down in Da Nang. The Company mail clerk kept all of it for me, as opposed to forwarding it on. Mail in this country sometimes has a way of getting misplaced or lost. He did me a favor by keeping it here instead of forwarding it on. Besides, most of the time I was in the hospital, my eyes were bandaged and of no use. Stretching out on my cot, I spend the rest of the afternoon catching up on mail. I save Sandy's latest tape for last and begin listening to her.

"Dearest Taylor, I miss you. R&R can't get here soon enough. I'm counting the weeks until we're together again. Things here are okay. Nothing really new to mention. It's been another pretty good day at school. The kids are listening to me a lot better lately, though they can still give me a headache. I have one now, but it gives me more incentive to teach them when I can motivate their desire to learn something. When they respond better, I teach better. If they tune me out for any reason, I'm not teaching them; I'm just babysitting them!

I received your latest tape yesterday, and you really sounded tired, but okay. The news has slowed down considerably about

Laos and moved on to other activities in the Saigon area. From what little you tell me, it sounds like you're not flying much around that area anymore. I sure hope so. From what we heard and saw on TV, that Laos' operation wasn't very successful and cost many men their lives. It may not be my place to question why, but I would like to know for what purpose they died?

What's this about guys who participated in the invasion of Laos getting to come home earlier? I heard from one of our friends there is a rumor to that effect going around. Let's hope it's true.

Angus just crawled up here on the bed with me and gave me a kiss. I'm lying on my side while dictating this, and he's trying to help. I'll see if I can get him to bark for you. I don't know what is so interesting for him, but he now has his nose right in my face and is trying to lick the microphone. What a pleasure he is to have here with me. It would be perfect if you were here too. Only a short time to go, and I'll not only hear "I love you" but be able to see it in your eyes, and feel you next to me! It's going to be so good to have you here with me!"

There's a knock on my door. I stop the tape and yell out, "Come in!"

In walks the Major. I start to get up when the Major says, "Relax, Taylor. Stay where you are. I just wanted to stop by and see how you're doing. Everything alright?"

Not feeling comfortable with lying on my cot, I sit up. "I'm doing okay, sir, thanks for asking."

He walks over to my desk, pulls out the chair, and takes a seat. "Stan tells me your eyes are good, and you were cleared by the Flight Surgeon to go back on flight status. You good with that?"

"Yes, sir. I'm ready. What's our operational status now, given the situation up north? Stan mentioned we are closing down Khe

Sanh and repositioning ARVN units around Quang Tri Province, and the 101st was redeploying back into our AO."

The Major, in a matter-of-fact voice, says, "That's it pretty much in a nutshell. It's been quiet the last few days, and Division is not expecting anything serious to happen right away. It seems we did a lot of damage to many of the NVA units that came out to fight. That's the good news. The bad news is they're a tough adversary and very serious about continuing the fight. We fully expect them to regroup and move south, probably back through the A Shau Valley again and across the DMZ."

Jokingly I respond, "I wasn't expecting them to pack it in and go home!"

"You got that right! Well, unless you have any questions for me, I've got one item to cover with you," the Major says.

"No, sir, I can't think of any right now."

The Major stands up and looking directly at me, with a big smile on his face, and says, "Good. I've taken the liberty of accelerating your R&R to Hawaii by a few weeks. You leave early tomorrow morning for Saigon. I'll take you over to the Phu Bai Tower area in the morning so you can catch your C-130 flight to Saigon. You're booked on a 747 flying out of Saigon to Hawaii late tomorrow afternoon. You have a room at the Royal Hawaiian Hotel, and Sandy will meet you at the Honolulu airport. I think that about covers it."

I leap from my cot with a spontaneous reaction, grab the Major's hand tightly, and shake it vigorously. I'm on the verge of being overcome with emotion. This was totally unexpected and most assuredly welcomed.

Looking directly at the Major and still shaking his hand, I say, "Thank you, sir. I don't know what to say or how I can ever thank you. Damn, this is great." I finally release the Major's hand and slowly step back, thinking to myself, *Oh my god, I've overreacted and just made a damn fool of myself.*

The Major, sensing my embarrassment, simply says, "That's alright, son, you deserve this. I'll see you off in the morning. Enjoy your R&R in Hawaii, and please give my best to your wife when you see her!" As the Major leaves the room, I set about packing for my trip as if I were a schoolboy going off to summer camp again.

# CHAPTER 32

## HAWAII-R&R

I'm flying in a luxurious 747 jetliner, enjoying the view and the beverage cart service. We are just a few hours from landing in Honolulu. To pass the remaining few hours, I decide to make an entry in my diary. The last thirty-six hours have gone by very quickly and once again seem like a big blur. My excitement about meeting Sandy is almost too much to bear. I can feel her in my arms and already see that beautiful smile of hers. *Come on, my fellow pilots, pour on the jet fuel into those four great big jet engines of yours, and let's pick up the pace.* I order another drink, take the diary out of my travel bag, and proceed to write an entry.

APRIL 1971

It has been a busy two days, and I'm very excited about spending five days with Sandy. This is going to be terrific! I feel like a kid again waiting for Christmas morning.

We're about two hours out from landing at the Honolulu Airport in Hawaii, where Sandy is waiting for me. Currently, I'm quite tired. I haven't been able to get much sleep since I was told about my R&R. I've been so anxious to be with Sandy and hold her in my arms again that all I do is think about it. It makes it tough to sleep.

Major Breckenridge surprised me with this early R&R when I got back to the Company from the 95th Evacuation Hospital in Da Nang. I was on the list to go to Hawaii within the next 30-45 days. The Major took it upon himself, with the help of our Company First Sergeant, to set up this whole thing and accelerate my R&R. I've only been in the Army now for a little over three years and have been around many career Officers and NCOs. He and Major Hutchins are cut from the same cloth. Both are men of character and courage, and they lead. I've been fortunate to have served with both of them.

Early yesterday morning, the Major took me to the Phu Bai terminal and saw me off on an Air Force C-130 flight to the Tan Son Nhut Air Base near Saigon. It was an uneventful flight down there, but we landed in one hell of a thunderstorm. It was a little concerning and made for a bumpy landing.

After landing, we were taken to the main terminal, where I checked in and settled down to wait for the call to board my aircraft. The lounge was a good place to wait, and to my surprise, they had many various brands of beer. Several Army guys were waiting in the lounge who were also going to Hawaii on R&R. I hooked up with a few. We enjoyed each other's company as we downed a few beers.

After being in Vietnam for over six months and living under very basic and crude conditions up north, the area down there seemed like paradise. It was like being back in the States at a major military Air Force or Army base with all the facilities that go with them. It didn't seem like we were in a war zone while I was there. Everyone I saw and interacted with was relaxed and didn't seem concerned about being attacked or rocketed. I could get used to that very quickly. I guess if I thought about it much, I could become pretty bitter about having to live like we do up north. We get shot at all the time and are still fighting this damn war. President Nixon can't turn this war over to the South Vietnamese fast enough for me. It's time to go home and end this madness.

I'm going to stop now. They just announced we're coming into Honolulu and will be landing shortly. I hope these next five days go by very slowly. I want to enjoy every moment with Sandy. God, I love her! It's going to be tough on both of us when I have to get on that plane headed back to Vietnam. But I'll do it, and we'll make it.

I love you Sandy.

A fter landing and taxiing to the gate, the pilot announces over the intercom they will be opening the doors momentarily and welcomes us to Honolulu, Hawaii. I gather up my belongings and wait anxiously for my turn to stand in the aisle and walk forward to the exit. They're moving too slowly for me. *Don't these people know I haven't seen my wife in over six months? They need to hurry the hell up and let me get off this damn plane!*

After walking down the ramp from the airplane and across the tarmac, I find myself in the concourse area. What seemed like an eternity was only a few minutes. Sandy sees me first and begins a dash toward me. Seeing her in the crowd, waving and moving toward me, I rush to meet her. As we reach each other, I drop my travel bag, tightly embrace Sandy, pick her up off her feet, and spin her around while giving her a long kiss. Oblivious to the people around us, we are swept up in the moment. We slowly draw back from one another enough to look into each other's eyes.

Sandy, with tears streaming down her cheeks, says, "Oh honey. Taylor, my god, how I've missed you!"

With one hand gently brushing her hair back, I wipe the tears from her cheeks. "Lord, how I missed you, Sandy. I can't begin to tell you how much I've looked forward to this moment. God, I love you!"

Once again, we tightly embrace and kiss. Then Sandy draws back from me and looks straight into my eyes. Then directs her gaze at the rows of medals on the summer uniform I'm wearing and then back into my eyes. With a quizzical look on her face and in a calm, questioning voice says. "I thought you weren't flying any dangerous missions! I'm no medal expert, but it looks to me like you've got quite a few of them on your chest. Where'd they all come from?"

Pulling her close to me again and feeling the warmth of her body next to mine, I respond. "I've been meaning to tell you but didn't know how. We'll talk about it later. We'll have plenty of time to talk. Right now, I have other things on my mind."

Sandy pulls back some and, looking at me with her longing eyes, says. "What could possibly be on your mind TJ? Don't think you're going to get out of talking. You made a promise, and I'm holding you to it."

"I did make a promise, and I will stick to it. Now let's get the hell out of here!"

Picking up my travel bag and holding Sandy close to my side, we walk through the terminal on our way to the baggage claim area. On our way, many of the people we pass look over at us. *Sandy is a stunning young lady and can turn heads. They're damn sure not looking at me.*

While waiting on the bags, I mention to Sandy, "Once I get my bags, I want to go rent a car. Do you think they have any convertible Corvettes or Shelby Mustangs?"

Sandy, smiling, looks at me and responds, "Taylor, dear... no, they don't. Sorry, I already checked. However, we do have a convertible car that I rented before you arrived."

"Really. Well, what'd you get?"

Sandy responds, "I think you'll like it. It's a 1971 Plymouth Cuda convertible, red..."

Sandy doesn't finish her comment when, without thinking about who I'm talking to, I blurt out, "No shit!"

Sandy responds without hesitation, "No shit! Is that enough of a muscle car for you?"

"That should do quite nicely. Well done, my love!" That rates another hug and a kiss. Out of the corner of my eye, I catch an older couple smiling at us. *I bet they're thinking, why don't those folks just get a room?*

After retrieving my bags, we head for the parking lot. With the same anticipation a high school teenager might have for a muscle car experience, I'm anxious to see the vehicle. Walking up to the car, I'm not at all disappointed. Looking at Sandy with an adoring look of appreciation, I say, "Well done...Well done!"

"Thought you might like it!" Sandy responds as she climbs in while I throw my bags in the trunk. Climbing in the car and settling in behind the wheel is almost like an out-of-body experience. It takes a minute to settle in as I'm looking for the cyclic, collective, and foot pedals. Once I realize it's a car and not a Huey, I regain my senses and fire her up. The sweet sound of a muscle car is something to behold. I push down on the pedal, and we take off for The Royal Hawaiian Hotel, where Sandy has already checked us in.

The Royal Hawaiian Hotel is a beachfront luxury hotel on Waikiki Beach in Honolulu. When you step out on the back terrace, you're looking at a beautiful white sandy beach, with long rolling waves coming in to rest on the beach. There's blue water, cool breezes, and the iconic Diamond Head off in the distance to the left of the hotel. The hotel opened in 1927, and with the unique bright pink hue of its concrete stucco, it earned the nickname "The Pink Palace of the Pacific." During WWII, The Royal Hawaiian was used exclusively by the US military as an R&R center. I think to myself as we walk through the lobby and out to the terrace with its stunning views. *I can get used to this real quick. Look at those waves. I wonder if Sandy will let me surf.*

Once in our room, I hang a sign on the door which reads, "Do Not Disturb," and then close the door and lock it. We are not seen again until the next day.

The following morning, we are lying in bed with our arms wrapped around each other and resting after having made love throughout the night. Our room is three stories up and has a beautiful view of the ocean. We left our doors open slightly to the balcony to enjoy the fresh sea air and hear the waves rolling onto the beach. Sandy looks at me with satisfaction and love in her eyes and says, "It's been a long time. God, what a night. You haven't lost your touch!"

Responding softly, "Neither have you, honey. The last twelve hours with you have been fantastic. You're my love; you're my life. I can't imagine living without you!"

Sandy can't help but be drawn to me again and rolls over on top of my body, and begins running her hands over me as she kisses me. I can't help but respond to her advances, and we make love again while we enjoy the fresh Hawaiian sea breeze and sounds of waves in the distance.

Later that afternoon, we are lying on the beach, watching the waves roll in. Surfers and outrigger canoes catch the waves out past the sandbars and ride them well into the beach area. I have been trying my best to convince Sandy that I should rent a board and show these folks how it's done. She is unrelenting, and I have to settle for taking her out on an outrigger canoe with me.

Neither one of us has ever ridden one before, but it proves to be an exhilarating experience for both of us. I find it like the thrill of catching and riding a wave into the beach, with one difference. With a surfboard, you must paddle out through the breaking waves by yourself to get far enough out to turn your board toward the beach and catch a wave. With the outrigger canoe, you have six people sitting in the narrow canoe, with one behind the other. The person in the back is your steerer, who is responsible for catching a wave and keeping you on course to the beach. The other five folks are the paddlers. Their job is to power the canoe through the breaking waves on the way out. On the way back, they help build up the canoe's speed until a wave takes over and propels it toward the beach. Sandy and I enjoyed it so much we went back several times.

That evening, we have dinner and some drinks at the Royal Hawaiian's oceanfront restaurant and bar. It's a beautiful moonlit evening, with waves rolling onto the beach and a cool, fresh ocean breeze. After dinner, I take Sandy, and we go for a long walk along the shore hand in hand, conversing as we stroll.

"Taylor, what's it like over there? What's really going on? I can tell from your reactions to noises, strange sounds, and your constant looking around that you're on edge and not really relaxed ...."

I stop and turn Sandy to look at me. The moonlight silhouettes her, and I can see in her eyes the look of concern. "Sandy, I've wanted to share with you many times some of what I've been going through, but I just don't know how. Where do I start? What do I say? How do I say it? When do I stop? This much, I do know. It's not like anything I expected."

Sandy looking up at me, responds, "We promised each other

never to hold back anything. Never to keep anything from each other. What do you mean by it's not what you expected?"

We turn back to looking down the shoreline and continue our walk on the beach, holding hands. "Before I left for Nam, I had heard all kinds of stories about the place. I didn't know what to believe or not believe. Hell, I'm not sure anymore what I even expected."

After a long pause and searching for the words to say, I continue. "When I was a senior in High School, I lost a good friend who had gone into the Army after graduating the year before me. He was killed over there. Until his death, I had never heard of Vietnam. From then on, it's been like a bad dream I can never shake. All through college, like everyone else, I lived in fear of being drafted. As soon as I graduated, they drafted me. Then, over the next two and a half years, I kept volunteering for every Army school I could, in the hope that damn war would end. It didn't, and now I'm over there. This has been no way to live."

Looking out over the ocean with the moonlight reflecting off the surface, I feel a sense of melancholia taking over. I do my best to subdue this feeling as we continue down the beach without talking for a short distance. Thinking I have it under control, I continue. "I know this much. I find it hard to believe and harder to understand what's going on over there, and I'm living it."

Sandy, sensing my sadness, and struggling efforts to open up to her, stops abruptly. She turns to look into my eyes and, pulling me close to her, says, "Talk to me, honey. I'm here. Talk to me."

In a hesitant voice, and searching to find the words to say, I respond. "You fight everything. The heat. The humidity. The bugs. The filth. The boredom. And the North Vietnamese and Viet Cong. Hell, some of us even fight each other. And for what? Why? I can't figure it out. I may never understand it."

With Sandy's encouragement, I'm finding it easier to talk to her and continue in a subdued voice. "I didn't tell you I was flying dangerous missions because I didn't want to add to your worry about me. I've certainly flown them. Several, in fact. Christ, I don't have a choice. I've got to do what I'm told. I don't like it worth a damn. It all seems like such a waste. Sandy, when I'm flying, I'm scared as hell. I'd be crazy if I weren't! And when I'm not flying, I live in fear of flying the next mission. God, I hate it over there!"

We resume strolling along the beach, hand in hand, as I tell her about some of my missions into Laos, the loss of Major Hutchins, and my roommate Scott. I also share with Sandy some of the highlights from my ordeal with Major Stewart. Sandy listens intently and slowly becomes more emotional, demoralized, and dejected. Sensing that I've gone too far with my candor, I bring the conversation to a close by asking her some questions. What is going on at home? How is the war playing there?

Sandy shares some of the news from back home involving the Vietnam War. She tells me that returning veterans are coming home to a nation divided. There are no parades, welcoming committees, or cheering crowds greeting them at airports or other ports of entry. Soldiers returning home from Vietnam are entering a country that is indifferent to them. Many times, disrespectful, and even hostile toward them. There has been a discernible shift in public opinion from rejection of the war to a rejection of the men fighting the war. Now it was my turn to be demoralized and dejected.

We have strolled up and down the beach for some time in silence, not wanting the evening to end or our time together in Hawaii to come to a close. Approaching the beach in front of the Royal Hawaiian, Sandy stops and clings to me, and won't let go. We stand there in a tight embrace with waves slowly rolling up onto the beach. A slight sea breeze washes over us while a bright moonlit night, with a heaven full of stars, shines above. We are frozen in time and don't want the moment to end.

Over the next three days, we spend our time wisely and visit many iconic locations around Honolulu. We go out each evening for dinner and some dancing. Driving our rented 1971 Plymouth Cuda, we visit Tantalus Lookout with its stunning panoramic views of Honolulu, Pearl Harbor, and Diamond Head. We drive over to Hanauma Bay Nature Preserve, where we enjoy the beach and snorkeling. One beautiful morning, we hike up Diamond Head Crater and enjoy more stunning views of Honolulu and the ocean. We visit the Punch Bowl, which is the location of the National Memorial Cemetery of the Pacific, and pay our respects to the men and women who are buried there.

Our most extended trip is out to the North Shore. Here we visit Waimea Bay, the Banzai Pipeline, and manage to get some beach time. While visiting that area, one of the local Hawaiians points out Elvis Presley's Estate on a hill overlooking Waimea Bay.

I particularly enjoyed this excursion as it allowed me to run the Plymouth Cuda and observe some incredible waves. It would have been fantastic had we run into Elvis, but we didn't. Maybe another time and place. We had a terrific time the entire day, and for the first time since arriving in Hawaii, I didn't think about Nam.

When our last day in Hawaii arrived, we were struck by how quickly our time together had passed. No matter how hard I tried to live these past five days in slow motion, they sped by in a flash. We resolved that nothing would prevent us from enjoying every minute of our last day together in paradise. After breakfast at the hotel, we went for a short swim on the beach, then headed over to the International Market Place for a light lunch and some shopping. From there, we drove to Pearl Harbor and the USS Arizona Memorial.

Our visit to the USS Arizona Memorial was a very somber and emotional experience for both of us. I grew up surrounded by

WWII veterans of the Pacific and European Theaters of war. These men are my heroes. I respect and admire them for what they did and the sacrifices they made. Sandy had an uncle who served in the Navy and was at Pearl Harbor on the USS Oklahoma that fateful morning. He survived the attack but was killed in the Battle of Midway.

The short ride on a Navy launch over to the USS Arizona Memorial is a very sobering experience as you think of the men who rest there eternally within the Battleship's hull. Many of them were still in their bunks or just starting to prepare for the day when it all came to a sudden and traumatic end. A Japanese bomb hit the main deck and penetrated several decks down to an ammunition magazine, which exploded violently, taking the lives of 1,177 officers and crewmen.

Arriving at the USS Arizona Memorial, we disembark the launch and move up the ramp to the Memorial, built across the ship's sunken remains. In the late 1950s, plans took shape to build the Memorial, and to raise the $500,000 that was needed so that it could be built. By 1960, less than half had been raised. Things changed when Elvis Presley performed a benefit concert for the Memorial on March 25, 1961. His concert raised over $54,000, and Elvis made a separate donation. His actions drew new attention to the USS Arizona Memorial, and more money poured in from private and public donors. The Memorial was soon built, and was dedicated on May 30, 1962.

In the back of the Memorial is a shrine room listing all the names of the lost crew members on a marble wall. From inside this area, you can look down on the ship and see small oil slicks still emerging from the ship's hull. Some say they are tears of the men who eternally rest inside the ship. Sandy and I move into this area and take it all in. This moment can be overpowering, and many people there are struggling to keep their emotions under control.

Standing together and looking at the names on the marble wall, Sandy says, "The names of all those men—all those names—my god!"

She turns to look at me with tears streaming from her eyes and continues, "You have to promise me you'll come back to me. I don't want your name on the wall of some memorial. I want you! Promise me! Promise me!"

*What can I say?*

# CHAPTER 33

## RETURN TO PHU BAI

I departed Honolulu on the evening of my last day of R&R, after visiting Pearl Harbor. Sandy drove me to the airport, where we both had a difficult time parting. I was the last person to walk out to the plane and up the steps to board. Turning to look back at Sandy for what could be my last time was heart-wrenching. We have endured many hardships since my deployment to Vietnam. Although I only have five months left on my tour, this was like starting all over again. I feel for Sandy. She is not leaving for San Diego until tomorrow morning and will be returning to an empty hotel room. This will be very difficult for her.

I left Honolulu on a luxurious Pan American 747 and flew back to Tan Son Nhut Air Base. From there, I caught a flight to Da Nang on an Air Force C-130. Not exactly a 747; no room, no beverage cart, no pillow, no stewardesses, and not very comfortable. Due to harsh weather, our C-130 was grounded and not able to continue to Phu Bai. The weather eventually cleared enough to reopen Phu Bai's airfield, and I was able to catch a ride back to my Company on a Chinook. My return to Vietnam was an exhaustive thirty-six-hour trip.

*Nothing's changed here. Welcome back to Vietnam.*

This whole time all I could think about was Sandy and how precious those last few moments were with her in my arms. It was very emotional for us both as we clung to each other until the gate attendants insisted I board the aircraft. My last visual of Sandy was of her crying, and her last words to me continue to haunt my thoughts. *Come back to me, come back to me. I love you!*

My trip over to Hawaii was exciting, as I couldn't get there fast enough. My journey back to Nam was a real downer!

The Chinook pilots, Richard and Alan, flying me back to Phu Bai, are good guys whose company I enjoy. Once airborne and clear of Da Nang airspace, I'm invited to join them in the cockpit area and observe. Chinook helicopters are enormous, quite fast, and have twin turbojet engines that produce considerable power. Some of their vital systems are dual, which provides back-up if they lose one. If my Huey were a Corvette, their Chinook would be a Rolls Royce Silver Shadow.

Landing in Phu Bai, we taxi over to their Company area and shut down. After performing their post-flight procedures, Richard and Alan are kind enough to give me a ride back to my Company. After a brief conversation, we shake hands and part company, agreeing to meet sometime at the Pilots Club.

As they drive off, I head straight to Major Breckenridge's office to report back. Walking through the trailer toward the Major's office, we meet as he's headed out for a briefing at Battalion. Turning around to join him, we briefly converse while walking out of the trailer together, heading for his jeep. He gives me the afternoon off to rest and asks that I join him for dinner later that evening. Climbing into his jeep, he casually mentions that he's assigned me a new roommate and suggests bringing him along tonight.

Entering my room, I notice something different about it and wonder who the new guy is. It doesn't take long to find out. After unpacking and laying down on my cot for a quick nap, the door to the room swings open. In walks a tall, lanky, dark-haired Lieutenant carrying his flight gear. Noticing me stretched out on my cot, he stops, throws his gear on a chair, and introduces himself. "Captain St. James, I'm Lieutenant William Connelly—I go by Bill."

Standing up, I extend my hand, "It's nice to meet you. Please call me Taylor or TJ. We'll just keep this informal, okay, Bill?"

As we shake hands, Bill says, "Not a problem. So, you just got back from R&R? How was it?"

"Too damn short. Other than that, it was great! Right now, if you don't mind, I need to get a little rest. It's been a long trip back."

Bill says, "Not a problem, I've got some errands to run, so you can have the room to yourself. I'll see you later tonight."

"Thanks, Bill. Oh, I'm having dinner with the Major, and he suggested you join us. Is that good for you?"

"Sure, about what time?" Bill responds as he heads for the door.

"About 1800. And would you wake me up about thirty minutes before then? I'm not sure I can trust myself to wake up in time."

Bill, looking back, says, "Not a problem. See you then."

That evening over dinner, Bill, the Major, and I, enjoy a light meal and some casual conversation. Early into our conversation, the Major asks how my R&R went and how Sandy was. I thank him again for his assistance in arranging it for us. I tell him Sandy sends her love and appreciation to him for what he did for both of us. I then share some of our highlights while in Hawaii on R&R. That place is a real paradise.

Bill enjoys our company. As the evening progresses, Bill

senses a strong bond has developed between the Major and me, one he hopes to emulate. Major Breckenridge is a good man. Bill should not have a problem bonding if he does his job and earns the Major's respect.

Our conversation slowly drifts toward the current situation in our AO and what might be headed our way. Looking over at Bill, the Major says, "Lieutenant, why don't you share with the Captain some of your background and how you got here."

Turning to look at me and with a business-like tone, Bill shares his story. "Well, Taylor, I just reported here yesterday. I've been with a Huey unit down south in the Mekong Delta area for the last six months. They stood down our unit last week, and those who had less than two months left in the country were sent home. The rest of us were reassigned to units located up in this area of operations. President Nixon has accelerated the draw-down of troops from Vietnam, particularly down in that area."

Pausing momentarily, he continues in a calmer voice, "Since being in Vietnam, I've managed to accumulate over five hundred flight hours and have been an AC for the last two months. However, all my flying experience up til now has been over flat land and wetlands. No mountains, hills, or valleys. Much of the terrain up here is different than down that way."

I respond, "We have that kind of terrain up here from the coastline inward several miles. Just on the other side of this base, you can see the hills and mountains in the distance. That's the location of many of the LZs we work with, and of course, it's the location of the infamous A Shau Valley. Flying in this area may require a few more skill sets, but I'm sure you'll pick them up quickly."

The Major cuts in, and looking at me, says, "Taylor, glad you mentioned that! I want you and Bill to fly together over the next few days so you can bring him up to speed. Is that okay with you two fellows?"

We both nod in the affirmative and the Major continues. "Taylor, it's been pretty quiet in the 101st Division AO for now. We've been busy repositioning troops and fortifying the LZs scattered around Camps Eagle and Evans and the mountain tops along the A Shau Valley. Those firebases are our main line of defensive protection. They also supply some for the ARVN forces. The South Vietnamese are taking over responsibility for the territory stretching from Camp Evans north to the DMZ. We are now out of the Khe Sanh and Quang Tri areas. All of that now belongs to our ARVN friends."

The Major pauses, and I take the opportunity to ask, "Major, are they ready for that? Laos was a disaster for them, and now they are going to take on all that responsibility? Are they being reinforced with fresh troops and hopefully some better combat leaders from the south?"

Bill has been listening intently and has grown more apprehensive about his new Division and our AO. He'd heard many dismal stories, while down south, about the Laos Operation and the poor performance of many of the South Vietnamese soldiers who participated in it. He doesn't feel good about what he's hearing.

The Major responds to me, "Well, we've been told the official version of the Laos operation is that it was a success, and the South Vietnamese are fully capable of taking on more of the fight. Unofficially, it was a rout and could have been a total disaster except for our helicopter pilots and their crews keeping them in the fight and getting them out of there as it became a total retreat. Maybe someday they'll make a movie about it. For now, we're still living through it and having to deal with whatever comes our way."

Upon finishing dinner and our conversation, the Major closes with, "Taylor, you might like to know that they completed Major Stewart's inquiry, and it wasn't good for him. He is being sent back to the States where he will be released from the service, on an "other than honorable discharge"! Whatever career he thought he had; it's gone."

Responding in a matter-of-fact voice, "I can't feel sorry for him. He really screwed things up around here for many of us."

The Major stands to leave, "I agree. Get some rest, fellows. You'll be needing it."

Over the next three days, Bill and I fly missions together to acquaint him with his new area of operations. I make sure to give him as much experience as possible flying in mountain terrain and around the valleys in our area. During this time, I record our daily activities in my diary.

MAY 1971

I flew 7 hours today with Bill, my new roommate. He is a First Lieutenant who was reassigned to our Company a few days ago, after his unit was disbanded under Nixon's plan to turn the war over to the South Vietnamese. He was flying down in the Mekong Delta area. The tempo of turning the war over to the South Vietnamese is picking up. But, from what we hear in our area, we'll be some of the last units to return home. The war still goes on in this part of the country. Just my luck!

I enjoy flying with Bill. He has a good head on his shoulders and has accumulated considerable hours of stick time. Not to mention, he is AC qualified. This time, I'm not breaking a new guy into the Company. I'm acquainting an experienced pilot with the area we fly in—a little less stress.

We flew several missions into LZ T-bone, delivering supplies and some fresh troops during the day. They have been beefing up all our firebases located out some distance from Camp Eagle and

Camp Evans. I think we are in for some more fighting. While working this firebase today, we observed a Chinook doing what they call "flame drops." This entails the Chinook carrying an external sling load of several 55-gallon drums filled with fougasse below their aircraft. Fougasse is a form of jellied gasoline, like napalm. It's highly flammable and can wreak havoc wherever it's dropped.

The Chinook, in a sense, acts like a bomber. It stays high and hovers over a designated target on the ground. When lined up over their target, they release the net holding the barrels. After the barrels hit the ground, a Cobra accompanying them rolls in, firing some of their rockets. When the rockets hit the barrels, the whole area goes up in a giant fireball. It looks like it could be fun, but I would hate to be flying one of those missions if they start taking fire. It could be a terrible situation if the barrels are hit. As the saying goes, "the worm will have turned." But, having said that, it was fun to watch them work. They were doing those flame drops all afternoon to clear the area around Firebase T-bone.

After we finished flying for the day, I took Bill to the Pilots Club and introduced him to Greg and some of his pilots. We all had a few beers and enjoyed each other's company. I believe Bill is going to fit in well and get along with everybody. I just hope I don't lose another friend over here.

I love you Sandy.


MAY 1971

Bill and I flew together again today and logged 8 hours. Most of our time today involved flying in and out of Firebase Capone. It is in the A Shau Valley on top of a 5,000-foot-high mountain. The view looking out into the valley is beautiful. But what evil lurks down there?

The weather was clear all day. However, on top of the mountain, we encountered some rough updrafts and downdrafts, making it hard for us to close in on short final and land. In this situation, you find yourself constantly adjusting your collective. If you're caught in an updraft, you push down on your collective, trying to keep from going up. If you're caught in a downdraft, you pull up on the collective to keep from dropping further. While you're playing with your collective, you have to keep pressure on your foot pedals and constantly move your cyclic to try and keep your nose into the wind. Flying in these conditions is very tricky, stressful, and can be deadly.

It's pretty easy to take off from up there, particularly with an updraft. But it can be a real pain in the ass to try and land with high winds. Needless to say, Bill got a chance to practice his mountain flying techniques.

Again, we flew in supplies and additional troops. Like we witnessed yesterday, a Chinook was doing flame drops around this Firebase much of the day. Firebase Capone sits on top of the mountain and has steep slopes extending out on all sides of the LZ. The vegetation and tree lines are about a hundred yards down those slopes, and this is where the Chinook concentrated their flame drops.

As we were finishing our last drop and headed home, we got an emergency call for a Medevac from Firebase Bastone. Two men were severely wounded by mortar rounds that landed inside Bastone's perimeter. We weren't too far from there and covered the distance quickly. As we closed in on their location, we could see they were still under mortar attack. It seemed to be sporadic and not well placed.

The Commander on the ground said his men were in bad shape and needed a MASH unit quickly. He wasn't sure where the mortar rounds were coming from but had requested artillery fire to be placed on several areas around his location. The barrage was to start any minute, and he advised us to wait until it was lifted. We didn't need any convincing. The last thing we wanted to do was fly in there while they were still receiving incoming rounds.

We informed him to have his men ready for us, as we would come in right after the artillery was lifted and the mortar rounds stopped. Once the ground Commander gave us the go-ahead, I had Bill take us in. Much to our relief, we were able to get in and out quickly without incident. We flew the two men back to the MASH unit at Phu Bai. When we got back to the Company, I checked to see if the men had made it. Good news. They both did and are going home because of the severity of their wounds. It's been another exhaustive day of flying, and I'm wiped out. No drinking tonight. It's early to bed.

I love you Sandy

## MAY 1971

This was an awfully long and frustrating day. Bill and I flew together again today for 3 hours. We were tasked with flying four soldiers to Da Nang for a special disciplinary hearing. I had no idea what it was for. A First Sergeant accompanied them, and all four men had their personal belongings with them. When we landed at Marble Mountain in Da Nang, we were met by several U. S. Army Military Police (MP) waiting on them. They had some drug dogs with them. As the men were getting off our chopper, the dogs got a hit on one of them. In short, one of those guys had several vials of heroin hidden inside his shaving kit.

As the AC, I was instructed to shut down our Huey. The crew and I were then taken to an MP building and subjected to several hours of questioning by some MP investigators. The Vietnamese and American military have been dealing with a drug problem for a while, and it has grown worse the longer this war has gone on. They have been running targeted and random drug searches, and we got caught in one. It seems these four idiots were into selling drugs. How that involved us in this situation escapes me.

We were not treated well, and it seemed as if they were trying to connect us somehow with this situation. It didn't take long for me to get pissed, and I jumped all over the Captain running the show. He called a Colonel, who jumped all over me when he arrived. In short, I told them, unless they were going to charge me with something, I was taking my crew back to Phu Bai. They could call any of my Commanders they wanted, as I had had enough of their inquisition. With that, I gathered up the men, and we flew back to home base. Arriving back at the Company, I was met by the Major and our Battalion Commander. We talked briefly about the situation. They enjoyed my story and even got a few good laughs from it. I was told not to worry about it and was given a cigar from the Colonel. End of story.

I love you, Sandy.

After writing my latest diary entry, I turn my attention to a letter from Sandy. It was on my desk when I returned from flying today. This is my first correspondence from her since returning to the Company. I miss her terribly as I struggle to regain the mindset of a combat pilot. There is no room over here for thoughts about home, wives, girlfriends, and family members when you're flying. You must stay focused and concentrate on your missions. If you don't, it could prove deadly for you and your crew.

I learned very quickly after arriving in Vietnam to live my

days in airtight compartments. It did not come easily, but proved very valuable and helped me to get through rough days. Thoughts of the war and what I had to endure daily receded from my mind during R&R with Sandy. That was the good news. The bad news is, I'm back in Vietnam and have to get my compartmental mindset back. With it, I may be able to deal with whatever comes my way until I catch the "Freedom Bird" home.

Stretching out on my cot, I open Sandy's letter and read it.

MY DEAREST TAYLOR,

Just a short letter to let you know, I'm back in our apartment in San Diego. Your parents met me at the airport and brought me home, fed me, and helped me get settled back in. They sure make it easier for me to deal with the loneliness and separation issues that come up. They are great in-laws.

God, I miss you, and it's only been a few days since we were together. After watching you walk up the stairs to the airplane and disappear inside, I couldn't bear it and just started to cry. It took a while, but I got it together enough to find the car and go back to the hotel. That wasn't any better, though, because I kept thinking you were right around every corner. Of course, you weren't. And that just made me cry again. It was an emotional roller coaster until I got on the plane to come home. I couldn't just sit there for hours crying on the airplane, so I did the best I could to keep a happy face.

If we ever do this again, I get to leave first!

I've been doing nothing but thinking about you constantly since we parted. I always think about you every day, but it just seems that no matter where I am or what I'm doing since we parted, you are on my mind. I love you so much. Seeing you for those five days in Hawaii surely did help me. I hope it did you as much good as it did me.

It seems as if I didn't get to say I love you enough while we were together. Come to think of it, I guess I could never say it enough. I tried to show you while we were together. I hope the message got through. Honey, you're the best husband anyone could ever have.

I finished taking pictures on our last roll of film and will be taking all the rolls in for development. Shouldn't take too long, so be patient! Angus was glad to see me when I got back. Your parents took good care of him while I was away. I think your Dad spoiled him some more, as if that's even possible.

This past week with you has been terrific, but I've been running on pure adrenaline, and it's about to come crashing down. I'm taking a few days off from school and catching up on my rest. Then I'm back in the game.

I'm going to close for now and get this in the mail. Take care of yourself and don't worry about us.

All my love, I miss you.

Your loving wife,
Sandy.

I can smell the scent of Sandy in her letter. Her sweet aroma and the words she wrote move me to tears, and my mood becomes quite melancholy. As if on autopilot, I get back up, put on my flight clothes, and head over to the Pilots Club for some company and a few beers. Lord knows I'm not the only man over here dealing with this sense of loneliness. Since misery tends to love company, going to the club might help me temporarily subdue my feelings of self-pity.

Arriving at the club, I have no problem finding Bill, Stan, and Greg with some of his pilots, and I join them. Light conversations and beer drinking ensue.

Greg, with a grin and some mischief in his voice, says, "TJ, how was your Hawaiian vacation, and how's Sandy doing?"

Looking over at Greg, I reply. "Before I answer that, I've been meaning to ask you if you ever hooked up with that nurse over at the MASH unit. So, did you?"

Greg laughing, says, "Well, a gentleman never talks about his "In like Flynn" behavior. But, yes, we did hook up. She's terrific! Maybe someday, when we get back to the States, we'll get together. One can only hope!"

Bill asks Greg what the expression "In like Flynn" means. Greg proceeds to explain that the actor Errol Flynn had a reputation for reputedly seducing women with considerable ease. This expression was coined to refer to that ability, so the story goes. This brings some laughter and a toast to Errol and Greg. After they calm down, Greg looks over at me and says, "So let's try this again. How was Hawaii?"

"It was fantastic. I'm ready to go back! What a beautiful Island. The Hawaiians were very friendly, and we had a marvelous time. And Sandy, what can I say. She's incredible!"

My response is followed by various questions from the group. "Where did you go?" "What did you do?" "How was it?" I answer them in general terms and within reason. Some things are just private. This helps me to deal with my melancholy mood as it begins to recede from my subconscious. Realizing that Greg started this line of questioning and how it was helping, I look over at Greg and nod my appreciation. As was typical of Greg, he just blurts out, "No problem, TJ!"

Later into the evening, Bill starts talking to the group about what he and I endured earlier in the day concerning our drug episode. Bill drives the conversation with me, occasionally adding my perspective. The pilots listen intently and have a tough time digesting what they're hearing. Sure, drugs are a problem over here, but we're still fighting a war. Treating men who are doing the fighting this way is difficult for us to understand and accept.

Greg brings the topic to a close with a final question to me. "TJ, Bill said you were called into Major Breckenridge's office and met with him and the Battalion Commander after you landed. Can you share anything about what happened? I think we're all a little interested in how that went."

With a smile on my face and some mild levity in my voice, I respond. "Yeah, sure. They both got a laugh out of it, and the Colonel even gave me one of his cigars. They both cautioned me about being careful and showing more respect to senior officers, no matter who they are!"

Stan asks me, "I'm curious. How'd you respond to their comments about showing respect to senior officers, or did you respond?"

Looking over at Stan and in a calm, measured voice, I respond. "Yeah, actually I did. I told them I didn't have a problem with that, but sometimes senior officers can get way out of line and show no respect for their men—case in point, Parker and the MP Colonel. He was a total jerk. Not everyone over here is a damn drug-head!"

I pause, and in a very matter of fact tone, say, "Just because I was the AC tasked with flying them to Da Nang doesn't make me responsible for those four idiots' dealing in drugs!"

Stan, in a low-key whimsical voice, says, "Okay, TJ. That pretty well covers it!"

Greg, with a smile on his face and a sense of anticipation, asks, "How'd they react to that?"

Responding with a grin, I respond, "The Colonel didn't take his cigar back." This is followed by laughter and the ceremonial beer tap in the center of our table.

# CHAPTER 34

## TYPHOON

For the past few days, the entire northern region of South Vietnam has been experiencing heavy rains and thunderstorms. The 101st Airborne Division has been advised that a typhoon will pass through our area within the next twenty-four to forty-eight hours. We are directed to prepare for the worst and hope for the best.

Major Breckenridge holds a meeting with his staff to go over the weather outlook and how he plans to deal with the storm. At this meeting, we are instructed to ensure that all necessary precautions are taken, and everything possible is done to tie down equipment and aircraft. Anything loose lying around the Company area should be gathered up and secured in our buildings. Extra water and food supplies are to be provided. Small backup generators need be available should we lose the Company's main generator, and the men should expect a few days of uncertainty due to the typhoon. During this meeting, I am directed by the Major to oversee preparations taken on the Eagles' flight line and securing of our Hueys.

Over the next few days, I record in my diary what our Company and I experience during the typhoon and its aftermath.

JUNE 1971

The weather around here has been bad for the last two days, and because of that, we've done very little flying. The Major held a staff meeting earlier today and informed us that a typhoon would blow through here sometime tomorrow. They do not expect it to be very damaging but can't be sure. Therefore, we have been ordered to prepare for the worst and do what we can to keep our Company from sustaining heavy wind damage. I've been tasked with ensuring we do our best to secure the flight line and our Hueys.

I've been in Vietnam for what seems an eternity and have experienced very poor weather and flying conditions many times. However, I wasn't aware that Vietnam was susceptible to typhoons.

It was not surprising, though, since I wasn't aware of many things about this country before I got here. The diversity of its people, which varies from well-educated to many living an agrarian lifestyle with little or no formal education. The country's geography includes tropical lowlands, rolling green hills, densely forested mountains, and coastal lowlands. Weather extremes over here range from hot and humid to cold and damp, but I haven't seen any snow yet. Their religious beliefs can include Catholicism, Buddhism, Hinduism, and Confucianism. Many Vietnamese place high importance on family and respect for their elders. Their political views are not as simple as we're led to believe. Most Vietnamese I've met impress me as people who just want to be left alone. They want to be free of foreign interference, have their own country, and many just want to live as their ancestors have for centuries.

Wow! I got a little carried away there. Back to the typhoon. I spent my day working with the men in the Maintenance Platoon and the Huey crew chiefs. We tied everything down on the flight line that we could and placed as many Hueys as possible in the hangar. We also put anything that looked like it might be blown away by the wind into the hanger and smaller company structures. The good news is, we were able to remove all loose and lightweight items to more secure locations. However, I fear that some of our structures will not hold up well if we experience sustained high winds. We could be in for quite a day tomorrow and have a mess when it's over. Since we can't control the weather, we just must deal with whatever comes our way.

I love you Sandy!

## JUNE 1971

Today has been very hectic. The typhoon hit us about mid-morning and got steadily worse. The winds were powerful and came in waves for hours on end. It's dark now, and the winds have slowed down considerably. I think the worst is over.

Earlier in the day, many of our buildings were taking a beating. Our pilots' barracks started to lose some of the metal sheeting on our roof to the winds. Several of us went out in the heavy winds and pelting rain, took sandbags from the closest bunker, and placed them on our roof. This worked okay as the roof did not lose any more metal sheeting. Many of the other barracks in the company area sustained similar damage. Sandbags were taken from bunkers all over the company area and used to hold down roofs. Now we must hope we don't have another rocket attack any time soon.

We have no power since turning off the generator earlier today. We had to do this when many of the power lines running through the Company area were blown down. I'm using candles and a flashlight to write this now. We'll probably be without power for a few days. Our room is leaking all over the place. Bill and I have been busy emptying water cans we've placed everywhere to catch it. From what I could tell late this afternoon, our hanger lost many of its metal side panels but did not collapse or do any real damage to the Hueys stored in the hanger. The Hueys we had to leave in their revetments seemed to come through the storm with little damage. Tomorrow morning at first light, we'll be doing extensive damage assessments to see where we stand. Good news, no men in our Company were hurt, but we're all tired, wet, and cold. I'm exhausted and need some rest.

I love you, Sandy!

JUNE 1971

What a day! The Company sustained a lot of wind damage. Luckily, none of our Hueys were seriously damaged, and we should be fully operational within a few days. However, we have no power as our lines are still down. They should be repaired sometime later tonight or by early morning. The few smaller generators we have for the Company were given to the mess hall and the maintenance hangar for lighting so they could work during the night. The rest of us are using candles and flashlights. All in all, it's not a bad situation, and could have been much worse.

However, our water supply is being severely limited. The main water plant that supplies Phu Bai was destroyed by the typhoon and will not be back online for several days. No showers, no washing of clothes, and only a rationed supply of drinking water for now. The mess hall must ration their limited water supply to prepare and clean pots and pans used to cook our food.

It's ironic, as there is water everywhere around here from flooding, and all we can do is look at it because we can't use it. We've been restricted from using water to shave and brush our teeth. Many of the men in the Company were looking forward to not having to shave when a temporary solution to our problem was found. Since we have an ample supply of Fresca soft drinks, we can use them to shave and brush our teeth. No one drinks the stuff in our Company anyway, so there's plenty of it around. Some fellows were disappointed about still needing to shave.

Repairs to our building structures and roofs are well underway, and we should be back to normal by sometime tomorrow evening on that front. We should have our power back on tomorrow morning at the latest, and then just deal with the water situation until it is restored.

It's been quiet around here for the last few days, given the typhoon and its aftermath. However, as always, rumors are circulating again about NVA activity. This time it involves the possibility that we may get hit by sappers in the next few days. Apparently, this typhoon and the massive flooding it caused all over the area doesn't bother them.

I'm exhausted, feel grubby, could use a shower and some hot chow, and generally just wiped out. I'm going to bed and sleep for twenty-four hours. One can dream, right? I've been up now for over forty-eight hours straight and need some rest.

I love you, Sandy!

# CHAPTER 35

## SAPPERS IN THE WIRE

Surprise attacks by North Vietnamese and South Vietnamese Communist units known as "sappers" are one of the most serious and feared threats to Americans in Vietnam. In Vietnam, we use the term sappers for Communists units that break through defensive lines using tactics similar to commando raids. Sappers have destroyed hundreds of supply and fuel depots, military bases, helicopters, and pieces of equipment, killing and wounding many troops in the process. The sappers' sudden and unexpected attacks create a fear that no place is safe, no matter how well-fortified or armed.

A sapper unit typically consists of three teams working together. One team is charged with penetrating the defensive perimeter, called the berm line, another with providing covering fire when needed, and the other is the assault team. These men are charged with destroying their chosen targets and inflicting maximum damage on soldiers operating the raided facilities. Sappers usually wear only shorts and a coat of mud or grease. Depending on their role, they could carry AK-47s, wire cutters, bamboo poles to lift barbed wire, Bangalore torpedoes, probing tools, RPGs, grenades, and scores of explosive charges.

It's been several days since the typhoon, and the Eagles have returned to normal operations. Flooding has receded, the Company area has been repaired, and is back to normal. I've been assigned the Officer of the Day (OD) duties and given some time off to relax and take care of any personal needs. This is customary when you're assigned to be the OD. This duty normally begins at 1700 hours and runs for 24 hours. All officers routinely fulfill this function while assigned to the Company.

Having been OD many times, I'm comfortable with this duty. Since we are a line combat unit, on a 24-hour, seven day a week schedule, the crux of OD duty is the overnight portion. It usually begins at dusk, runs through the night, and ends sometime after dawn.

At 1700 hours, I report to the Major for my OD assignment. Upon entering his office and rendering the customary hand salute, I'm directed to take a seat and make myself comfortable.

He begins with, "Captain, this could be a rough night. Division G-2 has reason to believe that sapper units might try and hit some of our larger base camps during the night, this being one of them. They are noticing more activity up north and around the A Shau Valley area."

The Major pauses and then continues. "I've assigned the First Sergeant to be your senior NCO tonight and three enlisted men from our security platoon to join you. Also, I'm placing the entire security platoon on the berm line tonight. They are gearing up now. As you know, we have a long section of the berm line and three guard towers to man. There should be enough men on the line to rotate them on two-hour watch shifts. I don't want anyone going to sleep out there tonight if it's their turn on watch. If we do get hit, we should be able to handle it."

Again, he pauses, and looking at me, says, "You have any questions at this point, Taylor?"

"Yes, sir, I've heard some rumors the last few days about sappers, but how credible is this information? We had these alerts many times during the Laos operation, and nothing happened!"

"This time, they believe it's very credible. There's a good chance sappers have already infiltrated the Phu Bai area over the last few days using the typhoon as a distraction."

Standing up, I begin to pace the office while talking. "Those bastards never take a timeout! Major, if it's not already being done, I would suggest we take some additional precautionary measures."

The Major, watching me pace around his office, says, "What do you have in mind?"

I stop pacing and look over at the Major. "Sir, I think we should issue weapons to all the men in the Company, particularly the maintenance crews that will be working on our Hueys tonight. We should also ensure that all lights in the Company area are turned on tonight, including the Huey revetments, staging areas, and our hangers. We need to bathe ourselves in lighting tonight."

Grinning at me, the Major responds, "Good ideas, see to it! Anything else?"

"I'm assuming that Division has plans to keep some helicopters in the air all night flying over our berm lines, and that artillery and night flare ships are on call to provide support if needed."

"They are! In fact, your buddy from the Butcher group is in charge of Cobra support for our area tonight."

"Greg. Good. We can count on him. With your permission, sir, I'm going to get some dinner and then get started!"

"I'll join you. Let's go."

After dinner, I meet with Captains Norton and Barnett,

Lieutenant Connelly, and the Maintenance Officer in the Head-quarters trailer operations room. The operations room serves as my command post for the night. I brief them on the situation with the sappers and the threat level we face, and instruct Captains Norton and Barnett to hold a meeting with all NCOs and pilots to inform them of our situation. They are also instructed to task the NCO's with informing their platoon sections of the situation, and ensure they are ready. I direct the Maintenance Officer to do the same thing with his men. After their meetings, the men are to draw their weapons with sufficient ammo. I emphasize the impor-tance of stressing to their men that we need to remain vigilant during the night.

I direct Lieutenant Connelly to ensure all lighting in the Company area is functioning and turned on before sunset. Having issued my orders, I secure a jeep from the motor pool and my weapons from the arms room. Given the threat level, I draw a .45 pistol, M-16, and M-60 machine gun. During my twelve months of Infantry training, I developed an affinity for the M-60. I have my driver mount the M-60 on our jeep, with a full belt of ammunition attached to the gun mount along with extra ammo cans.

Satisfied with the extent of preparations for the night, the First Sergeant and I drive out to the berm line. I want to inspect the security platoon's status and readiness. The Company's section of the berm line is over 300 yards long with three twenty-foot-high guard towers. These towers are evenly spaced along the line. Each tower is operated by three men on top and a machine gun crew of three men at the bottom. A searchlight is mounted on top of each tower which gives the crews an ability to illuminate areas out in front of their positions. The remaining men are staggered along the berm line in bunkers between towers, with three men assigned to each. Every position must always have one man awake and on watch for no more than two hours at a time. This should give each man a chance to rest between watches and hopefully provide a more effective defense against sappers.

Finishing our inspection of the berm line defenses, I remain on the berm line waiting for the sun to set completely. I want to check on the lighting situation from the berm line's perspective looking back into the Company area. The distance between the berm line and the Company area is about 100 yards, and the space is all open and cleared. If there is any weakness, this could be considered one of them. Not much lighting is provided between the berm line and the Company area. The idea is to keep anyone from getting through the wire, breaching the berm line, and making it into this area. Looking back into the Company area after sunset, I'm satisfied we've done what we can and hope we're ready for whatever the night brings. The First Sergeant and I head back to the Headquarters trailer.

Two of the three enlisted men assigned to work with me are responsible for radio communications. They will maintain contact with the men on the berm line, Battalion Headquarters, and any support units I may need to call during the night. The third man is my driver. The First Sergeant and I will alternate staying up and working two-hour shifts during the night. At 2200 hours, I instruct the First Sergeant to take the first watch and wake me at 2400 hours. Then I'll take over. Having done what I could up to this point, I stretch out on a cot in the Operations room and drift off into a light sleep.

A short time later, I'm awakened from my sleep by the First Sergeant. "Captain, you need to get up. It's your watch."

Slowly rising from my cot and trying to shake the cobwebs from my head, I say, "What time is it, Top? Everything quiet so far?"

"Yes, sir, nothing yet. It's about 0100."

Before he could finish his statement, I ask him in a calm,

inquisitive voice, "What? I thought I wanted you to wake me at 2400."

The First Sergeant responds, "You did, but it's been quiet so far, and you could use the extra sleep."

"Thanks, Top. Your turn. Get some rest. I'm going to take the jeep and check the Company area and berm line. I'll be back shortly."

Not looking back at me, the First Sergeant says, "Yes sir," as he lowers himself onto his cot. Checking with my radio operator on duty, I tell him where I'm going. I grab my driver, and we head out. It's a damp, misty night with no moonlight. I fear we may have some light fog settle in later as the conditions seem right for some. Even though the Company area is well lit, any significant fog cover could make things more intense. Not to mention what could happen if we do get hit and our lights are knocked out. Not pleasant thoughts, but that's the way it is. You deal with what comes your way and hope you do it right and survive the night.

Arriving on the berm line, I stop at each bunker and guard tower, and check on the men. Whenever assigned OD duty, I make it a point to check on them throughout the night. Most officers in the Company performing this duty follow the same procedure. However, the occasional few just sleep all night after delegating this responsibility to the senior NCO working with them.

On some of my previous OD assignments, I've occasionally walked up on a post and found all the men asleep. However, this evening almost every man on the berm line is awake and alert. Many of the men whose turn it is to rest couldn't sleep and are helping to monitor the perimeter. This gives me an added sense of comfort, and after our last stop on the line, we head back toward the Company area.

As our jeep pulls up to the Headquarters trailer, several explosions occur along the berm line I just left. Looking out at our perimeter, I see large explosions near all three of the guard towers. Two of them collapse to the ground on fire. The third one escapes a similar fate, and the men on top are frantically moving their searchlight across the open field to their front. As if a massive thunderstorm just rolled in unexpectedly, the whole berm line erupts with M-16s, AK-47s, and M-60s firing.

Claymore mines, set out in front of the bunkers and towers, are being detonated by men on the berm line. A claymore mine is a command detonated, directional mine, which is placed above ground. When detonated, it shoots a pattern of 700 steel balls into the kill zone like a shotgun. It has a devastating effect on anyone caught in the kill zone. Large explosions from satchel charges thrown by sappers are going off near the bunkers. Not ten minutes ago, all seemed fine out there. Now it's a bloody mess, and men are fighting for their lives.

Jumping out of the jeep and running into the Operations room, I find the First Sergeant working the radios. He's been talking with the men on the berm line that he could reach, to get their status. Turning toward me as I run in, he says in a matter-of-fact voice, "Sir, they've hit us with a large force, two towers are down, and several men are wounded already."

Before he can finish, I ask, "Did they see any sappers make it through the wire yet?"

The First Sergeant responds, "No, not yet, but there must be one hell of a lot of them out there trying to get through!"

I call Battalion Headquarters and give them a short and precise situation report. I request immediate Cobra support and flares to be dropped all along our berm line. Having done that, I instruct the First Sergeant to stay with the radios and keep communications up and running. The Major should be here any minute with some more officers. As I'm heading out the door on my way back to the berm line, the Major runs in with Captains Barnett and Norton.

The Major stops me and asks, "How bad is it?"

"It's bad. They're hitting us hard. Two towers are down. Several men are wounded, and they may have penetrated the berm line. Battalion has been briefed, we have Cobras inbound, and flares should start dropping any minute. I'm headed back out there now!"

"Captain, we'll take over in here. Let me know what you see out there. We'll establish some search teams and have them patrol inside the Company area. Hopefully, we can keep them away from our choppers. Good luck!"

"Yes, sir!" I run to my jeep after grabbing my M-16 on the way out the door. Once outside, I can already see flares starting to drop all around our area. This is a welcome sight as it helps to illuminate the berm line. Two of our three searchlights were taken out of action when the guard towers were destroyed. The fog I feared might settle in has not materialized. What has happened is smoke from the flares, explosions, and all the firing going on around us has become very thick. Our visibility is more limited, making it difficult to spot any sappers.

I have my driver man the M-60 as we head back out toward the berm line. The night sky all around Phu Bai is lit up with flares. In the distance, I see on the horizon some of the other berm line sections being hit with massive explosions.

The noise of combat is terrifying and very disorienting to your senses. Trying to stay calm and focused when all hell's breaking loose around you is incredibly difficult. Some men handle it. Others struggle with it. My experiences have led me to believe that a man can be a hero one day by his actions in combat, and the next time timid in his actions and response to the situation at hand. I'm thinking to myself, *Which will I be tonight?*

Arriving on the berm line and the first bunker, I find the men inside alive and firing out into the open spaces in front of them. Although they haven't seen any sappers yet, they tell me it sounds bad down the line. I leave them and move on down the berm line, checking on the next bunker and first guard tower. This guard tower hasn't been destroyed. No one has been hurt in the bunker or up in the tower. They tell me they've killed some sappers out in front of the guard tower and haven't seen anymore. I leave the jeep by the tower and trade my driver for one of the men in the bunker. We head out on foot to the next bunker with our M-16s at the ready. The noise level has increased and is very intense as firing continues all along the berm line.

As we approach the next bunker, I see two sappers with weapons and demolition satchels slung over their backs running across the open field headed toward the Company area. Their bodies are covered with mud and grease that make them almost invisible in the dark. Bringing my M-16 rifle up to my shoulder and taking aim at the running figures about 40 yards out, I open up and cut them down. Some rounds hit a satchel charge on the back of one of the sappers, and they both disappear in a horrific explosion. The infantryman with me, and I, are knocked to the ground, but we are unhurt.

Picking ourselves up off the ground, we rush over to the bunker and check inside. All the men inside are dead. There is nothing that can be done for them. The tower nearest this bunker was knocked out in the first attack. Covering the distance to the tower, as if we're running in a sprint race, we find three survivors, all of whom are wounded. Two of the men have dressed their own wounds and are still in the fight as they shoot at anything that moves in front of them. We do what we can to help the third man, but it doesn't look good. He's unconscious and losing blood. He bore the brunt of the explosion and has lost an arm and both legs below the knees. After placing tourniquets on his arm and both legs, I contact the Major on the bunker's field radio.

'Major, we're at the second tower now. Three of the six men manning this tower are dead. The other three are wounded, but two are still in the fight. The third man is unconscious and in bad shape. He needs medical attention ASAP. We also lost all three men in the bunker to the left of this location. I'm going to keep going down the line. Can you send some more men out here to help?'

The Major responds, 'Captain Norton is on his way out with two squads. What was the explosion between us and the berm line I just heard?'

'It was two sappers with explosive satchels on their backs. We cut them down as they were running toward the Company area. I'm afraid there are more of them that got through and headed your way.'

'Roger that, understand, keep checking the berm line, and we'll do what we can here! The Major adds, And be careful, Taylor!'

'Yes, sir!'

We continue to work our way to the next bunker. Once there, we find one man dead, another wounded, and the third man still firing his M-60 out into the area in front of him. He is very methodical in the way he moves his machine gun from side to side. This movement is highly effective in laying down suppressive fire across a wide area in front of us. I'm impressed with the man and let him know. We now have ample light to see what's in front of us and outside the berm line. The night sky has become very bright from all the flares raining down on our area. It may not be a thing of beauty, but watching those flares floating down from the sky is comforting. Looking out over the berm line in front of us, I see shapes of several bodies scattered everywhere out there. I think to myself, *This man is good. He's clearly an angel of death!*

Once again, we do what we can for the wounded man. I decide to wait for Captain Norton to catch up with me. I don't want to leave my machine gunner by himself. An M-60 can wreak havoc and is a prime target for your enemy to take out. Three men manning the bunker are better than one, and this position needs to be defended.

With all that was going on, I became oblivious to the helicopter support flying around us. Cobras are doing what they can all along the berm lines around Phu Bai. Light Observation Helicopters, called Loaches, are flying inside the berm lines and throughout the interior of the base, looking for sappers. The level of firing seems to have somewhat abated, with the arrival of helicopters flying everywhere.

Captain Norton makes it to my location, and as he approaches, I greet him. "Good to see you, Stan. This is one hell of a mess!"

Stan responds, "You got that right. Damn, they're hitting us hard. I dropped off some of the men at the last two locations and have these twenty men with me. We lost the wounded man back at the tower we just left. His wounds were too severe. There was nothing we could do for him. What do you want us to do?"

"You stay here with five men. Do what you can for the wounded man here. I don't think he's too badly hurt. I'll take the rest of the men with me, and we'll check the other two bunkers and the third tower. I'll let you know what we find, and we'll go from there. Alright with you?" Stan says, "No problem!"

I head out to the next bunker with the men following me. We stay low and spread out as we cover the distance to the next bunker. It was destroyed by a satchel charge thrown into it by a sapper. The men inside were killed, probably instantly. Nothing can be done there for them. I leave five men there to defend this area and move on toward the tower and last bunker.

Reaching the destroyed tower, we find two men clinging to life. They won't make it unless they get some immediate attention. I'm tired of seeing dead Americans out here and call for my jeep to be brought up. When it pulls up, we place the two severely wounded men in the back of the jeep and send it back to the HQ trailer with a rifleman riding along to provide some security. Once they are removed, and on their way back, I assign four men to defend this area. Heading for the last bunker, we are shaken by a series of horrific explosions occurring within the Company area. Some sappers have made it into the area and are detonating satchel charges. The explosions are followed by sporadic gunfire. I assume some of the Company's men are hunting them down and killing them.

There's nothing I can do for them from my position on the berm line, as I still have the last bunker to check. With the remaining men following me, we move toward it. There is no one firing from the last bunker, and I assume they're all dead. As we approach it carefully, with weapons at the ready, three sappers jump up from the bunker and begin shooting at us. Two of my men are cut down immediately as the rest of us drop to the ground for cover. We are only about 20 yards from the bunker and can see the sappers silhouetted against the night sky as flares continue floating down.

In a fit of rage, I crawl over to one of the men who was hit. He's practically cut in half, and his lifeless body still clings to his weapon. I take the M-60 he was using from his dead hands and begin firing on the sappers. Rising from the ground and staying in a low crouching position, I rush toward the bunker, shooting as I close in on them. An M-60 machine gun can do a massive amount of damage to the human body, and I'm in no mood to show any mercy. As I reach the bunker my machine gun goes silent as the last round tears into the shredded bodies of the sappers. I drop the M-60 and slowly turn around while looking back on the berm line and into the Company area.

The rage I feel and the adrenaline that has been rushing through my body slowly begins to subside as I look out over the devastation surrounding me. It's over! We have secured the berm line. Within the Company area, there are no more explosions, and the firing tapers off.

*I fear we have paid a heavy price to defend our Company area and Phu Bai base.*

Stan and I remain on the berm line.

# CHAPTER 36

## SAPPER AFTERMATH

After stabilizing the situation, Stan and I each take a small group of men and sweep the area between the berm line and the Company. This distance of about 100 yards is open, clear of vegetation, and offers no place to hide. However, it is not well lit, and sappers are very adept at concealing themselves in the open. Performing these sweeps is necessary to ensure there are no more live sappers within this area. Our sweeps only result in finding two sapper bodies, taken down during the height of the battle.

Meanwhile, Captain Barnett and several Warrant Officers and enlisted men sweep through the Company's staging area, barracks, hangar, and revetments where most of the Hueys are parked. They are searching out any remaining sappers. Their efforts result in flushing out four more sappers. Two were fleeing the Huey staging area before they had a chance to throw their satchel charges into some parked Hueys. They were cut down immediately. Two others were found working their way toward the Company's ammunition bunker. When detected, they were all dispatched quickly by several pissed off Americans.

At first light, the men of Eagles Company perform a thorough search of our area. This is done to determine the extent of damage sustained, the number and severity of casualties, and a body count of the sappers killed. This information is compiled and then sent up the chain of command to Division Headquarters. Division G-2 will perform an immediate assessment of the overall damage inflicted on the Phi Bai Combat Base.

When Major Breckenridge receives the initial assessment report from Division Headquarters later that afternoon, he calls a meeting in his office. Stan, Captain Barnett, the Maintenance Officer, the First Sergeant, and I are present. He reads us the Division's report summarizing the sapper attack we just experienced.

"Early this morning, Phu Bai Combat Base was assaulted by three sapper teams consisting of approximately fifty men each. They hit our berm lines on the north, west, and south sides of the base. The official count of casualties is 87 Americans killed and 114 wounded. The body count for sappers, 126 killed. Thirteen helicopters were destroyed and 18 damaged. The assault force slipped in silently through our barbed wire during the early morning hours. At this time, we do not know which NVA units were involved. However, their attack was well planned, coordinated, and executed. Those that penetrated the perimeter raced through the base, tossing grenades and canvas satchels loaded with explosives. They then directed automatic weapons fire at demolished or burning targets. Several structures have been damaged, and some are still burning. Had it not been for the men of the 101st standing their ground and fighting, Division Headquarters believes it could have been much worse. Phu Bai Combat Base is functioning at this time and should be fully operational within 48 hours. Well done, men of the 101st Airborne Division."

After reading the communique, he adds his comments. "The

men in this Company did an outstanding job last night. It could have been worse. We fared better than many of the other units that were directly hit. We lost only two Hueys, and four others sustained damage. Two will be repaired by tonight, and the other two within a few days. Operationally our aircraft readiness is still high."

He pauses a moment as he struggles to control his emotions, and slowly looking around the room, continues in a calm, compassionate voice. "Our casualties last night were twenty men killed and six wounded. We may have fared better than other units last night, but I realize that's no solace to any of us for the losses we suffered. We are in a war, gentlemen, and these bastards only play to win. Tonight at 1800 hours, we will hold a service in the Company formation area to honor the twenty men we lost over the last twelve hours. If there are no questions, you're dismissed!"

We are all exhausted, our adrenaline is wearing off, and I just want God to wrap me up in his arms and give me twenty-four hours of peace and quiet with nobody trying to kill me.

# CHAPTER 37
## THE NVA ARE COMING

The following night, Camp Eagle and Camp Evans are hit simultaneously by large sapper forces. Much of the damage done in these Camps was primarily inflicted on building structures and vehicles. Several men defending the Camps were killed or wounded. Since many of the 101st Division's helicopter units are stationed at Phu Bai, the Division's total helicopter force's damage was considered minimal. Although considerable damage was done to Camps Eagle and Evans, they too are considered operational and will be fully functioning within a few days.

For several days following the sapper attack, we are busy repairing structures within our Company area and the damaged Hueys. Routine missions are flown in support of the 101st troopers manning the firebases located in the A Shau Valley and near Camps Eagle and Evans. After the sapper attacks on the 101st, and considerable activity occurring up north near the DMZ against South Vietnamese forces, it's predicted that NVA forces will soon make a major push south.

South Vietnamese forces are now responsible for Quảng Trị Province. They are deployed over a series of strong points and fire support bases dotting the area immediately south of the DMZ and from the coast to the mountains in the west. Cam Lo Combat Base and Camp Carroll are two of the South Vietnamese northern and western defense lines situated on Route 9 and are heavily defended. Several firebases are scattered strategically across a wide area of Quang Tri Province. They include Mai Loc Camp, Dong Ha Combat Base, Firebases Nancy, Sarge, and Fuller. The terrain in much of the area being defended is relatively flat and easily traversed. As you move closer to the coast, sand dunes become more prevalent. Much of the area is devoid of vegetation due to years of fighting and the spraying of agent orange. This type of terrain is very conducive to conducting armored warfare.

Although the South Vietnamese forces have their own helicopter support, it is limited, and most of their aircrews have little experience. Vietnamization of the war has been slow to address the training of Vietnamese helicopter aircrews. This is an acute problem for the South Vietnamese forces, given that President Nixon's Administration has accelerated the pace of the turnover process.

The 101st Division and ARVN Commands are preparing for another major engagement with the North Vietnamese Army. It's believed they will cross the DMZ and attack ARVN forces across a wide area with armor and heavy infantry concentrations. It is also believed they will try to harass the 101st and keep us from reinforcing the South Vietnamese forces. Their goal is to capture and hold Quang Tri Province. Given the state of the ARVN's own helicopter support, the 101st Aviation Group will again provide the bulk of air support for the South Vietnamese forces in Quang Tri Province.

# CHAPTER 38
## SELF DOUBT

For some miraculous reason, the Pilots Club was spared during the sapper attack and has been busy every night since the attack. It's been five days since Phu Bai was hit. The usual crowd, Greg, some of his pilots, Bill, Stan, and I, are at the club having beers and enjoying each other's company. We have been experiencing relative calm in our area since the sappers' attack. However, the rumor mill has been running rampant again, and there is growing concern that it's soon going to change for the worse.

Greg, in a calm, matter of fact voice, says to the group, "What do you guys think of all these rumors we've been hearing about another major NVA offensive up north? Do you think there is any truth to them?"

Stan replies, "From what I've been hearing, yeah, there is another one in the works, and it could start any day now!"

Bill, with a melancholy and nervous voice, responds. "Damn, I was afraid you would say that! With the draw-down accelerating, I don't know about you guys, but I don't want to be the last American to die over here!"

In a low and calm voice, I say, "Given everything that has happened lately, I would say we're definitely in for another round of heavy fighting. Particularly up north. We all know the South Vietnamese have very little of their own helicopter support. You can bet we're going to be called upon to help them again!"

Our conversations taper off as we reflect on the prospects of more heavy fighting. Greg, who always tries to lighten things up when there's a down moment, proposes a toast to me. He looks over my way, and in a loud and boisterous voice, says, "I propose a toast to TJ, the Audie Murphy of the 101st, for his actions the other night against the sappers."

We raise our beers, tap them together at the center of the table, and finish them. Greg waves to one of the bartenders to bring us another round. As the beers arrive, Stan, trying to outdo Greg's attempt at injecting a little levity, says, "I thought Audie Murphy was awarded the Medal of Honor for his actions. They're' just giving you a Silver Star." Some light laughter ensues as I respond with, "I'm no Audie Murphy, and they can keep the medal. I'd rather they just send me home on the next flight back to the world!"

My response draws "amens" from the men around the table, and they all raise their beers in another toast to Audie Murphy. Audie Murphy was one of the most decorated soldiers of WWII. He did receive the "Medal of Honor" and every other U.S. Army combat medal for valor they could award, and in several cases, more than one. He was also presented with French and Belgian awards for heroism. When the group quiets down, I offer to share with them a little story about meeting Audie Murphy.

I begin, "When I was in the fourth grade, we lived in Riverside, California. The movie "To Hell and Back" was shown at the military base there. In case you're not familiar with the movie, it was about Audie's WWII experiences. It was based on his autobiography, and he played himself in the film. He was the guest of honor at the base when they showed his movie, and they gave him a military parade. My Dad had some connections and took me to see the parade. Most of the young boys I hung around with back then knew who Audie Murphy was, and his exploits."

I pause and glance around the table to see if there is still any interest. There is, and I continue. "When the parade was over, Audie walked down the long line of people viewing the parade on his way to a waiting vehicle. As he approached my Dad and me, I gave him a little boy's best impression of standing at attention and rendering him a hand salute. Damn, if he didn't notice me and stop. He came over, knelt down, and talked to me for a minute. I have no idea what he said then, but I've never forgotten that moment."

The table is quiet as they digest what I just shared with them. Stan, feeling a little foolish about his earlier comment, looks over at me and offers his apology. I assure him I was not offended by his comment. In fact, I consider his attempt to compare me with Audie Murphy a compliment.

After finishing our last beer, we call it a night and head back to our quarters for some rest. Several of us drove jeeps to the Club, and as we walk out the door, Greg offers to give me a ride back to my room. Sensing that Greg wants to talk, I accept, and on the way over to the Eagles Company area, we converse.

Greg asks, "TJ. Is that story for real?"

I respond, "Yes, every word."

Greg, "No, shit!"

"No shit Greg!"

As we approach my Company area, Greg pulls his jeep over to the side of the dirt road and brings it to a stop. He's been wanting to share with me for some time now what's been on his mind. Since we are good friends, with over two years of shared experiences, he feels comfortable talking to me.

In a reserved, almost melancholy voice, Greg says, "TJ, I'm

getting to be a short-timer over here. I'm less than ninety days out from going home. These last several months of flying in Laos and everything else that's gone on has been a shit storm from hell. Supposedly, the life expectancy of a helicopter pilot over here is about 30 days. I've certainly surpassed that and don't need any more of this shit! I don't know if I can handle this much longer."

I interject, "Greg, I know how you feel. But you're one of the toughest guys I've ever known. If anybody can deal with it over here, you can! Hell, I remember many times back in Infantry OCS, I'd look to you for that extra push to keep me going, and here we are!"

Greg cracks a little smile as he responds, "Maybe I didn't do you any favors in that regard!"

Grinning, I respond, "Maybe you didn't, but I'm not complaining!"

Greg resumes the drive back to my Company area, and upon arriving, pulls the jeep up near my quarters. Greg, looking directly at me, says in a serious, calm, and reflective manner, "TJ, the United States has been over here fighting this damn war since the early sixties, and we're still at it, with no end in sight. I don't know about you, but it pisses me off because many good men have died over here, and for what? If I'm going to be one of them, I would like to think it's for a good reason, and not in vain. I wonder what history will say about this war and the part we played in it?"

"I feel the same way, Greg, and I would like to think we are making a difference. But, like you, I have my doubts. As for history, I hope we're remembered for trying to do the right thing over here and that we did it with courage and honor. I guess time will tell."

Greg manages to work up a small grin and says, "Wow, that was deep!"

"Yeah, sometimes I even surprise myself."

"I didn't mean to get all that philosophical with you, TJ. I just wanted to get some of that off my chest."

Stepping out of the jeep and looking over at Greg and say, "I understand. Thanks for the ride, buddy. I wouldn't spend any more of your time worrying about what's coming our way if I were you. Hell, we have no control over it anyway."

Greg responds, "I guess you're right. Maybe we can't control what comes our way, but that sure doesn't make it any easier to deal with it over here. Damn, I wish I were leaving for home tomorrow!"

In a slow, calm voice, I respond, "Greg, that makes two of us! Being that you're a short-timer, you'll be on your way home before you know it! See you around, good buddy. Now go get some sleep."

Greg replies, "Yeah, no problem, see you around." Greg heads back toward his Company area. On the way back, he mumbles to himself. "I wish I had TJ's confidence; I'm going to need it."

As I'm crossing the short distance to my room, I'm thinking, *my god, if a man like Greg has these self-doubts, what about me?*

# CHAPTER 39

## QUANG TRI PROVINCE

I wake up the next morning to grim news. North Vietnamese units have crossed the DMZ and are on the offensive, attacking several South Vietnamese firebases in Quang Tri Province. Our helicopter air operations have been placed on hold. We are now on full alert to support the South Vietnamese up north and are awaiting orders. Earlier today, Major Breckenridge called a briefing for all pilots at 1300 hours in the Operations room. It is now the designated hour, and we are all present as he begins his briefing.

"Gentlemen, the North Vietnamese have crossed the DMZ in large numbers supported by tanks, armored vehicles, and heavy artillery. Several ARVN forward firebases are under siege. Initial reports indicate they're holding their own but taking heavy casualties. They will need troop reinforcements and supplies within the next twenty-four hours if they are going to stop the North Vietnamese from overrunning their bases. We'll be providing the bulk of their air support once again. This will include helicopter units from our Division, fighter jets, and B-52s if needed."

He pauses, collects his thoughts as he looks around the room, trying to gauge our reactions, and continues. "As you're well aware, we've been here before, so I'm not going to bullshit you! This is another bad situation. We'll be flying into heavy combat, and they have come to fight. Division believes the South Vietnamese forces can hold the line, but it's going to take a massive effort on their part. We'll need to get their men and supplies into all those areas under siege." He pauses again and asks, "Any questions?"

In a matter-of-fact voice, I ask, "How soon do we saddle up and go, sir?"

In a calm, measured voice, the Major responds, "I'm coming to that. There's a problem. The South Vietnamese must bring up several thousand troops and more supplies from the south. It seems they didn't fully prepare for this scenario. They failed to stage sufficient troops and supplies in reserve up north. Since this morning, they've been flying massive airlifts of troops and supplies into the Quang Tri airfield."

The Major pauses, collects his thoughts, and proceeds slowly as he chooses his words carefully. "They have already attempted to send in ground reinforcements to their bases under attack, but have met heavy resistance and pulled back. Apparently, they haven't airlifted enough troops and equipment up there yet to make an effective fighting force. They need more people and air support before they can break through to their bases being assaulted. While they're building up their forces for a counterattack, they want to fly in some reinforcements and supplies to those bases under siege. That's where we come in! It's now expected they'll have enough ARVN troops up there by early morning for us to airlift in. Therefore, we'll be headed out early in the morning to play our part."

The Major looks over at Captain Barnett, Stan, and me and says, "Captains Barnett, St. James, and Norton, you'll meet with me to make aircraft assignments and final planning requirements." He looks back at the group and continues. "One last point, gentlemen. Since the sapper attacks, the 101st has received several helicopters and replacement troops from units standing down in III and IV Corps. We are now at full strength. Unless there are any questions for me at this time, we'll meet back here at 1800 hours for our detailed briefing. Thank you!"

The room clears as the Major walks into his office, followed by the three of us. We spend the next few hours preparing detailed plans for meeting our mission requirements.

That evening our pilots and crews assemble in the mess hall for our briefing. The Major gives us an overview of the situation once again to benefit the crew members who were not present at the earlier meeting. He then turns it over to Captain Barnett, whose comments are brief, to the point, and presented in a calm and measured manner.

"We will be departing the Company area at 0500 hours. We need to be at our staging area in Quang Tri by 0545 hours. We've been assigned to airlift two ARVN Infantry Companies plus supplies into Cam Lo Combat Base. This base is located northwest of Quang Tri and is critical to the South Vietnamese defense of Quang Tri Province. It's a large Combat Base that is currently defended by a substantial force of Rangers and Marines. We'll be taking one Company in at a time. When we have them inserted, we'll begin resupplying the camp. You can anticipate flying several sorties into the camp. Several other 101st Huey Assault Companies, Cobra units, and some Chinooks are also supporting South Vietnamese bases under siege up there. Many of their bases are in dire straits. When we complete our missions, we could be called on to assist other units."

He stops for a moment to give us time to digest what we heard and a chance to speak out. We are silent, so he continues. "We'll have three flights of five Hueys each. I have the first flight,

Captain Norton the second, and Captain St. James the third. Major Breckenridge will fly the C&C chopper. Your aircraft and aircrew assignments are posted on the flight operations board. Our gunship support will be provided by eight Cobras from the Butcher group. Captain Owens, Butcher 12, is their group leader. Any questions before I turn it back over to Major Breckenridge?"

There are none, and the Major stands up and faces his men. He's looking out at a room full of young men, many of whom could be one of his sons. He speaks to us in a manner like that of a father to his son.

"When we head up north tomorrow morning, it will be the start of what will probably be several days of intense combat flying. Most of you men have been there before. For a few of you, this will be your first time. What we do, gentlemen, never gets any easier. It doesn't matter how many times you've been in a combat situation; the enemy doesn't care. They are dead set on winning, and to do this, they will throw everything they can at us to stop us from succeeding. Being scared is not a problem. I would be more concerned if you weren't. Rely on your training and the men you're flying with to get us all through this."

The Major takes a long pause as he looks across the room, making eye contact with each man, and closes with, "It's a privilege to fly with men of your caliber. Get some rest, and may God protect you. See you in the morning!"

# CHAPTER 40

## SADDLE UP AGAIN

The next day arrives very early for my fellow Eagles and me. I'm on the flight line checking my assigned helicopter with a flashlight after having breakfast with the crew. It's now 0430 hours, and the sun has not yet made an appearance. Jake, one of the newer Warrant Officers, is flying with me today. I flew with him when he first joined the Company. Our crew chief is Charlie, whom I highly regard, and the other door gunner is Joel. Joel transferred in two days ago from down south. He's an infantryman whose unit stood down. He has six months in the country and was not eligible to go home with his unit's redeployment back to the states. Joel carried an M-60 while in the field and should be comfortable with his new duty. The First Sergeant informed me that he had been awarded some combat ribbons and a Purple Heart. So, he's no novice when it comes to combat. He should prove valuable today.

After performing all necessary pre-flight checks, the Eagles crews board their choppers and fire up the engines. By 0500 hours, we're lined up and ready to launch.

We hear the Major over our radios, 'Phu Bai Tower. This is

Eagle 1, ready for take-off. We're a group of sixteen heading north. Over!'

The tower responds, 'Roger Eagle 1, cleared to launch, climb, and maintain 2,000 until you clear Camp Evans airspace and proceed at your own discretion. Good luck! Over!'

'Eagle 1, Roger Phu Bai Tower. Eagles, we're cleared to launch. Follow me, gentlemen. Over!'

One after the other, we bring our Hueys to a hover and follow the man in front of us as we slowly lift off and climb into the dark, early morning sky headed towards hell.

Reaching our assigned altitude as the morning sky is slowly changing from dark to early dawn, we go into our normal formation—three flights of five Hueys each, in a V formation, one behind the other. The Major is in front, leading us.

Arriving ahead of schedule at Quang Tri, we land at our assigned staging area, refuel, and shut down the choppers. We are directed to a small army tent near our staging area. Here we are met by the American Liaison Officer for the South Vietnamese Commander of the forces we'll be working with to reinforce and resupply. The Liaison Officer, a Colonel, is a large man who presents an overpowering figure and dwarfs any Vietnamese he's standing around. Upon seeing him, I think to myself. '*This guy must scare the hell out of the Vietnamese. He looks like the Jolly Green Giant.*'

The Colonel proceeds to brief us on the current situation and our mission. Speaking in a loud, gruff, authoritarian voice, he says, "The Marines and Rangers at Cam Lo Combat Base are hanging on. Those poor bastards have been in constant contact with the NVA for the past twenty-four hours and are taking one hell of a beating. They've been under heavy artillery fire most of the time. The North Vietnamese have deployed tanks. They are situated way back from the base, well-concealed right now, and have been firing shells into the Camp. However, they haven't been very effective. We believe they're waiting on us to resupply and reinforce the base. When we do, they will, in all probability, come out shooting. They are currently located to the north and west of the camp. Waves of North Vietnamese have been attacking the camp but haven't breached the outer perimeter yet."

After pausing for a moment, he continues, "Your landing zone is a long, narrow, cleared strip in the middle of the base, which runs east to west. It will easily accommodate five choppers landing in trail formation. Up to this point, the bulk of incoming fire has been from the base's north and west sides. Artillery is landing all over the place, and they seem to have zeroed in on many key areas in the base. This includes your landing zone."

He pauses again and looks over at the Major, "Major, it's your call, of course, but I suggest approaching from the south at a low altitude and land from the east. On your way out, head west, make a sharp bank to your left, and head south as soon as possible. This may help to reduce the amount of incoming fire you'll get."

Major Breckenridge responds, "Thanks Colonel, I think we'll take your advice on that. Any idea how many sorties we might need to make in there?"

"Best guess would be four or five. With your fifteen choppers, you should be able to get each Company in as an entire unit. Two trips, two Companies inserted. It's resupplying them that's going to involve at least two, and probably more flights back into the camp. They're desperately short of everything!"

Pausing, the Colonel, in a calm and almost inaudible voice, continues. "Your Vietnamese troops are ready and forming up at your staging area as we speak. If you don't have any more questions, you can saddle up. Good luck to you and your men!"

Major Breckenridge thanks the Colonel and then turns to face his men. "Good luck, gentlemen. Remember to stay alert, call your targets, and watch out for each other. Okay, saddle up!"

As we clear the tent and head for our Hueys, the Colonel walks over to Major Breckenridge and stops him. "Major, one more thing. There are about eighty wounded South Vietnamese in the camp. You and your men need to bring them out."

The Major responds, "Will do. Let the Base Commander know he's not to load his wounded on the first two flights in. We need to get in and out quickly. He's to have half of them ready to load when our third flight comes in. Those should be his most severely wounded troops. We'll get them and extract his remaining wounded when we come back out with the second Company of men. Again, on the third incoming flight only."

Responding, the Colonel in a curious tone, "Why just the third flight each time?"

Major Breckenridge responds in a matter-of-fact voice, "It's best we get in and out as fast as possible on flights one and two. If it gets really hot in there, the less time on the LZ, the better. Disembarking troops and loading the wounded takes more time on the ground. This way, we have a better chance of getting more men in there fast if it's really bad."

The Colonel responds as the two men shake hands and part company. "Got it. I'll coordinate with them. Again, good luck!"

# CHAPTER 41

## CAM LO COMBAT BASE-FIRST TRIP

Arriving at our helicopters, we saddle up. I check to ensure my chicken plate is where I want it in the chin bubble. I adjust the chicken plate and survival vest I'm wearing to make them as comfortable as possible. Climbing into my left seat, I strap in and extend the armored plate on the side of my seat as far out as it will go. Once satisfied, I slip on my helmet and plug the helmet's radio chord into the Huey's radio system. I look over at Jake, then Joel, to see how they are doing. Charlie is standing out in front of the Huey. He has removed the rotor blade tie-down strap and is ready for start-up.

Seeing that Jake and Joel are settled in, I begin communicating with them in a matter-of-fact tone over the intercom. It's all business now. This is going to be a rough day, and we'll need to stay sharp and be alert.

Looking over at Jake, 'Jake, you good to go? Everything set the way you want it?'

Jake responds nervously, 'Yes, sir!'

'It's TJ, Jake. Call me, TJ. Okay? When we're ready to lift-off, I'll do the flying, and you keep an eye on our instruments and what is going on outside the cockpit. Does that sound good to you?'

'Sounds good. TJ!'

'Joel, are you good to go back there?'

Joel responds calmly, 'I'm ready. The M-60 is locked and loaded. We're good back here.'

'Good, we're going to need you on that gun today, so stay sharp and shoot at whatever is shooting at us. This is a free-fire zone!'

The Major transmits to his men, 'Eagles, Eagle 1, start your engines and reply when you're good to go! Your packs are lined up and ready to board. Over!'

Yelling out my window to Charlie, "Clear!" Charlie responds, "Clear!" I start my Huey, bring it to full power, and we are ready. Charlie joins us in the chopper, straps in, and gives me a thumbs up. I transmit to the Major, 'Eagle 1, Eagle 25, good to go! Over!'

As the other Eagles bring their Hueys to full throttle and ensure all instrument readings are in the green, they too respond affirmatively to the Major. We are ready! The Major instructs the South Vietnamese ground commander to load his troops. While they're loading, the Major transmits to us. 'There are about eighty wounded South Vietnamese in the camp who need to be evacuated as soon as possible. I've instructed them to have their most severely wounded ready for us on this trip. They're to load no more than half their wounded this time in. We'll get the rest of them on the next trip. I've also instructed them to place their injured on the last flight in. That will be your group, TJ. Copy that Eagle 25? Over!' I respond in the affirmative.

The Major continues, 'I don't want this to become a cluster-fuck out there, so stay sharp and get in and get out quick. Over!' We acknowledge the Majors transmission with multiple double-clicks and some of us respond with 'Roger that!' There is no questioning of the Major's order on extracting the wounded. We're all aware of the reasons for doing it that way.

Over our radios, we hear the Major's voice loud and clear, 'Eagles, we're cleared to launch. We'll climb and maintain 1,000 feet. Stay in trail formation and follow me to our holding area. We'll hook up there with the Butchers. Over!'

Again, we acknowledge the Major's radio transmission as we take off, one behind the other. The sun is slowly rising to the east now and is very bright. The sky is clear, with a cool, mild breeze. It would be a good day to go flying if it weren't for where we're going. Reaching our assigned altitude and holding station, we go into a large circular flight pattern while awaiting the Butcher group's arrival.

Greg is approaching our holding pattern and calls the Major. 'Eagle 1, Butcher 12, we're approaching your location from the south. Over!'

The Major responds, 'Butcher 12, Eagle 1. Roger. I have you in sight. Over!'

While we continue to fly in a holding pattern, the Major and Greg have a conversation that we can hear. Greg informs the Major that his group has been providing fire support to the South Vietnamese at Cam Lo Combat Base since early last night. They've been flying out of Quang Tri base since they got here. He's already lost one Cobra due to a heavy concentration of machine guns and 20 MM (millimeter) fire. His pilots were able to get back to Quang Tri and crash land on the side of the field. They both survived but were medevaced to Phu Bai. Their Cobra was destroyed, so they're down to seven.

Greg shares with Major Breckenridge the situation he's seen while flying around the Combat Base. It's not good. The base is now getting hit from all sides. The best approach to the base is still from the south. Most of the heavy firing is coming from the other three sides. It consists mostly of machine guns and 20 MM cannon fire. They have seen several tanks set back a good distance from the base, but they haven't engaged yet. Incoming artillery fire has been constant and pretty accurate.

The Major conveys our lineup to Greg. Three flights of five Hueys each, led by Eagle 16, followed by 8, and then 25. The last flight in, on both trips, will bring out their wounded. We're inserting two Companies, one on each trip to the Combat Base. Once the troops are inserted, we will be flying several resupply sorties into the base.

Greg tells Major Breckenridge he will be sending in four Cobras on the first insertion, two on each side of the Eagles trail formation. They'll stay on station and continue flying cover for flights two and three during their insertions. Greg and his other two Cobras will fly high cover over them and take on targets of opportunity. Major Breckenridge agrees with Greg, and the plan is set.

I've been monitoring the exchange of information between Greg and the Major and am anxious to get started. I don't have to wait long. The Major transmits to his men. 'Eagles, Eagle 1. You heard Butcher 12s transmissions. When we go in, flight leaders keep your distance from each other. I don't want you stacking up in there. And remember, in and out. Over!' Acknowledgments of 'Roger that!' and double-clicks are heard.

I look around at my crew. I see Jake adjusting his shoulder straps and the chicken plate he's wearing, again. Then he looks down at the chicken plate he placed in the chin bubble. Jake is clearly concerned about what is to follow. Charlie and Joel are looking out at the helicopter formation we're flying in and the terrain below. Over the intercom, I transmit, 'Here we go, fellows. Stay alert and keep me out of trouble. Jake, what about your .38 revolver? This is gonna be a ball buster!'

With apprehension in his voice, Jake responds. 'Yeah, right. Okay, okay. Does that really help?'

As Jake pulls his holster between his legs and tries to get comfortable, I say, 'You never know. It might. I'll take all the help I can get right now! Charlie, how's your leg doing?'

Charlie responds in a joking manner, 'It's doing fine. But I'm not too sure about me. I wish I were back in Da Nang right now, enjoying the company of some nurses!'

'Ouch! That hurts, Charlie. You mean you prefer them over us?'

A moment of levity always helps, as the crew enjoyed the comment. I then ask Joel, 'You alright back there, Joel? How are the packs doing?'

Joel responds, 'I'm doing good, sir. The packs, they don't look too good. I know how they feel. I've been there myself a few times, poor bastards.'

Our conversation is interrupted when the Major transmits calmly and authoritatively, 'Eagles, Eagle 1. We're going in. Call your targets, and let's get it done. Good luck. Over!'

The Major pushes down on his collective and forward on his cyclic, which places his Huey in a steep, controlled dive. As he closes in on the terrain below, he pulls up on his collective and back on his cyclic, leveling off his Huey at 100 feet above the ground. His Eagles follow his lead down to the deck.

Following the chopper in front of me, I intermittently scan my instrument panel while maintaining visual concentration outside of the Huey. I notice that Greg has pulled up close to me, and I give him a thumbs up and call him.

'Butcher 12, Eagle 25, good to see you fellows. Here we go again. You ready? Greg gives me a thumbs-up as he responds, 'Eagle 25, Butcher 12. We're ready, remember, good buddy. Get in and get out fast. Over!'

As Greg pulls away from me and gains more altitude so he can provide cover for us, I respond, 'Roger that!'

Closing in on Cam Lo Combat Base, I see smoke from

artillery fire and Air Force bombardments rising high into the sky from several locations around the base. The radio traffic I hear from combatants on the base is intense and conveys a sense of urgency for more help.

Major Breckenridge has flown ahead of us and gained some altitude over the Combat Base. This gives him a better visual of what is going on around the base. From his vantage point, he directs Captain Barnett to take his flight in. 'Eagle 16, Eagle 1, proceed with your approach and watch your exit to the west and south. We have intense fire coming from the west. Over!'

'Eagle 1, Eagle 16, Roger, going in. Over!' Captain Barnett transmits in a calm, business-like voice. He conveys no fear in his voice and seems oblivious to the battle going on around us. Hearing the transmission, I think to myself, *Where do men like this come from?*

I can't see the action yet as I'm too far out, but I can hear the radio traffic. As Captain Barnett approaches the outer perimeter of the base from the south, he begins receiving heavy small arms fire. Some of the choppers are hit, but no one is hurt. They continue in and make a sharp left bank as the landing strip comes into sight. Captain Barnett leads his flight in and out, just as artillery begins to rain down around the landing strip. After take-off, they do an immediate left bank and head due south over the base and back towards Quang Tri. No one is hurt, but several choppers have holes from small arms fire and shrapnel from artillery shells that exploded near them on the way out.

The Major directs the second flight in. 'Eagle 8, Eagle 1, you're good to go.' Stan acknowledges the order and leads his flight in from the south. He follows the same route as the first flight, but as they close in on the landing strip, his flight starts receiving heavy fire from 20 MM and 40 MM cannons. The second ship in the formation is hit in the tail boom but manages to crash land near the east end of the strip. South Vietnamese troops scramble from the Huey and head for cover as the crew jumps out unscathed. The other four Hueys make it in and land. As their packs leap from the choppers, the crew from the second ship that was hit, run to the nearest Huey.

After confirming that his crew from the destroyed Huey is on one of his other choppers, Stan leads his men out. His Huey, along with the other three in his flight, have sustained some battle damage but make it out. Once again, I've been listening to the action over the radio. I've grown more concerned about the increasing fire being directed at us and wonder, *Where are our guys? What are they doing? Is anybody shooting back?*

The Major has been busy coordinating a response to the increasing heavy weapons fire directed at his men. The entire area around the base has poor visibility. This is due to the smoke from incoming artillery and mortar shells landing all over the base. The Air Force has also been busy dropping cluster bombs and napalm at specific targets outside of the base's perimeter. All this smoke makes it harder for the Major to locate enemy positions and direct Greg's Cobras in on them.

Coordinating with Greg, the Major can locate enemy positions on the perimeter's western and northern sides. This is where he believes the incoming 20 MM and 40 MM fire directed at his Eagles is coming from. As I close in from the south toward the base, I can hear Greg and the Major working together to destroy enemy positions on the ground.

The Major transmits to me, 'Eagle 25, Eagle 1, you're good to go. They have your wounded ready for extraction. Be advised, we have come under heavy 20 MM and 40 MM cannon fire. The Butcher group is working on that now. Over!'

'Roger, Eagle 1. We are inbound now. Closing in on the landing strip. Over!' Over the intercom, I say to my crew, 'We're headed in, fellows. Stay sharp. Remember, we're picking up some wounded before we bug out.'

They respond by clicking their microphones. Approaching the landing strip fast, I bank hard left, line up on the airstrip, and head toward the end of the strip. This gives my flight of Hueys room to land behind me. Bringing my Huey to a fast stop, I slowly settle to the ground allowing my packs to jump out. I've been so busy flying, I hadn't noticed we were not receiving any incoming fire on the landing strip. This was good, and on top of that, the South Vietnamese loaded their wounded onto our choppers very quickly.

We are lucky! We get in and out of there fast. Only a few of our choppers sustain hits from small arms fire. No one is injured. Just after we lift off, the airstrip begins receiving enemy artillery fire and what looks like tank fire. Clearing the airstrip, I make another hard-left bank and head south toward Quang Tri. Looking back at the airstrip, I see it taking several accurate hits from artillery. Thinking to myself as we head back to Quang Tri for another load, D*amn, that doesn't bode well for our return trips.*

# CHAPTER 42

## CAM LO COMBAT BASE-RETURN TRIPS

Arriving back at our staging area in Quang Tri and after hot refueling, my group hovers over to our staging area and falls in line behind the second flight. South Vietnamese troops from the second Company have already started boarding some of our Company's choppers when my flight settles in behind Stan's. Once we came to rest on the tarmac, South Vietnamese troops begin loading onto our choppers. We are headed right back out when all our choppers are loaded. Since we lost one of our Hueys while inserting the first Company, Major Breckenridge decides to take the troops that would have gone on that Huey with him for the second trip out.

The Major transmits to his men. 'Eagles, Eagle 1. I'm carrying some packs in with me and will lead the first flight in. Once they're out of my ship, I'll hang around until the third flight clears the area. Over!' Several double-clicks and radio transmissions of 'Roger that!' are heard. He then issues the command to lift off and follow him.

Once again, we take off following our leader and head north toward Cam Lo Combat Base. While we were refueling and loading troops, Greg and his Cobras refueled and rearmed, and headed back with us.

Approaching Cam Lo Combat Base, the Major is advised by the Vietnamese Ground Commander that they are under heavy attack from all sides now and have tanks in their northern and western perimeters. He informs the Major they have sustained many more casualties, which need to be airlifted out as soon as possible. The Major tells him to have them standing by and ready to board once they land. As before, he instructs them to place their more severely wounded soldiers on the third flight in. He tells the Commander we will continue to bring out their wounded every time we return to his Combat Base.

The Major transmits to his Company. 'Eagles, Eagle 1. I've just been advised that all four sides of the base are under heavy attack. Also, there are tanks on their northern and western perimeter. They have more casualties. We'll bring them out with the third flight. Over!' His flight leaders respond affirmatively.

Approaching from the south, he sets up his approach into the landing strip and transmits, 'Stay sharp, men, here we go. Over!'

As he leads the first flight in, they come under heavy fire from machine guns and cannon fire. Captain Barnett is flying behind the Major. Closing in on the landing strip, his Huey takes a direct hit from 20 MM fire and crashes to the ground just short of the landing strip. They hit hard and roll over several times, coming to rest on one side. Men scramble from the chopper and run for cover. Not all of them make it, including Captain Barnett, as their Huey explodes in a large fireball.

The Major's chopper and the three remaining choppers in his flight take multiple hits as they are riddled by heavy fire. By the grace of God, they manage to get in and out, with the Major leading them. After clearing the landing strip, the Major releases his flight to go back to Quang Tri. Gaining some altitude, he transmits in a calm, compassionate voice. 'Eagles, Eagle 1. We just lost Eagle 16 and some of his crew. We're receiving heavy fire from all sides—no change to your approach. I'm going to get more firepower to rain down on those little bastards. Eagles 8 and 25, hold south of the base while I see what I can do. Over!'

Both Stan and I acknowledge his transmission and stay south of the Combat Base. We gain altitude and settle into a holding pattern.

The Major contacts Greg, 'Butcher 12, Eagle 1. Can you see where all that 20 MM cannon fire is coming from? Over!'

'Eagle 1, Butcher 12. We've knocked out some of their guns and have a fix on three more locations. We're all gonna roll in there again and see what we can do. Over!'

Greg leads his Cobras on a gun run across the northern and western perimeters firing their rockets and 20 MM cannons at several targets. Secondary explosions are seen as his group scores several hits. As they fly out of the area, the Air Force rolls in with fighter support and takes on several targets, including the tanks. The entire northern and western perimeter areas are engulfed in explosions as fire and smoke rise toward the heavens. While this is unfolding, South Vietnamese Artillery units continue to pound several sides of the base's outer perimeter with artillery.

Observing from his vantage point that enemy firing has tapered off, the Major drops down from altitude and shoots an approach into the landing strip. He's checking to see if he'll draw any fire. It's quiet. Regaining altitude, he transmits, 'Eagles 8 and 25, resume insertions. They've been set back momentarily. Butcher 12, good work. Over!'

Stan, Greg, and I all transmit our acknowledgments back to him. Stan leads his flight in without incident. Although instructed to wait for the third flight to come in, several wounded South Vietnamese rush to Stan's choppers and jump in. His flight is delayed momentarily while the soldiers who rushed his choppers finish loading. He doesn't want any of them clinging to their skids as they take off. We dealt with that several times in Laos, and it makes for a very difficult take-off. Once they are loaded onto his choppers, he pulls pitch and leads his men out.

As Stan's flight clears the landing strip and makes a tight bank to the left toward Quang Tri, I lead my flight in on a low fast approach path. Coordinating my leg and arm movements in a flurry of activity, I bring my Huey to a quick stop. I then settle our skids on the ground. The packs jump off and run for cover. Men on stretchers and some walking wounded are loaded into our Hueys. They also bring with them the door gunner and crew chief from Captain Barnett's chopper, both of whom were wounded. They are placed in the Huey behind me.

Captain Barnett and his pilot didn't make it. Some South Vietnamese Marines pull their bodies from the helicopter and place them in body bags. Those same Marines bring their bodies over to my Huey and place them on the floor of the chopper. Once loaded, I lead my flight out of the area without sustaining any more damage to our Hueys.

I don't know how much more punishment our Hueys can take. I remember my Dad telling me how indestructible the B-17, Flying Fortress, bombers were that he flew over Europe in WWII. We're no B-17, but I do like the idea that we may be indestructible!

Arriving back at Quang Tri, I direct my flight to refuel, return to our staging area, and then shut down. I tell them I'll join them shortly. Leaving them, I land my Huey at the MASH unit set up near the Quang Tri flight line. The bodies of Captain Barnett and his pilot are removed by medics and taken inside where they will remain until our Company is released for the day. At that time, one of our Hueys will pick them up for our return to Phu Bai Base.

I'm remorseful and mad as hell, having lost another friend. Right now, though, my day is not over. It can only get worse. I must hold my emotions in check and finish the day out. I'll grieve later. Many men's lives are at risk, including mine. I must stay focused.

Returning to the staging area, I perform a hot refuel, hover over to our designated spot, and shut down. The Eagles' Hueys are parked in the staging area where supplies are being loaded onto our choppers for the next trip back. The aircrews need a break, some time to relax, and to regroup. Our Company has lost two pilots, two crew members have been wounded, and two Hueys destroyed. Greg's Butchers group has lost one Cobra, and two pilots were wounded. Our day is still young. We have at least three more missions to fly back into Cam Lo Combat Base to deliver supplies for the beleaguered Combat Base.

We only have a short time before launching again, so we try to use it wisely. I seek out a latrine area, then head for the tent where we met earlier, and the pilots are now gathered. Some are smoking, picking at some Army chow, drinking water and coffee. Most of all, they are making small talk among themselves. It has been a rough morning, and everyone is dealing with it in their own way. I think we are all trying to block what we've just been through from our thoughts. What is hard for me to deal with is knowing we're going right back out there again.

Greg and his pilots have also returned to the staging area. After refueling and rearming, they have joined us and are taking a break. They will launch again with us and continue to provide cover during our resupply missions.

I have been nursing a cup of coffee with Greg and Jake. All three of us are internalizing the loss of Captain Barnett and his pilot and are avoiding talking about it. My roommate Bill, who's been flying the last ship in my flight, seeks me out.

Bill walks over to where Greg, Jake, and I are standing. Looking at me and in a tentative and somewhat nervous voice, says to me. "TJ, this is not like any kinda flying we did down south. You're in a conventional war up here. My god, I've come under fire before but not like this. Tanks, 20 MM and 40 MM cannon fire, and artillery. We saw machine guns, small arms, and RPGs, but this shit—Damn!"

"Yeah, it can get pretty damn intense up here sometimes!" I respond coolly.

"Pretty intense! That seems like an understatement. We've only been in there twice and already lost two ships, two pilots, and have some wounded. And Captain Barnett." Greg cuts in on Bill and says, "Bill, relax. We still have a long day ahead of us. You did good. Keep it up, and just stay focused. We'll be back at the Pilots Club having a few beers before you know it."

I hand Bill a cup of coffee, and Jake offers him a cigarette. Bill takes the coffee from me, nods his appreciation, and looks over to Jake and says, "Thanks, but I don't smoke." I've been dealing with my own demons internally and wonder, *how many more friends do I have to lose before this madness ends?*

The Major calls all of us together by the tent to include Greg's men. "Gentlemen, our supplies are loaded. We're going back out. We have at least two more trips after this one, and maybe three. Activity around Cam Lo Combat Base is tapering off some. However, artillery fire is still pretty heavy. Get in and get out. As you know, it takes longer to unload supplies than troops, so have your crews help once you touch down. The quicker you unload, the faster you can get out of there." He pauses for a long time as he looks around at his men.

In a fatherly and somewhat emotional voice, he continues. "We lost two good men out there earlier today, and some were wounded. It's not over yet. We mourn our losses, but you need to put that in the back of your mind right now and stay alert and focused. I don't want to lose any more people out there today. Any questions?"

There are none, and we head back out to our helicopters.

Major Breckenridge will lead the first flight in on every resupply mission. He will then fly C&C over the base until his last flight is clear of the landing strip. The first resupply trip out to Cam Lo Combat Base is uneventful. We all get in and out with no casualties and minimal battle damage. We only receive light machine gun fire while flying out to the west and then south of the base. While on the landing strip, only occasional artillery fire lands near some of us. Returning to Quang Tri, we refuel, load up more supplies, and head back out.

Approaching from the south and just above ground level, the Major leads the first flight across the base toward the landing strip. Visibility is good as the smoke which has lingered over the base from previous fighting has almost dissipated. Approaching the landing strip on short final, they are suddenly and viciously set upon by heavy machine-gun fire and 20 MM cannon fire. Several Hueys are hit but manage to land, and men scramble to unload the supplies. Time on the ground is minimal as the Major transmits to his flight, 'Gentlemen, let's get the hell out of here now. Over!'

He takes off, with the other three Hueys following right behind him. On the way out to the west and turning south, the Major notices several tanks are closing in on the western perimeter. He also notices what appear to be armored vehicles firing mounted weapons into the base at them. Keeping his flight low to the ground, they clear the southern perimeter, and he orders his flight of three Hueys to return to Quang Tri. Climbing to higher altitude, the Major returns to his C&C responsibilities flying over the Base.

He transmits to Stan and me, 'Eagles 8 and 25, Eagle 1, be advised we have another hot LZ. Tanks are closing in from the west, and we have several armored vehicles firing heavy weapons. Flight one is out but took several hits. I'll see what I can do. Over!'

The Major calls Greg and is frustrated with all the NVA activity they keep running into and says, 'Butcher 12, Eagle 1, we gotta get those damn armored vehicles down there. We also have more tanks. Over!'

Greg responds to the Major. 'Eagle 1, Butcher 12. Roger. We see them. We're rolling in. Over!'

The Major responds, 'Butcher 12, Roger. Eagle 8, take your flight in, and good luck! Over!'

Stan responds to the Major, 'We've cleared the southern perimeter and are lining up for final approach to the strip now. Over!'

As Stan leads his flight in, I see in the distance Greg's Cobras working over the western perimeter area. Smoke from all the explosions is once again creating poor visibility. Just before Stan's flight manages to land, they are hit by a withering crossfire of machine guns. Looking out of his cockpit window, Stan sees red tracers streaming in from all directions. His door gunners are returning fire and cannot help with unloading the supplies. The South Vietnamese are slow to unload the choppers as they are also under fire. Stan, talking to his pilots over the radio, directs them to have all their gunners throw the supplies out now. They comply, and this speeds up the process.

Just as Stan orders his flight to take off and follow him, a 20 MM shell hits the right side of his chopper and explodes just behind the seat his pilot is strapped in. Shrapnel from the exploding shell hits the pilot in the throat. The pilot struggles to speak between desperate gasps for breath and a terrible gurgling sound. 'I'm hit! I'm...' Stan looks over at his pilot and sees he is grabbing at his throat, trying to stop the bleeding. Every time his heart beats, arterial spray squirts out from the wound in his neck, hitting the cockpit, instrument panel, and all over the pilot. Watching this unfold in slow motion, as his pilot struggles to breathe, Stan is shaken as he yells over the intercom, 'Stay with me! Stay with me!' It was then that Stan realizes there's nothing that can be done for the pilot who has slumped over his controls. The gasping has ceased. Stan struggles with the horror of what he just witnessed as he looks out over the landscape of mayhem with it's sounds and fury engulfing the LZ. The NVA tanks, which had been holding back, have now joined the battle and are firing at them. Tank shells are exploding around him and his fellow Eagles—the men he is responsible for. His vision is blurry from the dust and smoke, and chaos envelopes him and his aircraft. It's "Danger Close," and he knows he has to get his flight group out of the kill zone. Now! In an authoritative and matter of fact voice, Stan transmits to his group, 'Follow me, let's get the hell out of here!' Pulling his collective up, pushing his cyclic forward in a controlled manner, and applying maximum power to his engine, his Huey begins an agonizing slow ascent out of harm's way. The four choppers behind him follow him out.

Throughout this battle, his door gunners are busy firing at every target they see, and can't get to the pilot to pull him off the flight controls. Stan manages to keep control of his chopper long enough for his right door gunner to pull the pilot back from the controls eventually. All five Hueys sustain battle damage. But, they are all able to make it out and head back toward Quang Tri. Once clear of the base and hostile fire, the gunners pull the pilot from his seat and try to help him, but it's too late. The right door gunner tells Stan over the intercom, 'Sir, he's dead!'

The Major continues to direct Greg's group at the targets he locates. They have a devastating effect, as secondary explosions occur in many of the targets they roll in on. Once again, the Air Force is called in, and they hit the eastern, northern, and western perimeters of the base. It has become an all-out effort by the NVA to breach the perimeters and take the base. Unfortunately, for the NVA, that was a big mistake. The Air Force comes in with multiple fighter bombers dropping cluster bombs and napalm.

Artillery support from other South Vietnamese bases has started shelling the attacking forces with high explosive and white prosperous artillery rounds. The accumulation of all this firepower has a devastating effect on the attacking forces as they sustain heavy losses of tanks, vehicles, and men. They break off the attack and pull back.

I was ordered earlier by the Major to hold back my flight until they could gain more control over the deteriorating situation. After the firepower directed at the NVA abruptly ends, the Major once again dives down from his altitude. Shooting an approach into the landing strip, he receives no incoming fire. All is quiet. Regaining altitude, he transmits to me. 'Eagle 25, Eagle 1, we broke their back, I think. You're cleared to go in. Over!'

'Eagle 1, Eagle 25, Roger, headed in now. Will advise when approaching the landing strip. Over!'

The Major comes back with, 'Roger 25! The Ground Commander just advised me they have some more casualties remaining to be extracted. I requested they load them on your last three Hueys. Do you copy Eagle 25? Over!'

I respond, 'Roger, copy!' The Major transmits, 'Remember. Get in, get out! Over!'

Once again, I approach the Combat Base from the south and hug the deck. More smoke and flames are rising into the sky in the distance where we are headed. These are from massive fires outside the base to the north and west. I assume they're tanks and armored vehicles that are burning. It gives me some comfort that maybe we won't get shot at again.

Upon making our final approach into the landing strip, several troops are waiting for us to touch down. Landing my flight successfully, we stay ready and wait for the troops to finish unloading their supplies. Looking out my windows, I'm struck by the amount of damage the base has sustained from all the assaults and bombardments they've endured. It looks like a moonscape, with very few buildings left untouched. While looking around, the Major calls, 'Eagle 25, Eagle 1. You guys done down there yet? Over!'

'Eagle 1, this is 25. We are pulling pitch now. Over!' Just as I finish transmitting, a heavy barrage of artillery shells lands all over the landing strip. None of my choppers take a direct hit, but many sustain shrapnel damage from the exploding rounds, including mine. I yell out over my radio to my group, 'Let's get the hell out of here! Now!' After taking off, I bank to the left and head toward the southern perimeter of the base. All five Hueys make it out and follow me south.

After departing the airfield and gaining altitude, I call Bill, who's flying the last Huey in my flight. 'Eagle 13, Eagle 25. Is everyone out of the LZ and okay back there? Over!'

'Eagle 25, Eagle 13. Roger. We're all out. I think we'll have a hell of a lot of holes to patch up tonight on these Hueys. Over!'

Just as Bill finishes his transmission, his Huey is hit with ground fire from one of the surviving armored vehicles outside the perimeter. He calls out, 'Eagle 25, this is Eagle 13. We're hit. We took several rounds down the right side, and my pilot and right door gunner were wounded. We're checking them now. Over!'

I release my other three Hueys and instruct them to return to Quang Tri. I make a 180 degree turn and head back toward Bill. As I close in on the left side of his Huey, I see that he's visibly shaken and working hard to stay in the air. I call over to him, 'Eagle 13, Eagle 25. How are you doing over there? What's your instrument status? You have some smoke coming from your tail area. Over!'

Bill is busy flying his chopper while scanning his instruments for any problems. He doesn't see anything unusual. His surviving gunner checks out the pilot and other gunner and tells Bill they're both alive but badly hurt. They need medical attention right away. Bill responds to me, 'Eagle 25, Eagle 13. Instruments look good. Both men are alive but severely wounded. I need to get back to Quang Tri fast. We'll need the MASH unit waiting for us. Over!'

From his vantage point, the Major has seen the action unfold below him, and heard our radio traffic. He calls on Greg's flight to come down and work the area again. He then drops down from his altitude and pulls up on the right side of Bill. He sees him struggling. 'Eagle 13, this is Eagle 1. I'm out your right window. You're doing fine, son. Keep it in the air. We'll call ahead and stay with you. Over!'

Bill responds in a low, emotional voice. 'Eagle 1, Eagle 13. Roger sir. Thanks. Over!'

As we approach the south end of the base, I see Greg's Cobras rolling in again, firing their guns and rockets at targets somewhere on the western perimeter. I hear their radio chatter. I call out to Greg, 'Butcher 12, Eagle 25. How's it going over there, buddy? Over!'

Greg responds, 'Eagle 25, Butcher 12. It's been one hell of a day so far. They just keep coming out of the damn woodwork. Over!'

'Butcher 12, Eagle 25. You guys are doing a great job. But, damn, these little bastards are putting up one hell of a fight! Over!'

'Eagle 25, Butcher 12. You got that right. I think we sent several of them straight to ...'

Greg's transmission abruptly ends. 'Butcher 12, Butcher 12, this is Eagle 25. Come in. Over!' I repeat my last transmission, and still no response.

I look over at Jake, and over the intercom, I ask him, 'What the hell just happened? Do you see anything?'

Looking back at me, he points outside the Huey on the right side and says, 'Over there!'

I see it, 'Oh my god. Oh shit!'

Greg's Cobra was pulling out of a dive from another gun run when he was hit by 20 MM fire. His Cobra spirals into the ground, hitting hard on their skids. The Cobra flips over several times, coming to rest on its side just inside the Combat Base. Emotionally shaken, I call the Major. 'Eagle 1, Eagle 25. I'm going over and check on Greg. You've got Bill. Over!'

Knowing how close Greg and I are, and realizing he would do the same, he transmits back to me. 'Eagle 25, Eagle 1. Roger that. Be careful in there TJ. Over!'

Arriving over the crash site, I can see Greg is still in the Cobra, but his pilot has managed to crawl out. I land my Huey in as close to the downed Cobra as possible and have Charlie and Joel run over to help the pilot and pull Greg out. The pilot is wounded but can help them extract Greg from the Cobra. Greg is unconscious and badly hurt. My crew and the injured pilot struggle to carry Greg's limp body from the Cobra to the Huey. They make it and place Greg on the floor of the Huey. They then help the wounded pilot on board. With everyone on board the Huey, I take off and head for Quang Tri. Climbing into the sky, I pull in maximum power and push the cyclic forward, gaining all the airspeed my Huey can handle.

Once at altitude, I call the Major. 'Eagle 1, Eagle 25. We have the pilots and are headed at max speed for Quang Tri. Greg is unconscious and bleeding heavily from a head and chest wound. His pilot is complaining of his back and left arm but is alert. Over!'

He responds, 'Eagle 25, Eagle 1. Roger. Understand. I'll alert the MASH unit. Get there as fast as possible, and I'll join you as soon as I can. Over!'

Acknowledging the Major, I focus all my attention on getting Greg to the MASH unit as fast as possible. Closing the distance to Quang Tri and oblivious to anything going on around me, I'm not aware of the tears that have been streaming down my cheeks. As we close in on Quang Tri, I'm given immediate clearance to the MASH unit. At that moment, I realize my eyes are all watered up, and I'm having trouble seeing. Struggling to control my emotions, I'm thinking to myself, *Not Greg. Not another good friend. How many more friends do I have to lose God? How many?*

# CHAPTER 43

## HOW MANY?

A pproaching Quang Tri, we are given immediate clearance to land and proceed to the MASH unit on the southeast side of the flight line. I land and hover over to the MASH unit where medics are waiting on us. Once I settle the skids to the tarmac, medics remove Greg and place him on a gurney. I watch as they push his gurney through the doors and inside the building. Other medics help the wounded pilot out and place him on a gurney. He, too, is rolled inside. Once my helicopter is cleared of the wounded, I hover over to a parking area near the building, settle the chopper to the ground, and shut down.

Taking off my helmet and wiping the tears from my face, I take a moment to regain my composure to the extent possible. Climbing out of the Huey, I tell Jake, Charlie, and Joel, "I'm going inside. Will you fellows take care of our post-flight and secure our chopper?"

We're all in an emotional state. Greg is well-liked, and they know the friendship that exists between Greg and me. Jake speaks for all of them, "We've got this TJ. Do what you need to do. We'll join you when we're done out here." I nod my appreciation and head inside the building.

Entering the building, I'm overwhelmed by what I encounter. The facility is a beehive of activity. Wounded men are everywhere on gurneys awaiting their turn for medical attention. I can see several men being attended to by doctors and medics in the back of the facility. After several days of intense fighting, the South Vietnamese have sustained many casualties. They have their own medical facilities and personnel, but because they are overwhelmed, they've turned to the 101st medical units for help. The 101st Aviation Group has sustained many of our own casualties. This MASH unit was set up as a temporary way station for our aircrews, and was not intended to be a fully operational unit.

Wounded aircrew members are brought to this facility for immediate care and stabilization. Once stabilized, they are sent to Phu Bai Base for further care and evaluation.

Most of the wounded in the building are South Vietnamese soldiers. The others are American aircrew members. All the 101st Aviation units supporting the South Vietnamese are coming under heavy fire as we fly in and out of firebases we're assigned to support. It's not Lam Son 719, but the North Vietnamese are inflicting many casualties on American aircrews.

Before I left for Vietnam, Sandy and I saw the movie MASH. It left quite an impression on me as to what a MASH unit might look like. My reaction to the scenes in front of me is akin to being on the movie set. But this is no movie. It's not a dream. It's my close friend, Greg, on a table in the back, fighting for his life.

I'm directed to an area near the front of the facility where I can wait. While waiting, my crew joins me and asks if I've heard anything about Greg's condition. I tell them Greg is in the back where the doctors are working on him, but I don't know his status yet. Just as I answer them, a medic rushes up, saying, "Your

Captain needs more blood. We need a couple of donors. We're running out of plasma." He inquires about our blood types to determine if any of us are a match for Greg's. I am, and I volunteer to donate. The medic takes me back to where they are working on Greg, trying to save his life.

Approaching Greg's operating table, I'm asked to lay down on the table set up next to him. Greg doesn't look good and is struggling to breathe. Laying down next to my friend, I extend my arm. The medic inserts a needle into my arm and attaches a tube, which runs up a support rod, over to the table with Greg on it. Once everything is set, my blood begins running up the tube and over to Greg's arm. Greg is receiving my blood as they fight to save his life.

The medic monitoring me tells me I'm almost finished donating, and they have other men standing by if needed. Just as they remove the needle from my arm, the doctors working on Greg go into a frenzy of quick activity. "He's crashing. He's crashing." The lead Doctor says in a loud, matter of fact tone. After the needle is out of my arm, I turn to look over at Greg to see how he is responding. His breathing has stopped. I want to get up and shake him awake, but I'm too weak and exhausted to move. The last thing I hear from the other Doctor working on Greg before I pass out is, "He's gone!"

I wake up several hours later and am slow to realize where I am or what happened. I'm exhausted, having seen and experienced too many horrific events since arriving in Vietnam and flying with the Eagles. I'm asking myself questions. *When will it end? How much is enough? How much more can I take?* I've asked these questions many times since arriving in this country, and I know I'm not alone. These are the type of questions men in similar situations have dealt with in previous wars. Now those of us fighting in this war are dealing with the same questions. So will those who fight in future wars. I'm in good company and not alone, but I sure feel alone.

Shaking my head as I try to clear my mind, I slowly sit up and realize I'm in a tent. The flaps on the side of the tent are up and tied back. Looking outside the tent, I can see the MASH unit where I was earlier. Sitting next to my cot is Major Breckenridge. Looking at the Major, I ask him in a soft, tired voice, "Major, how long have I been out? How's Greg doing?"

The Major looks away and then back at me. He is clearly struggling with what he is about to tell me. Speaking to me as a father would to his son, he says compassionately, "Son, you've been out for almost four hours..." I cut in, "Four hours. That can't be!"

He resumes talking to me in the same manner, "Son, it's been a rough day, and you're exhausted and need some rest. You did good out there again today. No man could be asked or expected to do any more than you've done." A long pause, "Taylor...Greg didn't make it. He's gone!"

I'm silent and struggle to control my emotions from spilling out. I have lost two more friends today, Captain Barnett, and now my closest friend, Captain Greg Owens. Sitting on the edge of my cot with my head resting in my hands, I look down at the floor. I can't stop it, tears begin to well up in my eyes, and in a low, barely discernible voice, "This can't be. This can't be. How many? How many?"

The Major, looking at me, and in a calm, very compassionate voice, asks, "How many of what, son?"

"How many friends do I have to lose over here before it stops? How many?"

After a long pause, Major Breckenridge responds, "TJ, that's a question no man knows the answer to. No one! Son, we have to accept what happens to us and move forward and hope and pray that it ends soon."

With that last comment, I stand up, start pacing around my cot, and then lose it. Major Breckenridge stands, stops me from pacing, and places his hands on my shoulders. I just want it all to end! Wishing that God would just wrap his arms around me and give me a brief respite, I find the Major an acceptable substitute and embrace him.

# CHAPTER 44

## QUANG TRI PROVINCE AFTERMATH

Major Breckenridge flew me back to our Company later that evening in his chopper. After completing their last resupply mission, he had sent the other men in the Company back to Phu Bai Base. Stan lead them, carrying the bodies of our fallen comrades. The Major remained behind, waiting for me to wake-up so he could bring me back. It was a tough day for the Eagles as we lost some more good men and sustained heavy battle damage to several Hueys.

Over the next few days, we were able to bounce back and fly support missions up north to help the South Vietnamese beat back the North Vietnamese. The cost was high to the South Vietnamese forces. They fought well, held, and pushed the invading forces back to the DMZ for now. The 101st Aviation Group sustained several aircrew casualties and some fatalities. Damage to our helicopter companies was considered light and acceptable. To the men of the Eagles, it was more personal and a tough pill to swallow.

The NVA sustained the most losses and had to pull back inside their borders for the foreseeable future and regroup. They

307

tried a conventional warfare approach with massive troop movements, armor, and heavy weapons fighting in the open. Hitherto,
they had conducted mostly guerrilla warfare where they picked
their time and place to strike. It had been highly effective for
them. However, this attempt to take over and hold Quang Tri
Province was a defeat. The North Vietnamese units that participated in this ill-fated offensive sustained massive casualties and
equipment losses. Much of that beating was inflicted by American airpower, which was brought to bear very effectively on
NVA forces fighting in the open.

After the offensive failed, the NVA shifted their strategy to a
wait and see approach. The Nixon Administration continued to
accelerate their Vietnamization of the war and pull-out American
combat troops. The 101st Airborne Division, which is in the
northern part of South Vietnam, will be one of the last units to
rotate back to the states as the draw-down continues.

Our eventual withdrawal would leave the South Vietnamese
to defend the entire northern area of I Corps. The NVA believed
that once the 101st Airborne Division was withdrawn, they
would succeed in another massive attack across the DMZ and
planned to do so soon.

Following the latest battle for Quang Tri Province, the 101st
Airborne Division, as expected, began a slow draw-down. Our
mission requirements also slowed down considerably and became
much less intense. This is the environment that my fellow Eagles
and I found ourselves going into during the late summer and
early fall of 1971.

Stan, Bill, Jake, Major Breckenridge, and I continued to serve
and fly together. During my remaining time in Vietnam, I
fulfilled the duties of Operations Officer and then Executive
Officer of the Company. I flew my share of missions and helped
to train new pilots as they reported into the Company. My
remaining few months in Vietnam passed by very quickly.

Finally, the day arrived that all those serving in Vietnam looked forward to and kept a daily count of, "one day and a wake-up!"

On my last night in the Company, my fellow Eagles threw me a homeward bound party. Many in the Company participated with shared stories, making toasts, and wishing me well. Although there was considerable drinking, I did manage not to get wasted. I'm not being initiated. I'm going home.

Major Charles Breckenridge presented me with my wooden Eagle. The temporary tape listing my name had been replaced with a metal plaque. Inscribed on the plaque were my name, the dates I served, my unit designation, and my call sign: Eagle 25.

# CHAPTER 45

## HOMECOMING

I t will take me four days to return home to Sandy and my family once I am released by the 101st Airborne Division. During this time, I record in my diary what happens and the experiences I have while waiting for my turn to board the "Freedom Bird" home and take Sandy in my arms again.

DAY 1

I left Phu Bai early this morning and flew to Da Nang on an Air Force C-130. It was another lousy weather day with rain and low hanging clouds. I had no desire to take a helicopter, thinking I had used up my nine lives and many more over here. I thought to myself, "I am going home, no more risk than necessary. My year is coming to an end. Thank God!"

Upon arriving in Da Nang, the other men and I who were going home were met by a bus and taken to a separate restricted area of the base. This area was isolated and set up to process men who had completed their tour of duty in Vietnam and are leaving the country. Due to all the drug problems, everyone leaving is being screened and tested several times while in this area. If we stay drug-free during our quarantine, we are then cleared to board a "Freedom Bird" for home. I'm not clear on what happens to those who test positive for drugs, but the rumor is they are sent to a drug rehabilitation program.

This entire process can take a few days, and we are no exception.

After spending what seemed an eternity doing paperwork, we were given a drug urine test. Following that, we were given a basic draft board, "how do you feel," type physical. We were then sent back to our holding barracks, where we are restricted from leaving the area. In fact, it's surrounded by barbed wire! Apparently, they don't want anyone to sneak out of the area and go wandering around the main base looking for some drugs.

Not much to do in here but sleep, eat, read, chat and watch some TV. Time goes by very slowly. While at dinner, I ran into two Chinook pilots from the same Company that Richard and Alan were in. These were the fellows who gave me a ride back from Da Nang when I returned from R&R. They told me the sad news that both men were killed last month while flying in dangerous weather between Phu Bai and Da Nang. They became disoriented and crashed into the side of a mountain. They were good men. What a damn shame!

My last night in the Company was great, but emotional. I've left some good friends behind at Phu Bai, some good memories, and many more I just want to forget. I'm sure I'll run into some of these men again back in the states. I hope on my next assignment I work with Senior Officers of Major Breckenridge's caliber. He is a fine man, officer, and leader.

## DAY 2

Today was the same as yesterday, long, boring, and I thought it would never end. We were subjected to another drug urine test. I just can't get over what I've heard about the drug-related problems and racial tensions that some units have experienced. This war has gone on far too long. Troop morale and unit cohesiveness, necessary for a combat unit to be effective, have taken a real hit. It's a sad situation and will require a considerable, long term effort for them to be restored.

In my opinion, the vast majority of men and women who served in Vietnam did so in an honorable fashion. God knows, there have certainly been exceptions to this, but most of us gave it our best. My generation fought this war the way we were ordered to by our superiors. It is not our fault we are leaving, and there is no clear victory. If blame is to be laid anywhere, it is with those who set strategy and policy during this war. They are the generation that fought and won WWII. For those of us who actually did the fighting, it would be worth noting that we never lost a battle. We did lose many good men, but that happens in every war. The difference here is that our sacrifices may well go down in history as being futile. Not much else can be said. My year is up. I'm going home, that is if I ever clear this damn holding pen.

## DAY 3

I went to bed early last night as I knew it was going to be a long day. Didn't sleep well as I was too excited about going home and anxious to clear any remaining hurdles to get out of this damn place. We were finally cleared, and my flight, with 210 men, was going home. We departed Da Nang early in the morning of my third day of being in a quarantine and restricted area. When we lifted off from Da Nang, the pilot came over the intercom and announced we were leaving Vietnamese airspace and could look out our windows at the country below. I didn't see too many fellows looking out their windows. I'll just speak for myself. I didn't look out my window. As far as I'm concerned, I have no plans to return and don't care to see the country again.

I genuinely feel for the people of Vietnam. Their country is in shambles. They've been at war for decades with outside forces and between themselves. I believe many Vietnamese just want to be one country and left alone. The French, Chinese, Japanese, Russians, and now the Americans have all played a role in adding to their misery and contributed to dividing their country. I can only hope they eventually work it out among themselves and become one country, at peace with itself.

After several hours of flying, we approached Tokyo from a high altitude, and I could see snow-capped Mount Fuji in the distance. Upon our arrival in Tokyo, we were allowed out of the plane to stretch and relax for a short time while the plane was cleaned and refueled. While walking around the terminal, I was greeted by many Japanese who seemed friendly and respectful. I slowly began to relax and recall what a terrific feeling it was when we took off from Vietnam. Most of the fellows on the plane were exhausted from all the processing we went through before leaving, and there was very little talking or celebrating. However, the look on our faces spoke volumes. We were alive and going home.

After leaving Japan, we flew to Tacoma, Washington, and landed at McCord Air Force base. We arrived late in the evening and spent the night in a holding area.

DAY 4

Early this morning, we were sent to a processing center on base. Most of the men were given their discharge papers and sent home. The rest of us were going home for a well-deserved rest and then onto our next duty assignment.

I received my travel orders, and was then transported to the Seattle, Washington airport with a small group of Army returnees. At the airport, it was akin to an out-of-body experience. The place was packed with people going in all directions and absorbed in their own thoughts. But what bothered the men who were with me, and myself, were the disparaging looks we received from so many people. It was obvious we were returning veterans from Vietnam, but it became very discouraging to see the looks and stares we got. To hear the comments directed at us by many people, mostly our age, was very disheartening. Some of the comments were: "baby killers," "losers," "warmongers," and "Nixon's war boys." We were only in Tokyo, Japan, for a brief time, but were treated with much more respect. But now we are back home and are treated like this!

So much for "Welcome Home!"

After leaving Seattle, I flew into the San Diego airport, where I was met by Sandy and my family. Although exhausted, adrenaline took over, and I moved quickly down the ramp steps and into the arms of Sandy and my family. Airport personnel directed us into the terminal, where I took off my flight jacket. My father, who was standing near me, got a glimpse at the ribbons on my uniform. Being a retired Senior Military Officer, who saw action in WWII and Korea, he recognized many of the ribbons and became emotional. That was not his style, but he gave me a long embrace. I never told anyone about my experiences in Vietnam except for Sandy. I did share some of them with her while we were on R&R in Hawaii. Although I knew dad was sure I had seen action, I apparently caught him off guard with how much.

I'll close by saying it's been one hell of a long year. I made many friends, and I lost many friends. I don't believe I'll ever understand it all, but I hope if we ever go to war again, we do it right—whatever the hell that means. My year in hell is over, and I never want to do that again. Thank God I'm home. It's great to be home.

I love you Sandy.

# EPILOGUE
## REFLECTIONS AT THE VIETNAM MEMORIAL


## WELCOME HOME
## THANKS FOR YOUR SERVICE


I t is later that same fall morning in early 1990 when the lone
figure and the reflection in the wall are still touching hands,
with their heads bowed. The lone figure slowly raises his head to
reveal me, looking directly at the reflection in the wall. As I do,
the reflection slowly raises his head to reveal Greg's proud, defiant, and yet peaceful face. As we stare into each other's faces, the
faces of Scott, Rick, Bob, Captain Barnett, and Major Hutchins
become visible, one after the other, and all have the same look.
Tears stream from my eyes and flow down my cheeks.

I slowly step back from the wall as the reflections fade from
sight. Turning from the wall, I wipe the tears away while looking
for Sandy. The Memorial is now full of visitors, and I have to
work my way through the crowd. As I do, I run into other
Veterans who are having their own flashbacks. As only Vietnam

veterans can, we exchange glances and acknowledgments. The wall can be a very emotional experience for anyone, particularly veterans. Some hug, some shake hands, many say to each other, "Welcome Home!"

Working my way to the top of the walk, I spot Sandy standing back some distance from the Wall with our young daughter and son next to her. Our eyes meet, and we move toward each other. We come together, and Sandy looks into my eyes. She sees pride, contentment, and a sense of peace coming through. This is a look she has not seen in many years. We embrace tightly as our children join us. Standing there embracing, Sandy looks out over my shoulder, gazing back at that beautiful, black, granite wall.

Sandy softly whispers into my ear, "All those names, all those names."

# AFTERWORD

## LAM SON 719 AND ITS AFTERMATH

During an April 7, 1971, televised speech, President Nixon claimed that "Tonight I can report that Vietnamization has succeeded." At Dong Ha, South Vietnam, President Thieu addressed the survivors of Lam Son 719 and claimed that the operation in Laos was "the biggest victory ever."

Although Lam Son 719 set back North Vietnamese supply operations in southeastern Laos, truck traffic on the trail system increased almost immediately after the operation ended. The American Military command's claims of success were muted as they understood the operation had exposed grave deficiencies in South Vietnamese Military "planning, organization, motivation, operational expertise, and most importantly, leadership."

For the North Vietnamese, Lam Son was viewed as a complete victory. The military expansion of the Ho Chi Minh Trail to the west, which had begun in 1970, was quickly accelerated. The area that the Trail passed through in southeastern Laos expanded from sixty miles in width to ninety miles.

Another result of the operation was a firm decision by the North Vietnamese to launch a major conventional invasion of

South Vietnam in early 1972, known in the west as the Easter Offensive. This was an invasion across the DMZ and into Quang Tri Province. Had it not been for massive American airpower deployed in defense of the South, this invasion could have ended the war then, with a complete victory for the North Vietnamese. Their invasion didn't succeed, and the war would go on until April 30, 1975. On that date, NVA tanks crashed through the gates of the Presidential Palace in Saigon, effectively ending the war in Vietnam.

During Lam Son 719, U.S. planners believed that any North Vietnamese forces opposing the incursion would be caught in the open and decimated by American airpower. This airpower would be in the form of tactical airstrikes and air mobility. Airpower played an important role, but not a decisive one. American airpower prevented a defeat from becoming a complete disaster, but at a terrible cost for American helicopter pilots and crews.

It is difficult to ensure complete accuracy related to the various categories of statistical information compiled over the entire time of the Vietnam War. However, the figures presented here are believed to be reliable.

The number of helicopters involved in Lam Son 719 was over 750, most of which were assigned to the 101st Airborne Division. The 101st had 84 of its aircraft destroyed and another 430 damaged (20% of those were rendered inoperable). Combined helicopter losses totaled 108 helicopters destroyed and 618 helicopters classified as having sustained battle damage. During the two months of flight operations, seventy-two helicopter aircrew members were killed, fifty-nine were wounded, and eleven were missing when the operation was officially declared over on April 7, 1971. During Lam Son 719, American helicopter aircrews had flown more than 160,000 sorties.

The United States Military was shocked and unprepared for the severe losses sustained by helicopter aircrews and the number of helicopters that were damaged or destroyed during the two months of Lam Son 719. Advocates of United States Army aviation were forced to reevaluate their basic air mobility doctrine and tactics. Particular attention was directed toward the combat survivability of helicopters in a hostile environment.

## ACKNOWLEDGMENTS

I wish to thank my wife, Linda, for all her support, encouragement, and understanding as I endeavored to write this novel. It was a long journey we traveled together to arrive at the stage where my novel was published. Linda served as my first editor and helped make it a better manuscript for submitting to a Publisher. Thank you!

I also wish to thank Frank Eastland of Publish Authority, who accepted my manuscript for submission and subsequent publication. His professionalism, guidance, and support are very much appreciated. Working with him, his staff, Bob Laning, my editor, and Bob's wife Nancy, the initial manuscript I submitted was greatly improved upon over time and resulted in my first novel, *Chariots in the Sky*. I also wish to thank those members of my family and friends who have provided me with their technical support, encouragement, and comments during the writing, editing, and ultimate publication of my novel. My sincere thanks to all of you!

Writing this story has been a wonderful experience. It is a

story that I've wanted to tell for many years. You might say it was a trip down memory lane as I drew on some real-life events to help weave a story. To those who read my novel, I say a special thank you. I hope and trust you found your reading experience insightful, educational, and enlightening.

# ABOUT THE AUTHOR

Larry Freeland was born in Canton, Ohio and raised across this country. After graduating from College, Larry joined the U.S. Army and served one tour in Vietnam with the 101st Airborne Division as an Infantry Officer and a CH-47 helicopter pilot. He is the recipient of the Distinguished Flying Cross with one Oak Leaf Cluster, the Air Medal, with 10 Oak Leaf Clusters, the Vietnam Service Medal with 3 Bronze Stars, the Bronze Star Medal, and various other military service medals.

Larry is now retired and lives in North Georgia with his wife Linda, a retired teacher. They enjoy traveling together around the country, going on cruises and visiting historic places in Europe. They are both fans of LeMans racing and drive their Corvette to some of the annual races held in the United States. They stay involved in various activities, most notably those associated with the Cystic Fibrosis Foundation and Veterans related organizations.

For more information about the author visit his website at www.larryfreeland.com

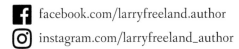

facebook.com/larryfreeland.author

instagram.com/larryfreeland_author

# THANK YOU FOR READING

**Publish Authority**

If you enjoyed *Chariots in the Sky*, we invite you to share your thoughts and reactions online and with friends and family.